The Journeys of Bertie & Winnie

by

Britt Gourley and Dylan Beckett

The dachshund in the photo below is the real inspiration for "Gretchen Schwartz" in the book. She is called "Gretchen" and lives by the ocean in America.

This is a work of fiction. Names, characters, businesses, places, events, and incidents are either the products of the authors' imaginations or used in a fictitious manner. Unless otherwise indicated, any resemblance to actual persons, living or dead, or actual events is purely coincidental.

The Journeys of Bertie & Winnie
Edition Copyright © 2021
[Britt Gourley,Dylan Beckett]
ISBN: 978-1-008-98615-2

Book Three of the 'Bertie & Winnie' Series.

Contents

A Note to Our Readers

We are very pleased that you have chosen to add *The Journeys of Bertie & Winnie* to your bookshelf! In hopes that you'll have the most delightful reading experience possible, we would like to make a few introductory remarks.

The story often references the past, and that past has important implications for the present and future. Because this is the case, the narrative does not necessarily move in a traditional, linear fashion, and various plots are intertwined. We hope that you will find this approach to be thought-provoking and pleasurable.

There are asterisks (*), daggers (†) and double daggers (‡) throughout the text that refer to explanatory notes at the ends of chapters. These describe places, people and objects that may be unfamiliar.

For those of you who may be curious, much of the American side of the story takes place in a fictionalised version of the North Shore of Boston, Massachusetts. The village of Badger's Bay is loosely modelled on the small coastal town of Swampscott. In particular, the spot referred to as "Bertie's cove" was inspired by Eiseman's Beach. Cape Berkeley bears some resemblance to Cape Ann, which is 25 miles north of Swampscott.

You will no doubt notice that certain real places—London, Paris and Venice, for instance—stand side-by-side with imagined ones throughout the book. The following map will guide you as you accompany the characters on their travels.

And now, we invite you to step into Bertie and Winnie's world with us.

Chapter One
That's Not the Ticket

"I'm sure I don't know how that could have happened, ma'am," Wagmore said smoothly, smiling at himself in the gilt mirror near the telephone at the duchess's residence. "I'm quite sure I followed your instructions down to the letter, and there was no mention of the SS Marlin being a "party" ship, as you call it. Why, I have the brochure right here with the itinerary. Let's see—various sightseeing opportunities along the way, Le Havre, Gibraltar, Valencia—all here, and a couple of stopovers in locations that you yourself agreed looked pleasant and interesting. Indeed, the masquerade ball piqued your interest, and also, I see that there are any number of night-time activities, including magic shows, live music and even dance lessons, which I'm sure Bertie will appreciate." Wagmore took pleasure in emphasizing the last point, after things didn't work out to plan at the tea dance several months ago.

There was no immediate reply, so Wagmore continued in soothing tones. "I am more than happy to get in touch with the tour operator if you wish, although I feel there is likely little, they can do at this time if you are indeed on the wrong ship."

The greyhound held the phone away from his ear, only half listening to the tinny noise of Muriel berating him on the other end, returning the phone to his mouth at various opportune moments and agreeing with her from time to time. When he finally put the receiver down, he was feeling very satisfied with himself, chuckling out loud as he imagined Bertie and Muriel feeling miserably out of place in the middle of a crowded ship, with all manner of young dogs and cats dancing to funky music in platform shoes.

By way of congratulating himself, Wagmore decided he would give Peel, the footman, a series of demeaning and arduous tasks around the London house and sit idly by while he performed his duties. His was the sort of personality that loved to pick up on any fault in others, despite his own shortcomings as the head butler. Peel's to-do list was long enough to keep him busy whilst his boss popped into town and dealt with some of his own personal business. Wagmore was beginning to get used to not having the mistress around and really couldn't imagine waiting on her again when she returned, however far away that day might be.

He had grown accustomed to being in charge and couldn't tolerate others knowing his own business or questioning his decisions. Most of the staff presented no difficulties in this regard, but Harry Nightingale, the chauffeur, was a different kettle of fish altogether. Muriel had definitely got a soft spot for him, and his attitude and general demeanour did not sit well with Wagmore. He was especially irked by the fact that he was not privy to the conversations they had when out in the car, since at the house he could hear most of the general chatter, whether on the telephone or in the drawing room. Information was power, and Wagmore revelled in knowing more than others and would use any opportunity to manipulate them when he could benefit in some way. It nettled him that he had little power over Harry, and he was always searching in vain for something he could use against him. When he exited the house and saw the golden retriever lounging contentedly after the morning's duties, the butler made a point of giving him something to do. "That car needs a second coat of wax," he said, fixing the chauffeur with his icy glare. He turned and peered through one of the windows, taking care to leave a pawprint on it. "And I'm sure the interior could do with a vacuuming too." Harry abandoned his tea and biscuits with a sigh and nodded briefly. It was a small victory but kept the lazy so-and-so on his toes and reminded him who was boss of this household.

Chapter Two
Winnie Loses Her Head

It was a raw sort of afternoon, already dusk, really, and Winnie's yellow woolly hat could be seen bobbing up and down along the sea wall at Bertie's cove. If anyone had been looking, that is. But no one was. School was out for the day, and no one had been tempted to hang about outside. Not even Digger and Rufus were braving the bone-chilling cold today, surmising that any buried treasure was likely to stay buried until tomorrow. Winnie, who was searching out drier bits of driftwood for the cottage fireplace, was beginning to tire of her task, and her attention wandered. Lost in thought, she stumbled over a protruding stone and fell, nose down, her armful of wood scattering about her.

"Jumping Jehoshaphat!" she exclaimed. Rubbing the sand off her face, she noticed a smear of black on the arm of her checked coat. "Blast!" She had fallen squarely into a pile of ashes. 'The Christmas bonfire,' she thought, gathering up the bits and pieces again. The festivities she and Douglas had arranged, and the magic of that evening, seemed ever so long ago.

As she made her way back to the cottage, with her bundle neatly tied and dragging behind her, Winnie had to admit to herself that she was feeling at rather a low ebb. It had been over a month since Douglas had returned to England, and whilst he had written to her, it was not the same as being in his company. The joys and excitement of the Christmas period—as well as the angst and adventure of the previous year—were but a distant memory, and she was finding it hard to transition back to her rather mundane life.

Of course, she still enjoyed spending time with Dino and Augie, although she was beginning to feel a little like a spare part, as Eddie was now so much a part of Sophia's and the pups' lives. Bertie was away in England with Muriel and unlikely to return anytime soon, if ever. In some ways, she felt a sense of annoyance with herself: she had been the one to instigate the contact with his sister, Samantha, all those months ago and she was the reason he was no longer in her own life. It was all for the best, of course, but selfishly, she sometimes regretted that she'd poked her nose in. Even Bertie's budgie, Stanley seemed to have found new interests lately. He had become chummy with a few of the seagulls after patching up his differences with Glenn, and Bryson the crow had introduced him to his own family and friends, so Stan was more often out in their company than at Bertie's cottage. Despite his cantankerous and demanding nature, Stan was at least a constant in her life, but even that had changed. She deposited her load of driftwood under the eaves and sat down on it with a sigh. 'If I don't watch out, I'll become a right old misery guts, as Bertie would say,' she thought.

But she knew that she wasn't just wallowing in self-pity. She longed for a new direction and purpose and wasn't sure if that could be found in Badger's Bay. She needed a change of scenery and to explore the world she had read so much about in her textbooks. The thought had crossed her mind that she could travel abroad, but she really could not face doing that on her own. Douglas had invited her to come to England—perhaps he could accompany her? She had broached the subject in one of her letters, but he hadn't really given any definitive answer, and he had responsibilities of his own. She was growing up, and the thought of staying in one place at present didn't appeal.

Winnie had had just about enough of her own thoughts when she caught a whiff of familiar perfume and saw a colourfully dressed cockapoo bounding towards her.

"What's happening?" Lottie asked. "You look like the cat's got your cream."

"Oh dear," Winnie replied, "is it that obvious?"

"Well, perhaps not to Joe Public, but I think I've known you long enough to see you are deep in thought and a bit down in the dumps," the cockapoo said as she gave Winnie a big bear hug to try and lift her spirits. "And I can't really see why, as you've just finished school early. You're free as a bird, and the world's your oyster."

Winnie smiled at her friend's exuberant mix of simile and metaphor. "Aha, so you can turn that frown upside down. And if you don't mind, let's continue this conversation inside. I'm getting frostbite. And yes, I know what you're going to say," Lottie said, before Winnie could tease her about her fashionable but very short and thin magenta coat. She pulled the doxie up off the driftwood pile and marched her inside. "I suppose this sort of chat will call for some tea, though I'm dying for a cup of joe," she murmured as she filled the kettle. "So, what's up?"

"Oh, you know," Winnie said, "the usual."

"Mm, the pups? Stanley, Bertie? Douglas? Shall I go on?"

"Not really," said Winnie. "Just...everything."

"That really narrows things down, doesn't it?" Lottie pushed a steaming mug of Assam towards her friend and wrapped her paws around her own cup.

"I think I need a break and something to look forward to and concentrate my mind. And I don't mean more studies."

"Hear, hear to that!" Lottie exclaimed, tapping a spoon on the side of her mug after having shovelled half the sugar bowl into it. "All work and no play make Jill a dull girl. I think we all have those thoughts. You need a holiday, a long break. Just jump on a Greyhound bus or American Airlines jet and see where it takes you."

"Really, can you see me doing that? I'd get down to the next town or over the ocean and be homesick before the day was out," Winnie said.

"Perhaps, but that's if you didn't have someone with you," Lottie beamed. "I'm a sociable dog and all, but travel can be a daunting thing to do alone, even for me. What do you say we give it a go together, a road trip or something? We might even bump into some friends or make some?"

Winnie remembered something Bertie had told her— "never look a gift horse in the mouth"—and, rather out of character, just said yes straight away, without even thinking about it.

"Decided, then," Lottie said. "Now where did I put my suitcase?"

"You're going to need more than one, with your wardrobe," Winnie giggled. But Lottie was too enamoured of her idea to take any notice.

"I know just where to get tickets in Piedmont Bay. I've been by a thousand times and looked at the travel posters. You get yourself together and talk your Aunt Bea round, and we'll be off by Friday!" Lottie left her untouched tea and dashed to the door. "And don't you dare have second thoughts, Winifred Wigglesworth, or I'll…" but whatever dire threat she uttered was lost as she fairly collided with Stanley in the doorway.

When they had disentangled themselves, the budgie burst through the door, still muttering imprecations, and was met by two deserted mugs of tea. "Fred?" he squawked, picking up the yellow hat in his claws and tossing it over a peg. But there was no reply. "What's she gone and done a runner for?" he wondered aloud. "Well, can't let this go to waste, anyway." And he drank deeply from one of the mugs. "Phlbbttt!" he spluttered and unceremoniously sloshed the remains of Lottie's tea into the sink. "Those two will be the death of poor Stan! Can't even get in me own front door and have a decent cup of tea anymore!"

Having made good her escape, Winnie fairly flew over the frosty ground, not caring where she went, a newfound sense of freedom tingling through her like electricity.

Chapter Three
Room Without a View

The room Bertie and Muriel had rented for the evening was compact to say the least. As they entered, they were greeted by an en suite bathroom on the left and two beds in the centre of the room, separated by a small bedside cabinet and lamp. There was a minute dressing table with tea stains on the surface, along with a small kettle and two cups, lit by the feeble glow of a fluorescent light above, its pull cord missing the handle. Someone had made an attempt to brighten the room with a yucca plant, but it looked a bit forlorn in its corner. Roughly textured wallpaper was coming away in various places and stained in others, while the blue carpet had bald spots and tucked up at the edges. The room was simply lit by an unshaded bulb, which was probably for the best, given its low wattage. Humble as it all was, it was ample for their needs, as they wouldn't be staying more than a night.

On the far side of the room was a large window, and Bertie placed his suitcase on the bed and walked over. As he drew the curtains, he realised why they had been left shut—ten feet in front of him was a brick wall. 'So much for the view,' he thought, quickly shutting them again before Muriel looked over.

"You take me to all the best places, Bertie," Muriel said as she studied the room.

"I'm afraid it was all we could get at rather short notice," Bertie replied apologetically. "But I'm glad we decided to disembark from the ship at Le Havre and go 'off-piste' so to speak. I know we only travelled from Southampton for a short while but that was enough. Really, I don't know if I could have taken a whole Mediterranean cruise with those others aboard.

"It's not as if we are getting old, is it, Bertie?" Muriel joked. "My, look at this painting on the side wall, it's...well..."

"Not to your taste," Bertie said as he approached and studied the artwork.

"Maybe we should have invited Hans along. He could have been our resident art critic," Muriel chuckled.

The painting portrayed a rather elegant bichon frise, dressed in a long robe and holding a silver topped walking stick. He was standing in the grounds of a country estate, a boxwood maze and manor house behind him. The plaque on the front was badly faded, so only 'Duke of Arting...' was decipherable. It was quite a dark painting, with a shadowy background, but the dog's facial features were well defined, and he held his superior nose in the air. They both turned away from it and looked around for something to divert their attention, but nothing presented itself.

"Well, we may as well have a go at the kettle," Bertie said hopefully, and made two cups of coffee with the powder and dried milk provided. He valiantly drank from the rather grubby cup, trying not to catch his mouth on the chip. Muriel thanked him and drank thirstily until she realised it tasted rather awful. She sidled over to the yucca plant. "Lovely cuppa never had anything like it," she said as she poured the contents into the pot.

"Never again," Bertie thought, and he covertly tipped his cup into the plant when Muriel had moved away and turned her back.

The pair were rather tired, and as they had already eaten before arriving, they decided to call it a night. They had left a packet of dry biscuits on the dresser for the morning, Bertie having managed to buy some before leaving the ship. It was lucky that he had, given the hotel did not offer breakfast. Tucking up in bed, he apologised for the room, but Muriel brushed it off casually, and he smiled at her graciousness.

Just as he was getting off, he heard a thud and flicked on the bedside lamp. Muriel was already asleep and didn't stir. Rubbing his eyes, he could see that the painting had fallen off the wall, and the aristocratic duke was staring back at him from an awkward position on the floor. Bertie hopped out of bed, picked up the painting and quickly hung it back on the wall. He slid quietly back into bed, glad he hadn't awoken Muriel.

In the middle of the night Bertie was once again awakened by a noise. Sitting up in bed, he could still hear Muriel's regular breathing, but nothing else. He looked around and didn't see anything so decided to ignore it this time and go back to sleep.

In the morning, Bertie awoke first. It wasn't the blazing sun shining in that ended his slumber, as there wasn't any. The room was pretty much as dark as the night before. His ears were assaulted by a banging and crashing next door as the tenants exited their room. He heard one of them screeching.

"That's the last time I'm coming away with you! This was meant to be a romantic weekend, but oh no, you had to go and book this dive!"

"My fault, is it? That is rich! You really are an ungrateful madam! Where did you think we were going to go on my wage, eh?"

The argument went on as the pair stomped down the corridor. Bertie yawned, looked around and spotted the painting on the floor again. 'Odd,' he thought. 'Maybe I'll tell the owner on our way out.'

Muriel was rising just as Bertie finished rehanging the painting. Sitting up and stretching her legs in the air she sprang into action with a glint in her eyes and dived into the bathroom, leaving Bertie standing in surprise, now crossing his legs. Needing something else to think about, he gathered their belongings, put the half pack of biscuits in the suitcase and closed the lid. He noticed the floor around the yucca plant looked rather damp, so he grabbed the pot and pulled it a little further into the room.

Muriel stepped outside the building into the fresh air as Bertie paid for the room. He didn't feel the need to comment on the decor and state of the place. He took one look at the cat behind the counter, a cigarette drooping from one corner of his mouth and a greasy bandana looped around his neck and decided that to do so would be pointless. But the memory of his interrupted night's sleep meant that he could not leave the establishment without comment. "One thing before I leave. The painting in our room seemed to keep falling off the wall. Maybe the hook needs fixing or something?"

The attendant looked down at the key fob on the counter and said very matter-of-factly, "Oh, Room 114, yup, that room's haunted mate, all the residents say that. I always get a cold feeling when I enter that room, steer clear myself. Old Bobby the cleaner swears he can hear voices too, and he told me some story about the subject of the painting coming to a rather sad demise round these parts."

"Really, you don't say." Bertie smiled cautiously and decided not to tell Muriel about what he had just been told.

"Good for the ghost hunters though, they love a bit of mystery. Always book that room, they do. And of course, we can't disappoint them, so we haven't renovated it in donkey's years, keep up the atmosphere, you know." The cat delivered himself of this piece of information with all the innocence of a young kitten who had just knocked over a vase and looked up at its mother with saucer shaped eyes.

Upstairs, in a small hole in the ceiling above the painting, a very content mouse in a beige turtleneck jumper lay quietly sleeping, tummy full, dreaming of the feast of dry biscuits he had eaten during the night.

Chapter Four
The Yellow Brick Road

Eddie sat at his desk with his chin in his paws, a stack of uncatalogued books unheeded at his elbow and his mug of tea growing cold. At present, his mind was on matters wholly unconnected with the Wagminster Library, or books, or tea. But the sight of a brand-new tin of Jaffa cakes made him smile in the midst of his reverie. His nephews, bless them, were under the false impression that he needed a monthly supply of these most British delicacies, and he had never had the heart to disabuse them of that notion. He had found a much more appreciative recipient, and it was to this particular dog that his thoughts now strayed.

He had been considering a particular matter for quite some time, riffling through various books of poetry on his own shelves and then poring over obscure volumes at the library, all to no avail. There was a notebook locked away in his desk that he occasionally pulled out and scribbled in, but he inevitably crossed everything out and slammed it shut impatiently before returning it to the farthest reaches of the drawer and turning the key. A bit absent-minded at the best of times, Eddie had excelled himself in recent weeks and became the talk of the staff lunchroom when he left his hat in the refrigerator and his bag lunch in the coat closet one morning. Of this he was blissfully unaware, as one of the kindest of his colleagues, a motherly Maltese named Mrs Pettifer, had quietly rectified the error. She took a genuine interest in his welfare, as he lived in the house the Pettifers once owned, and they were just up the road from him.

She approached him now. "Mr Kimber?" Eddie did not stir from his trance, so she laid a paw lightly on the shoulder of his tweed jacket. "Mr Kimber, those two little tykes Augie and Dino are asking for you." Eddie started and looked at her in confusion. "I tried plying them with graham crackers, apple juice and a story, but nothing doing. They want you," she continued, her dark eyes twinkling amid masses of white fur.

Eddie rubbed his eyes and smiled at her. "That's all right. Bring them in here and give yourself and Sophia a break," he said, pulling a basket of Lego bricks out from under his desk. "The little rascals know these are in here."

The two pups had been waiting outside the door, tails wagging in anticipation, and they now tumbled in noisily, grasping Eddie ecstatically by the trouser legs before diving into the coloured bricks and immediately scattering them to the four corners of the office. Eddie smiled at the prospect of a patron, Mrs Pumphrey most likely, appearing at his desk, waving a blue brick in her paw and causing a scene.

Dino picked out all the green and yellow bricks and set about a self-appointed task with intense concentration, whilst Augie happily tasted each colour in turn. Eddie gently replaced them with some larger bricks and sat back, returning to his musings. Absently fiddling with a few of the tiniest bricks he had confiscated from Augie, he looked down and realised that he had affixed them to the centre of a thin, flat piece. He picked at it with a claw for a few minutes and then tossed it aside. "Confound the wretched things," he muttered.

"Looky! Looky what Dino made!" The pup held his creation aloft, a green rectangle balanced on two yellow columns. "What is it? Can you guess?" And before Eddie could venture a reply, Dino bounced about the room, still holding the object above his head, and chanting, "Stan-ley, Stan-ley!" Augie eagerly lifted up his voice, too, though slightly out of sync.

And at that moment, despite the clamour and chaos, an idea came, thanks to this evocation of Bertie's cantankerous budgie. "Shhh, you two. Yes, very well done, Dino. Now, it's time to play the 'quiet game,' Eddie said. "Sit very still and don't utter a peep for five minutes. The quietest one wins"— he looked around desperately— "a Jaffa cake." Round eyed with desire, the pups subsided, and Eddie flicked through his Rolodex for a particular number.

At that moment a familiar white tabby cat appeared in front of him. "You've got your hands full there Eddie," she said, smiling. "Maybe I can help?"

Eddie looked up at his friend Cilla, a teacher from a nearby school who frequented the library. "I'm trying to organise an expedition, top secret, you know." He dipped his head in the direction of the pups. "What did you have in mind?" The cat should see the relief on his face.

"An ex-pupishun!" Dino cried, dropping his masterpiece and dancing about. "Ouchy! Legos hurt!"

"Augie win," the pup said to Eddie in a whisper, tugging at the sleeve of his jacket.

"Indeed, you did, my lad," he said, slipping a cake into Augie's paws and another in his pocket for the moment when Dino realised his loss.

A second later Cilla had placed her books and satchel down on the desk and popped around the counter. "Hello there, would you like to play a game together?" she asked. Dino and Augie jumped up in delight. The quiet game wasn't very appealing, and this cat looked so much more fun.

"Hello, Jack. Yes, it's Eddie. I say, you wouldn't be able to do me a small favour, would you?"

Cilla was leading the two bouncing balls of energy away whilst Eddie continued his call.

"Righto! We'll be round in shortly. Thanks!"

At this juncture, Sophia poked her head round the door and looked at him apologetically. Eddie grinned at her and finished his conversation.

"Oh, if you have somewhere to go, I'll get the two pups out of your way," Sophia said. "I did think they would be happy with Mrs Pettifer for a quarter of an hour while I dashed to the post office. I'm so sorry." She patted down the ruffled fur around her ears and looked at him anxiously.

"Not at all," Eddie said jovially. "They are currently being entertained elsewhere, and you mustn't go haring off. We're going on a little trip!"

Chapter Five
The Getaway

The journey by train and bus from La Havre to Paris had passed largely without incident, although Muriel had fallen rather spectacularly over an umbrella protruding into the centre aisle of the bus. Bertie had proven himself quite capable of catching her, thankfully, and he had given the offending passenger a suitably fierce glare before almost going head over tail himself. "I say, keep your clobber out of the way, will you?" he said a bit testily, looking back at the dog whilst guiding Muriel to their seats. "You could have injured the lady." Muriel smiled covertly, not entirely sorry that she had nearly come to grief, as it had given Bertie a chance to show his gentlemanly side. And she had to admit to herself, though she never would to Bertie, that perhaps she hadn't tried particularly hard to keep her balance.

Late that afternoon, the pair emerged into a bright forecourt and sauntered over to an outdoor café that afforded them a view of the spectacular entrance to the Louvre. A waiter set cups of café au lait and a plate of madeleines before them. "What service!" Bertie marvelled. "I don't recall ordering anything."

"I do believe it's their polite way of keeping tourists from merely stopping here to rest without spending a few francs," Muriel said with a smile. "Did you enjoy our little jaunt? There is so much to see! I could spend a week there, but I appreciate it might not have been quite your cup of tea." Muriel looked at Bertie questioningly.

Bertie chuckled. "I have to admit that when we began walking around the gallery, I was sure I would feel like I did when I was about six and Samantha took me, or rather dragged me, around clothes shops, when I would have much preferred to be in the fields playing. But I did find it very interesting. I know I'm not very artistic and don't know much about fashion or art in general, but I did learn a lot. Perhaps we can go back tomorrow?" he offered, smiling.

"I'm not sure if that last suggestion is quite honest or not. I wonder if I should call your bluff, Bertie," Muriel answered with a laugh.

"You can try, but I have a very good poker face," Bertie replied. He suddenly remembered the last time he had played the card game with Harry and Nap and hoped Muriel had forgotten. He swiftly changed the subject. "Shall we hail a taxi to get us back to the hotel? I'd rather not get on the Metro at this time of day. I'm sure it gets very busy."

Muriel agreed, and once the bill was settled, she looked around and spotted a taxi rank. "Oh, there's one, over there," she exclaimed as she waved her paw in the air. The taxi driver spotted her and pulled the rather woebegone-looking Peugeot estate up to the kerbside for them to enter. Bertie held the door open and gestured. "*Entree*, Madame," he said with a valiant attempt at the appropriate accent, and Muriel slid inside. Just as Bertie was about to get in himself, a rather out of breath cat with a bag slung over one arm ran up to them.

"*Excuse-moi*, I'm so sorry, would it be possible to share your taxi? I'm in such a rush, my son has had an accident, you see, terrible! I'm fraught with worry, and I need to get home as soon as I can," the cat sobbed.

"Oh dear, how sad," Muriel said from within the car. "Is he hurt?"

"I really don't know. I just had a call; it was all rather brief. He's always falling out of the tree at home or getting up to some mischief, but can't be too careful, can I?" the cat said, wringing her paws.

"Of course, we aren't going very far. That'll be fine, won't it, Bertie?" Muriel replied.

Bertie was a bit put out, looking at the cat with eyebrows lowered and with some distaste. He really wasn't sure she wasn't just after a free ride, but he reluctantly agreed. He walked around the car and got into the passenger side next to the driver and started to tell him the name of their hotel.

The taxi driver must have been listening to the previous conversation because the moment Bertie had finished talking, he jammed his foot on the accelerator and screeched off. Bertie clung to the dash, remembering he had been warned that drivers in France were quite aggressive, and he was proved right when the Peugeot's horn sounded more often than a police siren in an emergency. He slunk deep into his seat and tipped his hat down over his eyes, not wishing to witness the carnage that was likely to occur. As he did so, a couple of pedestrians regretted walking into the road and quickly jumped back onto the safety of the pavement, not before waving their paws at the taxi in disgust.

In the opposite direction, a fleet of police cars streamed down the centre of the street. One of them narrowly missed clipping the Peugeot as the driver deftly slipped into a gap behind a Citroen DS, pulling out immediately when the last car had passed. After what seemed like an eternity, Bertie and Muriel were deposited at the entrance to their hotel. "I do hope your son is unhurt," Muriel said kindly, looking through the open window at the cat, who was looking considerably less distressed than she had ten minutes ago. "Son...oh, *merci, Madame, oui. Au revoir.*" The taxi peeled away with its customary panache.

"Free ride," Bertie commented, bemused, as he stood holding the coins for the fare. "Not that we didn't nearly pay with our lives." Muriel gazed after the taxi and pondered but kept her own counsel.

Chapter Six
Salad Days

Bertie guided Muriel to her seat and then took up his own in the elegant dining carriage of the Pullman coach. They were due to set off from the station at Chartreux at any minute. It was certainly a novelty for Bertie to be eating in this fashion. He was not used to it and was constantly aware of others watching his every move—but perhaps that was just his over-enthusiastic imagination. Muriel had told him often enough that she was not interested in moving in society circles any longer, but that knowledge did little to calm his nerves, as the other passengers certainly seemed to fit that bill. She smiled at him, appreciating the efforts he was still making, and perused the menu. Bertie looked out of the window and brooded over events from the previous day.

After their death-defying cab ride from the Louvre, they had opted to travel to and from the Musée D'Orsay by the Métro. On the way back to the hotel, their conversation naturally turned to what they had just seen. Bertie had been rather more interested in the modern art exhibition, Muriel in the 19th-century sculpture and paintings, and they debated the merits of each. Deafened by the roar and screech of the underground train, Bertie had misheard Muriel's description of a particular painting, thinking she had said it was *garish*, and then hastened to agree with her, saying he disliked it too. "Awful colours," he'd said, nodding vigorously. In fact, she had been describing the shape of a particular dog's posterior and said it was *pearish*, as in the fruit, much to Bertie's embarrassment. Fortunately, no one else heard his faux pas.

After the pair had travelled along a few stations on the tube train, a family entered the carriage. A young pup was talking in English and chatting away merrily with her brother. The brother was carrying a rather nice-looking camera on his shoulder and in deep conversation. Bertie watched them as he held onto the grab handle, although he was really quite happy, as the swinging motion almost reminded him of being on his dory on the choppy seas. A moment later, he spotted a dog with a coat draped over his arm, and he thought he just looked out of place somehow. He continued to watch as this dog approached the young pup, then saw his other paw slowly emerge from under the coat, move towards the camera bag, unzip the cover and reach inside. A second later, the English pup had given the intruder's paw an almighty whack with a rolled-up magazine, which caused him to recoil and shout a series of expletives at her in French. Unbeknown to the miscreant, the pups' parents spoke fluent French, and they understood exactly what the dog had shouted out.

"What is the meaning of this, you young thug? There I was, simply travelling along in peace, when I was attacked in broad daylight! Did you see that? I have a train full of witnesses." The parents explained to their pups what the thief had said, and he was chastised in his own tongue by all and sundry. Another passenger apprehended him and held him until the next station, where he was duly taken away by the gendarmerie, despite his protestations. Bertie had admired the young pup's pluck and was reminded of Samantha, who certainly would have done the same, he was sure.

"Soup or salad, Bertie?" Muriel asked.

Bertie was awakened from his daydreaming, looked at Muriel and then at the waiter standing over their table with pen tapping his notepad. He could tell from her tone and cocked head that this was not the first time she'd made the enquiry.

"What? Oh, yes, that sounds lovely," he replied. "Never heard of a 'super salad' before, but I'm sure it will be delicious."

The waiter looked towards Muriel with a slightly exasperated expression.

"He'll have the salad as well," Muriel replied in French, saving Bertie from any more embarrassment, and smiling at him. The waiter turned on his heel. "Really, Bertie, I feel as if you left your powers of speech at the station. What is the matter?"

"Oh, nothing." He attempted to draw her attention to something else. "Do you know Muriel, there are two Cavalier King Charles spaniels over at the next table that look rather similar, both wearing the same dresses and matching silver hats?" Bertie said, as his glass was filled by another, more communicative waiter. He mopped up a small spill and leaned down confidentially.

"Oh sir, that is Miss Louisa and Miss Lucille.* They are mother and daughter, with us for the entire journey," the waiter explained. "They are *très magnifique*, are they not? Such *je ne sais quoi*." He warmed to his theme, lifting his paws expressively. "Seldom do we have even one such elegant passenger, and here, two!" He paused and corrected himself a bit sheepishly. "Oh, three...pardon, Madame."

Muriel looked up at the waiter and then back down to her glass but decided not to turn around. She remembered exactly who the two dogs were and really did not want to have to speak to them. She noticeably hunkered down in her chair. Bertie noted her reaction and tried to make light of the situation, whatever it was. "If I was to compliment the mother on looking like her daughter, she would probably think I thought she looked quite young. But on the other hand, I wonder if the daughter would think I was saying she was looking rather old?" He rubbed his whiskers in mock consternation.

"I would keep your thoughts to yourself, Bertie, and stay well away from those two—and whatever you do, don't compliment either of them," Muriel said with an unusual sharpness in her tone.

"Too late, one of them is coming over now," Bertie replied. "Stand by your beds!"

"Why, it is, I knew it! I thought it was you, Moo! I haven't seen you in years, I was just saying to mother I believed I saw you boarding the train and she didn't believe me. She said the dorgi looked far too old to be your good self. Oh, my, fancy that," Lucille said with a smirk and titter of laughter. "And who is this handsome gentle dog?" she said as she turned all of her attention to Bertie. "My, you've caught yourself a big fish here."

"My name is Bertie, and may I ask whom I am addressing?"

"Why, of course, fine sir, I am Lucille Meredith Hunter, but you can call me Lucy if you wish," Lucille replied in a flirtatious manner.

"Charmed, I'm sure," Bertie said in his finest imitation of a nasal aristocratic voice. "I do love the colour of that dress, oh and the pattern, just divine."

Muriel began to laugh, having heard Bertie's impression of a high society gent before, and nearly choked on an olive. Lucille turned around to find out what was so amusing.

"Sorry," Muriel said, feigning a cough as she reached for her empty glass. "Please excuse me for a moment, while I…"

"Yes, dear," Lucille said, "you go and sort yourself out." She lost no time in taking Muriel's seat and turning her full attention to Bertie. "I'm surprised to see old Moo Moo here actually, she's been a recluse for ever so long. Wherever did you two meet?" she said, with her eyes fixed firmly on her new companion. Bertie wondered what to say. He could either continue his little charade and have some fun or tell the truth. Whichever version of events he decided to recount he was certain he would be in trouble with Muriel, but his decision was made quite easy by what Lucille said next.

"Why, did I detect a slight accent in your voice, Bertie? Perhaps Australian?"

Bertie looked up and saw Louisa staring in his direction, sipping a cup of tea, and he almost thought he had double vision as he shifted his focus to the other dog in front of him. The suggestion was like a red rag to a bull, and he couldn't let the comment go unanswered.

"Why, that is very perceptive of you, my dear! I have been to those shores on many an occasion. In fact, I have a little villa in a spot called Kookaburra Island, a most beautiful and peaceful place. I've often sat on the porch at sundown and just looked up into the sky and studied the stars as I drifted off to sleep. Have you heard of the place?"

"I have, I have, Bertie, and I've always wanted to go there. But alas, I've not had anyone so dashing as yourself to take me."

"That is sad indeed, a fine dog like yourself, I'm sure you would love it there. Although it can be beastly hot at the wrong time of year."

"Oh yes," Lucille said, "that is very true."

"And you must watch out for the spiders, especially in the dunnies, certainly wouldn't want a black widow crawling up your leg and setting up home in your...undergarments," Bertie said, realising it really didn't matter what he said. Lucille was smitten with him, and he was afraid that if he allowed things to continue much longer, the mother might join them too. 'How do I keep getting into these blasted pickles,' he thought ruefully, though he had to admit that he was rather enjoying himself, too. It wasn't every day that a female of the upper classes—or any female, really—looked at him with such adoration. Never mind that she'd no doubt lose interest the moment he told her of his humble origins. Perhaps that should be his next revelation.

The waiter returned, poured Lucille a glass of wine and then turned to Bertie. "Sir, your salad will be arriving shortly," he said. Lucille looked up and immediately interrupted.

"Oh, splendid, I'm famished! Moo Moo can take something in her carriage, can't she Bertie? Waste not, want not as my mother always says." The waiter didn't really have a clue what she was talking about but simply nodded and disappeared to get the food as requested.

Behind the door at the end of the carriage, Muriel was peeping through the glass and getting a bit restless. She could see the back of Bertie's head and Lucille chatting away but could hear nothing over the clatter of the wheels. 'What is she saying?' she thought. 'It's a shame I can't read lips, but I'll be darned if I go back now. Still, I hope she's not torturing Bertie too much.' She cast about, wondering what to do. A stack of yesterday's newspapers sat in the corner, ready to be offloaded at the next stop, so she grabbed several and pushed them between the sliding door and the jamb, creating a small gap to listen through.

Lucille smiled at Bertie, leaning forwards. "I'm sure you are wondering how I know Moo Moo, aren't you? I was at boarding school with her, and we spent many happy years in the dorms together at St Cuthbert's."

"Really," Bertie replied, and decided he would try and flatter the dog to at least make things interesting. "But you look so much younger. Were you in the same year?"

"Oh, you tease, Bertie, but it's true! I have always looked young for my age, everyone says it. Lucille preened a bit, surreptitiously checking her reflection in the window.

"I'm sure there are some stories you could tell you about those years and the mischief you got up to?" Bertie suggested.

"Oh my, yes, there certainly are," she said with a wink.

*__Lucille and Louisa:__ The two King Charles spaniels were named by one of the authors, who, as a child, owned a train set with two Pullman carriages of the same names. They looked wonderful in their chocolate and cream livery with silver roofs.

Chapter Seven
A Seafood Saga

Lucille finished her plate of salad before Bertie had even had a mouthful. 'She certainly liked her food,' Bertie thought, as he watched her gulp down the wine, too, and then lick her lips contentedly.

"School stories you say. Well, there was the time when we got a new a French teacher. He was rather suave and debonair, wore a lovely brown checked tweed suit too and green tie. Every young pup had gooey eyes for him, except for Moo Moo. He spoke with an amazing accent and had a wonderful smile, just like you Bertie. Many girls used to give him a present at the start of the lesson or come up with an excuse just so we could be a little bit closer to him, and if he perched on your desk, well, we were in dreamland. One day we were tasked with practicing some conversation in pairs, but the class had an odd number of students that day. Moo Moo—the lucky devil—was the odd one out, so she got to speak with Mr Charpentier…"

Bertie was wondering when Lucille would come up for air. She didn't seem to ever stop talking. No wonder Muriel had made a hasty retreat.

"…All the other pups were very jealous, and one decided to play a trick on her. Constance, the head girl, sneaked up to the blackboard, grabbed the chalk and scribbled a large heart with an arrow through it with the words 'Muriel 4 Mr C' in the middle. Moo Moo was so embarrassed that she ran straight into the toilets and cried. Of course, I tried to comfort her, but it was simply ages before the others stopped teasing her, poor lamb."

"I can see…" Bertie began, but Lucille was off again.

"Oh, but that was nothing compared to the incident with the hamster, oh that was so funny, in fact mother tells the story so much better than I do. Mother, Mother!" Lucille called. "You don't mind, do you Bertie, of course you don't, three's company, two is a date, I always say…there you go, Mother, I can't have you sitting over there all alone when I'm enjoying such wonderful company in the form of this debonair young dog here."

Louisa got up, gathered her purse and walked up to their table.

"Bertie, this is my mother, Louisa Meredith Hunter, but don't call her Lou as she really detests it, don't you Mother? Now, where was I?"

Bertie courteously acknowledged the dog who had now taken up residence in the seat directly opposite him. His expression was a picture, as he was now looking at a second dog wearing a chocolate-coloured dress with the same pattern as her daughter. Louisa was just about to speak as she tidied the cutlery in front of her, but before she could get a word in edgeways, Lucille was off again.

"Mother, now what was the name of our headmaster at St Cuthbert's, Mr, err…"

"Mr Darby, dear," Louisa replied meekly.

Bertie smiled. This poor dog might have looked like her daughter, but Lucille must have inherited her loquacious tendency from her father's side of the family.

"Oh, lovely Mr Darby, I still send him Christmas cards, you know, and a handwritten note inside letting him know of my exploits over the year. Do you know, he was married to one of the teachers, but no one knew, of course? It was a secret, they had different surnames you see. Well, except for year five, they all knew, oh, and year seven, of course. I really don't know why he didn't just tell everyone. She passed away a year or so ago, very sad. I was at the funeral, lovely affair it was, shame about the vicar, wouldn't have been my choice of hymns either, but there you go, we all have our own tastes, don't we Bertie?"

'Oh my,' Bertie thought, nearly in agony. 'What am I going to do? It's only lunchtime! I'm going to be stuck with these two until it gets dark, at this rate. Lucille is like a Duracell bunny, she only needs a drum to complete her ensemble!'* His eyes started to glaze over as he saw the waiter returning, no doubt about to ask what they would like for their next course.

"A note for you, sir," the waiter said, as he handed a folded piece of paper to Bertie, who took it with some surprise and promptly read the two lines in Muriel's distinctive script.

Bertie, don't worry, I'll rescue you. Just order the shrimp.

Bertie couldn't help but wonder why ordering shrimp might be the solution to his problem, but he did as he was told. He didn't relish doing so, but if this was to be the means of his salvation, so be it.

"Ladies, would you like to order a main?" he asked.

Lucille evinced great pleasure at this evidence that she would be able to continue her conversation with Bertie and asked the waiter to bring their existing order to the new table when it was ready. Her mother showed no sign of emotion and picked a bit of lint off her skirt. Bertie then did as he was instructed, checked the menu, and requested the shrimp with a honey garlic marinade and a garnish of green onion. To his surprise the expressions on the faces of the two dogs opposite changed in an instant. Their eyes grew large, and their ears drooped. Lucille gulped a bit. At the same time the train slowed and started crossing tracks as it changed direction and the carriage rocked somewhat. Both dogs reached for their glasses of water and each took a sip. The waiter returned very quickly and presented the mother and daughter with their entrées, chicken with white beans and escarole, whilst Bertie was given his garlic shrimp.

"Mmm, lovely, thank you," Bertie said, as he watched the other two slowly pick up their knives and forks and take mouthfuls. Bertie noticed that Lucille had gone incredibly quiet, which was a blessing, but he politely attempted to make some conversation.

"Oh, I do love shrimp. You know, I've been on a shrimp boat and caught it myself, makes all the difference you know." He didn't get much of a reaction from the pair, so he continued. "You know, shrimp is so versatile. You can boil it, bake it, add it into all sorts of dishes, I've even had shrimp sandwiches cooked on the barbie, you know." Bertie waited a minute and noticed the dogs had put their cutlery down. "Oh, I hope there isn't something wrong with your food? Here, would you like to try some of mine? It is delicious." Munching on a bit of green onion, he proffered his steaming plate to Lucille.

That was the straw that broke the camel's back. Lucille immediately gulped, put her paw to her mouth, got up and ran down the aisle as fast as her legs could carry her to find the nearest convenience. Her mother, on the other hand, was not so nimble. She turned her head from side to side, her eyes wild, as if looking for something, and then proceeded to vomit into the handbag of the passenger behind her. The cat gasped in utter disgust, stood up and started throwing her paws in the air, trying to usher Louisa away from her table as fast as she could. "Get away you ghastly creature! I have never been so embarrassed in all my years! Benjamin! I say, Benjamin, sort this mess out at once!" Her companion called for the harassed waiter, who bore the handbag away.

Poor Louisa tried to make haste for the exit whilst the cat continued her barrage. The whole of the carriage had stopped eating their meals and were watching the scene before them, Bertie included. He quickly got up and took Louisa's paw, gently guiding her towards the closest door. Muriel, who had been watching from a safe distance, moved backwards and out of sight. After passing through the gangway connection, Bertie pulled down the window of the adjoining carriage and told Louisa to take several deep breaths. The wind rushed in, and she stood there a moment, doing exactly as she was told despite still feeling slightly wobbly on her paws. Bertie held her arm, ready to assist her if necessary. The waiter peered through the glass window, and Bertie nodded in his direction, waving a paw to tell him everything was under control.

"I think the fresh air is doing the trick," Louisa replied, seeming to have found her voice now that her daughter was not around. "I don't know what it is, but the whole family is the same, we have a rather abnormal reaction to seafood. I had hoped it may have jumped a generation with Lucille, but she is afflicted, too."

"I wouldn't worry too much about it, just one of those things," Bertie assured her.

Muriel stepped forward, feeling rather guilty, and offered some kind words, whilst patting Louisa gently on the back.

"I'm afraid Lucille will insist we get off at the next stop and change trains," Louisa said. "She really doesn't like being embarrassed like that and would feel ever so uncomfortable knowing all those other passengers might be gossiping behind her back."

"How are you feeling now, Louisa?" Bertie enquired, seeing her eyes brightening a bit again.

"Much better, thank you, Bertie," she replied. "Oh, Muriel, are you okay now too? I do hope so. Right, I must go and check in on Lucille. Do excuse me." With that, Louisa trotted off through the dining carriage and back to the sleeping quarters.

Bertie looked at Muriel. "Well. That was an experience I don't wish to repeat."

"I certainly hope not Bertie," Muriel replied.

"Oh, and by the way," Bertie said. "I hate to say this, but didn't you know, I absolutely detest shrimp. It's a good job there were some vegetables on the plate, or I'd have been sticking my head out of the window with your friends."

*Duracell Bunny: Lucille, one of the King Charles spaniels was said to look like a Duracell Bunny. This is a reference to an anthropomorphic pink toy rabbit which was powered by Duracell batteries. Mallory Duracell first launched the Duracell Bunny campaign in 1973, and the brand still features the characters to this day. A series of advertisements normally featured one Duracell Bunny competing against other bunnies who were using standard battery power. By the end of the ad spot, only the Duracell one was still running.

Chapter Eight
No Friends of Mine

"I'm so sorry, Bertie. I think I should have warned you about Lucille. You can see why I didn't want to speak with her, or, more to the point, listen to her drone on and on without respite," Muriel said apologetically.

"Humph," Bertie replied. He was not in a particularly good mood after the past tortuous half hour.

"Don't be like that, Bertie," Muriel said, nudging him. "You found a way out of the situation like you always do, and you must surely see the funny side?"

"Grump," Bertie mumbled as he turned and saw Muriel's obvious contrition over how the situation in the dining car had played out.

"I suppose I forgive you, Muriel," Bertie said in a slightly begrudging fashion. "Although perhaps it is not just me that you should be apologising to," he added.

Muriel's face fell as she suddenly realised, she should really do the honourable thing and make sure both Louisa and Lucille were bearing up after their ordeal. But she really did not want to get stuck with the daughter, and what with their proximity on the train, she was hardly likely to be able to escape easily.

Bertie smiled, "I won't hold you to it. You can let your conscience decide, Moo Moo."

"Mmm," Muriel said under her breath. She loathed that nickname but decided to let it pass just this once. "You do know that Mr Charpentier wasn't French?"

Bertie looked into Muriel's deep brown eyes. "Don't tell me you were listening to our whole conversation from behind the carriage door?"

"Why, of course, I was. I needed to make sure you were okay," Muriel replied.

"Oh my, that does put a different slant on things. So, you didn't escape after all," he laughed.

"No, I didn't. I sat, or rather stood, through the whole thing too!"

"You were saying," Bertie prompted.

"Oh yes, Mr Charpentier. He could speak fluent French, there was no doubt about that, but his real name was Mr Carpenter, and he was from Nottingham. He just liked to put on the accent in front of the pups. I was passing the staff common room one evening, not sure why now, but he was in there on the phone talking to his wife. I peered round the door, as I didn't recognise the voice at first, and there he was good as brass. He didn't see me, so his secret was safe. But ever since that day I felt his halo had slipped somewhat, unlike all my other classmates who simply swooned over his charm."

"I understand now," Bertie said.

"Oh, and you shouldn't believe a word of Lucille's story about the head girl Constance. She was a friend of mine. It was Lucille herself who wrote that message on the chalkboard."

"Oh. Not so much of the 'poor lamb Moo Moo,' then," Bertie said, his eyebrows lifting at this new information.

"Certainly not. And about 'lovely Mr Darby.' Lucille and her cohorts tortured him relentlessly, leaving little gifts and notes for him 'and Mrs Darby' where everyone could see, in the common room, and on his desk, and even at a lectern just before he was due to address the assembly one morning. They were the ones who ferreted out his secret, you know, went through Miss Forsyth's handbag and found a note to 'my dearest Mrs D' from 'your ever-loving Mr D.' " Muriel gave Bertie a sidelong look.

Bertie's ill humour was rapidly evaporating, and he relaxed a bit under her gaze. "She certainly had me wrapped around her paw, then," he said ruefully.

"Oh, Bertie, I almost thought you were going a bit far yourself with your upper-class impersonation of a well-travelled businessman. You never did say what your line was," Muriel said a trifle mischievously.

"Well, Lucille was a bit too willing to believe everything I said, and I don't think she was actually listening anyway. I nearly said a lot worse."

"Well, you didn't. And you were a true gentle dog in the end, seeing to her mother like that. Made me feel quite a rotter, really," Muriel said, before cutting herself short, not wanting to revisit the final moments of that encounter. "But I was proud of you. I really felt for you once the mother came over, though. She is perhaps worse than the daughter in some ways. She will sit there in stone silence and is extremely hard to make conversation with. She tends to reply with monosyllabic answers and end conversations before they even start. It's like talking to a brick wall."

Bertie smirked and patted Muriel's paw. "Well. It's over now. And I just saw them disembarking, so we'll be spared their company for the rest of the journey. Would you like some shrimp?"

Chapter Nine
Stanley Causes a Scene

Winnie burst into Bertie's cottage from out of the clutches of a chill Nor'easter and immediately began building a fire in the grate. She had a letter from Bertie in her pocket, and, on a whim, she had decided that she wanted to curl up in his favourite chair and read it there. She rubbed her paws and pulled her hat further down over her ears. "Stan! Aren't you freezing, you exasperating creature? And you've left the window wide open!" She shook her head in disgust, pulled down the sash, and looked around the snug little room. Silence reigned, as sure a sign as any that the budgie was not in residence.

Winnie shrugged. No doubt he was up to mischief outdoors somewhere with his newfound pals. 'Good thing, too. Blow the stink off him,' she thought. 'And maybe reduce that tummy of his, too.' The fire was crackling merrily now, so she sunk into the depths of the worn leather chair and opened her letter, smiling fondly at Bertie's somewhat childish paw writing.

26th January 1978

Dear Winnie,

I hope your Christmas was a particularly good one. Shame that young Douglas had to get back here to work, but we all have our crosses to bear. He's a good chap, and you'll not find many like him, my girl. But then he's not likely to find many dogs like you, either.

Winnie felt a little pang in the vicinity of her heart. She had always known that Bertie was a true romantic, despite his reserve when it came to his own love life. But Douglas's latest letter had been brief and rather distant, and she certainly wasn't the kind of dog to go chasing after him. Putting her chin up a little, she continued to read.

Your Aunt Bea sent me an announcement of your early school graduation. You never did tell me, you silly sausage. Though of course I am not surprised.

You will be pleased to hear that the bracelet Percy found in Lady Effingham's lake was at length returned to him. He was understandably not keen to have something so valuable in the house again, so after consulting with Lady E. to make sure no offence would be taken, he has sold it. And then the old so-and-so wouldn't rest until he had given me half the proceeds. I do not feel at all right keeping it all, though. After setting a portion aside for a trip with Muriel, I've decided that I would like for the rest to go to you.

Winnie dropped the letter in her surprise, and a previously unnoticed cheque slipped from its folds. She scooped it up and put her paw to her mouth.

It's not a princely sum, but it should stand you in good stead for a couple of nights at the Ritz (wink). All I ask is that you come and see Muriel and me sometime this year. She is eager to meet you, and I have missed you, my dear.

Winnie's eyes misted a bit. It wasn't often that Bertie slipped into calling her that.

Do write to us with all your news. We have missed hearing from you since the New Year.

Fondly,

Bertie

P. S. How is that curmudgeon of a budgie faring? If you need to withdraw any funds from my Post Office account in order to keep him in the style to which he is accustomed, then by all means do so.

As if summoned by the postscript, a green and yellow head poked through the little flap over the door, and the rest of a plump, feathered body tumbled through.

"Cawr! You look cosy enough! I 'ope you 'aven't been at the last of my fruitcake, Fred. Stan will not stand fer that kind of treachery. Oi! What's the matter with yer? Going to be swallowin' flies at that rate. You must be guilty, then." Stan took up a perch in the window and fixed her with a beady-eyed glare.

"Your fruitcake is safe from me," Winnie replied, folding the letter and cheque into her pocket. "Must be about as old as you are and nearly as mouldy. Now, before I get your tea, I've got something to tell you."

"Arrrrh, don't tell me. Ran right out of fish fingers, 'ave we? Not the sort of news I need today, with it blowin' a right gale out there." Stan glanced at his reflection in the window and smoothed down his poll.

Winnie took a deep breath and prepared for battle. "I'm going to take a holiday," she said, as calmly as if she were merely informing him that she was popping down to the library. "I'm going to be out of town for a while."

Stanley shot off the window ledge and installed himself on the arm of the chair. "Wot? You...you're joking, you can't go! I won't 'ave it!" he squawked.

"I can and I am," Winnie replied, firmly.

"What about me? You promised Bertie you would look after me!" Stanley said querulously, his feathers well and truly ruffled, both literally and figuratively.

Winnie refused to be moved. "I did, and I have been doing exactly that for many months, and Douglas did, too. Anyway, you have lots of new friends now," she replied.

"Friends, mmm, I wouldn't go that far, Fred. Acquaintances, merely. I admit I might have misjudged Glenn a bit in the early days, well 'e was a greedy little seagull wasn't 'e, there is no denying that, but we do share the same taste in cheese. I must say I'm surprised by Bryson—now, 'is taste in food is a bit on the disgusting side sometimes. He'll eat anything."

"I'm with you there," Winnie replied. "Eating out of trash barrels is not quite my cup of tea, either. But I deserve a break, and I'm afraid you will have to fend for yourself for at least a couple of weeks. You've done it before, and it will do you good. The cottage needs to be kept up to scratch too, so you'll be so busy you won't have time to miss me."

"Cor, you don't mean that, surely. Cook for meself *and* clean? I'll be working my wings to the bone, I will. Yer a 'eartless one, Fred. Turnin' on an old pal like this. An' I's heard there's going to be a storm, Chief told me, and 'e doesn't usually get these things wrong. I think you'd better wait a while, just to be on the safe side? No 'arm in stopping 'ere for a little longer, make sure old Stanley is safe, is there?"

"This old cottage has weathered many a storm before your time, Stan. Nothing's going to happen to you here," Winnie assured him. She wouldn't put it past Stan to have exaggerated some offhand remark from Chief.

"Hmph," Stan answered.

"Are you going to miss me?" Winnie asked.

"Wot a thing to ask, Fred," Stanley replied, knowing full well he would miss the company of the young dachshund very much indeed. The cottage could get lonely without her banter. Bry, Glenn, Gertie and the rest were not at all keen on coming indoors. And of course, there were the lovely meals she cooked for him. "How's you going to pay for this trip anyway, missy?" Stan said, quickly changing the subject. "Cost's money, it does, to go travelling."

Winnie touched the cheque in her pocket but decided not to mention it just now. "Well, you won't remember, as it has nothing to do with your tummy, but I did some research into my family history last year. Aunt Bea found out about it and told my great-aunt Gwen. She was extremely interested in what I'd discovered and gave me a little gift to help cover my costs. She said that I needed to experience the world and not just read about it."

Stan was shocked into silence for a moment or two. He certainly hadn't seen that coming. "Never can tell what eccentric old dogs might do, I guess," he mumbled. But he quickly changed tactics. "Hah! I've got it! I'll come, too. I could do with a 'oliday meself. Make a great team, we will!

You could cook me the local food, and I'll be the navigator, make sure we keep going in the right direction," Stanley suggested. "And I could do my famous 'Bumbling Budgie' act and pass yer woolly 'at 'round if ever we were skint. Great-aunt Gwen's few bob can't last forever, now, can it? Especially with yer appetite."

Winnie rolled her eyes at him. "Oh, no, you're not coming. I'm not having you shouting at me and eating your way across the country." Half thinking, she may have been a little too harsh, she quickly moved on. "Oh, besides, Lottie is coming, and she is allergic to budgies." Before she could stop herself, she let it slip. "And Bertie has very kindly made sure I have some funds, too."

"Wot!!!" Stanley crowed. "Don't talk twaddle, no one is allergic to budgies! We are very accommodating birds!" Suddenly the full horror of Winnie's last words broke upon him. "And where did Bertie get money from? And why didn't 'e give me any?" he shouted, his eyes bulging a little more than usual.

"If you're going to take that line, I'm not going to tell you anymore," Winnie replied. "Bertie has made sure you have everything you could want. Pull yourself together, Stan. No need to be getting into a two-and-eight, as Bertie would say."

"Harrumph! Bertie giving Fred money and not thinking about poor Stanley. We were stowaways together, mates fer life. Fine way to treat an old pal, that is."

Winnie knew that there was not much hope of settling the matter if she did not steer the conversation along a different course. "Bertie has asked me to come visit him, you know. In England. He'd like for me to use some of the money to do that," she said calmly.

"Pah! England! I've told you I'd not go back there unless I was stuffed and mounted," Stanley retorted as he flew up to the top of the kitchen cupboard. "Where are those fish fingers, then? Don't s'pose yer going to begin starving me just yet, are ya?" And he crossed his wings and sat mumbling a string of colourful unprintables to himself.

Chapter Ten
Watch the Birdie

"If I didn't know better, I'd say we were headed to Cape Berkeley. But it's not quite tourist season, and everything is shut." Sophia glanced out the train's smudged window as yet another town flew by, and then looked inquiringly at Eddie. He was doing his level best to keep Augie from diving head over tail into the row in front of them, where a Labrador sprawled over three seats with various parcels and was mechanically munching through a dozen cider donuts.

Eddie smiled. "You'll have to be a bit more cunning than that if you think you're going to get round me and my vow of silence on the matter," he said with a wink. Sophia tossed her head playfully and turned back to the window. It was late winter, and everything was brown and grey and bare without a blanket of snow to hide the ugliness. Despite the uninspiring vista, Sophia's heart was light. She had no idea why, really, except that she was content to be here, now, with Eddie at her side, even in a dingy commuter train, and with the afternoon before them.

Eddie let his eyes rest on the corgi's lovely profile and had just begun a pleasant daydream when the dog ahead of them broke into his thoughts. "Hey! That pup's droolin' all over my stuff! Keep 'im outta my space, mister!" The disgruntled Labrador glared at the little group while continuing to make steady progress on his sixth donut. "Parents these days," he muttered darkly, spewing crumbs over the front of his black jumper.

"My apologies," Eddie replied, and rummaged in his pockets, which admittedly housed quite a miscellany, for something to occupy Augie's attention. As he did so, something clattered to the floor, and he hastily bent to retrieve it whilst handing the pup a miniature pinball game.

"What was dat?" Dino asked, wakening from an all-too-brief slumber.

"Just a noise from the train, don't you worry about it," Eddie replied, sneaking a sidelong glance at Sophia. But she was frowning slightly at the back of their fellow traveller's head and keeping a paw gently but firmly on Dino's shoulder.

"Beahington Neck, next stahp!" the conductor intoned in the nasal accents of a dog born and bred in the area.

"Bearington? Wha...?" But Sophia's query was cut short by an almighty screeching of the brakes and the clamour of two dozen other passengers hustling toward the door, pushing and barging with no thought of queuing.

The four of them stepped out onto the platform, and Eddie shepherded them well out of the way of the stampede. "I don't understand," Sophia said, her ears growing pointier with her perplexity.

"Just follow me," the Great Dane assured her. And at length they found themselves halfway down a quaint, narrow little street with one-time fishermen's cottages cheek-by-jowl on either side. Most were still boarded up for the season, though a little café on the corner offered an array of tempting strudels, and another more rustic establishment proclaimed that fresh-caught lobsters were to be had within. "Here we are," Eddie said, with a little note of triumph in his voice, as he stopped in front of another shop, its bright windows shedding a warm glow over the dim afternoon. The shingle, lettered in gold, said "Whittier & Soule, Olde Tyme Portraits."

Sophia laughed, and the pups pressed their noses to the plate glass, ogling the racks of colourful costumes and shelves of props within. "You know, I've always meant to bring them here, but the thought of crowds of summer tourists always put me off." She peeped in. "There's no one else here. Ah, that call you made," she said, her eyes dancing. "Winnie says you know everyone, and I'm inclined to believe her."

"I have my ways," Eddie grinned, as he knocked lightly on the door. It was opened by a Sheltie, fastidiously dressed in the manner of an Edwardian gentleman, waistcoat, silk cravat and all. "You must be Mr Kimber," he said, looking unenthusiastically down at Augie and Dino, who were prancing about with excitement. "Jack said you'd be coming, but he didn't mention any—"

"Pleased to meet you," Eddie interrupted. "This is Mrs Pembroke and her pups Augie and Dino."

"Whitty," the Sheltie said, nodding briefly at Sophia. For a moment they were taken aback, wondering what had prompted this observation, as Eddie hadn't said anything remotely amusing. "Short for Whittier," he explained, with a sniff.*

"Pleasure," said Sophia.

"Now, if you'd like to step over here, you may have a look at samples of our photos from various eras. "Revolutionary War, Civil War…"

"Mmm. Maybe a more peaceful period?" Sophia suggested.

"Ah, yes, and you're Brits from your accents, so not really of interest, eh? There's the Old West," Whitty said, doubtfully, flipping to a photo of a rather voluptuous dog in a low-cut number with a gunslinger on each arm. "You could forgo the guns, I suppose."

Eddie looked at Sophia, who shook her head slightly.

"Oh, and the Roaring Twenties." The Sheltie sighed as the pups suddenly burst from restraining paws and dove toward a garish gold and red costume. "And, of course, Jack has insisted that we do pirates. Suppose that might do for you? Plenty of those where you come from," he said with a smirk.

Suddenly, there was a commotion in the back of the shop. "Well, shiver me timbers, we've got visitors!" came a voice that sounded vaguely familiar. Augie and Dino ceased their rummaging amongst the swords and paste jewellery and dashed with one accord over to a twitching red curtain. Dino nosed it aside. There stood a grey cat and a ginger kitten. The kitten was hopping from paw to paw uncomfortably in a pair of tall leather boots and struggled to get a view of the newcomers from under a wide-brimmed and plumed hat worthy of any Cavalier. The grey cat seemed more comfortable in eye-patch, headscarf, billowing shirt, and knee-length trousers. "Yarrr, matey! Who goes there?" he shouted in an attempt at pirate-speak. "Ye'll be walkin' the plank soon if ye don't watch yerself! Me mate Puss in Boots here'll see to that!" As he hoisted his cutlass above his head and brandished it about for emphasis, a row of feathered ladies' hats and gentleman's bowlers hanging from the roof beam came crashing into a heap on top of Whitty.

"Wilbur! Gabe! What are you doing here?" Sophia exclaimed, as she rushed to aid the poor Sheltie and Eddie collected the fallen headgear.

Wilbur pulled off his hat and looked at Gabe in disgust. "You doofus! I told you not to go waving that thing around!" Gabe looked abashed, and Wilbur clumped over to help sort out the mess. "We sort of, well, we've got a job," he said, turning a little redder under his whiskers.

Gabe had found his voice again and chimed in. "Yeah. We hitched a ride on the train a while back, lookin' for adventure, and we kinda ended up here. We didn't have any money to ride back."

"Mr Jack saw us at the lobster shack down the street. We were hungry, and he bought us supper," Wilbur continued. "And offered us a job. We're his models. Going to be in that book there," he added with a touch of pride. "Says we're exactly right for the pictures he wants to do. He's a genius!" Gabe nodded vigorously in agreement, his eye patch slipping.

Sophia smiled at them. "I wondered why you two hadn't been round in a while."

"We're going to earn enough to travel the world!" Gabe said expansively, stretching his paws wide. Luckily, Wilbur had snatched the cutlass from him before anything untoward happened again.

"Not today, you're not," Whitty growled at them, picking a stray purple feather from his waistcoat. "Be off with you. Shoo! I've got paying customers here."

"We'll just change out of these, then," Wilbur said. "Mr Jack told us to take some of the costumes and practice posing."

"Fine, fine, just scat," the Sheltie said irritably.

"Stay out of trouble, you two," Eddie called after them with a grin, as the kitten and cat disappeared behind the curtain again.

"So sorry about that," Whitty said, straightening his cravat and attempting to recover his dignity. "Now, what is it to be?"

48

"Pie-rats!" Dino and Augie cried in unison.

"I think perhaps we'll go with something a bit more sedate. Victorians?" Eddie suggested, catching hold of the pups again.

"Very well." Whitty gathered a pile of costumes and dumped them unceremoniously in the dressing rooms. After a bit of a scuffle with the pups, who were not particularly keen on wearing little velvet Fauntleroy suits after having seen Wilbur's and Gabe's glamorous get-ups, Sophia emerged, resplendent in a burgundy satin dress, gloves, and velvet hat with a little veil.

Eddie was already in place on a small dais, a top hat in one hand and walking stick in the other. "You do look the part, and quite lovely, my lady" he said with a courtly bow. "Now, promise not to notice how short these trousers are. It's a disgrace for a gentleman of my standing, but there's nothing to be done."

Whitty bridled and pulled himself up to his full height. "We do our best to accommodate everyone, sir," he said touchily. "But there are always exceptions."

"Oh, yes, I know. I don't mind being exceptional," Eddie replied, winking at Sophia, who flirted her fan at him playfully. "Now, how shall we stand?" Augie and Dino were already showing signs of extreme boredom, fidgeting, and panting in their costumes.

"The gentleman should be seated, as was customary. The lady to the side and slightly behind. Those two…" Whitty said, hopelessly.

"I can take Augie on my lap, and Dino can stand right here," Eddie offered.

"Fine." The photographer stepped behind the camera, and, for effect, disappeared under a black cloth.

Augie whimpered. "Where grouchy man gone?" Sophia shushed him, before quietly saying "it's 'where has the grouchy man gone.' "

"We're going to take an historically accurate photograph and a modern-style smiling one, all part of the package," Whitty said from beneath his shroud. "No smiles in the first one. Look up here." He held a bedraggled-looking stuffed parrot toy aloft. Dino giggled, Augie shouted "Stan!" and the camera clicked. "Argh! I said *no smiles!*" He waved the unfortunate bird around in frustration. "Again."

After half a dozen shots and just as many reprimands, Whitty emerged, his fur ruffled and his expression sour. "Will that be all?" It wasn't really a question.

Eddie cleared his throat. "If you could do just one more," he said. "The lady only."

"Oh, that's not necessary," Sophia said quickly, taking the pups' paws and guiding them off the dais.

"Yes, it is," Eddie replied, firmly. "You two need to play the 'quiet game' for just a few minutes, now."

Whitty, cheered a bit by the prospect of a further sale and an attractive, cooperative subject, instantly became more obliging and bustled around Sophia. "If madam will just sit here, so, with one arm on this table," he said, arranging the voluminous skirt in graceful folds. "Ah, a three-quarter profile, I think. And tilt your hat a bit that way. Yes, that'll do. You may smile or not, as you like." And he disappeared beneath the cloth again.

Eddie listened for the dog's low-voiced countdown and, in a moment, was down before Sophia, a tiny box open in his paw. The camera clicked, Whitty exclaimed in horror, the pups flung themselves at the pair, and Sophia sat with her paws to her mouth and tears in her eyes.

Eddie looked at her questioningly, his paw trembling a little. "Yes," she said in a choked voice. "Yes." And he lifted the little veil and did what was the only proper thing to do under the circumstances.

"Ewww!" said Dino, hiding his eyes, and they all laughed. Whitty hid a smirk behind the handkerchief he'd been using to wipe his brow.

The little group emerged onto the street, and, as if on cue, a whirl of fluffy white met them, scarcely touching the ground. "Feavers," said Augie, reaching out a paw.

"That's right," Sophia said. "The angels must be having a pillow fight today."

"A celebratory one," Eddie added, taking her paw.

A bit further along, where the street ended and a small jetty began, two cats in sailor's garb were sheltering from the snow under the eaves of an outbuilding, huddled together for warmth and looking around as if deciding what to do next. Presently, a ship's captain, a compact Boston terrier, sauntered by. "Oi! You two! What's the meaning of this? Get aboard before I dip you in the harbour! She sails in a quarter of an hour!" One of the hapless felines stepped forward as if to say something, but the captain hustled them both along before him. "You'll be swabbing the deck for this bit of tomfoolery," he growled.

*John P Soule and Harry Whittier Frees: This chapter was inspired by the actual experiences of one of the authors. The dressing up of Sophia's family, Wilbur and Gabe was suggested by the works of John P Soule and Harry Whittier Frees, 19th- and early 20th-century photographers who spent considerable time taking shots of animals in costume.

Chapter Eleven
Pulling out all of the Stops

The remainder of the train journey from Paris to Chartreux had been delightful—at last felt like they were truly on holiday. The countryside through which they travelled was quite green and lovely. Bertie had been content merely to laze in their sunny compartment and let his eye rove over the rolling landscape as if it were an open sea, with swells here and there in the form of hills and various cottages and churches riding along the billows like ships, the latter thrusting the masts of their towers and steeples skyward. "If we could be sure not to be haunted by any more spectres from your past," he remarked to Muriel, who sat opposite, trying her paw at a crossword puzzle, "then I'd be almost as happy in this train as in my dory for the rest of our trip."

"And if I know you, you'd be persuading the driver to let you take charge, too," Muriel teased, though she was secretly delighted that Bertie was relaxing and enjoying himself despite the unfamiliar luxury of the train's fittings and passengers. "What's a six-letter word for 'château'?"

The next morning was exceptionally fine, so Bertie and Muriel made an early start from their hotel after a light breakfast of croissants and coffee. They sauntered happily along a pleasant lane, paw in paw.

"This looks like a quaint little church, Bertie. Shall we look inside?" Muriel asked.

"Certainly," Bertie replied.

The pair walked through the lychgate and up to the main entrance to the church where there were two bench seats straddling the little alcove. The inside of the church was quite spartan, with long dark wooden pews on each side and large cylindrical stone pillar supporting the soaring roof. The pair walked reverently forwards down the aisle, admiring the stained-glass windows as they did so. The scenes had always enchanted Muriel, the strength of the colour, the mock shadows and the realism, despite the brittle medium. At the far end of the nave was the altar, and to the side the long organ pipes reached up towards the vaulted ceiling. An organist sat on the seat in front, and, oblivious to the new visitors, began playing the "The Bridal Chorus" from the opera *Lohengrin*. Bertie and Muriel looked at each other in surprise and amusement and edged away a bit to the side of the aisle. Coughing slightly, Bertie made their presence known, and the cat at the organ stopped, turned and smiled.

"Oh, jiminy whiskers, I didn't know we had guests. I thought I was alone," he said. "I'm practising for the weekend; a lovely young couple are getting married."

"We don't mind," Muriel replied. "I do love the sound of an organ, and it's lovely to hear it being played so well."

"Ah, *merci*, madame," the cat said, his whiskers twitching with delight at the compliment. "Forgive my rudeness. My name is Henry."

"I have to say that this fine instrument has not always received the treatment it deserves," the cat said as he turned around and got up from his seat. "We have had a number of organists over the years, some rather worse than others, as this is but a small parish and not able to pay well. Many years ago, my great grandfather used to play here. In fact, it was through his generosity that this organ is still in use today. But I digress. Before that, his predecessor, a grand old cat called Edmund, played for most occasions, from weddings to funerals and ordinary Sunday services. The church did not have a very large congregation, so he was not called upon too often."

"Really?" Muriel said. "Do tell us more."

"Well, Edmund was a funny old stick by all accounts. He loved his music, was a music teacher by day, you see, but there was no doubt he rubbed most people up the wrong way. He was rather an uppity character and not many got on too well with him, really. He had an acute sense of hearing and would often get quite gruff at the slightest of disturbances. Why, he even lost his temper once at a small kitten who was being baptised, so as you may imagine he wasn't extremely popular in the town."

"I know a few dogs like that," Bertie said.

Henry smiled and nodded, his large eyes settling on the dachshund for a moment.

"One particular Christmas, Edmund was said to have come into practice "In Dulci Jubilo," a staple of every organist's repertoire and often played after midnight Mass. He pressed down the keys and was most distressed with the muffled noises that came out. He couldn't quite understand why. Edmund battled on to finish the piece, but nothing changed, and his dissatisfaction remained."

"How odd," Muriel said.

"Now Edmund was a rather neurotic cat and had a bit of a reputation for being jumpy. He had once convinced himself that the hooting of an owl was a rabid beast roaming the moors, lying in wait to eat him for supper, and he had refused to leave his house even to play for a harvest service, much to the chagrin of the congregation. Now he shivered as he walked out of the church and had the strange sensation that he was being watched. He surveyed the area again, saw nothing to justify his apprehension and went home. The next day, he reported the matter to the janitor, but the old tom shrugged off Edmund's fears. "Just the wind, makes a horrible racket in the belfry sometimes," he assured the organist, and swore blind the sample of the music Edmund insisted on playing for him sounded just the same as at any other time. The situation continued; some nights Edmund had a bit of light relief and felt more at ease, and other times, alone in the church, he began to hear odd noises which gave him a fright, ghostly echoes which haunted the space."

"Oh, dear. Poor fellow," Bertie interjected.

"Not long after this, Edmund was adamant that his sheet music had gone missing, only for it to be found at a later date in the vestry. The vicar insisted that he didn't have a clue how it had ended up on top of one of the wooden beams, certain that none of his parishioners would play such a trick, and they had quite an argument. On several occasions, his seat had been raised a couple of inches, and once he refused to play for service when the bishop made a visit, so the choir were forced to sing very embarrassingly off-key. Old Edmund was very particular about the position of his seat and was most upset when it kept changing height and he had to spend time getting it just at the right level again. The vicar could only apologise, thinking either a chorister or a school pup must have been sneaking in and making mischief."

"How sad," Bertie said. "But the youngsters will have their fun. When I was in church once, the collection plate was being handed down the line, and a rather grand dog had just made a significant contribution, when the pup behind her thrust a feather from her hat under her nose. She sneezed violently, the coins and bills went flying everywhere and the pup and his mates scrambled under the pews to try and pick up the money. The dog who had sneezed stood up and apologised profusely, realising she had left a rather untidy mess on the back of…"

"That's quite enough of that story, Bertie," Muriel quickly interrupted, strongly suspecting that he had played his part in the tale. "Please continue, Henry."

The cat looked at Bertie and gave a little flick of his tail. "Where was I? Oh yes, the situation continued unabated for Edmund. Over the following weeks, he became obsessed with the idea that something was truly amiss. One night he lit some candles near the organ, only to find them continually being blown out; another time, the bells started ringing for no apparent reason, interrupting his playing. He really was at his wits' end. No one believed his rantings, accusing the poor fellow of drinking too much communion wine. Desperate, Edmund resorted to prayer, and kneeling down near the altar, pleaded aloud for these occurrences to stop."

Henry could tell that he had a captive audience, so he continued. "The next day, Edmund tried a new selection of music, ignoring the muffled noises, and played the organ louder and louder. To his surprise, the pipes seemed to be back to their old melodic ways. Cheered, he continued well into the night, doing what he loved most, and eventually fell asleep at the organ. He awoke from his slumber with a jump, having heard the G sharp key tinkle. He was a little blurry-eyed but focussed on the organ and found a little note wrapped around one of the stops. Opening it, he read a message in minute writing…Wait one moment—it is still here inside the stool. Bit of history, you know." The cat retrieved a yellowed slip of paper and read aloud.

"Monsieur,

I came to this village from Paris, seeking refuge from the noise and bustle of the city. I had worked long and hard on the Metro, seeing to the tracks, but I could no longer abide the noise and danger. I come from a long line of country dwellers, and it has always been my dream to return to the parish where my ancestors lived. I was uncertain as to its whereabouts, however, and wrote to a distant cousin for information. She directed me to this place and explained that they, and even she herself in days gone by, were church dwellers. So I decided to take up residence here, confident that at last I would find peace.

As soon as I entered this quaint edifice, I felt that I had come home. However, I quickly discovered that any number of others felt the same way. There is quite a colony of rats in the crypt and a family of bats in the bell tower. I cast about for a suitable spot and found a congenial nest in what I think are called the "pipes" of this contraption. I settled in very happily for a few days.

But then, my world was shattered! And you, Monsieur, appeared.

The noise! The horrifying, monstrous noise! The force of it jostled me out of my bed. I couldn't think or sleep or find anywhere that it didn't reach. I realised now why the rats had settled in the crypt. My ears are very sensitive, you see, and I could not bear it!

In my desperation I tried to stop you. I am not proud of this. I even enlisted the bats to help me ring the bells at odd hours in hopes of frightening you away. But you persisted.

I have been driven to distraction and cannot live this way any longer, but I have no other place to go. I blame myself for thinking there was any hope left for me. I am the last of my family here and gave up everything in Paris to come to this place. I have nothing left and not a soul to call my friend. But you will be safe from me from now, I will end your misery and not torture you any longer, nor you I.

I bid you adieu.

Napoleon"

Muriel and Bertie both started. "Napoleon?" Bertie asked, incredulously.

"Well, yes," Henry replied. "It is a common name in this area. In any case, Edmund was very wide awake by the time he had finished the note, and he feared that it sounded ominous. Where was this mouse, for a mouse he must surely be? Edmund was a decent fellow at heart and could not help but worry that he might come to some harm. He jumped up and dashed about the church with a candle. Finding no one, he climbed the staircase to the top of the bell tower and gasped when he spotted a small figure teetering on the edge of the parapet. Careful not to make any sudden moves, he slunk over to the creature, crouched so that he would not be seen, and then swiftly snatched the mouse from peril with both paws. Napoleon struggled and squeaked in terror, thinking his end had come in a different way.

" 'You are safe with me,' Edmund said gently, wrapping the shivering creature in his handkerchief. 'I will do you no harm. I am sorry that you have been so miserable. But you must not do this thing. Come with me. My wife and I will give you a home until you find someplace more suitable. I, too, suffer from misophonia, although the organ does not affect me, of course, but I have always been rather sensitive.' "

"Edmund was as good as his word, and his spouse knitted a tiny pair of earmuffs for Napoleon. He began accompanying the cat to church, wearing these, and gradually became accustomed to the organ's sound from a safer distance. In time, he learned to love it and even was known to turn pages for Edmund at some services as their friendship blossomed. He built himself a very cosy nest in the vestry, found employment at the cheesemonger's, and married a local lass. Edmund played for his wedding, of course. Napoleon's great-great-great grandchildren still live here, and they have always been on the best of terms with the organists, me included. One of them often talks about a relative who made his way to England when his master, a French bulldog, I believe, married a lady there."

Bertie and Muriel looked at each other and smiled.

"But I have taken much of your time, madame and monsieur. Pray forgive me," Henry said.

"Not at all, not at all. I've been known to spin a yarn or two in my time. And your tale was a corker. Sounds as though it's true," Bertie replied.

"Every word," Henry assured him, "every word."

Chapter Twelve
Mean Streets

The night had drawn in quickly and it was murkily dark on the streets. As much as Bertie hated to admit it, they were lost. They had left the quaint town of Chartreux and its surrounding villages behind several days ago, and he was sure this had been the right path to get back to their hotel in Burmilleux, despite Muriel's protestations. But now they were getting rather anxious and just thinking of a long hot bath and sleep.

A drinks can that was whipped up in a gust of wind startled both Muriel and Bertie as it tumbled down the gutter. The persistent drizzle dampened their clothes and spirits and blurred their vision. Despite clinging on to each other for warmth, they were getting very cold. A car screeched around the corner and drenched them both, and as Muriel shook out her coat, there was a metallic clatter. She immediately felt in the pocket and looked at Bertie with utter misery in her face, her ears sopping and drooping. "The hotel key," she whispered. "I knew I should have left it at the desk!" Bertie looked frantically around the pavement and saw nothing but an inconveniently placed sewer grate right next to them.

"It'll be alright," he assured her, though he was far from feeling sanguine. He'd met the night porter briefly and had found him to be pretty surly. "Let's just concentrate on getting back. Was that the café we saw earlier? They're all beginning to look the same to me."

A tall character emerged from the shadows of an alleyway and the pair froze. He stopped, turned and looked at Bertie and Muriel, his face covered in darkness as he was standing in front of the only working streetlamp. As he approached, Bertie started to clench his jaw. He released Muriel and stepped in front and slightly to the side to protect her in any way he could. The slow, precise steps of the dog ahead rang eerily on the cobbles as he approached. Bertie reached into his pocket and wrapped his paw around the stainless-steel D shackle he kept inside. It was something very innocuous from his dory but a useful tool in case of emergencies of this nature.

"Now, what do we have here?" the figure said in a deep voice as he removed his paws from his pockets. "This isn't the type of area anyone should be wandering in after dark."

"We're heading back to our hotel, and we just took a wrong turn," Bertie said, feeling the truth was the best policy.

"Lost, eh? Easy to do, I suppose," the dog said. "Should have been a bit better prepared, bad thing can happen to newcomers."

Bertie wasn't too keen on the tone this dog was taking, and if he had been on his own, he probably would have run off already. As it was, he had no choice but to stand firm.

"You'd better come with me," the dog said.

"Now, why would we do that?" Bertie replied. "Go off with a stranger? I think we'll just find our way back to the hotel, if it's all the same to you."

"Oh, it's not okay with me, sir. I take my responsibilities very seriously; I'll have you know. I think the police station will allow you shelter for the night and keep you safe. I'm Brigadier Guillaume, and I happened to notice that you lost your key just now. If I know anything about the proprietors of the hotels in these parts, they're not likely to look kindly on the two of you, given the state you're in. Come along, follow me."

As Bertie and Muriel watched the dog move aside and show the way, they noticed the officer's lapel and uniform. They let out simultaneous sighs of relief, and Muriel squeezed Bertie's paw in silent gratitude for his staunch approach to the situation.

The police station was a small building not far from where Bertie and Muriel had met Brigadier Guillaume. Like its English counterparts, it had a front desk and seating area, along with a small office at the back which was none too tidy.

The police dog led the pair down a narrow corridor. "There you are, take your pick," he said, as he flicked the light switch and guided the pair in.

"There are warm blankets on the beds and a toilet in each cell. Afraid there's not much privacy, but I don't think you need to worry about that."

"Thank you," Muriel said politely, not relishing the position they had found themselves in, but grateful that at least they were now warm and had somewhere to sleep. The closest cell had a set of bunk beds and was as good as any, so Bertie headed in and sat down.

"I'm on the night shift, be out on the front desk if you need anything," Guillaume said, and walked back to the main office, slamming the door behind him and flicking the lights off. A dim glow remained in the cell, moonlight through a small window that offered the only link to the outside.

"Don't suppose we can order a nightcap," Bertie said quietly to Muriel in jest, "or a sandwich." Although she was not really in the mood for his jokes, Muriel gave him a small smile and lay back on the bed.

Chapter Thirteen
Panic Mode

Wagmore brushed his paw over his head and shook it vigorously, removing the cobwebs that had attached themselves to his fur. The attic was not a place he liked frequenting and usually left such matters to Peel, but on this occasion, he didn't want to delegate the role. He knew Muriel left older documents in an array of boxes up there. Most of them would be of no use to him, but he was sure he would unearth some nuggets of information that would prove useful, so he made a habit of disappearing into the loft space when the house was empty. Given the staff were at lunch, this seemed as good an opportunity as any. A couple of small arched windows supplied enough daylight to get his bearings, and for the darker spots he had brought a torch with him. Never one to be caught short, he'd also brought a jam sandwich to keep him nourished. The house was large enough to have a small staircase giving access to the area, so there was no need to run up and down loft ladders.

Wagmore pulled some cardboard boxes from under the eaves and noticed the distinctive papery cone of a wasps' nest in front of him. There didn't appear to be any of the insects buzzing around so he began studying the contents of the topmost box. There were several discoloured hardback books inside, covered in a thin layer of grit and dust. Under those were some society magazines from the 1950s, again, rather brown and frail looking. As much as it might be a waste of time, he decided that, to be thorough, he would take each item out one by one and check for anything of interest. Just as Wagmore had flicked through the last of the monthlies, he heard the gravel on the drive disturbed by a returning car. 'Drat,' he thought. 'Nightingale's back early.' He threw everything back in the box and shoved it under the eaves again with some force. A moment later, he heard the unmistakable noise of angry wasps, and within seconds several started swarming in front of his face. He looked around quickly for something to brush them away with and found an old hat which must have been worn at Ascot or some such prestigious event. He grabbed it, fanning the air as he ran for the door, shutting it firmly behind him before they could invade the house.

As Wagmore calmed down, he turned the headgear around in his paws, and a wicked thought came into his head. A good few months ago, Peel had let him down with a particular task involving Bertie and his hat. In fact, Peel was a bit of a let-down all round, and while he was willing to let some things pass, that incident had really stuck in his throat. He—Walter Wagmore—whose father had stood shoulder to shoulder in battle with the then-master of the house—*he* had been subjected to a demeaning lecture from Muriel over the gaffe. It was not to be borne, and he had bided his time long enough. Wagmore walked back down into the kitchen where he saw the offending footman polishing the silver candlesticks from the dining room. "Well done, lad," he said genially. "While you're in this industrious mood, you may as well fetch the second-best serving set from the attic and give it a rub-down, too." Rather taken aback by the praise, Peel did as he was told without question, putting down the rags and polish and disappearing in the direction of the attic. Wagmore chuckled to himself as he imagined the scene the footman would now encounter and moved within earshot of the attic door to make sure he heard everything clearly.

"What the…?" Peel said as he entered the roof space. Within a moment he was fleeing back downstairs, carelessly leaving the door wide open, racing past Wagmore and knocking his shoulder in his haste to get to the back garden. Wagmore laughed out loud, ignoring the young lad's clumsiness. But his mirth was abruptly cut short by the sound of some angry wasps circling his jacket pocket. His mind reeled for a moment. "Blast! Jam sandwich!" he yelped and dashed out the front door as quickly as Peel had the back. Seeing the Bentley in the driveway, he headed straight for it and slammed the back door shut after hurling himself inside. Outside, the wasps had followed him and were now buzzing furiously around the windows, and Wagmore congratulated himself that he was safe as houses.

Harry put the oil can back on the workbench in the garage and looked out to see the cause of the disturbance. Inside the Bentley he could see the narrow, anxious face of a greyhound peering out. He approached the car and peered inside, his eyes falling on an unexpected object in the dog's possession. He shook his head. "I don't know just what you're playing at," he said, loudly enough for the butler to hear through the glass. "But just because you have filched the duchess's hat and she's away, don't expect me to act as your chauffeur. But I do think it's just your style," Harry added with a smirk. Wagmore looked very sheepish as he realised how foolish he appeared, gripping the ribboned and feathered hat in his clenched paw. He opened the door at the opposite side and stood up tall. "Just inspecting the car, making sure you've been keeping it clean and tidy in my lady's absence. And it seems you overlooked this hat in the back seat. Tsk. Can't get into bad ways, now, can we?" he said gruffly and scurried quickly back to the house before he got a response from the smiling driver.

Chapter Fourteen
Locked Up

The night was long and Bertie couldn't sleep. He could hear that the wind had picked up outside and was wailing like a banshee, while the rain beat down on the metal roof and sounded heavier than it probably was. Glad for the shelter and relative warmth, he sat at the top of the bunk bed and thought back to his days in the merchant navy. Many a time he had been in strange places, awake, and hearing noises he was unfamiliar with. It was a time when he was excited by travel, seeing new places, meeting new people. Much of the crew became good friends, and they had his back just as he had theirs. 'Poor Duffy,' he thought as he recalled one friend in particular. Bertie had done his job well, took orders and got used to a consistent way of life, embracing the challenges that presented themselves with vigour. His humdrum existence in Badger's Bay was a stark contrast to his younger days, and whilst he still hankered for a quiet life at times, he did not feel he wanted to return. He had made new friends—Harry, Nap and Percy—a thing he'd thought impossible at his age, and England could perhaps become home again. Percy...he wondered how he was getting on. The Welsh terrier had been spending some time with that young artist who seemed to look out for him and keep him from becoming too melancholy. Bertie resolved to write him a note as soon as he could get his paws on some hotel stationery.

The cell was quiet and void of any atmosphere—too quiet, really. Bertie could hear Muriel asleep in the bunk underneath and at least felt some comfort that she was safe. He decided to get up and stretch his legs, as he tended to get cramps if he stayed in one position when asleep for too long. He eased himself down from the bunk, stepping on the frame below and trying to avoid waking Muriel. Before he hopped to the floor, he looked up and peered outside. He still wasn't tall enough to see out the window, so all he could see were raindrops cascading down the pane. Sighing gently in frustration, he decided to investigate the cell area instead. He slipped out the door, walked about in the semi-darkness and realised the cells were all the same, with a toilet, a sink and either a single or bunk bed. 'Is it normal for the place to be empty, or have we just hit upon a quiet time of week?' Bertie wondered as he tiptoed around the cold and loudly echoing concrete floor. He turned on the tap in the cell opposite and cupped his paws, capturing just enough water for him to have a little drink. Noting a tummy rumble, he wished he had brought along some of the small packs of guest biscuits from the hotel.

Bertie plodded aimlessly back to his own cell. The sooner he was out of this gloomy place, the better. Lost in unsatisfactory musings, he grabbed one of the steel rungs without thinking and pulled the door shut, hearing a clunk as the lock fell into place. 'Cripes,' he thought. 'What have I done?' He tried tugging on the door, and while it rattled, raising his hopes for a moment, a few more yanks assured him that it was firmly shut. He felt up and down for a handle to turn, but there was none. They were well and truly locked in. Bertie decided it would not be the best idea to shout for assistance, as it would likely just scare Muriel. It would be light soon enough, so he resigned himself to going back to bed and trying to get some sleep. Feeling too stiff to climb back up to the top bunk, he shivered and slid in next to Muriel. She sighed in her sleep and relaxed into him. Smiling to himself despite their circumstances, he drifted off.

Chapter Fifteen
A Night to Remember

The sun rose and started casting a bright light across the cell floor. The warmth of the rays caused Bertie to stir, and as he flipped over and opened his eyes gradually, he saw the deep brown eyes of Muriel staring back at him. Sleepily, he rubbed his eyes, yawned unabashedly and started to rise from his slumber.

"Good morning, dear," he said. "Looks like the rain must have stopped at last."

Muriel did not reply at first.

"What's up?" Bertie said, as he flipped his legs over the cell bunk and sat up straight. He knew that look, and although he felt he couldn't be blamed for the fact that they had ended up in the cell the previous night, it was a bit of an embarrassment.

"We're locked in," Muriel replied, tapping her foot on the floor with frustration.

"Locked in," Bertie repeated. Surely not! He was still a bit groggy, but his memory was coming back to him fast. 'Oops,' he thought. 'It was my fault. I remember now.'

"Hasn't Officer—what was his name—come round?" Bertie asked, postponing his admission.

"Yes, a guard has come round, but it wasn't Guillaume. He was called Arnaud," Muriel said. "That wretched Guillaume must have closed the door on us in the night."

It took a moment for Bertie to realise that he was not the object of Muriel's annoyance, but once he did, he decided that Guillaume's shoulders were broad enough to take the blame. "So you think Guillaume told this other fellow to keep us in here?"

"Possibly," Muriel replied. "But he said that he had no record of us in the prison logs and couldn't release us until he found out more information."

"The rotters!" Bertie shouted.

"Keep your voices down over there, please. I'm trying to sleep," a quiet voice said from across the way.

"I'll shout as much as I like," Bertie replied, looking out from the bars. In the cell opposite he could just make out the pointy ears of a cat above a pillow, the suggestion of a frilled collar and a long tail swishing over the side of the bed, just touching the floor.

"We're so sorry," Muriel said to the ears and tail, while giving Bertie a warning sidelong glance. "Please don't mind us."

"Why shouldn't she mind us?" Bertie grumbled. "At least she's here for some offence or other. All we did was wander down a wrong alley and lose a key."

"Right now, the quieter we are, the better. We don't want to upset the inmates or the guards," Muriel advised in an undertone, and Bertie had to concede that she was right. His shoulders sagged.

The voice came again, soft, yet impossible to ignore. "Have you lost something? Funny old world when the local gendarmes put us behind bars for absent-mindedness." Muriel and Bertie looked at each other and then peeped out of their cell again. Though her vocabulary was British enough, the cat's accent proclaimed her to be American, possibly even from the vicinity of Bertie's bit of coast. There was a bit of a rustle behind the pillow, and then it was moved aside.

Even with this partial view, they could see that she was a magnificent creature, mostly white with delicate ears that hinted at calico colouring. But there was very little else they could tell about her, as most of her head and face were expertly swathed in a beautiful paisley scarf. Even her eyes were scarcely visible, and she looked askance rather than straight at her neighbours.

'Guilty conscience can't look us in the eye,' Bertie thought, somewhat uncharitably, still feeling a fool for having landed them in this mess. 'Or she's toffee-nosed and trying to avoid being recognized.' He walked back to the bottom bunk and sat down again, with his head in his paws, 'I wonder what advances in science they will have achieved when we finally leave this place?' he mused miserably.

Chapter Sixteen
Calico Confession

"Yes, we're in a spot of bother, certainly," Muriel answered the cat, in the even tones of one well used to smoothing things over. She was taken aback by their neighbour but was no stranger to the commonness of crime amongst the well-heeled, as she had immediately taken this cat to be. "We hope to explain ourselves and be out of here soon. This is Bertie Longfellow, and I am Muriel...Berkshire." Good manners kept her from mentioning her title.

"Pleased to meet you," the cat murmured, and turned her head to one side. There was a pause before she added, "I'm Anipe Amourby. Ani, usually." Muriel was surprised that she had so little to say, after that initial dryly humorous remark about foreign police dogs. With her well-bred and kindly instinct to avoid embarrassment for all parties and keep conversation flowing, she ventured an explanation of their situation.

"I was rather an idiot and dropped the key to our hotel room down a gutter. And Bertie here forgot the map. Brigadier Guillaume brought us here to keep safe until morning, but it seems there's been some sort of mix-up."

The folds of Ani's scarf twitched, and it was difficult to tell whether she was laughing to herself or merely nervous. "I see," she said simply.

Bertie sat back with his bushy brows raised slightly. 'Tough nut to crack,' he thought. 'Hardened criminal, I expect,' and decided to leave things to Muriel as he kicked a piece of grit on the floor.

Muriel saw that the onus of the conversation was going to be on her but decided to persist. Perhaps the cat was just shy, whatever her present predicament seemed to suggest. She glanced away and continued talking nonchalantly about the previous evening's mishaps. "That's the last time I let Bertie tell me he doesn't need a map," she said. "And I'm no help. All the streets look the same to me here. Even in London I've been known to lose my way." This wasn't strictly true, as Harry saw her safely to most destinations, but she thought she'd go along with the cat's mention of absent-mindedness.

There was a slight rustle across the way as the cat shifted position.

"Perhaps you had a similar mishap?" Muriel suggested. "It seems this is a rather seedy part of town, and the police are on the lookout for clueless tourists like us."

"Imagine an entire jail full of innocent bystanders while the baddies run free," Bertie said with a chuckle.

"I'm innocent too," came a slurred voice from the shadows of a cell further down the corridor. "Always knew the French had some peculiar ideas about things." Muriel rolled her eyes at the suggestion and wondered who else had been brought in during their sleep.

There came what sounded distinctly like a giggle from across the corridor. Ani's tail swished a few times, and she cleared her throat. "I suppose it was a mishap, really," she said at length. "But it's all been rather harrowing."

"You don't have to tell us if you don't want to," Bertie interrupted hurriedly, thinking that perhaps Muriel shouldn't have drawn the cat out of her shell. This Ani might actually be a felon for all they could tell and knowing her secrets could get them both into trouble whenever they managed to get out of this place.

The cat hesitated. "Oh, I think I will. I've been going over and over it, trying to think of some way to convince the gendarmes, but the truth sounds so improbable."

Muriel had had the same thought as Bertie, but she reasoned that a real criminal wouldn't tell them the whole story anyway. And she had a good feeling about this reserved feline. "Go on," she urged.

"Well, I was in Paris, you see, doing a bit of research," Ani began. "I have been in France for some weeks and hired a car, as I do not like the Metro and was planning to travel here. A few days ago, I had spent most of the day at the Sorbonne, and I was rather cross-eyed from my labours. I'd forgotten to take note of where I had left the car, and to my horror, I couldn't find it anywhere. All the cars looked alike to me, either green or blue, and the car I hired was apparently red. You'll laugh at me, but I didn't think to write down the license number and left the hire documents in the glovebox."

"Easy enough to do," Bertie said, thawing a bit. He was beginning to warm to the cat despite his reservations.

"I panicked and went to the nearest station to report the car as stolen. I couldn't imagine that I'd actually lost it. How does one lose something so large?" Ani shook her head ruefully. "And I just couldn't imagine what the hiring company would charge me for that sort of disaster. The next day, I retraced my steps and suddenly remembered that the car should have a label from the company on the back bumper. I did finally find it, much to my relief, and was soon on my way. But when I had nearly made it here to Burmilleux, I heard that distinctive French police siren."

"Oh no," Muriel said.

"Yes, you guessed it. I had forgotten to report that I'd found the car," Ani said, shaking her head in self-disgust. "I'd been so engrossed in my work that I'd probably have lost my tail if that were possible. And I'd somehow gotten my passport and license mixed up with some papers I left in the hotel safe before I left. The officer I spoke to in Paris was very blasé and hadn't bothered to take a copy of my passport photo for the file, so of course I'm under suspicion for theft."

Bertie's distrust had evaporated. The cat's story was too self-deprecating to be false, he thought. "Surely they can contact the hotel or the hiring company and sort it out? Seems easy enough to me."

Ani sighed. "I'm afraid there's more to the story," she said. "The officer spotted my camera on the passenger seat and said they'd had one reported missing from just the area where I had been staying. So, they confiscated my Leica and banged me to rights, no questions asked."

"Is there anything on the film that might prove the camera is yours? Did you have someone take your photo at the Eiffel Tower, perhaps?" Muriel asked.

"Oh no. Nothing like that," Ani replied, visibly shrinking down into herself. "I don't like having strangers take my picture. Only family."

Bertie sensed her embarrassment and tried a different approach. "Well, I'm inclined to believe you. But if there's one thing I learned in the merchant navy, it's that you have to look into a chap's eyes to know if he's telling the truth."

Ani drew back into the dimness of her cell. "I understand if you don't think my story is true. I know it sounds rather ridiculous."

Muriel and Bertie looked at each other, at a loss what to say next to this mysterious feline. Muriel spoke first, trying to put the cat at her ease.

"That is a lovely scarf," she said. "I've never seen anything quite like it."

"It was my mother's," Ani replied. "I always wear it. I didn't take it off even for the police. I know that made them even more suspicious. But I really couldn't." Her voice shook a little. "I feel naked and vulnerable without it."

"It's okay, my dear. I'm sure you have your reasons," Muriel said soothingly, giving Bertie a nudge with her foot to stop him saying anything further on the subject. She got up and gestured for him to follow her to the opposite corner of the cell. "What do you think?" she asked in a low voice.

"I think she may be a bit barmy, but she seems harmless enough," Bertie whispered back. Muriel gave him a look. "Alright, maybe not even barmy. We all have our little eccentricities." She glanced at his woolly hat and grinned at him. "Yes, yes," he said, patting it fondly. "I don't see why we shouldn't trust her. Do you?"

"No," replied Muriel.

"Right, then." They both moved back to where they could see Ani. "Seems like we're all more or less in the same sort of pickle," Bertie said genially. "Perhaps we should put our heads together and see if we can find a way out of it."

Chapter Seventeen
Whose Baby?

Winnie and Lottie descended the steps from the transatlantic jet and rubbed their eyes a little groggily as they stepped onto the tarmac. The cockapoo had slept like an infant, though perhaps a bit more noisily, for the duration of the flight, whilst her companion had oscillated between bouts of sheer terror when she remembered the 35,000 feet below them and half-waking dreams about castles and country hedgerows. "Ugh! Rain!" Lottie muttered in disgust, trying ineffectually to shelter her head with a magazine swiped from the cabin. They rushed for the terminal and then realised that they had no real itinerary—well, to be fair, Winnie had urged her friend to see the sense in making some sort of plan but had not prevailed. After getting through customs, they deposited their damp selves and their luggage on an uninviting green plastic bench and looked about them. "Not impressed so far," Lottie commented. "That guy I gave my passport to didn't even crack a smile. Sheesh."

Winnie refrained from pointing out that his was no smiling job, and probably a dull one to boot. "So where to now?" she prompted.

"How should I know? You're the one with the travel book. I just want to get out of this dreary airport."

Winnie pulled out her well-thumbed Baedeker. "Well, we can start traveling north, and if we do, we could start at St Albans. Or we could head south toward the coast."

"Toss for it," Lottie decided, and pulled out a quarter. "Heads, north. Tails, south."

Heads it was. After navigating the tube and St Pancras station—Winnie was never quite sure afterwards how they'd done it—they found themselves in a little village just outside St Albans. After a nap and a ploughman's lunch, they headed out from their room above the Fox and Grapes.

"Now isn't that the cutest thing you've ever seen," Winnie said to the rather distracted Lottie, as they approached the village green.

"What? Oh, sure, whatever," she replied.

"Look, over there," Winnie insisted, pulling on Lottie's paw and trying to draw her attention to the scene in front of them. It didn't make much difference. Lottie was not interested, so Winnie left her friend to her own devices and moved positions to get a closer look.

A small crowd had gathered for the event, and a makeshift rope boundary had been set up to keep the audience from disturbing the entrants. A board on the far side showed the titles of the competitors and their weights, with names such as "Rocker Bye Baby," "Tiny Totter" and "Creepy Crawler." The Diaper Derby was about to start.*

A firing gun had been replaced by a baby's rattle, and with a vigorous shake by the judge, they were off. Proud parents began encouraging their pups to crawl to the line-up of various toys a short distance away. Many of the pups sat in their diapers, glued to the spot, wondering what on earth all the fuss was about. A fair few started howling the minute their parents moved a distance away, but some began crawling towards one of the toys, eyes eager. As the minutes passed, a couple of contenders for first place appeared from the mix, edging ahead. Suddenly, though, there was a bit of a kerfuffle, and from amidst the crowd an affenpinscher pup shot through and tumbled over. As he got up, a diaper thrown from the crowd landed on his face. He fell and rolled about a few times, clawing at the thing until he finally disentangled it from around his head and ears. Thrust aside, the diaper fell squarely on a minute Yorkshire terrier, completely enveloping it. The poor pup froze in panic and caused a general pileup amongst the crawlers. A pandemonium of booing erupted from the onlookers as the affenpinscher continued a clumsy run-crawl, tripping up at various places along the course. Behind came calls of "stop that rotter!" But nobody was paying any attention, merely thinking that "Rotter" was the entrant's name.

Jostling for position with a lead pug, the affenpinscher headed towards an older St Bernard gesturing from behind the line up of toys, perhaps a friend of the family, Winnie thought, although no one else seemed to notice.[†] As the affenpinscher crawled its way to a soft rabbit sitting on the finishing line, he was promptly picked up by the terrier judge in a long white overall, held aloft and pronounced the winner. A giant red rosette was pinned to his little jumper, and flashbulbs nearly blinded him. Other pups gradually found the finish line in time, with a little persuasion and a lot of patience, and the St Bernard quickly hustled through, collected the prize money and trotted off with pup in tow, leaving a forlorn representative of the diaper company standing next to the main prize—a year's supply of diapers with "Bumco" emblazoned across the seat—gaping after him with a bemused expression on his face.

Winnie turned around as the excitement waned and decided to hunt for Lottie. She looked back to where they had been standing earlier but couldn't see her. 'Perhaps she's gone to get something to eat,' she thought, and decided to head towards the burger van. She spotted the cockapoo in the queue and, waving at her, decided to wait away from the throng. Behind the small tent for customers, she heard some voices.

"There you go, that's your share. Now be off with you before we get caught and give me that wallet before you go too. You can't be seen with that."

"Right you are, Mr Weinstein, but the pints are on you when we next meet. That was just about the worst experience of my life out there! See you anon," the second, squeakier voice said.

Winnie didn't have to wait long before she noticed the same St Bernard walking one way and the affenpinscher walking the other, now lighting up a cigarette.

'The cheating little scoundrels,' Winnie thought as Lottie pushed a burger in front of her and asked why she had a peculiar expression on her face.

Winnie didn't respond. "Earth to Win-Win," Lottie said, waving a paw in front of the doxie's nose.

"Hey, stop right there!" Winnie shouted, and Lottie jumped away.

The two dogs both stared in Winnie's direction, panic written on their faces. Instantly realising that there were no police in sight, they laughed at the doxie and continued their way. Winnie knew she would never catch the St Bernard, and even if she did, she would never be able to hold on to him, so she flew off after the affenpinscher instead. Unfortunately for her, the St Bernard saw what she was intending, having covertly watched her movements. He spun around, and before she knew it, she was being held aloft in his large paws. Winnie started to kick and scream, but no one paid any heed, as she merely looked like a typical tired, squally pup in the giant dog's paws.

A moment or so later the St Bernard's vision became impaired, everything went very dark, and a strange pungent smell started filling his nostrils. He dropped Winnie while frantically trying to remove the appendage from his head, but it was too late, as his legs were now being tightly wrapped, around and around, with a roll of terry cloth. By the time the diaper had been removed from his face, he had lost his balance and toppled onto the ground, his eyes resting on a pair of red Doc Martens. Lottie looked at her fouled paws in disgust, wiped them thoroughly on the grass, and glanced around, hoping Winnie had made good her escape. The affenpinscher had already hightailed away, but Winnie was on his heels. Seconds later the small dog was grabbed by a passing police dog, who was sure he had lost his parents.

"Well done, Lottie! Thank you!" Winnie said, as she returned, panting, her hat all askew. With uncharacteristic demonstrativeness, she threw her arms around the cockapoo and felt a sob in her throat. Lottie patted her and gently pulled away.

"Enough of that, now, Win-Win. We can't let these miscreants get away with whatever it is they've done!" Lottie exclaimed. Winnie opened her mouth to explain, but their eyes were drawn to the struggling St Bernard. He was inching towards something on the ground several feet from him. As soon as he saw the two dogs regarding him, he stopped and tried to look as nonchalant as possible with a dirty diaper around his shoulders and his legs pinioned like a turkey's.

Winnie edged over to the object of his attention and picked it up. She flipped the wallet open and pulled out a driving license issued to a

Malamute named Roger Dodgerson. Lottie looked over her shoulder. "Well, looks like you've either had a pretty major makeover, or this isn't you at all," she said a bit sardonically.

At this moment, a leather-jacketed Irish setter lounged towards them. "You need any help, ladies?" he drawled. "This bloke giving you two any trouble to speak of? Looked like there was a bit of a set-to just now."

Lottie and Winnie looked at each other and then at the setter. They had no idea whether he was in league with the other two dogs, but they had to find the affenpinscher, and fast. Winnie spoke first, as Lottie seemed temporarily robbed of speech. "You could give us a paw by keeping company with Mr Weinstein here. Must dash, but we'll be back," she called over her shoulder, pulling Lottie after her.

"Gorgeous…just gorgeous…" Lottie was murmuring as she tumbled after the doxie. Winnie ignored her.

"Keep your eyes peeled for that little pipsqueak," she said. "What did that knuckle-headed police dog do with him?" Just as she finished speaking, she spotted the uniformed bloodhound handing the dishevelled affenpinscher to a motherly looking dog and motioned for Lottie to follow her. "Oh! My Ralphie! I had no idea you'd wandered off! That's what comes of leaving the pram in the car, isn't it my little shnookums?" And she began bouncing the dog about. "But where did you get that jumper, you rascal? That's not yours, is it?"

As she shook the dog playfully and continued bouncing him at her side, a shower of bills and cigarettes fell from the jumper's pockets.

"Hi! What's all this?" the police dog exclaimed. "We's been told to look out for a pup like you! Freddie Fast Paws, that's who you are!"

"That's all my dough. I won it fair and square!" Freddie yelped.

"Not so fair, I'd say, if you're partaking of these," Lottie retorted, having been woken from her daze. She picked up a handful of cigarettes and handed them to the bloodhound. "Or else you're pretty precocious."

"And what about this, eh? We found it with your friend back there," Winnie chimed in.

"Weinstein ain't no friend of mine! And you can't blame a fella for having a bit of a lark, now, can ya? I'm the right weight and all. Always gets taken for a pup, so I thought I may as well have a little fun," Freddie whined, squirming out of the mother dog's surprisingly firm grasp. She had suddenly realised her mistake and tightened her grip further.

The bloodhound scratched his jowls. "Nooooow," he drawled. "How come you to know that the fella's name is Weinstein? Is that who you're talkin' about, girls?" Winnie and Lottie nodded.

At that moment, another police dog came dashing up. "That's him! Well, Freddie, you've always prided yourself on staying out of the papers, but you're going to be front page news, you first-prize rotter!"

"Where's that Weinstein feller you two were talkin' about?" the bloodhound inquired. They all looked up as a commotion came their way.

"Lookin' for this?" asked the Irish setter, winking at Lottie and Winnie. He'd finished the job Lottie had begun, and the St Bernard's arms were tied securely behind him with another few diapers. He howled with rage as he was dragged along by his shirt collar.

As the police dogs converged on the two felons, Winnie's eyes were on Lottie, who was brushing the dark hairs off her pale jumper and tossing her ears a little.

"Pleased to meet you both, I'm sure," the setter said with a charming lilt and held out his paw. "Name's Ted Tierney. You two were pretty entertaining to watch back there," he added with a roguish grin.

Lottie subtly edged in front of Winnie and took the proffered paw. "I know an excellent place to get burgers," she said demurely. "I'm Charlotte. And you must be starving after wrangling down that monster."

*Diaper Derby: This chapter was inspired by an old photograph of a "baby crawling race" or "diaper derby," a fad which began in the middle of last century. From 1946 until 1955, an annual event in the US was sponsored by the National Institute of Diaper Services, although there were similar races across the globe. One notable event took place in Sydney, Australia on New Year's Day 1957 when a mother used a glass of beer to coax her baby in the race. The baby had two mouthfuls, stopped crawling and sat groggily on the ground, refusing to move. Other mothers used cigarettes, matches, orange juice and dolls to coax their children to the finish line.

[†]**Bernie Winters:** The authors chose to make Mr Weinstein a St Bernard as a reference to English comedian and comic foil Bernie Winters and his dog, Schnorbitz. In 1984, Bernie presented the second series of the game show "Whose Baby?" during which celebrity panellists met the children of a well-known person and tried to guess who their parents were.

Chapter Eighteen
Hustling the Hustler

Harry settled down on a stool at the end of the bar and waited for his friend, Tully, to arrive. He recalled the last time he met up with him at Dolphin Square with Bryn, Bertie and Nap and the resulting furore wasn't far in his mind. There would be no repeat of those scenes, that was for certain. The bar dog, "Humphrey," as his nametag proclaimed him, was dressed in a white shirt and red waistcoat to match the decor, and he was quick to ask Harry if he would like a drink. Harry declined, snacking on the peanuts in the bowl instead, rather to Humphrey's annoyance. The hotel and bar were not really Harry's cup of tea, but Tully had suggested it as it was a good place to pick up fares who tipped big after a hard day in the city. 'Being a cabbie has its perks over being a chauffeur,' Harry thought, but Muriel paid well enough, and he did get board and lodgings thrown in, so he really couldn't complain. On the adjacent side of the bar was a cat sipping a glass of what looked like milk. Harry shook his head. "Can't account for tastes," he murmured to himself.

Behind Harry a couple of dogs at a pool table, perhaps not the most obvious thing to have in such an upper-class establishment, but this was no seedy pool hall. He could just about see a plush games room along the way for guests to have a flutter on the wheel if they were so inclined. Savile Row was in evidence everywhere, and Harry felt quite underdressed. Although he wasn't in his oily overalls, he certainly wasn't in his chauffeur's get up either. He looked down at his simple pullover and plain trousers and smoothed out a crease. 'Tully certainly knows how to pick these places,' he thought.

Harry hadn't played pool himself for a long while, though he was sure he remembered being quite a dab hand at one time. He preferred 8-ball over 9-ball and even had his own cue, although couldn't remember where it was now, perhaps lost in a bet. As he emptied the bowl of peanuts and was calling the bar dog for more, the British blue cat arrived, with a cheeky grin on his face.

"Hello Harry," he said, "fancy seeing you here at the Palace Club. However, did you get in without a tie?" Tully teased.

"It's okay. I pulled up in Muriel's Bentley, so they thought I was some maverick millionaire who liked to dress down," Harry laughed.

"Fair enough," Tully said. "I came in the cab, and the doorman thought I was here to pick up a fare."

"Drink?" Harry replied.

"Yes, thanks, a shandy will be fine," the cat said.

"A shandy and a beer," Harry called to the bar dog, who nodded in acknowledgement.

"Did you bring the Fiat then?" Tully asked.

"Oh, no," Harry said, "I'll get a cab, shall I? I don't think I'll have much trouble finding one, just don't expect a big tip," Harry joked.

"Never would, not from the likes of you, my friend," Tully replied. "Anyway, what do you think of the place? Not bad, eh? Wouldn't mind spending a night in the penthouse here?"

"Seems okay," Harry said. "I'm not sure even Muriel would be keen to be seen here though. A bit ostentatious, isn't it?"

"Just a bit," Tully said, "Those paintings on the wall are ghastly, modern art they probably call it, looks like something found on the bottom of a chicken coop if you ask me. And those thick gold frames, hideous. Always fancied my own pool table though and that one is a beauty. Just haven't got the room, not unless I used it as a dining room table too, or perhaps cut the cues in half and shimmied round to take the shots. Don't think the missus would be too keen though, especially if the lads came round, and we would be like sardines stuck in a can. Stick to poker, eh, Harry?"

"That's still a bit of a sore point Tully, as well you know. Poor Nap had to throw his clothes out after his little dip, couldn't get the smell out whatever he tried. Fortunately, I don't think any permanent harm has been done. Bertie and Muriel are away on a holiday and seem to be enjoying themselves by all accounts."

"Really," Tully said. "You mean to say you have the whole house to yourself then?"

Just as Harry was about to speak, the cat from across the bar called out, "Hey, who's been drinking my cocktail?" with a perplexed look on his face. No one seemed to take any notice of his little rant, though, and after a quick look up, Harry continued.

"Not quite. Wagmore is still around, lording it up over everyone, but I tend to keep myself to myself as far as he is concerned. I really need to catch up with Bertie, but if he called the house, Wagmore would of course answer the phone. I'd never get a look in."

"Tough gig," Tully said. He took a gulp of his shandy and picked up a peanut from the refreshed bowl, threw it in the air and landed it deftly in his mouth. "Still got it." He then turned to look behind him. "Aye, aye, looks like the basset has just won. Will you look at that?"

Harry turned too, though he had already been observing the game from the corner of his eye. A large grey mastiff with a gold collar had just lost the game. Frowning fiercely, he walked back to the bar. "That's a hundred down the drain, but I'm sure you're keeping a note of all this?"

Humphrey replied, "Yes sir, I've got the money right here, Barney, as per the company policy, no cash on the tables. Not that we've ever had any customer money stolen, you understand, but we like to keep things strictly professional here, everything above board. All initial stakes and any winnings are safe and sound, don't you worry about that."

"Perfect," the mastiff replied in a condescending manner and returned to the table. "Fancy another, double or nothing?" he said to the basset as he grabbed the triangle and racked up the balls.

The basset smirked ever so slightly and agreed, "One more game. I'm not in the habit of losing though."

"Fine then, but if I don't win the next game, I'm done," the mastiff declared.

As Harry continued to watch, he half wondered if the mastiff was being hustled. He was sure that the basset had pulled a few shots and made some calculated misses, too. Harry and Tully got up from the bar, at which point the cat exclaimed, "I'm sure someone has been drinking my White Russian, you know!" Humphrey glared at him, but Tully nodded in agreement, and the cat subsided.* If nothing else, his years in a cab had taught him to humour eccentrics. He joined Harry at a table where they could more conveniently watch the game.

"My break," the basset said and smashed the cue ball into the pack with a venom in her shot. The number seven ball went straight into the corner pocket, and the rest of them spread across the pale blue baize evenly. The green six ball was next, screwing back to the blue two ball. The basset seemed to be holding no punches and in control, and both the onlookers were impressed by her shooting skills. It looked like some beads of sweat were forming on the mastiff's forehead, and he was beginning to frown and look worried. Harry considered the position of the balls and thought it looked odds on the dog had been had. The basset moved around the table and smiled at Tully as she dipped down for the next shot on the orange. Sipping his shandy, Tully whispered to Harry, "odds on." The basset hit the shot but got the forward spin on the cue ball all wrong, ending up placing it behind the black and blocking a clear shot to another pot.

"Damn and blast," the basset shouted and glared at Tully. "You caused me to mess that up. Keep your mouth shut the next time." She turned back to the table and to assess any options. 'Touchy creature,' Tully thought to himself. She grabbed the chalk from the side of the table and dusted the tip of her cue, mulling the shot in hand.

"Trying to lemonade, are we?" Barney said, clearly thinking he had caught a bit of luck and that the basset was stalling for time.[†]

"Knows his pool terms," Harry said quietly to Tully, being careful not to incur the wrath of the basset, too. She leant down again and lightly tapped the cue ball off the cushion and into the three ball. Her turn at the table over, she went back to the other side of the bar and had a drink from her glass. Harry watched her and the reaction from the bar dog. It was only slight, but he was sure he saw a nod as she approached. Maybe the hustle was now in play after all. In the meantime, the mastiff was cleaning up and was grinning with satisfaction as the balls fell into the pockets. He finally potted the thirteen ball, "unlucky for some, but not for me," he pronounced, and was onto the black. Tapping the middle pocket with his cue, he made a show of his prowess at the table, much to the annoyance of the basset, who had her arms crossed as she waited for what looked like the inevitable. Predictably, the black dropped down, the white bounced off a cushion and stopped mid table and the mastiff had indeed won.

Harry and Tully both watched as the basset walked back to the table and graciously congratulated the mastiff. "Don't fret, you can win your money back another time. Back to the bar to even up," the mastiff said. "And to show there are no hard feelings, I'll buy you a drink. What's your poison?"

"Whiskey sour," she said to the bar dog, who grabbed the bottle, poured the liquid into a shaker with a squirt of lemon, added some sugar and began to rattle it around. Within a minute he was pouring the cocktail into a rocks glass.

"Cheers," the mastiff said. "Now, where can we get a cab out of here?"

Humphrey was about to answer, but Tully piped up, "I can give you a ride, my friend here needs his beauty sleep, and my cab's out front if you want a lift?"

"Looks like my evening is over too, then," Harry said, not particularly wanting to stay in the company of the bar dog. He emptied the dregs out of the glass and walked out with the others leaving the luxurious surroundings behind him. Outside, Harry said his goodbyes and headed off to where he had parked the Fiat. Tully pointed to the black cab, unlocked it and showed the basset and mastiff into the back. The diesel engine fired into life with a puff of black choking smoke from the back, and Tully asked where the pair wanted to be dropped off.

"Wilton Crescent, Belgravia. Know it?" the mastiff asked.

"Yup, not many places I don't know in London, guvnor. Be there in two shakes of a tail," Tully said, as he turned the wheel and car full circle and headed off down the road. Tully always marvelled at the tight turning circle of the Austin FX4 and was proud of his ability to manoeuvre the vehicle around some of the tight streets in London, although it wasn't the most comfortable of cars to work in. The roads were quiet, and for the most part he enjoyed driving at this time of night. All the better if it was raining or cold outside, as that normally meant he picked up more fares.

"Visiting or on your holidays?" Tully asked but got no reply. He looked in the rear-view mirror and could see the dogs in the back canoodling, so he decided to keep himself to himself for the rest of the short journey.

Outside the exclusive property, Tully pulled down his window and reached his paw backwards to open the back door for his passengers. "Safely home," he said.

The mastiff got out of the cab, closely followed by the basset clinging on to his shoulder. "There you go, keep the change," he said.

Tully checked the notes handed to him and was pleasantly surprised to see a hefty tip, even though he had not told them the price. He watched as the mastiff pulled out his keys, and the pair disappeared inside.

*The Humphreys: The chapter contains a subtle reference to a series of TV commercials created in the UK in the 1970s for the British milk company. Characters called Humphreys were milk thieves whose only visible presence was a red-and-white striped straw which was used to suck up the milk. Several TV personalities featured in the adverts, but the campaign is best known for the slogan: "Watch out, watch out—there's a Humphrey about!"

†Lemonade: This is a pool term that means the act of intentionally playing slower than one normally would, with the intention of disrupting an opponent's rhythm.

Chapter Nineteen
Lottie Makes an Old Friend

Lottie looked at the maroon and cream livery of the AEC Reliance coach standing before her and folded her arms. "What was Winnie thinking?' " she muttered to herself. The coach had the words "Beeliner Tours" emblazoned on the side, and from the looks of the guests boarding, Lottie was in for a new experience, that was for sure. Reggie the driver was a portly, middle-aged chow, his fur rather in need of a comb and the remains of the morning's breakfast down his shirt. 'Perhaps he should have avoided the beans,' she thought.

"That's right, put your bigger bags down by the side of the coach and I'll have them stowed away by my new helper here. Hand luggage can be brought inside." Reggie stood next to the coach, pointing this way and that like an air traffic controller while his passengers happily disburdened themselves. Lottie looked on with a distinct lack of enthusiasm. Winnie had turned into a little charmer when she had met Reggie at the Fox and Grapes and had managed to convince him to let them travel on his coach. The catch was that they would pay their way by doing the heavy lifting, as he had a rather bad back. As Lottie began lifting some of the cases, she groaned. 'No wonder he's got lumbago,' she thought. 'What do these old dogs take with them on holiday? A week's supply of tinned beans and pineapple chunks?'

Winnie tried to help Lottie with the smaller bags, but Lottie was having none of it. She was in too much of the hump with the dachshund to want a partner and claimed that she wanted to do it all herself. Winnie noted her thunderous look and rather doubted that this was the case but decided it best to give her some space. She slipped away and found a seat at the front of the coach where she could keep out of the way.

Reggie slammed the hatches down, fastened them and proceeded to the driver's seat. "Come along Lottie, a good job done, only got to unload them at the other end and you'll be done for the day," he shouted cheerfully, just inches from her ear.

"I'm not deaf, you know," she said testily.

"Sorry, luv. I've gotten used to raising my voice a bit with my usual crowd," he answered with imperturbable good humour.

The pair stepped into the coach, and Reggie lowered his large frame into the driver's seat, squashing the already flat cushion still further. "Arhhh, that's better... oh Lottie, I spotted a seat in the middle of the coach, the last one left I'm afraid."

"Whaaat! Why can't I sit up front next to Winnie?" she exclaimed.

"Sorry, luv, that's reserved. Best grab the seat before one of the old dears puts a bag on it. Don't want to stand all the way, do you?" Reggie nodded, gestured backward, and started the engine.

Lottie was not best pleased and stomped down the centre aisle of the coach, looking for the empty seat. It didn't take long for her to spot the only one remaining, and then she realised why no one had taken it. A snoring Airedale terrier was sitting on the aisle, blocking the seat next to the window. 'The cheeky devil,' Lottie thought. 'Obviously one of the first to board, and none of the others wanted to disturb him.' She tiptoed in front of the dog, trying not to wake her new neighbour, which was hard when wearing her Doc Martens. As slowly as she could, she eased into the orange and brown striped seat, then gently placed her bag in front of her and tried to relax. "At least I don't have to speak to him," she muttered to herself.

The terrier opened his eyes ever so slightly and peered inquisitively at his new seat mate. Having satisfied himself on one point, he addressed her quietly. "That's not a very pleasant thing to say, young lady. You ought to be a bit more careful who you mumble about in future. We're not all deaf you, know!"

Lottie jumped in surprise and looked across at the dog. "Ooops, thought you were asleep," she admitted, feeling rather embarrassed and beginning to blush under her whiskers.

"No harm done," the terrier said genially. "I was faking it actually, but don't tell anyone. Pays to have your wits about you on these trips sometimes. You don't know the half of what goes on—coach politics, really."

"Coach politics?" Lottie had recovered from her gaffe and looked puzzled. "What's that?"

"Oh, you have much to learn, I'm afraid. I'll just clue you in on one point. As far as seats are concerned, I like my window seat. Beryl, on the other hand, always sits right at the back so she can make faces at the cars behind. Maxim loves an aisle seat, so he can play cards with Brian on the way. Eileen, she likes to sleep the whole trip, so it doesn't matter where she sits, and Edward over there, well, he has a reputation for getting a bit travel sick. The driver always likes to have him up front so he can make a quick exit, especially as he's the one that usually has to clean the coach at the end of the day..."

Lottie gasped in horror, fervently hoping that Edward hadn't had a large breakfast, as she didn't know what Reggie might ask her to do next.

"...although if I was in his shoes, I'd avoid sitting above the wheels, especially when we hit bumps in the road."

"I see. So why were you only pretending to be asleep, then?" Lottie asked. "Wanted the luxury of a spare seat next to you? Or are you just an unsociable grump?"

"What, like you?" the terrier replied with a smirk.

"Point taken," Lottie conceded.

"No, not that at all. Ms Chasemoore is the reason. She is the rather flirtatious Afghan hound sitting a couple of rows behind. Now, don't laugh, but she has a thing for me as you younger dogs would say, and I do all I can to avoid being on the same holidays as her, let alone being on the same coach. But when all else fails, I do my best to prevent her from sitting next to me," the terrier said. "I've used this ploy in the past, but I think it's wearing a bit thin."

Lottie turned her head and tried to look behind her and in between the headrests for this temptress, but she had no luck. Instead, she saw the greying faces of two dogs looking back at her blankly while delving into a bag of boiled sweets. She briefly wondered if the Airedale was pulling her tail. "Chasemoore"? Really? Maybe he just had an overactive imagination. She shrugged and turned back to him.

"My, I'd never have guessed there was so much to worry about, and there I was thinking that all you oldies just popped a Werther's Original in your mouths, wrapped yourselves up in your cardies and had forty winks," Lottie joked.

"I like it when you smile, young lady, make sure you do it more often, it suits you," the terrier said. "While you still have your teeth," he added, as he pulled out his false ones and waved them in front of the cockapoo. A string of drool slid onto the floor.

"Ewww, gross," she said, laughing. "I'm Lottie."

"Arthur Barclay is what my doctor calls me, but I'm Artie to my friends," he said, offering a paw. "Pleased to make your acquaintance." He popped his teeth back in with the other paw.

'There might be life in the old dog yet,' she thought, and the last bit of her ill-humour evaporated.

Chapter Twenty
Shaggy Dog Stories

Curling more comfortably into her seat, Lottie regarded Artie with interest. "How long have you been doing these trips, then?" she asked.

"A fair old while, not sure exactly when I started. It was probably not long after I lost my wife. I was at a bit of a loose end, and a friend suggested I try and meet some others, so here I am. You'll find there are plenty of couples on these tours, as well as some dogs and cats who don't drive anymore, but there are also many who are just lonely. So there is a fair bit of camaraderie too, shoulders to cry on, advice given and anecdotes exchanged," Artie replied.

Lottie looked sympathetic and felt a little chastened. She really hadn't grasped that notion before, and had tended to think, as the young do, that the elderly were all more or less alike and rather a dull lot.

"The way I see it, Lottie, is that I have my own personal chauffeur, my luggage gets taken to my room for me, I don't have to worry about how to get to where I am going, what route to take or where to park, and I can even sleep while travelling if I want. What's not to like?" Artie said.

"Hey!" a voice called from the opposite side of the coach. "Do you know you look really silly wearing that clobber? And those nose piercings. Really, you look like a bull!"

"Ignore Tabatha," Artie said to Lottie. "She's just jealous and also a bit eccentric. She planned to go on a cruise once, but the boat company had inexplicably gotten her name wrong on the manifest and wouldn't change it. Her bright idea was to change her name by deed poll just so she could go."

Lottie wasn't sure if Artie had made that up or was telling the truth, but he had made her laugh. "I once knew someone that broke up with her boyfriend just before their holiday and put an advert in the paper asking for anyone with the same name to go with her. Todd, I think."

"Really, a total stranger?" Artie said.

"Straight up, and she was chill about it, thought it would be different. She found someone, too, and they went away, spent a week on a blind date, so to speak, and came back home. This Todd didn't sweep her off her paws or anything, but she said they had a totally fab time. I told her she was just lucky he wasn't a serial killer."

"What is the youth of today getting up to?" Artie said, shaking his curly head. "Wouldn't have happened in my day, you know, although Billy often dines out on the little excursion he had when he was younger."

"Who's Billy?"

"His nickname is actually 'Smiles,' on account of him looking rather morose all of the time. It's not his fault, the cat just looks that way. He got rather drunk one night after spending too long in the company of some rather rambunctious friends in Holland. While he was waiting for a taxi back to the hotel, he decided to hop into the luggage bay of a coach to keep out of the foul weather. Unfortunately for Smiles, he fell asleep, only to wake up several hours later across the border in Belgium. All of his belongings, including his passport, were back at the hotel, so he had a devil of a job to convince the border police of the nature of his visit."

"Really, I think that trumps my story," Lottie said.

"It may well do, at that. It only happened last month too, and I was three sheets to the wind, so I didn't take much notice," Artie said.

"Wowza. You were one of the raucous friends?" Lottie asked, her eyes wide.

"I'm afraid I was, so now you know," Artie said laughing. "We aren't all past it and can still have some fun given the chance."

"Certainly, is an eye opener," Lottie said. "I'm sure you're full of interesting stories?"

"I think every one of us has weird and wonderful stories to tell and being old just means we have more of them. We might sometimes look rather grumpy and unapproachable, but when you get to our age it is often unavoidable with the various aches and pains and strain of trying to remember where we left our glasses. We certainly don't all smell of lavender and live by the seaside. It just takes a little patience, though, and most of us will open up in time, not that many of the younger generation have much of that."

"Oh, I don't know. Don't be so sure about us," Lottie replied with a smile.

At that moment, Reggie's voice bellowed out down the coach. "Stopping soon! Edward needs the restroom."

"Looks like he did have too much for breakfast after all," Archie remarked.

"I'm glad I'm down here out of the way—looks like Winnie might be called into action," Lottie said.

As the coach pulled up to the service station coach park and stopped with a jerk, Winnie made her way back to the middle seats, having just narrowly escaped the fate Lottie had imagined for her. "Oh, there you are. Sorry we couldn't sit together," she said, a little sheepishly. She glanced shyly at the Airedale, who had leaned back in his seat with a handkerchief over his eyes.

"Oh, I've been having a groovy time. Mr Barclay here, Artie, has been telling me about all the stuff he gets up to on the road. Isn't that right, Artie?"

There was no reply. "Keep your voice down," Winnie said, gesturing at the older dog.

"Don't sweat it. That's just a ploy to keep a certain overenthusiastic admirer away," Lottie replied, nudging the dog in his side. Artie snorted, and his head nearly hit the roof. "Where is she? Where's Ms Chasemoore? Not coming this way, I hope?" he said hoarsely.

"Here I am, *dahling*—you called? You've been dreaming about me, have you?" Lottie and Winnie gawped at a reed-thin Afghan in a purple pantsuit and silver heels, a wide rhinestone-studded belt cinching a tiny waist. She was not without a certain kind of personal charm and looked like the sort of dog who usually got what she wanted. "But you're still calling me 'Ms Chasemoore.' Now you know that's my last ex-husband's name, you sly devil. I'm Alfie to you," she cooed, laying a bejewelled paw on the bewildered Airedale's shoulder. "Artie and Alfie. Absolutely perfect. Can't these two pups give us a little space? We've got *so much* to talk about, haven't we, my love?"

Lottie nearly burst into hysterical laughter at the woebegone look on Artie's face, and Winnie stood transfixed, taking in the situation. Then she gathered her wits and sidled up to the Afghan. "Excuse me, ma'am, but I think you might want to check the back of your outfit...looks like there may have been something sticky left on your seat?" The dog instantly began to wriggle around to look. "Where? Where?" she said, in panic. "This is an Antony de Rossiter creation, I hope you know, though you probably don't, from the looks of you. Oh, I must get it off! That wretched Reggie never cleans this coach properly! I'll be sending him the bill if I have to replace this suit, and his boss will get a tongue lashing, too," she growled. And with that, she fled out of the coach and towards the door, narrowly avoiding a collision with Edward outside, who was bending over and wiping his mouth.

Lottie looked at Winnie with her head cocked to one side. "That was quite the performance from you, Win-Win. Couldn't have done it better myself. You have my undying admiration." Winnie glanced downward, smirking a little. "Well. Let me introduce you to Winifred Wigglesworth, up-and-coming Hollywood starlet," she said, turning to the bemused Artie.

"Pleasure to meet you, sir," Winnie said demurely, offering her paw.

"The pleasure is all mine. You just about saved my life just now."

"Why does she call herself 'Alfie'?" Lottie asked. "Weird sort of name."

"Her full name is Alfreda," Artie replied. "Got it on authority from Reggie, as she'd never own up. Now, young Winifred, why don't you take a seat for a mo and tell me all about yourself."

"Oh, I'd rather hear about you," Winnie said hurriedly. "Lottie says you were telling her about your travels."

94

Chapter Twenty-One
The Legend of Bertie Longfellow

"I'm telling you, Pierre, that's what happened. If you don't believe me, that's your lookout," the parakeet said, drinking a glass of Roussillon red.

"Come, come, Nicole. That's not what I'm saying, but you know you were in rather a state when you were taken in. You always are. so how do you know you didn't just mishear something?" her companion replied.

"If I must, I'll tell you again. You obviously weren't listening well enough," Nicole said. She put her glass down, tapping the rim with a claw. "It was like this. I was out on the razzle, and I admit I had a few too many glasses of Château Margaux, it was a special occasion after all."

"Every night is a special occasion for you, Nicole, but please carry on," Pierre interjected.

The parakeet fixed him with a beady-eyed glare. "As I was saying, the fine young officer brought me in and showed me to my cell to sleep off my excesses. I normally have the place to myself, so I was rather put out to find my usual cell occupied by two dogs snoring away. Even worse, I was left in the cell next to one with a cat. I overlooked it all and settled down as is my routine, hoping for a peaceful night, but I got rudely awakened at about eight o'clock in the morning. I ask you, I need my beauty sleep, and to wake up to that lot yammering going on. I nearly blew a gasket. I was still a bit groggy—I'd had a late one after all—but decided there was little chance of getting any more shuteye, so I listened in. I assume the boss of the outfit had been brought in earlier that night along with his partner. They were sharing, you see."

"Really, yes, I understood that bit the first time," Pierre drawled. He preened his feathers in a bored sort of way. Nicole hastened on to the gist of her tale.

"The cat was telling them about the getaway car, or trying to come up with a good reason she shouldn't get a hiding from the dogs, if you ask me. Very reluctant to say the wrong thing, she was. Red car, or perhaps white, it doesn't really matter. She tried to tell some tale to the gendarme, said that it was a hire car, but *les flics* were having none of it. They knew it was stolen, as it had been reported earlier in the day. Not a clever enough story, anyway, so they threw her in the slammer. Well, cats are a bit stupid, aren't they? Not like us birds."

"Quite," replied Pierre, cocking his head in agreement.

"Now, apparently the cat had left the plans for the robbery at their hideout, although it was probably a good thing they weren't found on her, actually. This Longfellow chap got in a bit of a sulk and left his partner to try and coax the info out of the cat. I'm sure he was going to give her what for once they got out, and I couldn't blame him. Cats are always up to something bad, it's bred into them from an early age. The second officer that took over, smart fellow, he was having none of their lip. He told them they were in for a long stretch as he handed them their breakfast, the usual, a croissant and a bit of muesli and a cup of tea. Thanks to them, I was last in the queue, tea and croissant both cold, pah."

"Did you have any jam with that, and a silver knife, too?" Pierre enquired.

"No," Nicole huffed, fluffing her feathers in disgust. "But I brightened up a bit after I got some food inside me. A few moments later, all hell broke loose. The door to the cells burst open, and Longfellow's gang turned up, tooled up good and proper. They had cunningly disguised themselves as a set of protesters with placards and flags and were shouting about the conditions in the cells. Well, I never had any complaints, bit off the mark I thought. Anyway, they could have come up with something more believable, but in they came, causing a ruckus, diverting the attention of the only guard on duty. He didn't have a clue what to do. Bertie's number two came up to the cells and unlocked them—let the cat out and even opened my door. Well, they had no choice, did they? It was all part of the ruse. The mob barged their way out of the lockup area, and this Bertie fellow and his moll hopped it with the rest of them. I couldn't believe what I was seeing! A breakout, in broad daylight, the cheek! Well, this guy knew his onions, must have, since he was hightailing it out of there in the middle of the crowd, holding one of the placards in front of his face. The guard, well, he put up a bit of a fight and got a couple of quick slugs in the stomach and head for his trouble. It all could have been much worse, but I stopped it. Pushed him into a cell and slammed the door for his own protection."

"You are a heroine, you really are, Nic. I'm sure you'll be given a medal for that piece of bravery," Pierre quipped.

"Quite," Nicole replied, taking this compliment as her due. "So, on my way out, I had a quick rummage and spotted a wanted poster on the wall. The artist's impression was not the best, but I recognised that Longfellow chap, all right. He's wanted in connection with the Van Cleef & Arpels heist, you remember? It was all over the news, a daring robbery by all accounts. The perps just walked into a jeweller's in broad daylight and got away with a suitcase-load of the sparkly stuff, and I'm not referring to champagne, either.

"Are you sure about all this? It sounds very far-fetched, Nic," Pierre said. "Last time you were in, you were convinced that you'd seen that notorious bank robber, what's his name again? Mesrine?"

"I told you, that's what I saw. The gendarmes are none too happy though, reckon the gang has gone to ground now, and they'll be impossible to find unless there is a lagger out there willing to give up some information. Wouldn't want to get on the wrong side of Longfellow though. I expect he has contacts all over the place. I'll be off to Gran Canaria for a few weeks to keep a low profile, don't want a visit from his sort—nor that cat, she gave me the willies."

"That's as good an excuse for a holiday as I've ever heard," smirked Pierre. "I just hope the cells there are up to your exacting standards."

Chapter Twenty-Two
Safe Passage

"It's a good job those football supporters caused such a ruckus when they did, Bertie," Muriel said. "If it wasn't for them, and the need for space in the cells, and the officer showing some leniency towards us all, I think we could have been waiting a long time to be released. Although I didn't appreciate having my derrière slapped by one of them."

"The rotter!" Bertie said, with lowering brows. "They were a noisy lot, weren't they? I wouldn't have wanted to be sharing a cell with those scallywags. A little too tipsy for my liking, so I was glad that their team had won."

Ani was not engaging in the conversation, instead trying to work out where she could get the next bus to somewhere a bit more civilised. She was busy looking for any signs that would direct her to a larger town where she could either hire another car or get on a train to her destination. Muriel watched her consternation as she tried to decide which way to go.

"So, where are you heading, Ani? We thought it best to head back to the hotel. Our luggage and belongings are still there, so we really need to return," Muriel asked.

Ani was silent for a few moments while she considered what to say. She wasn't keen to seem too helpless in front of these new acquaintances. "I don't know this town very well at all, I'm afraid. I'll need to get a map."

"In the meantime, why don't you come along with us?" Bertie suggested. "At least you can get your bearings, freshen up and have a nice meal?"

Ani felt torn. She really didn't know these two dogs from Adam, but considering her current predicament, she thought it was better not to be wandering about Burmilleux on her own, at least until she got herself in order. "That's exceedingly kind of you. If you don't mind…"

"Of course not. Given it's now Sunday, I don't think we are going to have much luck with public transport, but perhaps if we head down that street there," Bertie pointed, "we can see if there is a taxi rank somewhere. It looks like there is at least some more activity."

Muriel and Ani agreed, and the three set off along the narrow-cobbled street. As they walked, Muriel attempted to make friendly conversation with Ani, but she seemed to have shrunk into herself, her scarf once again wrapped securely round her head, and she returned polite but brief replies. Muriel didn't want to push the cat. They had all had a rather traumatic night, and it was certainly the first time she had seen the inside of a prison cell—although she didn't know if that was true for Bertie. She'd have to ask.

They had turned onto what appeared to be a high street of sorts, but the various shops were all closed. It appeared that most of the town's citizens were just out for a walk rather than actually doing any shopping. The end of the street opened out onto a river with a light amount of traffic ranging from a few rowing boats to the odd narrowboat. On the stone jetty there were two red and blue craft moored up, day boats, each with a small inner cabin and a covered deck. Several passengers were grouped around each boat, loading up their provisions for the day's outing, whilst two already on board were being shown the controls at the rear of one of the boats. Bertie had an idea.

"Give me a moment," he said, and a few minutes later he came back to Ani and Muriel with good news. "Enough of this wandering blindly about. I've got us passage on one of those day tripper boats. Wonderful chap, knows just where our hotel is."

Ani seemed to perk up a bit. "Trust you to find a handy boat anywhere," Muriel teased.

Chapter Twenty-Three
Heaven Help Us

Bertie eagerly stepped aboard *Achilles* first, nearly banging his head on the metal roof as he did so. Ani was helped in next, though she showed some reluctance as the boat swayed from side to side slightly from the wash of a passing boat. Muriel entered last, her face also betraying some trepidation. She was used to travelling on the water, but not in such small vessels, with every eddy making itself felt, and she wasn't much looking forward to the trip.

"How long did you say we will have to be on board?" she asked Bertie.

"It's only a couple of miles," he replied, and Muriel rewarded him with a small smile. Bertie decided not to remind her that travelling by boat was much slower than by car, about four knots, which was akin to walking pace. It would likely take several hours for them to get back to their warm room, especially as there were a couple of locks to navigate, too. The other boat, *Aphrodite,* was unhitched from its mooring and cast off first. As it did so, it turned hard left and disappeared upriver. *Achilles* had a somewhat less smooth departure. The captain, a volunteer from among the passengers, had given the boat engine some revs and tried to pull away, but he had forgotten that no one had unhooked the ropes from the jetty, so all that happened was that the boat pulled the ropes tight, stretching them in the same way a young pup on a lead might while trying to get away from its parent. Most of the group were unaware of this hitch, having gathered in their seats and expecting the boat to magically move under its own power. Bertie was watching intently but decided to stay by Muriel and Ani. He could tell that the cat was rather nervous of being within a couple feet of the water, and she was also obviously anxious about being in the company of so many others in such a small space. She tugged her scarf more securely around her and kept her eyes on the bottom of the boat. Muriel kept up a pleasant monologue in an effort to calm Ani, recounting various enjoyable and successful journeys on cruise liners and yachts.

The well-built tom cat at the helm called to his partner, an equally gingery tom, to hop out and untie the ropes. "Alright, Tango, that should do it," the cat said to the captain as he leapt back onto the deck. Bertie felt some relief as the boat pulled away, scraping the sides of the mooring, until there was finally clear air between the boat and the pontoon. The yard assistant looked up nonchalantly and shook his head, having seen it all before. He never would understand the need to repaint the hulls every year, as it only took a few trips out by inexperienced holiday makers to return them to their former inglorious state.

The river ahead looked clear of any obstructions to hinder their journey, and while their course remained straight, Tango seemed to have a firm hold of the tiller. Unfortunately, the first bend created some mayhem. The other ginger cat, who appeared to be his brother, screeched and shouted, waving his paws and tail about. "We're going to crash! Watch it!" Indeed, they were heading for the trees and bushes on the bank. Despite this, Tango remained unperturbed. "I know exactly what I'm about," he called back. "Mind your own business, or you'll get a face full of this!" He lifted both paws heedlessly from the tiller and batted his sibling away from the engine controls. Within about a minute, it was clear that the tom didn't know what he was doing, as the boat turned hard a port and then hard starboard before finally careering into the tree straight ahead. Thankfully, the boat was made of steel, and the tree came off worse, having a large gouge cut into it from the anchor at the front of the boat. Unfortunately, Muriel and Ani were now mired in the brambles and nettles which were growing out of the riverbank. The cat and dorgi heroically held their tongues, Muriel clutching Bertie's paw and Ani grasping the railing with an iron grip born of terror.

The other passengers, who had been busily chatting away without a care in the world, had now become aware of the slight panic up front and began reacting accordingly, shouting at the helms cat to watch what he was doing. Tango ignored their demands and threw the boat hard in reverse, causing a large swirl of muddy water to appear as they moved backwards. Then he shoved it hard forwards, turning the tiller, and the boat fortunately returned to the correct course. He beamed with satisfaction, and buoyed by his success, forged ahead.

"There you go! You should have had more trust in me. I know what I'm doing!" Tango shouted blithely down through the cabin. "And for my next trick, I'll navigate this stretch blindfold," he announced, whilst his brother cringed and shook his head violently, making no move to oblige him on this point. "Although someone really must bring me up a snack first. All this driving of boats is making me awfully peckish."

The journey continued for another half a mile before another bend presented itself. To Bertie's surprise and relief, all seemed to be going smoothly—or it was, until Tango's brother decided it was his turn to take the helm. Tango reluctantly agreed but immediately started to give him instructions as if he was now the fountain of all nautical knowledge. "Push the tiller left to go right and right to go left," he explained. "That's right. NO! Push left, I said! There. You must listen, you know. I'll control the power for you." His brother was not best pleased, and as soon as a couple of canoes up ahead appeared in the middle of the river, the boat was all over the place again. Tango was waggling the power controller back and forth from forward and into reverse and shouting. "Ginger!!! Push right! No, left! No!" But it was all to no avail as the boat ended up straddling the river lengthways, and the two canoeists just stopped to watch the pandemonium, laughing at the scene before them.

Tango noticed their derision and got rather angry with Ginger. "You're hopeless! Simply hopeless! I should dump you overboard, and you can see how you get on with them!" he said, shaking a paw toward the canoeists. Ginger scowled and muttered something to the effect that just such a fate would suit Tango himself. He somehow managed to salvage the situation, and both tipped their hats at the grinning canoeists as they passed.

"Good day, lovely weather we're having," Tango said, charmingly, before turning to his brother. "I think you'll find it's my turn again, now?"

Bertie was glad they were close to the first lock, as it would mean they could at least have a break from the bad helmscatship. Unfortunately, the fun had only just begun. "Lock ahead," Tango called out cheerfully, whilst Ginger sat sulkily with his arms folded, huffing to himself. Tango was as confident as ever, whistling a happy tune and looking happily from side to side as if at an appreciative audience on the banks. He'd been rather distracted when the boat hand had given instructions for operating the lock gates but felt no qualms. Fortunately, they were open, so the boat drifted inside and then slowed to a stop, only bumping the gates at the far end. Tango called out again for someone inside to shut the gates. "I'd do it myself, but someone needs to stay in control," he said with a wink at the nearest attractive feline.

Bertie laughed to himself when he heard this and watched as two of the other passengers popped their heads out of the cabin, only too willing to escape for a few moments. The boat stood enclosed by the two gates as everyone waited.

"Are we going up or down?" one passenger asked, and Bertie put a paw to his head, wondering how on earth the cat thought the boat could travel any higher than the level of the water upriver. "Down," he said, with great effort stopping himself from speaking his mind.

"You have to open the sluices," another passenger shouted, as he rummaged around inside the cabin and threw out the lock key while continuing to chat with his friend. Tango took charge once again, now half remembering that the metal stick was to be used somewhere on the gate and walked confidently to the front gates. He stopped a moment, quickly spotted the ring on the end of the handle that matched that of the protruding metal of the sluice gate, connected the two and began opening the sluice. Unfortunately, Tango's strength knew no bounds, and he continued winding the sluice up, all too quickly, without considering the mayhem he was causing behind him. Tango mistook the cheers inside the boat as a sign that he was doing a sterling job and continued, but soon even he could tell that the plaudits had turned into groans. Bertie realised that no one had tethered the ropes to the bollards at the side of the lock above, and the boat was soon tossing and turning, buffeted from side to side and hitting the front gates as the turbulent water emptied from the lock.

Muriel and Ani's nerves were now getting rather threadbare, and both were looking very tense. Bertie was equally worried, having not experienced this kind of violent battering since he was a young pup racing his sister Samantha across a boating lake, but there was little he could do.

Once the water level on both sides of the front gate had restored itself, Tango tore open the gates with another show of masculine force, and his brother, not wanting to be outdone, did the same on the other side of the lock. Each then found himself in a predicament—the boat was now six feet below and drifting out of the lock. Before he looked any sillier, Tango climbed down the slimy lock ladder and deftly leapt onto the roof of the cabin. Wiping his hands on his trousers, he then threw the lock key on the deck with a loud clatter, resumed the position of captain and pushed the controller forward. "You'd better get on! We're off!" he called up to Ginger, which only antagonised the cat further. He was wavering a tad, slightly fearful of heights. As the boat bounced off each side of the lock, there was just enough time for him to hang precariously from the tips of his paws, drop down onto the roof and re-join the captain, who gave him a conciliatory high five. A beagle who'd been watching from inside congratulated the cat. "Top marks, but a double somersault would have topped it off," he said with a grin. The boat emerged from the lock entrance with ironic claps from the members of the public above who had been watching the events unfold, much to the chagrin of those inside.

It didn't take long before the river ahead provided yet more opportunity for mayhem. Various other day boats were meandering along the water, and Tango saw this as a new challenge. He revved up the engine and decided he was in a race to the next lock. Fish was on the menu for lunch at the pub on the other side, and after all his exertions of the morning, he was getting very hungry. The craft started to create a large wash, pushing waves of water up and over the banks. Aghast walkers stopped and waved their arms in annoyance, which the tom took as encouragement to go even faster. The engine noise increased, and the boat frame started to rattle and vibrate. The boat ahead approached too quickly, and the *Achilles* met it just as it had started turning starboard. Tango, still filled with bravado, realised too late and slammed the boat into reverse, but the forward momentum caused the boat to collide broadside, and the *Athena's* lovely gold lettering and the idyllic painted castle were scratched through. The *Achilles'* daring captain fell in the water, pulling Ginger along with him. Bertie had already sensed the danger and was running through the inner cabin to the helm, falling forwards when the accident happened. He picked himself up quickly and climbed the steps to see no one at the helm. Shaking his head in disgust, he flicked the engine into neutral, and whilst the two boats were momentarily joined like Siamese twins, everything began to calm down.

The two cats were waving their arms around and shouting for attention, so Bertie grabbed the life ring and threw it to the loudest one, who grabbed hold and started paddling towards his brother. Once Bertie was satisfied that both were safe, he pulled on the rope and brought them back. Slowly the two reached the side of the boat and climbed aboard, looking rather like drowned rats. Those onboard were recovering from the shock of the recent events, and as the cats stepped down inside the cabin to dry off, they were rounded on by a pair of annoyed poodles closest by. Bertie had little sympathy and hoped they might have learned a lesson. Turning his back on them and toward the tiller, he took control.

Muriel and Ani joined him at the stern, and despite being rather shaken themselves, were ever so glad to see him in charge. The pair sat down and breathed a sigh of relief as the controller was nudged forward, the engine picked up its revs and the boat moved slowly but surely onward. Bertie deftly moved the tiller like the professional he was, and with slow and precise movements, carefully navigated the river ahead. A terrier popped his head out from the cabin to see what was happening. "I'm so glad someone knows what they are doing! Here, do you fancy a paste sandwich?" he offered, before returning inside.

Tango and his brother stood, dripping wet, slightly isolated from the rest of the group, each trying to dry themselves down with a tea towel grabbed from the galley. Tango found it easy to do by taking off as many clothes as was decent and was then quite pleased when he spotted a Bengal cat eyeing his svelte physique and numerous tattoos. Ginger sat down heavily and put his face in his paws, 'Here we go again,' he thought.

Chapter Twenty-Four
Cold Call

Johanna Voigt rubbed her paws together in an attempt to keep warm. She was going about her usual business of organising her next trip when a call came in from the office. Johanna worked as a tour guide in the district of Tolville, and she loved being able to share her knowledge of the area, the sort of information no one would ever find out unless they had lived there for as long as she had. Her particular interest was in the region of Theitenbach, where there were many unexplored caves. The most well-known and largest underground caverns were now a popular tourist spot, and the village nearby had gradually come to accept the constant stream of visitors as a boon to the local economy, although many residents were still set in their ways and hated the intrusion.

The caves themselves still managed to retain some of their mystery, as there were numerous unexplored, unmapped passageways. It wasn't clear where these routes ended, and from time-to-time Johanna had ventured down them just to learn more. A number were dead ends, although one did open out into an amazing cavern, with water falling down from several hundred feet. Johanna had been thrilled by the discovery, and over the course of the years that followed, it had been added to the tour, along with the adventure that led her to find it. Every so often a particular tourist would show such an interest that she would tell them that it was indeed she who had found the place, although normally she was too modest and spoke of the event in the third person.

Her office was located in the village and was really nothing more than a small shed located at the back of the post office, which also now sold souvenirs and postcards. A small electric heater was all there was to keep warm, and except in summer the space was always cold. The friendly postmistress acted in an unofficial capacity, mostly to help Johanna, as nearly all of the bookings came by mail through other agents. This arrangement made the call seem all the stranger. Johanna answered it, and what she heard was even more surprising. An American cat by the name of Anipe Amourby was requesting a private tour of the caves, or rather a set of caves in the same area, and she was hoping to engage her services for an entire week. Whilst Johanna loved being a tour guide, she usually had to make do with cut-rate packages for coach tours and the like, so she was rather dumbfounded by this prospect. 'Well, I'm never going to get rich, and I really do need to buy a kettle for the office,' she mused. She agreed a date to meet Anipe and noted it in her diary.

After getting off the phone, Johanna exchanged the Arctic climate of her office for the tiny but well-heated library to do a little research. The caller's unique name had caught her interest. After consulting various books, she found what she was looking for: 'Anipe, or daughter of the Nile.' This struck Johanna as rather peculiar and piqued her curiosity still further. Returning the books to the librarian, she decided that the cat's heritage was obviously something she would like to get to the bottom of when they met in a few weeks' time.

As she sipped her tea, alone at her flat, Johanna realised that she was very much looking forward to this meeting. And it wasn't really the prospect of a good fee that cheered her. Most of her tours were afternoon affairs, during which she met a great many dogs and cats but never saw them again, though some of them sent her notes of appreciation afterwards. These she kept in a tin and glanced through them from time to time, smiling over her memories of the writers.

But this would be an opportunity to share the trials and triumphs of her explorations with someone who just might be as fascinated as she was, over the course of a number of days. Ms Amourby had certainly sounded enthusiastic, in a quiet way that Johanna understood. As she looked out across the village rooftops at the overcast afternoon, her head resting in her paws, she reflected that life had been rather grey lately. Piercing through those thoughts was the memory of a lovely find that she'd only shared with one other fellow enthusiast and that had given her much pleasure. Perhaps this visitor was the one to appreciate it fully. "Yes," she said aloud, as the shadows began to fall and a ray of sunshine broke through the bank of clouds, touching the red gold of her fur. "We will go there."

Chapter Twenty-Five
Pistons at Dawn

As part of the agreement Winnie had made with Reggie, both she and
Lottie would be required to help on a couple of the excursions the company
had laid on for the holiday. Winnie saw this arrangement as an excellent
and economical opportunity to explore England and thought the work a
small price to pay for the privilege. Lottie was somewhat less enthusiastic,
but as she was on a budget and saving up for a new pair of Union Jack Doc
Martens, she didn't argue. The group of passengers that had decided to take
the trip had assembled and were boarding the coach. Artie was hiding
behind a couple of taller dogs in case Alfreda appeared, although in this
instance he was on safe ground, as she was not the type to get up early,
favouring her beauty sleep instead.

Reggie was in a rather foul mood. He had been called up by the manager in
the night after a customer decided to sleepwalk around the grounds in a
petticoat, and he'd had to calm down poor Mrs Chivers, who was adamant
she had seen a ghost. Fortunately, Winnie and Lottie's only task before
they set off was to do a head count. It was just as well that the coach wasn't
full, so they could sit further back away from the grumpy chow.

During the journey, Reggie started grumbling to himself about the
congestion of traffic on the narrow roads of the quaint villages. His coach
was a large vehicle, and he often relied on other drivers to be considerate of
the manoeuvrability issues he suffered, so when they came upon a large
tractor parked on the kerbside and blocking the left side of the road, his
temper started to fray. It wasn't long before a queue had backed up behind
the coach, while he waited for a convenient time to pass the vehicle. After
only a minute of waiting, the car behind started honking its horn, and the
excitable driver, a large retriever, was sticking his head out of the window
shouting at Reggie to get a move on. Reggie was aware of the tailback but
could only proceed when things were safe. Despite this, the car behind

pulled out, roared past, and then hooted its horn, narrowly missing the Anglia coming the other way.

"Miscreant," Reggie muttered to himself, but otherwise ignored the incident and finally drove past the offending tractor. A few miles along, the coach passed a petrol station, and the driver of the black Ford Capri Mk II could be seen filling up. Before long the Capri was once again stuck behind the coach, darting in and out of the middle of the road, trying to pass, but with no luck. Reggie, normally a rather placid dog, was starting to become agitated. Checking his mirrors, he could see the retriever was getting impatient and was certain it would result in an accident, so he pulled into the first bus stop he could find to let it pass again. As the Capri shot by, Reggie looked down at the boy racer and aggressively waved his clenched paw at the annoying creature. Much to his surprise, the car stopped quickly just a few metres ahead. The door opened, and the retriever got out and ran back to the coach. Within seconds, he was banging on the door, looking for a confrontation. Reggie was no stranger to road rage incidents and would normally be the one watching from a distance as others made fools of themselves, but on this occasion, there was no escaping being the centre of attention himself. He flicked the lever to open the coach door and jumped up from his seat.

The dogs and cats in the seats behind him were already alert to the situation and most anxious that no harm would come to Reggie. Not only were they dependent on him to get them to their destination, but most of them had developed a certain fondness for him, despite his perpetually food-spattered shirt fronts. Reggie walked down the steps to the combative retriever, who was gesturing to come and fight and making threatening lunges towards him, whilst the coach load of passengers had now all clambered to the nearside seats and were gawking out of the side windows. Reggie stepped back a touch when he saw the size of the muscles on the dog before him, realising he was somewhat out of his depth.

"Give it to him, Reggie," one dog cried. "Kick him where the sun don't shine," croaked another whilst banging on the glass with her stick. Winnie was surprised by this newfound vigour among some of the older passengers and half thought about corralling them into a mob as a show of force, given she felt no words would calm the situation down. But Lottie had other ideas, and she whispered in Winnie's ear before jumping off the coach and running stealthily towards the Capri. Reggie was still exchanging fighting words with the retriever, and both continued to gesture without landing any punches. Winnie waited a few more moments and then shouted out, "someone's stealing your car!" Reggie and the retriever froze for a second and then turned to see the Capri's door slam shut as it disappeared up the road in a puff of exhaust. The retriever broke off the argument and dashed desperately after his car, whilst Reggie stood back, huffing, rather annoyed that he hadn't given the other dog what for. Winnie tugged at his sleeve. "Come along Reggie, we need to pick Lottie up. She'll be two hundred metres away by now."

Passing the puffing retriever jogging up the roadside, Reggie's mood lightened, and he waved cheerily at the dog. Up the road and just over the brow of the hill, the black Capri was parked on the verge with a rather smug-looking cockapoo standing by. Reggie pulled the coach to a stop and opened the door to a beaming Lottie, who leapt in and threw a pair of fuzzy pink dice into Reggie's lap. "Thought you might like these as a memento, better than a black eye," she giggled as she returned to her seat.

Chapter Twenty-Six
The Crown Has Fallen

Hans was on the phone to his friend Percy while sitting comfortably in his flat. The pair had met some time ago in the theatre and developed a friendship. After Hans had moved to England, he had found it hard to meet others, and the charming older dog was good company. He had found he was speaking to him more often, and they occasionally took in a matinee together.

"I've just had a letter from Bertie," Percy told him.

"Oh, good," Hans said. He wasn't well-acquainted with the dachshund but knew he "a good sort of chap," as the British would say. "How is he faring? And Muriel?"

"Well, it appears that their original cruise itinerary has been scuppered, but he sounds cheerful enough. If I know Bertie, he's probably happier traveling here and there on a whim anyway rather than sticking to a pre-arranged schedule. They're just about to move on from France, but he doesn't really say where they're headed."

"Sounds like a pleasant trip." Hans stretched his toes closer to the electric fire and realised that he didn't envy the travellers at all. He'd been leading a peripatetic existence for some time, and it was rather pleasant to have settled in London for a while. There was silence for a moment, but it wasn't uncomfortable.

"So, how's life treating you, Hans?" Percy asked. "Anything new happening? Someone special in your life? When will we see some little Hans puppies running around?"

Hans laughed at the thought. "You'll be the first with an invitation to the wedding if it happens, you know that, and you can finally buy that new hat you were after. Although I dare say you have something dapper enough already."

"That's a real shame, you deserve some happiness." Percy paused. "I thought you were getting on quite well with Mila at one time, someone you mentioned from your days at Birkbeck College—if my memory serves me correctly, which it normally doesn't."

"That was a long time ago," Hans replied. "I haven't heard from her in quite a while."

"Right. What happened then?" Percy asked.

"Oh, we grew apart, things like that happen. She was a supply teacher for a long time and got offered a job further afield. She couldn't refuse the opportunity, and I didn't want her to, but it meant we only met on the weekends. Eventually she was working at the weekends, too. We spent less time together, and it just didn't work out unfortunately," Hans said solemnly.

"I'm sure you will find someone special, Hans, you are a handsome chap," Percy replied, trying to boost his confidence. "You'll be whisking some lovely maiden off her paws soon enough. Or perhaps you might try again with Mila? At least find out how she's doing? Faint heart never won fair lady; you know."

"Perhaps," Hans said. "So, how are things with you?"

"Oh, I can't really complain," Percy said quite sombrely.

Hans could tell his friend was holding back, as the tone of his voice had changed.

"What's up? You can tell me," he assured Percy.

"I've just been thinking. It's funny how your memory plays tricks on you, isn't it?" Percy said. "I could recall Mila, who we talked about only a few weeks ago, but I can't remember what I had for breakfast. I suppose I've come to accept that I'm never going to be the same dog I once was and to adapt as best I can. In fact, I consider myself to be one of the lucky ones."

"Why is that?" Hans replied encouragingly.

"I haven't told you all the details of my past. It would take too long, perhaps another time, but since the war I have met several other veterans on days of remembrance and come to see the effect it has on us all. One such dog had a rather big impact on me. I won't forget him—he was called Samuel, but we called him Samson. A colossus of a dog, he was, to look at him you wouldn't think he could be afraid of anything, so strong and muscular, even all these years later. We got chatting and he opened up to me, albeit in a confusing manner. He was in the army, posted overseas for much of the war, first seeing action in France. He went on countless missions with his unit. One time he was in a night attack behind enemy lines, and they got split up and lost. Eventually, he was picked up by the French Resistance and fought alongside them for a few weeks until re-joining his unit. War-weary, he was sent straight back to the front line. The fighting continued from country to country, moving on to Italy. He started to have bad dreams. He lost his friends, and only one of the dogs remained that he signed up with. He got no rest and was perpetually moving or fighting."

"That is sad indeed," Hans said, continuing to listen.

"At one time, he told me that at one of his final postings, that there were coconut trees growing in the woods where he had set up camp, although I had my doubts, unless he had mixed up the location. He recollected seeing the dogs climbing up the trees and knocking the coconuts down, which seemed natural enough, until he said he ran for his life as they fell, hitting the ground with ferocity, great amounts of earth being shot up into the air as they exploded. He was at pains to say how he felt, the sheer terror of having nowhere to hide and escape the onslaught of these coconuts. Perhaps this was a dream. I'm not sure."

"That sounds awful," Hans said.

"Oh, it was, horrific," Percy continued, "The shelling and bombardment of positions he was defending continued with no let up. Then he jumped to the next recollection, where he was lining up with another mass of troops, waiting to go into battle, standing in the ditch of a long road. Within minutes, a hoard of enemy soldiers appeared across the way, attacking them all. He turned his weapon on them, but although the gun fired, the bullets simply fell away, hitting nothing. Having checked his jacket for more ammo, he found he had none and was forced to improvise. He attached some shrapnel between his paws, pushed it through a glove and was ready for paw to paw and the reality that he was probably going to die very soon."

Hans looked more and more concerned.

"Despite this, the troops seemed to overcome the attack and push it back, eventually forcing the enemy to retreat. Again, the battle took its toll, as he saw lots of dogs being blown up by the German artillery. He became so disillusioned that he found himself walking aimlessly into a forest. Three other dogs did the same. Lying down by a tree, he looked up into the sky and fell asleep. He recalled being taken away from the conflict in a jeep driven by another soldier. The jeep was travelling too fast, swerving around bends at high speed, and it crashed into a bank. The driver was severely injured and lay motionless against the steering wheel. Another army dog saw what had happened and helped, and the next thing he knew, Samson was in the driver's seat, speeding to the nearest medical station. He drove through muddy fields, crashing through wooden gates and passing other troops' lines on their way forward to another skirmish."

"He was a hero, then. He saved this dog's life?" questioned Hans.

"You may think so, but his memory was playing tricks on him all along. Samson was indeed in that jeep, but he wasn't taking anyone to hospital. He was actually being taken back away from enemy lines, and he was court martialled and sent to prison for desertion."

"My," Hans said.

"So, those memories had been mixed up, the coconuts were mortars, the journey was being taken by an MP to barracks, and his military career was over," Percy said. "Long after the war, he was assessed, and the doctors discovered he was suffering from post-traumatic stress. The court martial was reversed, but he was a changed dog. He would come on memorial days to honour the fallen. Other family members would admire their relatives, and he would be envious in some ways, seeing how proud they looked of the medals on their chests, where he had none.

"Surely he was honoured too?" Hans said.

"Perhaps one day, my lad, one day when the world realises that mental scars may not be seen but are felt just as much," Percy replied. "Anyway, I don't want to depress you anymore. We need to have something to look forward to. Have any of the upcoming shows in London taken your fancy? I'd be delighted to join you again soon."

"Let me look at the listings and get back to you. We can definitely do that, it would be my pleasure," Hans replied.

He sat pensively for a while after ringing off, gravely considering what Percy's own experiences of the war may have been and the toll they must have taken. His eyes were drawn to the teddy bear on the sofa opposite.

Chapter Twenty-Seven
Bertie Goes for a Drive

After some consideration, Muriel and Bertie had decided that they would offer to accompany Ani on the next stage of her journey. They were at something of a loose end and thought they might be of use to her. Bertie, especially, was concerned for her safety. "If she goes about losing cars and is terrified of water, I don't think she should be left to herself," he declared.

"Oh, I think she's quite capable," Muriel said in Ani's defence. "Just hesitant. Remember, she came all the way from America on her own. And there are such things as trains and buses, not just cars and boats, Bertie."

"I still don't like the idea," he maintained, stubbornly.

Muriel smiled at his chivalrous instincts and let the matter rest. "She does seem a bit of a lonely soul, though, and the company may do her good."

Ani had nearly declined their kind offer, but the rather harrowing trip on the canal boat had weakened her defences, and she agreed to the plan. And so it was that she came to be seated next to Bertie in a hired vehicle on a bright morning.

"It's a manual transmission, Bertie. Are you sure?" Muriel said a bit sceptically.

"That's not a problem," he replied, with renewed zeal and confidence in his voice. "I can do it." He slid eagerly into the driver's seat and began fiddling with various knobs. Ani's whiskers twitched a bit as she took the seat next to him, and Muriel hoped for the best as she settled in the back.

The car they had hired was in fact not a car at all, but a Volkswagen Transporter pickup. Despite Ani's pleas with the car hire company for a camper van, they only had the one, and it was up on ramps in the workshop having the brakes looked at. Apparently, the cat who had rented it previously drove into the front window of a clock shop and had blamed the company for not servicing it properly. They allowed themselves to be convinced that the workshop pickup would suit their needs just fine, and they managed to get a steep discount on the rental price, although the luxury of having a cooker and perhaps somewhere to relax might have been nice. It did, however, give them an excuse not to stay out at night and camp under the stars. Bertie was keen to stress this point further, given he didn't want a repeat of what happened the last time he went camping—after arriving too late at his destination to find lodgings for the night, he had pitched his tent in the dark and awoke to find he had spent the night sleeping only several inches from a rather inert armadillo. Muriel was keen to stress that the chance of finding an armadillo in Germany was so remote that, if they did, she would be more than happy to kiss it, much to Bertie's disgust.

"You know they carry leprosy, don't you?" he said.

"I suppose that's one of those risks a girl has to take," was Muriel's rejoinder. "Just because you have a knack for waking up next to roadkill doesn't mean sleeping under the wide sky isn't frightfully romantic."

Bertie lifted his brows and grinned. "We'll have to agree to disagree on that one. If you agree to sleep one night out in the dory, I'll have a go at your version of camping."

As the dory was safely several thousand miles away, Muriel readily agreed, giving him a playful peck on the cheek.

Bertie waggled the gear level and fired up the pickup. The diesel engine clattered to life under the flatbed behind. "I might not have a clue how to drive on the left-hand side of the road, but we are in Europe now, and they drive on the proper side here," he said.

"If you say so Bertie. But you have to remember, these things can be a bit awkward. They have a dogleg first gear, the mechanic told us, so whatever you do don't put it into reverse when we are going along or he will have our guts for garters," Ani said, trying to convince herself that handing over the reins had been a good idea.

"I know, I know," Bertie crowed. 'I'm not an imbecile,' he muttered under his breath. He depressed the clutch, shoved the gear lever backwards and left, a bit too aggressively for Ani's liking, and they set off kangarooing forwards.

"Change gear, Bertie," Ani called out, "First gear is so short that you need to change up quickly."

Bertie tried to keep his head firmly looking forwards while he wangled the gear lever about to find second, but by that time he had stalled the pickup. He didn't need to look right to know what Ani's face would look like. He would almost prefer having Stanley in his ear, telling him off. He restarted the pickup and tried again. This time he had a bit more luck, getting it into second gear before realising that a rather wayward pair of cyclists on a tandem up ahead were veering all over the road, and he was forced to slow right down again. Bertie put his foot down on the accelerator and passed them slowly. As he did so, he heard one of them calling to the other, "this is the last time I let you decide what we are going to do for a day out! I told you these things were harder to ride than they looked, but oh no, you had to impress that young Bengal girlfriend of yours." There was no reply from the other rider.

The pickup continued on its way without mishap until it reached a T-junction and had to come to a stop.

"Which way?" Bertie asked.

"Let me check," Muriel replied, as she whipped the map from the bench seat and studied it. "Left... no right, definitely right," she called out.

Just as Bertie had checked that the road was clear, he heard a squeal of brakes. Glancing in the rear-view mirror, he saw the tandem hurtling towards him. The ginger cats' ears were flat against their heads and their eyes bulging.

"Tangooooo," the rider in the rear called out, but it was too late. They had got up too much speed on the steady decline in the road and hadn't realised the tarmac was about to end. Tango deftly twisted the handlebars to avoid Bertie's Volkswagen and whizzed by. "It's as easy as driving a boat," he called back to his passenger, but the next moment they were bouncing across the ditch opposite and crashing headfirst into a wooden fence bordering a field.

Bertie jumped out of the cab, followed by Ani. He needn't have worried though, as Tango was already up and about when he got there, dusting himself down and picking his poor brother up from the bushes. "That was fun. Pity the bike looks a bit worse for wear though," he said cheerfully.

'Oh no, it's him!' Bertie thought, as Tango turned and spotted him.

"Look Ginger, it's that chap from the boat, what a coincidence! He always seems to appear when trouble is around. I say there… yes, you. I don't suppose you can offer us a ride in your pick up? Least you could do after causing this little incident," Tango said.

Ginger looked embarrassed but decided to say nothing. Bertie was not amused by the cat's accusation, but before he could say a word, Tango and his brother had pulled the bike from the ditch and were hoisting it into the back of the pickup.

'The cheek,' Bertie thought, helping Ani back into the pickup. "Look here…" he started, but he was interrupted.

"So good of you to oblige. I don't suppose you have any chocolates or some grub? All this exercise has made me hungry."

Bertie was still dumbstruck by the audacity of this cat, but given he could see the tandem was in no fit state to ride, and they were in the middle of the countryside, he found himself with little choice.

"I'm Bertie," he said, "Muriel and Anipe are sitting in the cab."

"Terry Rumbelow is the name, but friends call me Tango," the ginger cat replied. "And this here is my brother, Ginger. So good of you Bert, just drop us off at the next village and we'll sort ourselves out, no point in crying over spilt milk now is there?"

Bertie smiled begrudgingly but was glad the cat could cause little mischief whilst sitting out the back, until he realised that Tango had slid open the glass window and was peering inside the cab.

"Cosy in there, isn't it? Don't suppose there's room for one more?" Tango laughed.

Ani didn't look best pleased at having drawn the attention of a new admirer, and Muriel replied politely, "I think we are doing quite well enough as we are, thank you."

Bertie wiped his brow and hopped back into the driver's seat. 'Perseverance and resolve,' he thought. The road followed the curves of the hillside, meandering in and out, thankfully with only a smattering of traffic. The Volkswagen seemed to be getting easier to drive with every mile, and Bertie started to enjoy himself, swinging the steering wheel from left to right, completely forgetting that he had passengers aboard until Tango started to speak again.

"Oh Muriel, you remind me of a someone I once met, on a farm it was, ooh, I was a teenager, I used to get up to all sorts of trouble, none of it my fault though, I can assure you. Anyway, I was on holiday, staying on this farm, and I got friendly with the farmer's son, a Pembrokeshire Corgi. We were hanging about in the barn when we started to smell smoke, frightened the life out of me, it did, as the barn was full of straw. We stubbed out our cigarettes and thought we'd better investigate. Strike a light! On the other side of the barn, we found a blazing fire, so we rushed off to get a hose and give it a good dowsing. I managed to sort that out with no problem while the corgi had alerted the farmer, big mistake. He thought we had caused it, didn't get our supper that night. Shame too, fish pie was on the menu."

Ani eyed the orange cat narrowly, convinced that he was to blame, despite his protestations. But Muriel played along a bit. "What happened next?" she asked.

"Oh, would you look at that, an orange bubble car, don't see too many of those, do you? Did you see that Bert? Of course, you did, you are driving. Oh, sorry, Muriel, you asked what happened next. Well, two days passed, and blow me down, another fire, this time in the second barn! The farmer looked daggers at me, but I had an alibi. I'd been flirting with the rather attractive tabby from next door all afternoon, and the farmer's wife could vouch for me," Tango said triumphantly.

"Was it another cigarette?" Muriel asked. "The farmer's lad perhaps?"

"Oh no, nothing of the sort. In fact, I learnt something that day, and so too did the farmer. He shouldn't have baled hay that was too wet and should have allowed plenty of ventilation within the stacks. According to the firedog, he also had forgotten to regularly check the temperature of stacks just after storage, too."

"Really?" Muriel said, a bit sceptically. "I've never heard that before."

Tango, happy to be an authority on the matter, continued. "Oh yes, the Dalmatian told me that the heat and humidity from the wet hay reacts with the dry hay, and the insulation provided by the stack can allow a fire to start. Who'd have thought, eh?"

A signpost at the side of the road marked a layby ahead, and Muriel, wondering if Ani was feeling a little car sick from Bertie's exuberant driving and Tango's voice in her ear, suggested they pull over for some air. Bertie decided he had better do as he was told and pulled into a spot where he found a number of other vehicles parked up. He turned off the engine, opened his door and jumped out to stretch his legs. Ani and Muriel did the same. Tango and Ginger hopped down from the load bed. As Bertie took in the views of the countryside, a small pup in a diamond studded collar and gold necklace came up to him.

"Nice vehicle you got there; can I look at the engine?" he asked.

"Why is that?" Bertie replied rather suspiciously.

"Oh, my dad is a mechanic, and he tells me if I study hard enough I might one day be a great engineer, just like him," the pup said, smiling and pointing over to his father.

"Oh, I suppose it can't do any harm," Bertie answered amiably and moved to the front of the Volkswagen. He started looking for the bonnet release catch without any luck. 'Drat, must be here somewhere,' he thought, realising that he was looking rather silly in front of the pup. "I know," he said triumphantly, and then pulled at the silver VW badge on the front of the van.* The thing promptly came flying off and landed on the gravel in front of the pup.

"Oops," the young pup said. "You didn't want to do that. The engines in the back of these things. Even I know that, and I'm only four."

Feeling utterly humiliated, Bertie grunted, "Why didn't you tell me that when I started tugging the badge, clever clogs?"

The pup didn't say anything and had a certain look about him. Bertie didn't know if he was about to burst into tears or run off and tell his father how the silly old dog in the Volkswagen didn't know where the engine was, so he picked up the VW badge and offered it to the pup.

"Here, keep it, it's busted now anyway. Why don't you hang it from your gold chain? It would go nicely with that."

The pup looked at the offering, took it from Bertie's paw and skipped merrily off back to his family.

Tango had been covertly watching this exchange, and he noticed Bertie's shoulders sagging as he approached him. "You definitely made that pup's week, Bert," he said, warmly, though with a wink. "He can show it off to his friends now."

Bertie leaned back against the vehicle and looked at him, his frown relaxing. He was soothed somewhat by the cat's failure to mention his gaffe. "I hope so. Now, will the next village be okay to drop you off at? Looks like it's not far."

*Volkswagen Badges: In the late 1980s, a US rap group called the Beastie Boys became popular. Their biggest hit at the time was "(You Gotta) Fight for Your Right (To Party)." Band member Mike D (Michael Diamond) typically wore a VW badge swinging from a thick metal chain around his neck, and fans across the world tried to emulate the look. Within days, the VW badge became a must-have Beastie Boys lover's accessory, and thefts of the badges from cars became rife. The problem escalated, and the car company itself even got involved, replacing customers' emblems free of charge in an attempt to avoid an impact on future car sales.

Chapter Twenty-Eight
Ani Arrives

Several weeks later, Johanna was locking her office and feeling both anticipation and a frisson of anxiety about the day ahead. She hoped that her estimation of Ms Amourby had been accurate, and that the cat would be intrigued by what she saw. Apparently, she was an historian who had been born in Germany and had always intended to revisit the country, but she had never found the time to make it happen. The phone line had been slightly crackly when Johanna had first spoken to Anipe, and she had also had trouble with her accent, but she could understand enough to know that the caller wasn't the average tourist. Johanna couldn't help but remember some of the sillier things she had been asked when coordinating a tour. "When I saw the brochure said it had a pool, I thought we would be going swimming!" one dog had grumbled loudly. Another had naively enquired, "Now the tour is over, can you tell me how to get to Germany from Düsseldorf?" Cringeworthy moments, but it was all part of the job.

Anipe had requested her services for a week, with a proviso that the tour might be cut short, or perhaps even extended, and she was willing to pay whatever the going rate was. Johanna was thankful, for whilst spring had arrived, it wasn't until the summer that she got really busy and earned her keep. The arranged meeting place was in the village, outside the post office.

The Volkswagen pulled up in Tolville and Bertie turned off the ignition. After travelling several hundred miles in the vehicle, he was now quite a dab hand with the clutch and dogleg first gear and was pleased with himself for persevering, despite his relief at finally getting to the destination. The pickup started coughing and sputtering before the engine finally cut out, and Bertie secretly hoped they could find another car hire company and leave the vehicle there for the owners to pick up, although he knew the idea was rather fanciful.

Along the way, Ani had phoned ahead to inform their tour guide that they would be delayed, purposely neglecting to mention the cause. She wasn't exactly eager to explain why she had been holed up in prison for a night.

They had arrived a few minutes early, so Bertie, Muriel and Ani stood looking about them before making their way to the post office. The place looked like a typical German town, a picturesque scene of the sort that might be seen on any postcard depicting the country's more rural locations. It was the type of place one might imagine appearing in a fairy tale: a small magical town with a web of winding cobblestone alleys, medieval townhouses, numerous monuments, and places of historic interest perfect for photos. The old town was full of immaculately preserved half-timbered buildings painted in an array of colours. All three of the new visitors were immediately entranced, although no doubt the day trippers that would be drawn to such an idyllic place in summer would ruin the peace they were now enjoying. The townscape of higgledy-piggledy houses and gabled roofs had certainly cast a spell on Ani, whose historian's eye had already noted the remnants of the ancient town walls. Seeing the town illuminated by the festive lights of the annual Christmas market would be especially magical, she thought.

Johanna looked at the two dogs and the cat standing outside of the Volkswagen and wondered if these were the visitors she was expecting. She hadn't intended to play host to three and wondered if she should consider increasing her costs. Certainly, the dog with the woolly hat looked hardy enough to take on the rigours of the mountains, although she wasn't sure the same could be said about the dorgi. All three of them looked to have come dressed for a pleasant jaunt around castles and museums rather than an expedition up mountain paths and through muddy fields, so she would have to politely suggest a visit to the camping shop before they started.

"*Guten Tag*! Hello there," Johanna said, smiling, as she walked over to the new visitors. "I'm Johanna Voigt. I assume you must be Anipe Amourby?"

Ani stepped forward and shook paws, nodding in answer. Johanna was a white tabby cat, slightly larger than most, with deep green eyes and petite pink nose. She looked to be in her late fifties, and was wearing staunch hiking boots, a thick green Barbour jacket and tortoiseshell glasses.

"Very pleased to meet you Ms Voigt," she replied. "I have unexpectedly made friends on my journey, and we had a stopover in Loutier just to recharge our batteries. Muriel Berkshire and Bertie Longfellow. I trust that they can join us?"

Johanna greeted them warmly. "You are all most welcome to Tolville. Would you like to warm up in my office, while we discuss the plan?"

"That would be great, thank you," Ani replied.

Muriel was slightly surprised by Ani, who was seeming a bit more confident and had allowed her scarf to slip down slightly, exposing a lovely beauty mark aside her nose and a unique patch just below her mouth. She was keen to learn more about the real reason Ani had come to this place.

"And I am not really one for formalities," Johanna said, "so you must call me '*Schatzi*' or 'Sweetie.' It's kind of a—what would the English call it? —a pet name, and all my friends use it."

The group followed Sweetie through the post office to the shed behind, eager to begin their next adventure.

Chapter Twenty-Nine
Hearing Voices

Wagmore was sitting in the high street café, deep in thought. He had already had cause to send back his first latte, with a hint of cinnamon sprinkled on top. "Tepid," he'd snapped at the waitress, with a glare that sent her scurrying. Now his second was going cold as he fell into a reverie. The hustle and bustle of the traffic outside and pedestrians walking past the window did nothing to distract him, instead seeming to enhance his trance-like state. The waitress briskly passed him by, clumsily knocking into the back of his chair and toppling over a cup and saucer on her tray at the same time, bringing Wagmore back to reality. He awoke with a start. Luckily for the waitress, she was already a good few metres away and had regained her composure, so she escaped blame.

Murdo McLoughlin entered the establishment five minutes later, puffing a bit. He was a portly cat, and the buttons on his uniform were doing their best to stay attached. He was on his lunch break from the block of flats he worked at and had limited time, but he had told Wagmore on the phone that it was important that they see each other sooner rather than later, as he had news that might be to his advantage.

"Hello Walter, how's things?" Murdo said as he pulled up a chair and took the last bite of a sardine sandwich. "Haven't seen you in a while. Are you still that dorgi's butler—what's her name?"

"She's the Duchess of Berkshire to you, Murdo," Wagmore replied. "What was so important that you dragged me down to your neck of the woods? Time is precious."

"You don't have to tell me that. I've not got long before my next shift starts. Working on the security desk in that place isn't a bed of roses, you know," Murdo answered a bit defensively. "Anyway, let's get down to business. I have some information for you. Usual rate?"

"I presume that will be acceptable as long as the information is useful," Wagmore said. "What have you got?"

"Well, you know I like to keep my ear to the ground, so to speak," Murdo said.

Wagmore rolled his eyes at him. "I know you like to listen in on the tenants' calls in your block of flats, yes."

"Quite. I thought you might like to know that this German fellow, been living there a couple of years, has been calling some old chap who blathers on about the seaside and such."

"That's not really the sort of information I'm after," Wagmore sneered, leaning back in his chair.

"Maybe not, but they really do talk all the time. Very odd. Why would a young chap like the German be interested? And the old geezer—Piers? Percival? Not sure, but a highfalutin sort of name anyway, keeps yammering on about how he can't remember this or that. The chap Hans keeps himself to himself, although I don't really see hide nor hair of most of the tenants, to tell you the truth. He's some sort of artist, so moves about, does some work in a place up town. He mentioned moving to London to escape his past. Maybe in his youth he was convicted of some minor misdemeanour or other? 'Not wanting to go back to that place' were his exact words. Perhaps a spell in juvenile prison or the like," Murdo said. "And if that's the sort of dog he is, then maybe he's got his sights set on relieving the old fellow of some extra assets. You might be able to get in first, maybe."

"Vaguely interesting," Wagmore said. "Anything else?"

"Not really. The older one mentioned something about someone named Bernie, I think, but it didn't sound important. Just another coot like himself, probably."

"Very well," Wagmore said. "But I'm really losing patience with your terrible memory for names. I presume you have some details written down for me?"

Murdo pushed a scrap of paper across the table towards Wagmore, whilst Wagmore returned the favour, pushing a small brown envelope the other way.

"Nice doing business with you, Walter, always a pleasure," Murdo said as he got up and walked out of the café. Wagmore sat back again, wondering how he could use his new-found knowledge to his advantage. He looked at the details on the piece of crumpled paper and recognised the Libertine Gallery listed as one of those la-di-da places where the upper crust went to discover the next up-and-coming artists. This chap and his phone pal seemed like a small fry, really, maybe not worth his trouble, but he didn't have anything pressing to do for the rest of the day so decided to go and take a look.

Chapter Thirty
The Cat Vanishes

"Actually, I had an interesting commission once," Hans said. "It was for an elderly cat who supplied me with an old black and white photo. She asked me if I could paint a replica, in colour, on a large canvas for her living room, which I was more than happy to do. She explained the colours of the various elements for my benefit. The only proviso was that she wanted to make a change to the original. The scene was of a beautiful country cottage garden from her youth with lots of colourful wildflowers in bloom. A wooden bench sat in the middle under a gazebo and stone slab walkways led to some wilder areas. It was all very natural and charming."

"What was the request?" Wagmore said, as he studied the Wowauzer in front of him.

"Oh, yes, I was coming to that," Hans replied. The customer took the photo from my paw and pointed to the wheelbarrow and gloves on top. 'Please remove that,' she said. 'It reminds me of Frank, the gardener, a rather cantankerous old soul if ever there was one. I never did get along with him. He was forever telling me off when I was a kitten for tramping on his roses, and anyway, it just shouldn't be there.' I thought nothing of it at the time. I had a grasp of what needed to be painted and took on the work without any concerns. I could easily extend the climbing ivy on the back wall behind the wheelbarrow and make it look and as if the wheelbarrow had never existed."

"The beauty of being an artist then. You had a chance to use your imagination? But there must be more to the story," Wagmore prompted.

"Oh, you are quite right. When the cat returned to collect the painting, I unveiled it in my customary fashion—I had the artwork on a wooden easel standing in the middle of the room, with a piece of black velvet covering it. When the cat and her husband were positioned in front at the right distance,

I pulled off the cloth and watched the reaction. At first, she looked quite happy, examining the detail and nodding in appreciation of my work. She put a paw to her mouth. 'Oh, my, I do love the composition! And the framing of the view is perfect, just as I remember!' Then her eyes fell on the area where the wheelbarrow had been in the original, and she frowned."

"She didn't like it then. Perhaps you had painted a watering can there she was upset with?" Wagmore asked.

"No, not quite, there was no watering can. In fact, I was very pleased with the change I had made, and it blended in perfectly. No one could have told you it wasn't exactly as it should have been," Hans replied.

"What then?" a clearly baffled Wagmore said.

"She turned and asked me a question. 'Where is Timmy?'

'Timmy,' I said. 'Who is Timmy?' I had not a clue who she was talking about.

'Timmy Tootles! Why, he was my neighbour. He was bending down behind the wheelbarrow at the time the photo was taken. He said he was trying to pull up a rather troublesome dandelion out from the stone path, but he was always a bit camera shy, so I think when he saw me whip out my Brownie he went into hiding.' Now what do you say to that?" Hans said.

"My, my," Wagmore remarked, as he began studying some of Hans's other works. "You'd have had to be a mind reader to know that. What happened?"

"I had to take the painting back, since the customer did not approve. She turned her head in a huff, swished her long fluffy tail and walked straight out of the room. Her husband was left with me and the rejected artwork, and he began apologising profusely. 'Don't worry, son, there's a charity ball coming up, and I needed something to take along. This will do nicely, should fetch a pretty penny."

Wagmore smiled. "So, from the sounds of it and the looks of your paintings here, you are quite an accomplished dog. This one here," Wagmore pointed at a lone teddy bear sitting on a wooden sleeper in the middle of a railway line, looking sad and forlorn. The bear was covering its eyes, and its trousers were askew, revealing an embroidered heart on its leg. It was titled *Ich Liebe Dich*. "This looks like an immensely powerful image, very moving. I love the colouring. I get feelings of both loss and hope—would I be right?"

"That's not actually for sale. It's one from my personal collection. I just like to have it on display as it holds a lot of meaning," Hans said with a tear in his eye.

Wagmore decided to move on. He didn't want the dog blubbering on about some past emotional experience. ", after hearing that tale of yours, I'm wondering something. I recently had a painting stolen, dreadful business, insurance paid out, of course, but the painting was never retrieved. Would you be experienced enough to reproduce it if I supplied a photograph? I suppose someone with your obvious skills can turn your hand to anything?"

Hans was pleased by the compliment and replied, "Oh yes, I could probably do that, no trouble at all. I'm assuming you're just looking for a reproduction for your own pleasure, not to sell?"

"Oh yes, the painting only has sentimental value, you know. Jolly good to hear that you're willing. I'll have a think about it, but in the meantime, I think I might just purchase this little number." It was the same teddy bear, but this time he had a big smile on his face, was wearing a red bow tie and playing a piano.

"I think it would fit nicely in the dining room. The wife is always telling me to brighten the place up, and this charming picture will do just that."

"Marvellous choice," Hans said, lifting the frame off the wall and taking it to the desk to be wrapped and paid for.

Wagmore left the shop quite satisfied, his restless mind teeming with various schemes.

Chapter Thirty-One
A Confidence Under the Constellations

"Are you sure about this?" Lottie asked, as she dropped her rucksack onto the scrubby ground. "I'd much rather try for a room at the Lamb and Crook back there. I'm plumb worn out after looking out for Reggie's lot all day, and I can't imagine getting a wink of sleep out here."

"Too expensive," Winnie replied. "And as you know, our agreement with Reggie doesn't include the hotels. We'll sort something out with him in the morning. Sorry. But what could be more adventurous than sleeping under the stars?"

"And when's the last time you did that, exactly?" Lottie retorted. "I just know I'm going to get brambles in my fur, and the last time that happened, I had to get it all shaved off." She shuddered. "This is not one of your cleverest ideas, Win-Win. And no way am I changing into my pyjamas out here. There could be all sorts of weirdos around. And I hope there aren't any sheep in this pasture," she added. "I'm terrified of sheep."

"Sheep?" Winnie replied, incredulously. "What would that be? Ovinaphobia? Anyway, you wouldn't want to go to that pub, then," she teased, trying to sound as nonchalant as she could, though she had just stepped in something unpleasant and was beginning to regret her penny pinching. The pub's bright windows winked at them from a mile or so off, and she couldn't help but imagine it laughing derisively at them. She shrugged into a nightgown and pulled her jumper and jeans off from underneath. "It'll be fine. It's a beautiful night, and Reggie was good enough to lend us all these blankets," she said, appropriating a couple and snuggling down underneath.

"They'll probably smell of beans and pineapple," Lottie muttered ungraciously as she followed suit. She'd kept her boots on, just in case there was a need to make a dash for it. Pulling out her torch, she put it under her face and flicked it on. "You're going to owe me for this," she said in a breathy growl that made Winnie yelp and then giggle. "No laughing matter, young Winifred," Lottie scolded playfully, her ill-humour dissipating. She was never grumpy for long, Winnie thought with a smile.

And then, as she pulled her blankets more securely around her nose and ears, she reflected that she really didn't know very much about Lottie's life before their fateful meeting over a yellow hat at a shop in Piedmont Bay. Or even after that. For all she was cheerful and outgoing, Lottie never said much about her past. Of course, Lottie was the kind of dog who seemed to live almost entirely in the present, but she had skilfully extracted most of Winnie's life story from her while avoiding saying anything about herself.

Winnie looked up at the stars, even brighter and more plentiful here than at Badger's Bay, and tried to think of a way to win her friend's confidence. She spotted a constellation she knew well, having often seen it out the window above her bed at Aunt Bea's house. "Orion!" she exclaimed happily, though with a twinge of homesickness.

"What was that?" Lottie said, a little sleepily. "Why are you talking about Ryan?"

Winnie turned to stare at her, though of course she could only make out a ghostly pale shape in the complete darkness. "What do you mean? I just noticed Orion the Hunter up there. You know, the constellation."

"Yeah, I guess," Lottie replied. "I was half asleep, and you just reminded me of someone, that's all." Winnie said nothing, hoping that her friend would continue.

The profound silence of the night, silence that Winnie could almost hear, was suddenly splintered by a lorry screaming past with all deafening clamour of several jet engines. The two dogs put their paws to their ears. "Well, I won't be getting to sleep anytime soon after that," Lottie said.

"Me, neither" Winnie admitted. In the darkness, with no earwigging fellow travellers and only the friendly stars above, she felt her courage rise. If she didn't ask now, she never would. "So, who is Ryan?"

Lottie didn't reply, and Winnie's heart sank. 'I'm always poking my nose in,' she chastised herself.

"Oh, yes, that guy," Lottie said at last, turning toward Winnie, her eyes catching a ray of moonlight. She didn't look affronted, and Winnie relaxed a little. "Well, he's a first-class scuzz, you know. A Rottweiler. Cousin to a certain Rufus of our acquaintance. Except that he never reformed. At first, I thought all his bad-dog stuff was just for show, like his spike collar and motorcycle boots. I was still pretty young and wet behind the ears when I met him. Much younger than you. I thought he was pretty cool, and I was sure there was a nice dog underneath, that he was just hanging with the wrong crowd."

"You gave him the benefit of the doubt," Winnie said. "Nothing wrong with that."

"No, I suppose not. Anyway, we had this ridiculous prom where we girls picked names out of a hat to find a date. Teachers thought that would keep all the teenage angst and hormones at bay. Well, they tried. I ended up with Ryan, and I thought myself a lucky dog. Most of the other girls did, too, and were looking daggers at me. One of them even said I'd cheated somehow. But I ignored them. Ryan gave me a corsage, I pinned a boutonnière on his jacket, and we were soon taking our places at the banquet table. I was feeling a little shy, if you can believe it, but Ryan kept cracking jokes, and soon all the dogs at our end of the table were relaxed and laughing.

"I was really looking forward to the dance after the meal. I'd practiced hard, and I knew Ryan had some pretty good moves. We were being served our dessert, and I was feeling impatient, probably eating a bit faster than I should, though not shovelling it in. At just the wrong moment, Ryan said something that had everyone roaring. Except that I didn't roar. I snorted."

"Oh, no," Winnie interjected. "I've done that myself. So embarrassing."

"Well, yes. I suppose everyone has done that at one time or another, and it's not as if I'd had punch streaming out of my nose or anything. No one actually noticed until Ryan said, 'Hey everyone! Did you hear that? My date is a pig! Did ya know? A pi-ig, a pi-ig, she snorts just like a pi-ig.

Shave her fur off, and she'd just be a little pink piggy underneath, wouldn't she?' "

Winnie gasped.

"If anyone said anything like that about me now, I'd sock it to 'em. But I was a bit drippy in those days, so I'm afraid I just fled to the bathroom to get away from the laughter. I was totally mortified. After a little while, I tried to buck up, though, and decided I had to face the music, so to speak. And I still wanted to dance. I thought maybe I could trade partners with one of the airhead dogs who had been so jealous of my date."

"I mustered up my courage and peeked out from behind the bathroom door. I could still hear all kinds of laughter, but I thought that the moment must have passed. There was a dog standing on a chair, though. My chair, I realised. Gyrating around and jumping and chanting something. I couldn't quite see or hear what was going on, so I edged back out into the dining hall.

"It was Ryan hopping around on my seat, and he was yelling, 'Pigs can't dance...pigs can't dance,' over and over, while some of the other dogs were clapping in time. I thought I was going to be sick, so I dashed outside—I didn't need to draw attention to myself again—and ended up running all the way home, actually, though I don't remember it at all."

Lottie stopped, and Winnie lay in shocked silence, feeling the pain her friend must have felt. She could never have imagined that something like that would have happened to Lottie. To herself, yes. But Lottie was so confident, so self-assured, able to bounce back from anything. She tried to think of something appropriate to say. "Well, I'm sure you can dance like anything," she said into the darkness. "Ryan was just a first-class idiot."

"Oh, he was that, all right. Still is. I think he's usually in jail, actually. But I've never been able to shake that off. I can't 'dance like no one's watching.' "

Winnie hunkered down under her blankets again and tried to block the image of the taunting Rottweiler from her mind. She felt a sort of kinship with Lottie that she never had before. 'Everyone has memories like that,' she thought. 'But not everyone is brave enough to share them. Maybe if we

135

all did, we'd be kinder to each other.' She kept pondering along these lines, and sleep eluded her, so she reverted to her puppyhood habit of counting sheep.

The next morning, she woke to a peculiar sound, the crunch of frost-stiffened grass bending under some considerable weight, a pause, a clatter, and then a sound like a large sack of flour falling. It repeated several times. Rubbing her eyes and shaking her head to clear it, she sat up and glanced around. There, across the road, was a drystone wall, with a small area where some of the blocks had fallen away. On the other side of the wall were three sheep, ambling towards them down the small hill. A woolly head then emerged at the gap in the wall, climbed over and dropped to the other side. It then joined its compatriots. Winnie watched, fascinated, as two more sheep did the same. Beside her, she heard a groan and a yawn. And then a shriek. Seconds later, a pair of red Doc Martens were pelting pell-mell away from their little camp, while half a dozen pairs of startled ovine eyes looked on.

Chapter Thirty-Two
Breaking Point

Wagmore placed the small painting of the bear down on his dresser and sat on the end of his bed, thinking. The bear looked much like any other bear, a common enough subject to paint, even if it was playing the piano, but it was the other painting in the gallery that had caught his eye. The subject and the title, *Ich Liebe Dich*, were familiar. He was sure he had read that somewhere before. 'Hans, talking to someone called Piers or Percival, a bear, those words,' he thought. It was all coming back to him.

He quickly put two and two together with the information that Murdo had overheard and recalled that those were the words he had seen on a tatty bear in a house he had been in last year when he was searching for a gold bracelet. 'Surely not,' he thought. Was this the same "Percy" he had loathed, the friend of Bertie's, the senile old coot that was losing his marbles, the dog that had those medals hiding under his bed gathering dust? Medals of the kind his own father had deserved but never received?"

Wagmore started to get agitated, thoughts of his own past whizzing through his mind. He grew angry and picked up the small painting he had just purchased, threw it on the floor and stamped on it hard, shattering the glass and breaking the frame. The canvas became distorted, and the bear now was no longer smiling, instead wearing a contorted expression. Wagmore walked over to the window and looked outside. It was a grim looking day, grey skies, damp, and drizzling.

"Are you okay in there?" Muriel's maid Flora asked, as she peered through the doorway. She was a kindly sort and didn't like to pry, but she had seen Wagmore come in and was going to ask him for some time off to visit her sister who was unwell. She wasn't sure now was the best time.

"Go away and get back to work!" Wagmore growled, walking quickly over to the door and slamming it in her face. He was in no mood to speak to the staff. He returned to the window, and a brace of crows flew by as he considered his next move. He had enough contacts to implement some elaborate operations if he needed to. 'Maybe something simple will suffice,' he thought to himself. 'But it has to be entertaining for me, too.' What would work? He didn't want money, that would be too easy. He was now fairly sure Hans could be coerced into doing something to prevent Percy getting into some spot of bother, but what could it be? Percy was a bit of a theatrical character, of course. Wagmore had overheard Muriel talking to her friend Lady Effingham about how he was the one that had taught Bertie to dance and scuppered Wagmore's plans there. And the dog was losing his memory, too. Perhaps that could play some part. Silly, broken-down, pretentious old pensioner! What had he ever done to deserve all those military honours? 'My father was a fine specimen of a dog, just the sort this country should have been proud of, and look where it got him. He could have really made something of himself. And me. Things could have been so different.' Wagmore clenched and unclenched his fists.

Everything was beginning to crystallize in the greyhound's bitter mind. He would play a long game with this one and enjoy every minute of it. He was about to start a little campaign that would affect both Hans and Percy. Looking down at the floor again, he picked up the pieces of the broken painting and tossed them in the waste bin. It wasn't the only thing that would be shattered after he had finished with those two dogs.

Chapter Thirty-Three
All Kitted Out

"How do I look?" Bertie said, as he emerged from the cubicle in a new thick green jumper and brown hiking boots.

Muriel looked him up and down and replied, "dashing, and that hat is just the thing. You were meant for these clothes, apparently." She looked at herself disapprovingly in the full-length mirror. The field coat swallowed her up. She held out her arms and flapped the too-long sleeves playfully at him. "I think this was made for a Bernese mountain dog!" Bertie pulled a smaller size from a hanger and helped her into it.

"I didn't expect to be going shopping," he said quietly, "but I think it's the right thing to do. Best to be prepared with the right gear. Mountains are much the same as the sea, really. The weather can turn very quickly—one minute you are peeling everything off in bright sunshine, the next you are walking in the fog, mist, drizzle or even mizzle and getting frostbite." Muriel didn't doubt Bertie's opinion, and she was rather glad he was there to help her choose her new attire.

Ani covertly watched the pair from a few metres off. She was secretly pleased with her new company. As shy as she was, she had warmed to these two dogs whilst on their travels together. She had come prepared, knowing what type of terrain they would encounter, but had decided to pick up some essentials locally rather than take them with her on the flight over. In her basket was some parachute cord, a couple of small torches and several thermos flasks. She offered to pay for Bertie's and Muriel's items, but they were having none of it.

The shopkeeper looked on and rubbed his paws with glee. His shop was usually quite bare of customers at this time of year, so he was certainly happy to see three of them. "Anything I can help with, do let me know," he said in perfectly enunciated English. "You must get boots that fit and don't rub. I have all sizes out back and am only too willing to fetch them for you," he assured them.

"Thank you," Ani said. "I don't suppose you have some batteries, too?"

"Oh, yes, definitely," the shopkeeper said. "A must have, and if you need some more, you know where I am. Here you go." He paused for a moment and decided to avail himself of the opportunity to talk to someone other than the moth-eaten brown bear in the corner, humorously kitted out in lederhosen and an Alpine hat. Bruno's expression had never been encouraging.

"The last customers I had told me a funny story, you know," he ventured, leaning comfortably on the counter, and looking at Ani, who pulled back a little but appeared to be listening. "They came all the way from Spain to visit and hired a car for their journey. They were stopping off at various hostels along the way for the night. Early on in their trip, they stocked up on food, just in case they couldn't find lodgings and a place to eat. When they drove over some rough ground, the fish they had bought leaked out of its container, and it really reeked. They tried everything, even washing the floor of the boot with bleach and scrubbing it really hard, but after an hour or so, the smell always returned. Anyway, they persevered, mainly by opening the windows as they drove. When it came to returning the hire car, they pumped the car full of air freshener, and the hire company didn't even notice. Woe betide the next customer who borrowed that car, that's all I can say."

Ani smiled, but Bertie, who had also been listening to the tale, was sure he could do better than that. "A pity," he said, leaning on the other end of the counter while he waited for Muriel to try out her boots. "You may not have heard about the smugglers off the Cornish coast who had a similar problem. They were persuaded, with the aid of a few extra shillings, to take a long, heavy crate on board that they hadn't bargained for. After launching into the night, they began looking at each other suspiciously as a pungent odour permeated the cabin. When the choking smell didn't disperse, their attention was drawn to the crate."

The shopkeeper listened, agog. "Must have been a body," he said, knowingly. "I have read enough of your English mysteries to know that most of your stories have at least one corpse in them."

Bertie cocked his head. "The smugglers feared exactly that. 'Oi! We never shoulda let our 'eads be turned by a few quid,' they said. A couple of them were already sick. Even the salt sea air did nothing to alleviate the stink, and the wretched crate appeared to be leaking. The two dogs with the staunchest stomachs heaved the thing overboard and swabbed the deck, but to no avail. A day or so after their trip, several of the village folk began complaining of a rotten odour in the vicinity of the beach. The vicar went to investigate."

"Oh, yes, there is always a vicar in these stories, too. Sometimes he is a detective himself," the shopkeeper said, nodding sagely.

Bertie grinned at him. "Well, this one found, to his sorrow, that his year's supply of *Brie de Meaux* was strewn over the sand."

"Hah!" the shopkeeper burst out. "You had me there."

"And the boat was never the same again. The smugglers ended by selling it for a song to a dog who'd lost his sense of smell."

Muriel fetched up behind him, giggling, and jostled his elbow. "That's quite enough of that," she said. "We're keeping Ani waiting." But Bertie had noticed that the cat had been shaking a little with politely suppressed amusement. 'Not at all toffee-nosed,' he mused. 'Just not one to push herself forward.'

Outside the shop, the three of them presented themselves to Sweetie, who had ducked into a coffee shop next door while they made their purchases. At least they now looked the part, despite everything being spotlessly clean and unmarked. She smiled, knowing how quickly that situation would change, and, pulling out maps for them, led them out the ancient town gate and up a steep hill toward their destination.

Chapter Thirty-Four
A Cut Above the Rest

"Now darling, if you'd be so kind to take my cases to the room," Ms Chasemoore said to Lottie as she was pulling them out of the compartment under the coach. "And be careful, they are genuine crocodile skin, can't have them scratched or torn now, can we, mmm?" Having delivered herself of these suggestions, she trotted off to the service desk inside the hotel lobby and left Lottie to it. Other passengers were a bit more civil, thanking the cockapoo for helping them out, and luckily a rather brusque but well-built hotel porter had brought out a trolley and was helping her load them up.

Inside at the service counter, Ms Chasemoore was ringing the bell impatiently. "Arh, there you are. Now, someone told me there was a hair salon in the village. Can you please tell me which direction that is?"

"Of course, madam, just follow the footpath down to the road and turn left, you can't miss it," the rather surprised desk clerk said.

"Oh, that close? I must pop along as soon as I can. Please make sure my mattress has been turned and that there are adequate towels for when I get back."

"Of course, madam, it will be my pleasure," the clerk said, realising this guest was probably going to be trouble. 'There's always one,' he thought.

Ms Chasemoore walked the short distance to the high street of the small village where they were staying. It was quaint and somewhat lacking in modern amenities, but there was an old-world charm about the place. The sign "Belle Curls - Beauty Parlour" looked promising, and the photos of elegantly coiffured dogs and cats in the bay window impressed her. "Not quite Parisian, but it'll do," she murmured to herself. Peeking through one of the small glass panes, she saw no customers and thought her luck was in.

On entering the establishment, Ms Chasemoore was met with the scents of country flowers and rose potpourri dotted about the shop and approved. There were a number of unopened boxes on the far wall and several pieces of seating furniture still wrapped in plastic covers. As she admired the sophisticated look of the immaculately clean decor, Ms Chasemoore looked around for a staff member to assist her. Instinctively, she trotted up to a sleek black table, and she was greeted by a young bichon frise wearing a white shirt with lime green apron sporting a small motif.

"Oh, I'm afraid we're… I mean I'm…." he stammered before he was interrupted.

"Good morning to you, I'm just after a bit of a tidy up really, but after looking at some of the pictures here I think I might fancy a slight tint. What do you think?" Ms Chasemoore replied.

"Oh, erm, I really… " the bichon said as he pondered. "I suppose… I, erm, Donna will be…"

"Come along, I haven't got all day, my lad. Shall I go over there?" Ms Chasemoore pointed.

"Of course, of course, come this way. Erm, I'm Oliver," the bichon said as he guided the Afghan further into the establishment. "Can I take your coat? I'll just pop it on the hanger over here and in the meantime if madame would care for a peppermint bonbon, I think I saw a selection over there." He pointed to the small table nearby with a white dish placed in the middle. The wall behind the table had a door frame painted on it, open to a tranquil garden scene with a range of wildlife in abundance. Ms Chasemoore picked one of the delicately wrapped sweets up, studied it and popped it carefully in her mouth.

"Now, if madame would wait here just a moment, I will find something for you to sit on, and then perhaps I can begin with a simple wash and rinse."

Ms Chasemoore willingly obliged and took her place on the leather barstool Oliver had pushed from across the room, tilting her head back into the porcelain basin, which oddly didn't have any neck rest and was rather like her Belfast sink at home. As she did so she puzzled over where the other staff members were. 'Perhaps the receptionist was just the junior and oversees the more menial tasks,' she mused. Oliver reappeared from another room, looking relieved and holding a squeeze bottle in each paw.

"You do have such silky-smooth fur, madame, it's glorious," the bichon frise said, as he gently placed his paws over Ms Chasemoore's head and washed it through with warm water from the tap. "Now, I mustn't forget to just pop a bit of conditioner on too, as mother always tells me." He looked at his watch with some consternation. "Drat, I've splashed some water on my glasses. I'll just give them a clean," Oliver said.

Ms Chasemoore was warmed not only by the water but the fact that she had now had it confirmed that the professional of the salon, the mother, was obviously going to be dealing with her very soon. She relaxed, listening to the music playing in the background.

"So, going anywhere nice on your holidays?" Oliver asked nervously, thinking on his feet.

"Why yes, here, as a matter of fact," Ms Chasemoore said. "I arrived today and thought I would just nip into town to get my hair done and then have a lovely meal with Artie later."

"Ohh, Artie, is that your admirer? And have you come away for a naughty weekend? I notice you aren't wearing a wedding ring," Oliver said, buoyed by being brought into the confidence of the customer before him.

"That is a little presumptuous of you. I think you are a little bit young to be talking about such things," Ms Chasemoore remarked. "Now, haven't I been under this tap for a little too long now? I'll be shrivelled up like a prune before long."

"Oh, yes, sorry, you are right, my mistake," Oliver said as he reached for the tap and turned off the water supply. 'Now where are those towels?' he thought and made for the bathroom again. 'Arh, there they are.' He unfolded one of the beige towels and placed it a bit clumsily over Ms Chasemoore's head. "There we go, ready for drying," he said chirpily while looking around at the front door to see if anyone had entered the shop.

Ms Chasemoore was taken slightly aback by having a towel thrown on her head, as she had expected to have her head dried by the assistant. 'The sooner this mother arrives the better' she thought. "Where do you want me now?" she asked.

"Oh, someone has put a mirror up over there by the two poodle figurines, go and sit on the chair in front. Then just let me just grab this plastic sheet and..." Oliver said. "Right, a trim you said, erm, I think I can do that, just a bit off the top perhaps, eh, can't have Arnie thinking you look like a tramp now, can we?" Oliver said.

"Artie—his name is Artie. And he would not think that would he? Stop being so flippant! I'll have to have words with your boss when she arrives. Well, I never!" Ms Chasemoore huffed. She turned to glare at Oliver and noticed a large dog peering in through the window with its paw over its eyes.

The bichon walked over to the large black table and picked up the scissors he had been using to open some of the packing boxes before this dog had come into the building. He started snipping the air, keeping his paws firmly behind Ms Chasemoore's head so she couldn't see what he was doing in the mirror, and glanced at his watch every couple of minutes.

"You seem to be cutting a lot off there. Are you sure it's not getting too thin?" Ms Chasemoore said with concern in her voice.

"Oh, no, you're fine, madame. It's looking just superb, it really is," continuing his air-snipping and wondering if his customer would notice that there was no hair on the floor when she rose. He'd have to keep her in the chair long enough to do a mock sweep-up. "So, this Arnie fellow, is he big and strong?" he questioned while he grabbed a comb from his back pocket to make himself look more professional.

"He is a fine gentleman, actually, not that it is any of your business. Now I think you are done, aren't you? I don't want to be late getting back to the evening meal. Can you hurry it along please?" the Afghan said, tapping the arm of the chair with her paw and forgetting all about the hair colouring she had considered when she arrived.

"Of course. I will see if I can find a hair dryer in the bedroom and give you a blow over. I'll be back in a mo," Oliver said. Luckily the boxes' contents had been scattered on the dresser in the other room, and he found what he was looking for. Something about what he had said struck Ms Chasemoore as odd, but she had no time to consider it. In moments, he was plugging in the device and wafting the hot air over her head. "Ta-da! You look a million dollars," Oliver shouted jubilantly.

She tried to take a critical look as Oliver pulled up a mirror behind her, but he was so quick moving it about that she really didn't know what it looked like. But it was nearly time to board the coach, and she decided it would do. She got up from the chair and pulled her coat from the coat hook. "Now, what do I owe you?" she asked.

Oliver had a look of puzzlement on his face. "Erm, what do you normally pay?" he said without thinking.

Ms Chasemoore had had enough. "Well, if you don't know what you are going to charge me, then I think I'll come back when your mother is back and settle up then. Good day," she said a bit testily and flounced out of the shop. Oliver let out a big sigh of relief, though he had no idea why she was referring to his mother, who lived a hundred miles away. 'What a strange dog,' he thought.

Just as Ms Chasemoore passed through the shop door, a few large dogs elbowed past her. "Mind your back, luv, dogs at work here," one said as he carried a heavy box inside. The other pair were panting as they tried to lift a large, white ornately framed mirror carefully out of the lime green removals van. The driver, who was chewing gum in the cab and reading a newspaper, looked out as Ms Chasemoore passed by, and then gave a wolf whistle. "Looking splendid, m'dear. Which hair did they cut?" he called after her, smirking as he returned to the sports pages. Ms Chasemoore favoured him with her most supercilious scowl and trotted off.

A sleek sports car slid into the space ahead of the van, and a poodle stepped out. "I say, I thought you said you'd be done by now," she said, turning a dissatisfied glare on the gum-chewing dog, who had instantly stowed his paper, picked up a clipboard and begun studying it intently. Shaking her head, she entered and pulled the photographs out of the window. "And you—Oliver, was it? Get your skates on and take down that ridiculous sign. Really! I may as well have done it all myself! I'll be having a word with your supervisor."

"Yes, Donna," Oliver replied meekly, and scurried off.

Chapter Thirty-Five
Seeds of Doubt

Wagmore woke with a start as Peel pulled his curtains open to a brilliant day. "I've just put your tea and the *Times* on your table there. You're usually up by now," he commented, looking curiously at the greyhound.

"That's quite enough out of you. I've got as much right as anyone else to have a lie-in, more so, in fact, what with having to chivvy you and your lazy cohorts all the time." He gestured curtly towards the door. Peel took the hint, and not wanting to get the rough side of his boss's tongue or worse, departed forthwith.

Wagmore sipped his tea and reflected on the invigorating dream from which he had just been rudely awakened. Only a couple of impressions remained before his mind's eye, which frustrated him, but they were quite vivid. In one scene, a Welsh terrier was dancing on the end of a pier to the applause of a gaggle of moronic tourists. The dog was wearing checked trousers, a bow tie, and flourishing a ridiculous bowler hat around on a walking stick. Several funhouse mirrors around the railings distorted his image and at one point distracted him. He made a misstep...but a pleasure boat below him had broken his fall, and he landed safely on the roof. Percy popped up like an irrepressible jack-in-the-box and continued dancing on the prow of the boat, a chest full of medals glinting in the sun. He pulled one off and carelessly tossed it skywards. That bit of the dream had not been so gratifying, but the next was much more satisfactory.

For no reason at all, Wagmore had suddenly found himself in the water, though the setting was quite different. His own svelte physique had been transformed into the shape of a speedboat, and he was eating up the racecourse marked out by buoys on the water. He was pursuing another boat, a rickety old vessel with a wide brimmed hat atop its mast and a Victoria Cross adorning its bow instead of an anchor. It was no match for him, and smoke billowed out the back as if the engine had caught fire. But he could remember no more except the dazzle of the sun reflecting off the water. He was sure that there had been more along those lines, however.

Wagmore pulled on the ratty brown jumper and a pair of equally uninspiring corduroy trousers he'd borrowed from the ragbag, probably ancient remnants of Harry's kit at one time or other and pulled a flat cap well down over his aristocratic brow and sleek ears. He rubbed his paws together with pleasure. All of the staff had been given the day off, so he made his way down to the scullery and gathered the tools of his new trade into an old golf bag which had once belonged to his master. He chuckled as he imagined what Captain Randolph would have thought of the use it was being put to now. But what gave him even greater pleasure was the fittingness of his approach. If only his victim could be in a state to appreciate the dramatic integrity of his scheme.

Having slouched his way safely to the familiar Wood Lane address, he pulled out one of Peel's cigarettes, appropriated from a pack left carelessly around the kitchen, and inserted it in the corner of his mouth without lighting it. He'd looked into the matter thoroughly and discovered, through several of his contacts, the dog who did Percy's housekeeping. A tidy little roll of pounds had convinced her to stay home that day and, if asked, tell the tale Wagmore had concocted: namely, that her husband, never yet seen in that neighbourhood, had had a sudden fit of conscience about his laddish ways and insisted on giving her a day's holiday. The housekeeper had assured him that Percy always stayed out of the house when she was working.

So, it was as Mr Louis Belcher that the greyhound easily entered the house and slipped his missus's key in his pocket. Dropping the bag with its broom, mop and brushes, he set to work on a task that had little to do with any of those things.

On the kitchen table were some opened letters, so Belcher had a peek. Utility bills mainly, although there was one for an annual subscription to an allotment society. A packet of Mr Fothergill's Calendula Seeds for Hardy Annuals sat next to the kettle. Perhaps he was about to plant them. 'Excellent,' Belcher thought, as he made a note of the society address to investigate at a later date. The house looked pretty much the same as it had the last time Belcher was there, perhaps a bit tidier, although he really hadn't had time to notice before.

A mere three-quarters of an hour later, he lounged against the bedroom door and surveyed his handiwork with immense satisfaction. Belcher's final act was to pull out the button from the ear of the Steiff bear and thrust it in his pocket. The bear was thrown back on top of the wardrobe to gather more dust.

Chapter Thirty-Six
Are you being Served?

Alfreda darted across the hotel lobby and out of the front entrance in a rush. After her rather odd experience at the hair salon, she decided it best to avoid making eye contact with the watching desk clerk at reception and did not reply to him when he asked about her visit, tossing him a smile instead as she headed out.

"Dinner will be served from 6pm," he called after her, hoping for an acknowledgement which didn't come.

A couple of dogs, waiting calmly on a bench outside the door, smiled smugly as they spotted Alfreda, her fur ruffled a bit by her hurry. "Always primping at the last minute, she is," a Scottish terrier remarked.

"She'll be late to her own funeral, that one," her companion quipped.

Reggie had pulled the coach alongside the kerb and started to usher them in. Unfortunately for Alfreda, Artie was not one of them, although she was sure he must have wanted to come along to see her delightful self. She would find him at the evening meal, he could be sure of that, and he wouldn't escape her clutches. At the last second, the blurred shapes of an Airedale terrier, red dachshund and cream cockapoo darted into the back of the coach, putting their paws to their lips to make sure Reggie didn't say anything. He was aware of the problems some customers had with others and didn't want trouble on his coach, so he let it pass and made his way to the front.

When they arrived at the nearby town, Reggie opened the doors and let the three late arrivals get out unseen. Winnie had slipped up to the front during the journey to tell him that they would make their own way back to the hotel.

Reggie was thankful that he had been updated. He remembered a trip not more than a few months ago during which he took a coach load of passengers to a shopping centre. The day passed like most of the excursions: customers made their way around and bought their own lunches, while he either had a snooze in the coach or passed the time reading the racing post until they all returned. On this day, two of his more awkward passengers didn't re-join the coach at the 5:30pm deadline. Time passed, and Reggie still hadn't seen the couple. Passengers already on the coach were getting restless, as was Reggie, so he looked in at the shopping centre's office and asked them to put an alert over the tannoy with the names of the missing pair. The car park was quite large, so he decided he had best go and check out the coach stop on the other side. It was a fair walk but worth looking, and if they weren't back when he returned, he would leave. Beeliner Tours' policy in these instances dictated that he couldn't wait longer than an acceptable time frame, depending on the circumstances. Lo and behold, the elderly couple were sitting at the bus stop, and when they saw Reggie they gave him a piece of their minds.

"I'll have you know that we've been sitting here for three quarters of an hour! What's the meaning of this?" the tom whined.

"We'll be missing *Days of Our Nine Lives* now, and it's all your fault!" his wife moaned. "It's a season premier, too."

Reggie had had to suck up the criticism and the resulting complaint promised.

The rest of the group of passengers disembarked and headed off to the more populated area of the town, and Alfreda was happily chatting away to her friends. They were looking forward to the lunch at the castle restaurant later on. Artie, Lottie and Winnie were also due to go to the same luncheon and started making their way there, too. They had booked an earlier start time and also only a main and dessert in the hope that they could avoid seeing Alfreda. Lottie and Winnie were dressed in their usual informal clothes, while Artie had made an effort and was wearing a checked blazer with a red carnation in the pocket. He was also sporting a particularly fine wooden stick with a silver handle.

They entered the castle grounds through a stone archway and walked along the path. In the distance was a closed wrought iron gate and to their side were a series of outbuildings. A sign outside an open door promised "extraordinary cuisine" and informed guests that the property boasted a 100-person stone patio, for seasonal dining overlooking a small lake; herb and scented gardens; a solid hardwood bar; a full kitchen; and a wine cellar. Artie was keen to taste some fine wine and licked his lips with delight at the prospect of the upcoming meal.

The three walked down the shadowy passageway and out into an area where a table was already laden with a roast partridge in a *purée soubise*. Smaller, steaming porcelain dishes held creamed *haricots blancs* and pickled *girolle* mushrooms. Behind them, on a dresser, they could see a strawberry cheesecake with a biscuit base.

They couldn't see any of the restaurant staff, so decided that it was best to start straight away before anything cooled off. Artie took his place at the head of the table and began expertly carving some of the partridge. Winnie passed round the vegetables whilst Lottie filled their glasses with some water and studied the wine bottles.

"Burgundy or Bordeaux?" she called.

"Go for the Burgundy," Artie said. "I find the soft tannins won't overpower the delicacy, and it's sprightlier on the palate."

"I don't have a clue what you just said, but it's good enough for me," Lottie replied, uncorking the bottle and pouring the red liquid into their glasses.

"Cheers," Artie said, as he held his goblet aloft. The others followed suit.

"This is all very pleasant," Artie said.

"Last time I had a meal like this, I wasn't old enough to sample the wine," Lottie said, as she put down her glass. "I was just a pup, and my mom took me to a swanky joint with her then-boyfriend. I remember thinking that all the fancy entrees sounded odd or disgusting and that I just wanted macaroni and cheese. I probably made my opinions known, too, in no uncertain terms. Mom tried to shush me, and her boyfriend was horrified. They cringed when the snooty-looking waiter came round. I repeated my request to him, and he lifted a bushy eyebrow but said nothing. A little later, he came back with a lovely plate of farfalle pasta in a creamy sauce. Mom and the boyfriend had escargot and pretended to like it, but by the end of the meal they were shamelessly sneaking bites off my plate, much to my disgust."

Winnie smiled, "I think Stanley would have had something to say about that."

"Stanley?" Artie enquired.

"Oh, he's a friend of mine, never lets anything get in the way of a good meal. I dare say if he had an allotment and caught a family of snails munching on his prize cauliflower, he'd pick them all up and cook them for his dinner."

The three laughed before hearing a noise from another room and footsteps approaching.

"What on…. Who are you and just what do you think you are doing eating my dinner?" the Burmese screeched as the five little faces of her kittens appeared behind her. She fixed her flashing green eyes squarely on the three dogs.

"I beg your pardon?" Artie said, putting his fork down. "We did book our places. There must have been some unfortunate error."

"Oh, yes, there most definitely was an error, and you're going to make it right by marching straight out of that gate! I've got my in-laws coming any minute and look what you've done. A beautiful dinner ruined!" And she put her paws over her face.

Artie, Winnie and Lottie looked at each other in utter confusion. "Your in-laws?" Artie said helplessly. "You invited them to have dinner with you here, at this table?"

"Yes, at this table! It's my table, isn't it?" the cat snapped.

Artie sat up straighter and put his napkin on the table. "Yes, madam, that does seem to be the question."

"And I'll tell you the answer. It is my table. It was my mother's, and she let me have it. My name is scratched on it underneath, if you care to have a look. Now please do go away, or I will have to call the police," the cat replied, her whiskers trembling. The kittens were gambolling around the room, repeating "my table, my table" in little sing-song voices.

"Aha! That must be where the mistake lies," Artie said with some relief. "No one realised that your mother was keeping the table for you, and then when she was gone, we came as we had arranged. Simple communication error," he said soothingly. "I'm sure you can get another table, as the next seating is very soon. When are your in-laws coming?"

"How dare you say my mother is gone! Who do you think you are? She's alive and well, thank you very much! And I'm very happy with my table, the finest walnut, it is. Communication? I have a few things I'd like to communicate to you. One of them is that my in-laws are here now!" she exclaimed, sweeping a paw behind her.

"Granny! Grandad!" yelled the kittens and rolled about with glee as a pair of sleek Siamese came through the creaking gate. "Althea, do you have other guests? Are we late?" the elegant mother-in-law asked, surveying the dogs with distaste.

"No, no, just getting something sorted," Althea replied, looking daggers at Artie.

Artie looked bemused, but Winnie had just noticed a sign on the door next to them which read "Kindly DO NOT Deliver Parcels for the Castle Restaurant Here." She instantly had a terrible sinking feeling and nudged Lottie, nodding towards it. They rose as one. "Artie, I think we have to go," Lottie said, urgently. "I believe a certain dog is coming in our direction."

Artie leapt up with the vigour of a dog half his age. "Well, then. So sorry to have had this disagreement, Mrs um—er, we'll be off now."

"You owe me a partridge!" the cat called after them.

"We really do, you know," Winnie said, but Artie was preoccupied, darting glances around, ready to dodge behind a tree the moment he needed to.

"Don't forget that we must go in and settle the bill," she added, gently pulling at his elbow.

They walked up to the main castle, edged through the now-open iron gate and ducked inside the main entrance. "Arthur Barclay here, just finished that splendid meal—my highest compliments to the chef. Although there is a terribly upset cat outside, not sure what happened with your bookings. You really must be more careful in future." The maître d'hôtel looked at him in confusion. "But sir, we have been looking for you. You missed your booking, I'm afraid."

A familiar voice echoed from the doorway of the dining room. "Artie, darling! In here! We're just starting on a glorious partridge. If I lived near here, I'd always be having them cater my parties. They do that, you know. But wherever have you been, you naughty dog?"

Chapter Thirty-Seven
Ups and Downs

Hans was getting slightly worried about Percy. During their last call, Percy had sounded somewhat distressed and had explained that the bedroom furniture had been moved around.

"I'm afraid this all sounds rather mad," he'd said. "But my bed was facing the window, and it's now under it. The pictures have been moved around. And I know that I didn't change the light pink blanket on the bed for the darker magenta one. It's too lightweight for this time of year. I know I'm forgetful, but surely…" His voice trailed off. "I feel as though I'm in Wonderland with everything topsy-turvy. I'm sorry. I just don't know what to think."

Hans had tried to reassure Percy, but he could tell that the terrier was still very anxious, so he decided to go and see for himself.

In the afternoon, Hans knocked on the door at Wood Lane and Percy promptly answered, showing him in. Upstairs Hans had a look around the bedroom. Unfortunately, though, he had never been upstairs at the property, so he couldn't tell if anything was out of place. He studied the wallpaper and noticed that there was a small hole in the wall where a picture could have hung in the past, but there was really no way to tell if this had been there a long time or not. The floors upstairs were wooden, so there weren't any indentations as there would be on carpet, and the skirtings were clean of dust. Hans offered to move the furniture back, and Percy gratefully agreed.

Hans thought for a moment. "It looks like your housekeeper is very thorough. Do you think she might have moved things and run out of time to put them back?"

"Oh, I wondered about that, but I called her to ask, and she swore she hadn't."

"Has anything else changed recently?" Hans asked when they came back downstairs.

"What do you mean?" Percy replied.

"Well, have you noticed any other unexplained happenings?"

"Not really. I often misplace things, like my watch, or even my glasses, but I usually find them in another room soon enough. I just don't always remember where I last set them down," Percy said.

Hans looked around the downstairs and strolled out into the small backyard. He could see that everything looked normal. Opening the fridge, he found a tin of baked beans and pulled it out to show Percy.

He gave a little laugh. "Oh, don't worry about that, I often put them in there. I like a plate of cold baked beans, it reminds me of the days in the scouts. That's not anything to worry about."

Hans smiled. He had noticed a box of cereal in there, too but didn't like to ask.

"Shall we have a cup of tea?" Percy suggested, clearly anxious for a bit of normalcy.

"That would be most welcome," Hans replied and sat down at the kitchen table and watched the dog go through the familiar, soothing routine. "You know, I've been reading up a bit on caves recently. I've got a commission from a cat in Germany who sent me a photo of a particular cave she wants me to paint. Friend of a friend she is. Quite a beautiful place. But I can't ever seem to remember the difference between a stalactite and a stalagmite." He said this nonchalantly, thinking he might catch Percy off guard.

"Oh, that's easy," Percy volunteered. "Stalactites come down and stalagmites go up."

"I always was taught to remember by thinking of 'tights,' but I'm darned if I can recall if they go up or down, surely they do both, don't they?" Hans asked, not sure of the answer to his own question.

"Very true, Hans, but you have to look at how the words are spelled. They might sound very similar if you say them fast, but stalactites have a 'c' in the middle, and stalagmites have a 'g'—'ceiling' and 'ground,' very easy once you know that fact," Percy replied.

Hans couldn't argue with that and was very impressed by Percy's recall. He might have had his off days, but he certainly was on form today, which just left the quandary about the bedroom.

"Does anyone else have a key to the house? Think carefully. Maybe you gave one to someone long ago?" Hans looked earnestly at the older dog as he was handed a steaming mug.

Percy paused, adjusted his monocle and rubbed his temples before answering. "No. Only Mrs Belcher, and she's been with me for years. And anyway, she didn't know anything about it." His eyes were wide with worry.

"I think you'd best put it out of your mind," Hans said reassuringly. "Just let me know if anything else out-of-the-ordinary happens. Meanwhile, let's have our tea and then get out of here for a bit, think about something else. What say you we stop at the gallery, and you can advise me on my 'cave painting'?" He was gratified to see Percy smile at his little witticism. But he was not feeling nearly as cheerful as he sounded. The situation was certainly perplexing.

Chapter Thirty-Eight
Wish You Were Here

After promising to write to Artie about their adventures and bidding him a fond farewell, Winnie and Lottie thanked Reggie, who surveyed them with a bit of concern.

"Where to next?" he asked. He was a kindly dog beneath his rumpled and sometimes gruff exterior and had taken an avuncular liking to this pair of innocents abroad. "Bye the bye, I did the maths, and I actually owe you a bit. I noticed that you two went without breakfast and always shared a portion at dinner time," he said with a wink, and produced an envelope from his shirt pocket.

"Thank you," Winnie replied with a wide smile, not suspecting that the extra had come from Reggie's own wallet.

"We don't have any idea where we're going next," Lottie piped up, with a frankness that made Winnie blush. She was a little embarrassed that they still hadn't agreed on a proper itinerary, despite her efforts.

Reggie scratched his chin. "Well, you can't really go wrong if you take the 578 bus to Rushing Beck. There's a pub there—know the landlady. She's a very good sort, runs a tight ship, lets out rooms above her establishment. It's the 'Cat and Cradle,' can't miss it. Couple of nice villages around there, too, worth a look."

The next day, having had an enormous cooked breakfast at the pub, Winnie and Lottie made their way down a quiet lane. The day was before them, and they were going to make the most of it. Granted, Winnie was a bit more enthusiastic than Lottie, who was less enchanted with rural life than with the thought of the bright lights of London. But she welcomed a day without a schedule planned by the coach company and whistled tunelessly as she sauntered along next to Winnie, who was so engrossed in her Baedeker that she nearly walked into a cow meandering across the road. The cow looked at her impassively and lumbered on. Lottie shook her head at her. "You're going to come to grief one of these days, Win-Win. I suggest that you get your nose out of that book and actually see the sights."

A ten-minute walk had taken them directly to the village green, currently strewn with a miscellany of stalls arranged around a tea tent, which also housed the entries for the baking competition. There was a general atmosphere of joviality, with no one seemingly in a hurry and pups chasing each other around the perimeter. Winnie tucked her guidebook away and gazed, fascinated, at the kaleidoscope of colours, the various handmade and donated wares and the smattering of carnival games. Lottie sighed audibly.

"I thought you said that there'd be rides," she said, irritably.

"I didn't. You did, and I didn't contradict you," Winnie replied. "Now, don't start whining, Lottie. There's plenty to see and do. Oh! Even a bookstall."

Lottie rolled her eyes and made for the tea tent. "Knock yourself out," she said. "I'll meet you here in an hour?"

"Sure," Winnie replied, somewhat relieved that she wouldn't be obliged to listen to her friend's running commentary on the oddity of English forms of recreation.

Lottie sipped stewed tea from a heavy mug and grimaced. 'I miss coffee,' she thought, feeling at the same time ever so slightly homesick. And a little heartsick. She and the charming Irish setter Ted Tierney had got on like a house on fire after the diaper derby, and he had just happened to turn up at a few of the coach's stop-offs. He had ended up by giving her his phone number, and she had called it once or twice but not had an answer—and then she's been an idiot and lost the number. One of the old dears behind the tea urn was watching her curiously, so she forbore to toss the tea away, lest she give offence. Gulping it down, she returned her cup with a smile and left the tent, hoping to find something that might hold her attention for a while. After passing stall upon stall of knitted pup clothes, handmade beaded jewellery, macramé projects, and jumble sale bits, she was getting rather fed up, but then spotted a small tent in a far corner of the green with its flap fluttering invitingly in the breeze. This was just the sort of thing to pique her interest.

"Got to be more interesting than the rest of this malarkey," she muttered, unconsciously using one of Ted's preferred adjectives. She poked her nose inside. It was rather dim, despite the open flap, and she thought at first that perhaps it only housed odds and ends needed by the stall holders. There were indeed some stacks of dishes and crates of miscellaneous items in one corner. But as Lottie's eyes adjusted to the low light, she saw something else glowing dully in the other corner, half obscured by a carelessly discarded tarp. Holding her breath, she tossed the covering aside and then let out a long, low whistle.

Before her was the turbaned figure of a Sphinx cat, gorgeously arrayed in a purple caftan spangled with various constellations. Its topaz eyes were mesmerising, and its head moved slightly back and forth, then up and down, as if sizing her up. It took Lottie a moment to realise that the cat was behind glass. Beneath it was an ornately decorated compartment with a coin slot and lever. A mirror behind the cat reflected Lottie's own puzzled face. Above, painted on the glass in ornate red and gold script, were the words Xanthe, Mistress of Your Fate. "Well, Xanthe. What's your racket? And why are you in here instead of out on the green where all the fun is?"

"I tell fortunes," the cat said, its mouth moving rather realistically in time with the words. Lottie nearly jumped out of her fur. "Place your coins in the slot, and you shall see." For a moment, she hesitated. She knew it was all rubbish, of course, but like many a dog and cat before her, she didn't care. She fished ten pence out of her pocket and slid it in. "You hold my services so cheap?" the creature asked, its eyes seeming to flash.

"Smarter than the average," Lottie grinned to herself, popping in another couple of coins.

Suddenly the thing went dark, and Lottie shuddered involuntarily. A moment or two later, the eyes glowed again, and a crystal ball lit up. "Vat is your vish?" came the low, unearthly voice.

Lottie was surprised into truthfulness. "Ted," she heard herself say. "I want to see Ted Tierney."

The cat didn't reply, and the backlights glowed once again. Lottie remembered herself and pulled the lever. "You're better than the one at the arcade in Piedmont Bay," she said. "Why are you hiding your light under a bushel in here?" A mechanical noise could be heard whirring inside the machine, and then a card fell into her waiting hand. "You will see Ted" was printed on it in scripted writing. She jumped back, almost dropping it. "Oh my gosh," she muttered. "That's some fancy piece of equipment."

Once the cockapoo had gone, a small sigh echoed through the dimness. The sound of a needle on vinyl preceded a click, and something fell to the floor. "Rats," said someone in a squeaky voice.

"Don't say that, Zofia, you might well summon one." Behind the machine were two white mice, one panting from exertion on something that looked like a hamster wheel. She gave the thing a few turns, and the lights above flicked on and then off. The other picked up a pen that had rolled into a corner.

"I know, I know, Zosia. That's the last thing we need. Hopefully they'll be kept busy with all the rubbish from the fête. I say, why can't we just pop out those pre-printed cards that say 'Your wish is granted'? I get a cramp in my paw trying to write that fast."

"Stop your whining. Just be glad we had a customer. I can't believe we got stuck back in here. The last vicar would never have stood for it, rest his soul. Folks came from miles around just for the pleasure. But the new 'fête committee' has no imagination whatsoever. Now, you'd best get a move on and alert the troops. There's work to be done."

Zofia sighed and slipped out of the tent. She and Zosia had 487 brothers, sisters, cousins, and second cousins scattered over the length and breadth of England, and they had developed a complex network for transmitting messages. She saw her first contact squatting under a bench, happily devouring some ginger biscuit crumbs. "Zach!" she called. "We're looking for a Ted. Ted Tierney. No description of the bloke. Recently seen with an American cockapoo. No name for her, unfortunately."

"I'm on it," the plump mouse replied, brushing down his jumper.

Chapter Thirty-Nine
The Cleaner, the Better

It had been several weeks since Wagmore had adopted his disguise of Mr Louis Belcher and rearranged Percy's bedroom furniture for him. He decided it was time to repeat the episode and increase the stakes. According to Murdo, the calls between Percy and Hans referred to his handiwork, and Hans was getting more worried. Hans had suggested that the older dog spend more time at the allotment where there was more company, just in case. Percy's anxiety had waned somewhat, but he was obliging enough to agree and told Hans he had more than enough to be getting on with down there. He had even branched out, and instead of just growing flowers, he had decided to turn over a small plot for vegetables. "I've despaired of making my benighted fellow gardeners understand that flowers are just as important as their marrows and peas—after all, they attract bees to the plots," he remarked. "A few cucumbers and courgettes will hopefully keep the peace."

Belcher arrived at 4pm, checked for any twitching curtains and unlocked the front door. The house was the same as he left it and he couldn't resist going upstairs to Percy's bedroom to see if it had changed. He wasn't surprised to see things restored to the same layout as before his first visit. Today's work was not going to be a repeat, though. The indefatigable Belcher had other plans.

He went back down the stairs, entered the kitchen and took out a saucepan from the cupboard. Lighting one of the gases with a match, he placed the steel saucepan on the hob and waited. With the gas dial turned to full, the saucepan started warming up, and Belcher watched, tapping his paw on the counter. After a few minutes, he turned, exited the kitchen and went back to the front door. Just as he was about to turn the handle, he stopped. A sudden urge caused Belcher to return to the kitchen. He noticed the slight burning smell as the bottom of the pan grew hot, but no smoke had filled the room. Belcher flicked the gas knob to the off position, picked up the saucepan by the plastic handle and placed it in the sink, turning the tap on to cool it down. After a few minutes, he dried it off, put it back in the cupboard where he had found it and left the building, leaving the front door unlocked.

Chapter Forty
Unwelcome Visitors

Percy was lost in his thoughts, remembering back to the time he spent at Lady Effingham's estate. What a glorious day that was,' he mused, a lopsided smile lighting his face. He did miss Bertie. 'Don't be selfish,' he thought. 'He deserves to see the world with Muriel. But I do wonder where they are now.' He neglected to pay much attention as he entered the property and heard voices, subconsciously thinking he must have left the radio on in the kitchen. When he entered the living room, he was flabbergasted to see a dog sitting there, bold as brass.

"Just what do you think you are doing here?" Percy exclaimed, as he put his house key back in his pocket. A large grey mastiff was lounging in his favourite armchair, munching on some snacks and watching television.

"I live here," was the simple reply.

"No, you don't. This is my house! Now get out before I call the police," Percy said, quivering slightly as he realised the size of the dog before him.

The noise in the room brought another new face to join them. A burly bull terrier appeared from the kitchen carrying several packets of ready-salted crisps and pork scratchings. He threw one to his friend.

"Who's that, Barney?" he enquired in a gruff voice to the mastiff, flashing a row of shining gold teeth under his top lip.

"Said he lives here, mate," the mastiff said.

Percy started to get slightly confused. He half wondered if he had come into the wrong house, or even the wrong street, as these two certainly seemed to look at home. As he was about to apologise for the intrusion he looked at the dresser wall and saw the framed picture of the River Thames, a photo Bertie had shot from his flat in Dolphin Square.

"Hang about, gentlemen. What is the meaning of this?" Percy said, anger getting the better of his nervousness.

"Look, bud," the bull terrier said, "we found this place empty, the front door was open, and we ain't moving. Nice little pad we have got ourselves here. Been a long time since we found a little number like this! Go to the police, see if we care. We know our rights, and there's nothing you can do about it."

"Beat it," the mastiff said, throwing the last couple of his peanuts in the air and catching them in his mouth, "before I throw you out," he gulped, scattering the shells on the rug.

Percy didn't like the looks of these two characters and was in no position to try their patience any longer. He had thought it slightly odd that the key hadn't needed turning in the front door, and now he knew why. In a resigned state of mind, he withdrew to fight another day. Nothing like this had ever happened to him before, and he couldn't explain it, but he wasn't going to take it lying down. He just needed some help.

As the slim figure of the Welsh terrier retreated and walked past the window, the mastiff got up from his supine position, picked up the phone and dialled a number.

"Mission complete. The old buzzard has gone on his way. What do you want us to do next?" Then, nodding in agreement, "yup… okay… will do." The mastiff put the phone down and smirked. "Pity we haven't got a pool table, eh Mason? I could right fancy a game just now. Any beer in the fridge? I'm parched."

Chapter Forty-One
The Long Walk

Th Bertie, Muriel and Ani kept up a good pace behind Sweetie. The path rose very gently and gradually before them, and Bertie suspected, though he hated to admit it, that their guide had been none to certain about their abilities. Muriel thought the same but kept her conjecture to herself, not wanting to embarrass Bertie by mentioning it. The way was pleasant enough, with violets making little pools on either side of them and the sun filtering through the tree-canopy above. After having travelled many miles by rail in the course of their journey thus far, the two were content to stretch their legs and enjoy the forest's sights and sounds in companionable silence.

Ani was silent for another reason. She had been thinking long and hard about whether she should divulge the reason she had come to Germany. Although she hasn't spent too much time with Bertie and Muriel, she had learnt to trust her judgement and felt they were dogs she could rely on. After all, they had stuck with her this long and had kept their promise to get her where she needed to go. Now that she was close—or as close as she was ever going to be—to her final destination, she had made up her mind to show them the letter that had precipitated this journey. Sweetie was up ahead on the gravel path, so Ani unfolded the brittle paper from within her side pocket. "Muriel," she said, starting slightly at the sound of her voice as it cut through the murmurings of the forest. "I'd like for you to read this, if you don't mind."

The dorgi slowed her pace a bit and took the letter. "Of course," she replied.

15th September 1949

My Dearest Ani,

If you are receiving this letter then I fear these may be the last words you hear from me. I have instructed my solicitor to send this to you if I fall ill or in the event of my passing.

It feels like years since your last leTTer and even longer since we spoke. I now very much regret sending you to live with your aunt in + America and not deciding to let you stay here with + me in Germany. I was also fearful of being called up to fight in the war and couldn't let you be taken into care. I always did what I thought was right for you and wanted to keep you safe. I do hope you can forgive me for the Time we were not able to spend together.

You must allow me to explain some things that I have never Told you before. When you were born and your mother sadly died, I was given a + gift for you. Its value is immaterial, it means so much more to + me than that, because it is a connection to your mother's past. Our work brought us together but also led to some consternation among our colleagues. Some began to believe this gift + was stolen, a falsehood which was perpetuated by a rumour, and That didn't help given that after the war much looting of treasures came to light. I decided that the only thing I could do was to hide the object in one of the caves I + used to visit near the old village of Beckenstein.

If you follow the stream north out of the village +and head into the Black Forest, you will find a waterfall. There is a narrow crevice behind which opens into a cavern. Inside I know you will be able to follow the SIGNS I have given you+. I have also decided to leave you one more item in the cave, a small journal which will explain something about our family tree and my own past.

Good luck.

Your loving father,

Elias

Muriel didn't know what to say. It seemed that they were on a real-life treasure hunt. "This letter is dated 1949, though. I don't mean to seem nosey, but why has it taken you so long to act?" she asked Ani.

Ani looked rather embarrassed. "I didn't receive the letter until a couple of years ago. It was lost in transit, must have ended up in some dusty old post office. I had believed that Elias had stopped communicating with me, as my letters did not get replies, and I'd felt rather lost and betrayed for a number of years. Anyway, I contacted our solicitor, and the son, who had taken over the running of things, relayed some new information to me. Elias had passed away in late September 1949, and this letter was sent to me after his affairs were set in order. Many of his possessions, papers and journals were passed to a colleague—which reminds me, I must try and find him, too. He will surely be able to help fill in many unanswered questions. The rest was sold off to pay for Elias's debts. He didn't own much, really. He spent his life travelling to new sites of archaeological interest and had little interest in wealth, as long as he could provide for his family. He had a particular interest in Egyptian history. And here we are."

Bertie had been listening, despite having to constantly stop and start because he had a stone stuck in his boot. He could see Ani's pain and vowed to make sure they were successful in helping this shy cat. "So, what do you expect to find?" he asked.

"I don't know, really. But since he took all this trouble, then surely it must be quite special," Ani replied.

'I hope it's not the bones of a long-dead pharaoh,' Bertie thought, but decided he'd better not say that aloud. "Maybe it's a rare emerald or ruby?" he suggested.

"Oh, I really don't think that would be the case," Ani remarked. "I have done some digging of my own, and although there may be gaps in the records, there is no evidence of any missing or stolen Egyptian antiquities. I think it is perhaps something with chiefly sentimental value. After all, it was given to him when I was born."

"I'm sorry you never met your mother," Muriel said, realising that perhaps not having had an important figure in her life may have caused her to be a timid cat.

"It's not something I think too much about. I have never known anything other than having a loving father, despite growing up with kittens that had both parents," Ani replied.

Muriel was pleased that Ani seemed to be opening up. Perhaps this quest was exactly what the cat needed, she mused. Making peace with her past might help her move on with her own life. Her reflections were interrupted by Sweetie's voice.

"Now, make sure you keep to the path and don't stray," she said as she pointed to the right. "Oh, and listen."

"Listen?" Bertie replied, wondering what they would hear in the middle of nowhere. To his surprise, in a few minutes he could definitely hear something. At first, he thought it was coming from the village they had left behind, but they were surely now too far from that location.

"It's a bell," Muriel said, after a moment. "But where is the sound coming from?"

"Just wait, all will be revealed," Sweetie said with a smile.

A few moments later, after the group had climbed higher up the path, they reached a ridge and could see what lay below them. The clouded sky was perfectly reflected in the water below. The expanse was contained by the mountains, but judging by the difference in colour at its edges, it was lower than it should be.

"Looks like someone's forgot to put the plug in," Bertie quipped, "or you have a leak."

Sweetie smiled again, but suggested they all stop and look a little closer at the far side of the lake.

"Look," Ani said, pointing at the source of the sound. "It's a spire... and a bell tower." She lapsed into silence, realising what had happened.

"That's right," Sweetie said. "This was the location of the village of Beckenstein. It was submerged in 1921, when the valley was flooded and turned into a reservoir. It is one of the beautiful moments in time, when the water level drops enough for the tallest buildings to reveal their past glory."

"Does it go any lower?" Bertie asked.

"Not normally, no, but there have been several years when there have been long hot summers and water from higher up ceased to trickle down. Rare droughts such as these have revealed the entire village," Sweetie replied.

"Oh, that does sound rather creepy," Muriel said. "What about the villagers, where did they go?"

"Some stayed until the bitter end, refusing to leave, but most were resigned to their fate. There is a stone monument further down the path in the opposite direction to commemorate them. It is a poignant reminder," Sweetie said.

"But how is it that the bell is ringing?" Bertie asked, ever the practical thinker. The bell bonged a final time and left a profound silence in its wake. Sweetie did not answer for a few moments.

"Some people say it is the ghost of the former vicar," Sweetie suggested, "but in all honesty it is most likely just the wind and a happy coincidence. Anyway, we can't stop here all day. There is still a lot of walking to do. A quick drink from your flasks, and let's carry on, shall we?"

Bertie ambled on but was determined to keep his wits about him. Perhaps he had merely been startled by their encounter with the sunken church, but he was feeling a little uneasy. Now that Ani had confided in them, he felt it was doubly his duty to look out for her.

Chapter Forty-Two
Revenge is a Dish Best Served Cold

The sun was most definitely not shining as it was on the picture postcards of Portpenny Island, and the clouds out at sea were threatening to blow in soon with another rainstorm. Despite the foul weather, Winnie and Lottie were sheltering in one of the promenade beach shelters, pondering Winnie's latest idea. The coach crowd were staying cosy in their hotel, playing cards and swapping stories, and the cockapoo was heartily wishing that she were doing the same. But Winnie was thinking ahead to the day when the tour would end, and they would have to fend for themselves.

"Are you sure about this, Win-Win?" Lottie asked. "It seems like 'a hiding to nothing,' as the Brits say, if you ask me."

"I know what you are thinking and agree, but the advert in the window said, "Paid work guaranteed, enquire within," so I did just that, and here we are," Winnie replied.

The advert in question was displayed in the window of the "Portpenny Island Ice Cream Parlour," whose premises sat with pride of place on the town's seafront. Winnie had been keen to point out that there was no such island, and that it had only been given the name in order to lend the place some semblance of believability for the area's rather anaemic tourist trade. The proprietors, a Mr and Mrs Baker, another misnomer, had emigrated from New England, where the residents ate ice cream all year round. It had been this couple's dream to move to the sunny coast of England and set up the little shop in their retirement. Despite their enthusiasm and substantial investment in the glowing neon sign and a large plastic ice cream cone above the shop door, things weren't quite going to plan. The ice cream flavours on the menu left something to be desired, including such rarefied delights as Pink Peppercorn, Acorn Squash, Sweet Potato, Whortleberry and Salty Liquorice. Winnie laughed when she saw that the last choice was "Oyster," written in ornate capitals and illustrated with two baleful looking shellfish, and wondered what on earth possessed them to add that.* 'We don't eat nasty stuff like that back home,' Winnie thought. It was obvious that Mr and Mrs Baker's business plan to take over the world with their ice cream concession had not considered one minor detail—inhabitants of Portpenny Island did not eat ice cream in minus temperatures.

Winnie handed Lottie the sandwich board extolling the virtues of the ice cream parlour and the various price reductions on offer and told her to head west, while she would walk towards the high street to drum up some trade there. Surely there would be some eager customers if only they knew what joys awaited them, or at least that is what Mr Baker passionately believed. Lottie harrumphed at the thought of demeaning herself by walking up and down the seafront in the rain.

"Who on earth is going to see you?" Winnie asked, and she could hardly refute that, given there wasn't a soul in sight.

After what seemed like an eternity, Lottie had had enough. The constant drizzle had dampened her spirits as well as her curly fur. She looked at her wrist and realised that her watch had stopped. "Drat," she said, cursing her luck. 'I must have been doing this for hours. Surely it's time to stop now?' she thought. Lottie looked around for someone to ask the time, but all she could see were a couple of horse boxes on the sand and a small corral where three donkeys were braving the weather. Their owner must have been related to the optimistic Bakers, given his hope that any young pup and holidaying parents would be giving him a ten pence piece to take one of the donkeys for a jaunt along the sand. Just in front was a phone box, so Lottie decided to take shelter from the wind and rain. On opening the phone box, she could see it was in rather a dilapidated state. Several of the glass panes were missing, some were cracked, and the red paint was peeling off the exterior. Lottie had a thought and rummaging around in her pocket for some loose change, she popped one in the coin receptor, picking up the phone and turning the dial. "The speaking clock will know," she said aloud as she waited.

"At the third stroke, the time will be twelve thirty-two precisely. Beep, Beep, pause, Beep."

Lottie wasn't impressed and slammed the phone down, realising she had another one and a half hours to parade aimlessly up and down the promenade. Even though she was down in the mouth, she was a girl of her word. After five minutes, she pushed open the door of the telephone box, turned right and continued her thankless perambulations.

"Well, I never did," one of the donkeys said to his companion. "I didn't know dogs could talk," he mused, as he munched on the hay bale hanging on the railing next to the phone box. "Nor did I," the other said, "but you're horsing around will get us into trouble one of these days. At least you got the time right this time. Just don't ever pretend someone has got the wrong number and is speaking to the queen. That would be pushing your luck a bit too far."[†]

Lottie walked past the two horse boxes, ignoring the wooden plaques pinned to the side, one of which said "Edward" and the other "Freddy." Winnie was having the same experience as Lottie at the other end of the seafront. The weather meant that any potential customers were rushing by with their heads down, well hidden under umbrellas. She was pleased that there was not long left to go. After shouting "ice creams, ice creams, come get your ice creams" times until she was hoarse, she realised it was like trying to sell ice to the Eskimos. She turned around and headed back to meet Lottie.

Back at the shelter, Lottie handed the sandwich board to Winnie and slumped into the bench seat. "That is an experience I don't want to have again. I hope they pay well?"

Winnie looked away sheepishly, not wanting to admit that the agreement with the proprietors of the shop was based on the number of customers that came through the door during their advertising stunt. She walked back to Portpenny Island Ice Cream Parlour with an uneasy feeling in her stomach for having been rather liberal with the truth. Inside the shop, Mr Baker was busy cleaning the work counter with a jay cloth, and Mrs Baker was noisily unwrapping a packet of flakes and placing them in a container on the shelf. "Here's that doxie that came in earlier," she announced and disappeared out back.

"You look like a drowned rat," Mr Baker said as he looked at the bedraggled Winnie.

"I feel like one, too," she replied.

"I'm expecting you'll be wanting your pay, then?" he questioned.

"I would be grateful," Winnie said. "We've been up and down that promenade and high street a hundred times. I hope at least a couple of customers came in?"

Mr Baker moved to the till and pressed a button to open the cash register. Winnie started to get excited as she held out her paw.

"There you go," Mr Baker said.

Winnie looked at what he had just placed in her paw and groaned. There were three vouchers for 'ice creams of your choice.'

"Sorry, but you look like a clever dog. You must have read the small print on the advert, so you knew my terms," Mr Baker said. "I'm being generous at that. And make sure you tell all your friends, the best ice cream in town, don't forget now," he said as he waved her out of the shop. Winnie returned to the shelter dejectedly, dreading the reaction she would get from Lottie.

"Whaaaaat? You're joking, Win-Win!" Lottie said as she was handed her reward for the morning's work. She was livid. "We can't even catch a bus with that!" she groaned, as she scrunched up the voucher and was about to throw it in the dustbin. "Hang on," she said, with a twinkle in her eye, "I have an idea."

Lottie disappeared in a rush and left Winnie sitting in the shelter. Fifteen minutes passed, and Winnie looked up to see Lottie walking back towards her with three donkeys in tow. Each one had an ice cream voucher pinned to its harness like a rosette. Lottie waved as she continued by. A moment later, Lottie had entered the ice cream parlour, holding the door open for the donkeys to go in too. Within seconds Winnie heard a commotion, and outshot Mr and Mrs Baker, fleeing from the scene. Inside, the donkeys were helping themselves to the delicacies from New England, including the famed oyster flavour.

Lottie emerged soon after, and as she walked past the Bakers she called out, "Not sure what the problem is. Your vouchers did say 'Ice creams of your choice.' It just so happens that the donkeys wanted to try them all. Perhaps you should have added some small print!" And she laughed merrily as she returned to Winnie's vantage point, where the doxie was unsuccessfully stifling giggles with her paw and had pulled her hat down about her ears.

"Well, we've fixed up the Bakers with customers, but we've still got no hope of a bus fare," Lottie said, her initial hilarity beginning to fade. "Looks like we're hoofing it, I guess." Winnie nodded ruefully, and they splashed along for a while, ears and noses dripping.

An odd sort of whirring noise began to make itself heard over the dispiriting patter of the rain on the pavement. The dogs looked at each other questioningly and then over their shoulders. A peculiar sort of vehicle was buzzing along just behind them, its single headlight beaming like a Cyclops' eye. As it slowed to a crawl beside the kerb, the driver, a moggie rather too large for his vehicle, poked his head out and tipped his peaked cap. His jacket was embroidered with "Ernie" in a delicate script. "Sorry it's rained on your parade, loves," he called out genially. "But I can offer you my float, if you have a mind."

Again, Winnie and Lottie exchanged bemused glances, but even riding under cover at walking pace was preferable to trudging along as they had been for the last fifteen minutes. "That's awfully kind of you," Winnie answered, and they crammed themselves into the small space next to the driver.

"Arh, I can hear from ye accents that ye ain't from these parts," Ernie said over the rattle of the empty milk bottles as the machine lurched into motion again.

"No, we're from New England," Lottie replied, wriggling into a more comfortable position.

"Oho! Ye should be tryin' that new lolly shop in town, then. Owners hail from those parts. Mmm...they've got all sorts there. Oyster." He licked his lips. "Wish as I could have that one, but it don't agree with me tummy. Keep tellin' 'em they should make a tuna or salmon flavour. I got my Auntie Mildred's recipes." He tilted his head dreamily. "Think I might quit this lonely life and start up me own ice cream stall. Give 'em a bit of competition, don't you know."

Winnie and Lottie smiled at each other. Perhaps the faith Mr and Mrs Baker had in their own recipes and business model was justified after all.

*Oyster Ice Cream: It has been suggested that First Lady Dolley Madison served oyster ice cream in the White House around the 1810s despite claims that it was invented in 1842. A recipe for it appeared in Mary Randolph's cookbook *The Virginia Housewife,* and it was a luxury food that only the "upper classes" could indulge in, mainly because of the scarcity of ice. Mention of oyster ice cream is also made in Mark Twain's novel *The*

Adventures of Tom Sawyer. The authors made up the notion of tuna or salmon flavoured ice cream.

†**Donkeys:** The donkeys in the chapter were added as homage to the American television sitcom 'Mister Ed,' a show which detailed the lives of a talking palomino horse and his owner Wilbur. The horse exhibited precocious human-like behaviour and was also rather obnoxious and inconsiderate. The concept of the show was derived from a series of short stories by children's author Walter R. Brooks, which began with "The Talking Horse" in September 1937. Brooks is best known for the *Freddy the Pig* series of children's novels which also feature talking animals that interact with humans.

Chapter Forty-Three
Trouble Comes Thrice

An exasperated Percy arrived at the allotment and quickly headed for the potting shed. A lone gardener looked up and wondered what he was doing wearing his Sunday best to the place but didn't question him. Inside, Percy sat down on the wicker chair and sat back. Anastasia was his only company and even she was wilting slightly and had lost some buds. Forgetting his troubles for just a moment in his anxiety for the plant, he automatically tipped some water into a dish and placed it under her. "That'll put you to rights," he murmured. "Wish it were that easy for me." He could hear the quiet digging over of soil outside but didn't want to be disturbed. He knew that one of the chaps had left a small bottle of Aberlour single malt whiskey in a small cupboard, along with a glass tumbler. Fetching it out, he rubbed the glass clean and poured himself a large helping. Percy wasn't used to drinking alcohol, normally partaking only on special occasions or at Christmas, and he coughed loudly after he swallowed. Sitting in despair, he poured himself another glass and swigged that back too and within fifteen minutes he was fast asleep, snoring heavily, head tilted back and sitting awkwardly in the chair.

The creaking of the potting shed door awakened Percy, and he squinted his eyes at the shaft of bright sunlight that fell across him. The silhouette of a dog filled the frame.

Hans had dismissed the notion of knocking, as he was too worried about what he might find after peering in through the misted-up window. His ears drooping and bushy eyebrows lowered, he gazed at the awakening Percy.

"Hello Percy, what's up? You don't look too good," Hans said, slipping inside and closing the door behind him.

"Oh, it's you, I'm so glad," Percy said wearily.

"Who did you expect?" Hans asked. "Anyway, I called you last night and got no reply. I knocked on the door this morning too, and again, no one answered, so I was worried. I thought of coming down here on the off chance you were out attending your patch."

"Now you have found me," Percy replied in a rather disgruntled tone of voice, very unlike him.

"What's wrong?" Hans said, sitting down next to him and looking at him earnestly.

Percy was immediately ashamed of his gruff comment, and when he glanced at his rumpled trousers and creased jacket, he was disgusted with himself. He began to recite the events of the past day, and Hans exclaimed in astonishment and anger.

"You mean you've essentially been evicted by a couple of squatters?" he said.

Percy nodded. "That's about the long and short of it. What could I do?"

"That's awful...and you don't know who these dogs are, you've never seen them before hanging about the place?"

"No," Percy responded glumly. "It's not as if I'm really attached to the place, I only rent it."

"That's not the point, Percy," Hans said.

"I've been there a good few years but often thought about leaving the area," Percy continued, resigned to the fact he was unlikely to be able to do anything about his situation.

"You can't say that it's not right." The younger dog began pacing the length of the shed. "Have you been to the police?" he asked.

"No," came the short reply.

"Look, Percy, I think you'd better come round to mine, get yourself cleaned up a bit and have a good square meal. I'm going to go have a look for myself and then stop at the station to see what they say. Here, take my key and make yourself at home."

Percy's face brightened up a bit, although he was far from his normal self. When they emerged from the shed, he gasped as he spotted the bulbs, he had planted strewn across the soil. The netting and frame he had constructed for his runner beans languished on the ground in a pile of broken wood and torn threads. He walked quickly by, whilst Hans made a right turn and walked in the direction of Wood Lane.

When Hans tried the front door, he found it locked, which he thought rather odd. 'How would a squatter have keys to the door,' he wondered, 'unless they have changed locks?' He tried the key Percy had given him and found the Chubb lock still turned. Entering the house carefully, he listened keenly for any noises, but there were none—the place seemed empty. He crept into the living room, where everything was in its place, and then through to the kitchen, where all was similarly neat and tidy. Looking inside the rubbish bin, he found only an empty bin liner. Upstairs the same situation presented itself. Hans could see the bed hadn't been slept in, the bathroom smelled fresh, and the spare room was still full of a random assortment of items. He pondered for a moment. Could Percy have got this so wrong? Surely not.

Hans returned to the living room for one last look. He noticed a white folded piece of paper in the shadows under the phone table and reached for it. On closer inspection, he realised that it wasn't a piece of paper at all, but a complimentary packet of matches, and it was embossed with the insignia of the establishment in gold lettering: "The Palace Club, Islington." Hans didn't know if Percy had been there or not, seemed a funny place for him to have visited, so decided to put it in his pocket and made a note to ask Percy about it. He deliberated with himself for a moment as to whether or not to go to the police but given that Percy had suffered a good bit of mental anguish already, he decided to return to his flat with the latest news.

It didn't take long for Hans to get back to his flat, nodding to the cat at the reception as he entered the stairwell. Inside, he found a worried Percy sitting stiffly on the sofa, reading one of his art magazines.

"Everything okay?" Hans asked.

"Fine, thank you Hans, I've just been reading an article in *The Burlington Magazine* about a new gallery opening up in Europe, although I have to say it is all a bit highbrow for my tastes."

"Oh, that, I was given it a while back by someone in the gallery. I only flicked through it myself, not quite my cup of tea," Hans replied, "Speaking of which, let me put the kettle on, and I'll update you on what I found out."

Chapter Forty-Four
Degrees of Separation

There was a saying amongst the mouse fraternity that you were never more than six paw shakes away from any mouse in the world.* As a result of this chain of contacts, a clever mouse would always be able to find someone who could help with a request for information. Zach's job was a little difficult, as he had been tasked with finding a dog—well, presumably a dog, but not necessarily—with a rather common name, place of residence unknown, even the region of the country he hailed from uncertain. But therein lay the pleasure of the challenge, and he relished it.

Some might have thought him a fool for having let his sisters Zofia and Zosia convince him to take up with them, what with their antics at the travelling fair. He used to have a steady nine-to-five job in the city, a modest residence, and a life which, although rather tiresome, did at least keep his head above water. Why had he given those things up? Yet here he was. He'd come to realise that his sisters had actually saved him from himself. He had grown tired, lacked ambition and drive and had no enthusiasm for his work.

In all honesty, Zach loved what he now did for a living. At first, he had become a traveller and couldn't complain, since it gave him the opportunity to meet lots of interesting characters he would never have known if he'd been stuck in his old office job. In a short time, his energy returned, and he had a new focus for his considerable energy. Working with his sisters at the coconut shy or hoopla would never make them rich, but that really wasn't the point. The change had done him good and, even better, allowed him the opportunity to do good.

Thinking about it now, he laughed at the sheer impossibility of it all, that he had managed to escape the rat race and become a successful business mouse in his own right but on his terms. Zach had always had an uncanny ability for storing information in his head and an excellent power of recall, which was one of the reasons everyone had wanted him on their quiz teams back in the day. Over time, Zach had created a network of friends and colleagues, as well. These two strengths had allowed him to create a thriving business, fittingly named "NiceMice." The network grew and grew, and as word spread, more and more mice wanted to join. There was always someone who was willing to pay for information, and through a credit and bartering system Zach capitalised. The fortune telling machine was a way of repaying his sisters and allowed them to have some fun now that they were all more than stable financially. Zosia had found the case discarded in an old refuse tip. The broken glass was easily replaced, and the Sphinx cat was found in an antiques shop where the proprietor was only too glad to find a new home for it, having seen customers' reactions every time they visited the store. A jumble sale had yielded a suitable costume, and some paste jewellery completed the ensemble.

Zach nibbled some more of his biscuit and considered who he needed to speak to first for his latest mission of mercy. He decided that the cheese shop would be his first port of call. The owner soon contacted his neighbourhood of friends. One of these was Hubert, a brown mouse who helped out at a nearby castle's kitchens. He informed Zach that a rather loud cockapoo had been a customer at the restaurant a few days earlier, when there had been a scene involving some coach tourists, a rather angry cat and her mother-in-law. This bit of information in turn led to a mouse called Marshall, who worked at a pub in a village near St Albans. It was here that the cockapoo had previously stayed for a couple of days. He confirmed that her name was Lottie. Part one of the request was done and dusted.

Part two, finding Ted Tierney, was a slightly more complicated matter, as it involved widening the search somewhat. Marshall had been friendly with Lottie, and she had told him that they had just arrived in the country. Zach deduced that she had probably met Ted before she had joined the coach tour, when her schedule and opportunities to socialise would have been much more regulated. So, the village seemed the likely spot. Apparently, one of the year's most celebrated events was a diaper derby, and it had occurred at just about the right time. But there were still at least two dogs by that name in the area, one of them a plumber. A bit more research and a letter to the police station's resident mouse revealed that Ted Tierney, a young Irish setter, and a Detective Constable in the police force, had been at the derby in an undercover capacity.

There was a certain element of luck involved with connecting people, and Zach seemed to have it in abundance, although he liked to call it skill and perseverance. The final piece of the jigsaw, getting the cockapoo and Irish setter to meet, would have to rely on just that. Through yet more connections and small favours, Zach arranged a few free football tickets to be handed to the constabulary where Ted worked and presumed, he would be one of those attending the match. Meanwhile, Lottie and her friend Winnie (Marshall had found the dachshund's name in the guest register) were due to continue their way, just in time for the match. Marshall set about asking a friendly cat to pose as a passenger waiting for a bus. He instructed her to direct the pair onto the supporters' coach when the driver took a break at the stop nearby. The whole situation did seem quite far-fetched, but Zach's plans always had a habit of working out.

*Six Degrees of Separation: There is an idea that all people on average are six, or fewer, social connections away from each other. Because of this a chain of statements can be made to connect any two people in a maximum of six steps.

Chapter Forty-Five
Mouse of Mystery

Nadine adjusted her glasses and twitched her whiskers as she listened to her instructions. "Just make sure that DC Tierney gets a ticket. Maybe pop one in his cubbyhole to be sure. You could even put 'from a secret admirer' on the envelope. Whatever works." The white mouse assured Zach that all would be well. She was one jump ahead, having already done what he was suggesting, but forbore to say so, as she was a bit shy of putting herself forward. When she rang off, she began her nightly job of sorting the unholy mess of documents left by the desk sergeant and pondered what it would be like to run such a business or help run it. She herself had been able to track down an uncle in London by availing herself of Zach's services, and she looked forward to her occasional visits, during which they would inevitably patronise his favourite patisserie, the oddly named "À Bon Chat Bon Rat." The waiter would always thoughtfully pile the chairs high with menus so that the mice could comfortably reach the table top. Thinking of this, she fell asleep over a pile of schedules and had a pleasant dream of madeleines and mauve waistcoats.

She was awakened by the desk sergeant, a morose malamute named Mac, who seldom took much notice of her nocturnal efforts. He sat down heavily, slurping his well-sugared tea and tipping back his chair at a dangerous angle. Taking this as her cue to depart, she skipped nimbly down via a couple of desk drawers left slightly ajar for the purpose but stopped short the moment her feet touched the linoleum. Her ears twitched.

"Oh, go ahead, take it, Poppy. I should stop at home and get my garden in shape, anyway. And I've been to most of the matches this season already." Nadine recognised DC Tierney's pleasant tenor with its slight lilt. "You and Fiona deserve a bit of fun. Lord knows we don't get much of it here."

Nadine peeped around the corner of the desk and watched in horror as the calico, their only female constable and not used to such kindness except from the Irish setter, hesitantly took the proffered ticket. She stifled a squeak. It was all going wrong, and on her watch! She slid down onto the

185

floor and tried to block out the voice in her head, the one that told her she was a failure and that nothing she did would ever go right. 'No time for that!' she told herself. 'You must make it work!'

Mac's breathing had become very regular and a bit nasal, so Nadine hopped back up on the desk and carefully removed the mug of tea from his paw. The last thing she needed was a mess to mop up. She studied the dog for a moment, and when she saw a bit of drool forming in the corner of his jowl, she felt she was safe for a while. 'Think, girl, think!'

She glanced around the desk and straightened a few piles before her eye fell on the stack of schedules she'd been labouring over the night before. Could she manage it? Maybe just. She reached for fresh forms and dragged them to the typewriter. After a bout of gymnastics on the keys and a bit of a struggle with the carriage—whilst frequently looking over her shoulder at the somnolent Mac—Nadine looked with some satisfaction at the two sheets before her. Gavin would be delighted to know that he would be spared duty at the football match. She had it on good authority that he wouldn't be upset about his ticketless state, either, as he was staunchly a Welsh supporter and had no love for either team.

There was a snort from behind her, and she nearly jumped out of her fur. "This tea is rubbish," Mac grumbled. "Why didn't you make me a cup this morning? I had to cadge some of the slop from the urn this morning. That's why I've got you, what?"

"Sorry, sir," Nadine replied, hastily replacing the schedules. "I'll make you a cup now, if you'd like."

"Oh, don't bother. I'm sure you have far more important things to do," he said irritably. Nadine sighed inwardly and reached for the cup.

Home at last, she had settled into a corner by the electric fire, having decided that it was worth forgoing her favourite bakery buns for a week in order to turn on all three bars and have a thoroughly warm tail and ears for a change. Her latest mystery from the library lay unheeded on her lap as she reflected on what promised to be a successful gambit for NiceMice. Perhaps Zach would be pleased enough that she could become a full-time agent…

The telephone bell shattered her reverie. It was Harvey from the pub. "Nadine!"

"Yes, Harvey," she said with deliberate calm. Really, he could have at least said "hello."

"Poppy has been in," he squeaked down the line.

"Yes, what of it?"

"She said Fiona absolutely can't make it to the match—family 'do, apparently—and she was looking about for someone to give the ticket to. Said DC Tierney gave it up for Poppy, and they felt ever so bad about it. What's going on? Didn't you get the Chief's message?"

Nadine felt her paws going cold. "Of course, I did."

"Well, she tried to give it back to him, but he wouldn't hear of it. And you'll never guess who wanted it!"

"No, I have no idea," Nadine replied.

"Gavin, that's who. Says he needs a good laugh and plans to sing 'Sosban Fach' the whole time."

"Oh, okay."

"But his pal Owen, he's from the same village, wants to come, too, so Gavin passed on the ticket to him, and switched schedules with Ted, so Gavin will be on duty but still in on the fun." Harvey ended with a wheeze.

Nadine's head whirled. "He *what*?"

"I know. Sorry, love. I tried to think of something to stop them, but what could I say? Sounds like a right pickle."

Nadine hung up the phone, sat down again, and put her head in her paws. The voice in her head started up again, but she found herself saying "pickle sandwich" aloud to drown it out.

It was well into the night before Nadine managed to get to sleep. Her mind was racing—she couldn't let Zach down and desperately needed to find a way for Ted to get to the football match of his own accord. She had a mind to call Uncle Napoleon for some advice, but then thought better of it. She couldn't go running to him every time she had a problem. As she told herself, 'when you find yourself in a pickle, get out your knife and fork and start making sandwiches,' and that seemed the best thing she could do.

After waking bright and early, she sat at the kitchen table, buttered her toast, and tried to consider her predicament with a fresh pair of eyes. She knew Ted was a conscientious type and that Gavin could be rather lazy, with a habit of doing what was necessary and no more. The best solution to her problem seemed to be to slip a new note into Ted's pigeonhole and tell him that there was the potential for some crowd trouble at the game. But that might look odd. Who at the station house would write an anonymous message like that? Surely Detective Inspector Plunkett would make it an official memo. Mac didn't take notice of anything, and in the unlikely event that he did have some sort of tip to pass on, he would certainly want to take credit for it. The other constables would feel duty-bound to inform DI Plunkett as a matter of course. Nadine sipped her rapidly cooling tea and tapped her paw on the table. 'Think, Nadine, think! They're counting on you.' Her only consolation was that it was her morning off, so her time and thoughts were her own for a change. She rose and pattered over to her favourite corner of the couch, pulling off the knitted pink blanket preparatory to wrapping herself in it. As she did so, her book clattered to the floor.

"Rats!" she exclaimed, allowing herself to utter one of the worst imprecations in mousedom. "I'll not find my place for ages now." It lay splayed open on the floor, spine up. She reached for it, sighed, and sat down, not yet bothering to search out her chapter. Her eyes fell on the page to which the book had opened itself.

Gina rose from her desk and slipped into her mackintosh. She knew exactly what she needed to do next.

"Bully for her," Nadine muttered grumpily, and then reproached herself. Really, she would end up as sour as Mac if she wasn't careful.

Pulling on her hat with a determined air, she exited through the half-glass door with "Goud & Associates, Private Enquiries" in gold lettering and made her way through a maze of streets until she came to a phone box never frequented by those in her office's neighbourhood. After a quick glance to make sure there were no other mice about, she dialled the number she'd memorised. "Mr Hersham," she intoned in a deep and resonant voice. "Something has come to my attention, and I must relay it to you..."

Nadine tossed the book aside with a fervour that would have made the town librarian weep and jumped up, forgetting that she had cocooned herself in the blanket. She ended up in a heap on the floor, but the mishap didn't faze her. She lay there for a few moments, smiling, then reached for the book and kissed it. "Thank you, Gina Goud," she said aloud.

Saturday morning dawned in an equivocal fashion, committing neither to sunshine nor showers. Ted opened one eye and remembered that he had the whole blessed day off, though in his pleasantly sleepy state, he couldn't remember why. He pulled the coverlet over his head and began drifting off into a dream that involved curly cream-coloured fur. With the inevitability of telephones on Saturday mornings the world over, the instrument on his bedside table began ringing shrilly. "Oh, argh, you bally nuisance," he groaned when it refused to stop. He fumbled around for the receiver. "Ted here," he mumbled into it, heard nothing, and then realised the thing was the wrong way round. He righted it and repeated himself.

" 'Ello, Mister Ted? Ted Tierney?" came a cracked voice. "Listen, mate, I don't wanna get into trouble meself, but I 'ear tell there's some sorta shenanigans brewin' this afternoon. At the match, mind. Could be them rotters from next town over, not sure. And ya didn't 'ear it from me. Just a concerned citizen, I am."

"Who is this?" Ted asked, rubbing his eyes and considering the possibilities. Most of them would have spent the evening before at the local and wouldn't be in any state to be calling him at this hour. But the caller had rung off.

Now fully awake, Ted stretched his long, lean body and shook his ears. "Some sort of crank, probably," he said to himself as he shuffled into the kitchen. "Same as they've been getting at the library lately. But how did he know my number?" He couldn't very well ignore it, and he knew Gavin would laugh it off. He looked out the window at his tangled garden and sighed. "Sorry my lovelies. Ted's off to the races, it seems."

A few days later, an envelope appeared under Zach's office door. He finished his buttered crumpet, dabbed at his whiskers with a handkerchief and slid off the chair to investigate. Inside was a neatly written document headed "Nadine Lefevre." The said applicant seemed to be seeking permanent employment with the agency in any capacity. Among the list of qualifications, the words "voice impersonations" were underlined twice. Zach scratched his chin as an image of the tidy little mouse with large glasses and an unconsciously winsome manner presented itself. "Yeeess,"

189

he said to himself. "I think the firm could do with someone like you."
Returning to his desk, he picked up the phone.

Chapter Forty-Six
Sandbags, Sausages and Stubbornness

As the wind howled like a proverbial banshee, Stanley remembered back to one of his last conversations with Winnie, when he had suggested there was a storm on its way. At the time, he hadn't much believed in the possibility himself, merely intent on trying to convince her to stay for a while longer or even prevent her from going on her trip. Sitting in the classroom of the Badger's Bay primary school, with a red and blue checked blanket across his shoulders, he now somewhat regretted that he'd had cause to tempt fate.

Chief had arrived early that morning at Bertie's cottage, along with Marlon and several other of his old rescue colleagues and was knocking on the door ferociously to wake Stanley up. If the bird hadn't already been awake and eating his second helping of sausages and fried bread, he would have been most upset at the interruption of his beauty sleep. On opening the door, he had seen a very worried Newfoundland, who insisted that a squall off the southeast was turning into a force ten gale.

"It will most likely cause a high tide with very real potential for damage, especially to this little cottage. It's too unprotected," he'd said. The dog was insistent that Stanley move to safer ground. But the budgie had heard several the tall tales of past freak weather occurrences and had shrugged them off as stories that grew in stature with every telling. He really didn't feel inclined to leave his home.

"I'll be fine enough on me old roof beam," Stan insisted. "Been through worse than a bit of rain and wind, ya know. And Bertie left me to keep an eye on things. Take that very seriously, I do," he said with some pride, puffing out his ample green chest.

"And both Bertie and Winnie asked that I watch out for you," Chief said firmly. He'd expected some recalcitrance from the bird and was prepared to stand his ground. Stan cocked his head and considered what Chief had said. Suddenly his mood changed.

"I can take care of meself!" he squawked. " 'Ow do they think I've managed to survive this far? They goes off an' gallivants 'round the world without so much as a by-yer-leave, and then they tells you ta 'watch out' fer me? Bosh!" He had rumpled up his feathers so that he appeared twice his usual size and, he thought, rather fierce. Flying up to the beam, he glowered down at Chief, forgetting the remainder of his breakfast in his fit of pique. "I's stayin' right 'ere, come 'ell or 'igh water."

The Newfie let the torrent of words roll off of him. "Suit yourself," he said. "But are you certain you've got enough provisions to last out the storm?" He sidled over to the plate with its lone remaining sausage and extended his paw. In a flash, Stan whipped down and filched it, nearly swallowing it whole before his feet touched the chair.

"So 'ow long do ya reckon this squall's gonna last, then?" he asked, as nonchalantly as he could, considering that he was slathered in grease.

The cottage was constructed of heavy stone walls which would protect from strong winds, but rising water was a different matter. The reason Chief had come mob-handed was because he had intended to help move some of the contents to higher ground, which in this case meant the loft space. The most valuable possessions, such as those in the memory cabinet, were wrapped in newspaper and boxed up. Clothes, books and papers were also moved into the loft. Most of the furniture had to stay where it was, except for lighter items that were stacked onto tables. At Stanley's insistence, though, Chief hauled Bertie's well-worn leather chair, the little cabinet with brass handles filled with packets of letters and the driftwood coat tree up the ladder. Much to the bird's dismay, though, Chief insisted that the food be left in the cupboards. "Time to head for shelter," he said, nodding toward Stan's flap at the top of the door. Stan took one last longing look at his home and departed.

The team of workers outside had set about filling bags of sand, which was of course in plentiful supply, and bolstering up the front and back doorways. There was little else they could do, and saving lives always had to be prioritised above preventing property damage. Within the hour, the wind started picking up and rain began to fall, heralding the coming storm. Stanley had packed a suitcase of belongings and jammed as many of his favourite Garibaldi biscuits in as possible, despite crushing them in his rush. Chief had finished his tasks, and they prepared to move to the safety of the local primary school where an emergency shelter had been organised.

Chapter Forty-Seven
Lottie Meets a Dragon

"Excuse me," Winnie said. "I wonder if I could trouble you for just a moment. Is this the bus we should get to go into Cooper's Wood? We would like to settle a disagreement. I think it is, my friend here thinks the opposite, and we would value your opinion."

"Oh, yes, dear, if you want to get there, then this is the one for you, although there might be a little hold up as we have some guests," the portly cat said, pointing to a queue of passengers waiting to board.

"It's only a short ride, and we'll be waiting an age if we have to catch the next one," Lottie said impatiently. Winnie turned to Lottie, who persuaded her to sneak on. "Okay, but on your head be it," Winnie replied. There were a few protestations from the waiting football fans at the front of the queue, but Lottie quashed their grumbling easily. "Ladies first, I'm sure you would agree," she tossed over her shoulder as she hopped on. Most of the supporters were dressed in various yellow attire, from hats to scarves, so in fact, Winnie fitted right in.

Strangely, there was no one taking payments, but they soon forgot that when they had settled in on the back seat and got comfortable. The pair watched as the supporters started to pile in, some pushing and shoving for the best seats while the driver commanded them to be civil. In between the yellow t-shirt-clad supporters, the team mascot appeared, heading down the aisle in a lion's costume.* "I love the colour of the shirts," Lottie said, "but I wouldn't want to stay in that costume all this way. Whoever is inside that lion must be baking hot."

"I agree," Winnie said, but quickly lost interest in the doings of their fellow passengers. She pulled out her map and started studying it.

The lion worked its way to the back of the coach and sat alongside Lottie, promptly ducking down a little in the seat, though the vast head remained firmly on. The mane flicked in Lottie's face, much to her annoyance. The lion was surprisingly big close up and wobbled a bit as the coach engine started.

"Are you okay in there?" Lottie asked.

"Sssshhhh," came the reply. "I'm hiding in here. I don't want my parents to find out I came. I should have been staying with Aunt Maude, but I so wanted to see the match."

Lottie did as she was told for once. She had been in enough scrapes as a puppy to feel a bit of sympathy. She grabbed a couple of wine gums from her bag and began chewing on them instead of being her usual talkative self.

"Everyone here?" the driver shouted over the tannoy system. "We'll be off in a mo," he assured them. A cheer sounded from the supporters and chorus of "we're on our way, this is our day, hurrah."

"Alright there, Parsley?" a supporter said as he appeared from behind the seat in front of Lottie. There was no reply, just a nod, so Lottie covered for the lion.

"I gave it some of my wine gums, probably got its jaws stuck together. Here, would you like one?" She offered the pack to the cat in front of them, who thanked her after grabbing a handful. He popped one in its mouth and then threw the others at his compatriots in the seats ahead.

The journey progressed as expected, with various team songs sung and merriment all round. Winnie had her nose stuck to the window watching the signs to track their progress. When they passed the town, she gasped and quickly turned to Lottie, holding the map up. "We've missed our stop! Look!"

The cat who had thrown the wine gums turned around again. "We thrashed that borough two weeks ago, keep up." Lottie looked at Winnie, and it finally dawned on them that they weren't on a bus at all and were now stuck for the rest of the journey. Resigned to the fact, they sat back in their seats, not wishing to embarrass themselves any further.

When the coach pulled into the parking area of a relatively small football ground, the supporters let out a big cheer. Dogs and cats started gathering their possessions and jumped up, ready to disembark. During the melee, a rather concerned dog started running down the aisle. "Cleo, quick, you need to get out of that suit, someone has told your parents! Jump out of the emergency door or something."

The head was whipped off, and a small pup's worried face appeared.

"I can't do that. The alarm will go off, Mitch," she replied in a panicky voice as she started removing various other bits of the costume. Lottie was watching with interest.

"Here, give it to me," she said, giving her coat to Winnie. "Duck down there," she commanded, taking the costume just as Cleo's mother appeared

"You really are the giddy limit, my girl. There will be trouble when I get you home. Now take that disguise off this instant before you dehydrate, you silly pup!" The dog promptly reached for the lion's head and pulled it off.

"Oh, my goodness," she gasped as she realised her mistake. "I'm so sorry." The cockapoo smiled back at her.

"That's okay," Lottie said, laughing. "Looks like someone was pulling your chain."

Cleo's mother disappeared back down the coach, and the pup unfolded herself from the scrunched position under the seat. "Thanks for that! You saved my bacon there. I think I'd better go and mix with the home fans and keep out of sight. Don't want any repeats of that—my dad would have my guts for garters."

"Looks like we have a new mascot," Mitch said with a laugh. "Don't worry, old Leonard doesn't do much, just a short walk around the pitch before kick-off and a wave to the kiddies and that's about it. Just don't ask about the nuns."

Winnie looked pleadingly at Lottie, hoping she would get out of the suit and they could be on their way, but she had a sneaking suspicion that the glint in Lottie's eyes meant she had other ideas.

"I think I can do that," Lottie said as she jumped up with the lion's head in her paw, handed her bag to Winnie and hopped off the coach with Mitch at her side. Winnie sighed as she realised that Lottie had got a free pass into the game, whilst she would have to pay to get through the turnstiles. 'Typical,' she thought, 'always the bridesmaid.'

Winnie found a quiet spot at the top of the small stadium and watched as the players began to warm up below. The rows of red and white seats beneath her started to fill as the music blared over the tannoys. Down on the pitch, she spotted the lion mascot striding into the centre circle, waving at the crowd. Cheers erupted from the away supporters on the terrace as they sang out "Lenny! Lenny!" It seemed that the crowd's adoration, along with the change in music to "Go your own way" kicked something off in the lion, as it now started dancing wildly in the centre spot and strutting up and down. Even the rivalry between the home and away fans seemed to be forgotten as both sets concentrated on the spectacular dancing rather than taunting each other. Winnie remembered her friend's story about the disastrous prom and smiled. She jumped up to cheer her on.

Unbeknown to Lottie, the home mascot, a dragon called Sid, was not amused. He had been making his way to the pitch to do his usual routine when he'd been hijacked by Lenny. Running towards the lion, he grabbed its paw and swung it round causing the mascot to fall down. Thankfully, the lion suit didn't have a long tail, as it kept getting covered in mud and needing to be cleaned. Dazed, but not for long, Lottie got up. Both sets of fans started cheering and jeering in equal measure, wondering what would happen next. Lottie decided that, rather than engage the dragon, she would simply walk around the centre circle as if she had captured the dragon, getting back into her rhythm with the music. This didn't go down well with Sid at all. Realising that he had been made to look foolish, he steamed head-first into the lion, rugby tackling it to the ground. During the scuffle, the lion's head rolled off, and the crowd let out a collective gasp. Many young pups started booing, others started crying. One member of the audience couldn't believe what he was seeing, stood up and rushed to help.

Ted wrestled the dragon away from Lottie and led her safely off the pitch to avoid any further confrontation. Smitten with her exploits, he squeezed her paw and smiled down at her. "If only my name was George, eh, Charlie?"

"I think you saved the dragon from me, actually," Lottie replied, tossing her head playfully. "I was just about to give him a slug in the chops."

*Shane the Lion: The chapter was inspired by the true story of a lion called 'Shane' who lived in Woking, England. In the 1970s, Ron Voice bought the cub from a Birmingham pet shop. The lion became a much-loved member of the family and a regular at the public house in Woking, The Albion. Ron worked at his town centre taxi firm, and Shane would sit in a van parked in the road nearby. Parents were often seen lifting their curious children to peer through the windows of the van where Shane spent much of his day, and the RSPCA was inundated by worried residents. Later, the pair lived in a double decker bus. However, the adolescent Shane caused a scene in the town when he spotted bookkeeper Poppy Hull on her way to work, dressed in a faux leopard skin coat. Shane pulled the bumper off the van he was tethered to, bounded over and pounced on the unsuspecting Mrs Hull, causing her to fall over. She was unhurt, but outraged councillors claimed the lion had given the town a bad name and vowed to push new legislation through parliament to outlaw the keeping of unlicensed wild animals as pets. Shane was eventually banned from being exercised in public unless caged. Ron and Shane had left Woking by the time of the hearing on March 23, 1976, and the exact fate of the lion is unknown, although he is rumoured to have gone to a safari park.

Chapter Forty-Eight
The Railway Cat

Winnie was sitting on a bench on platform one of Pawbury railway station, chewing on the end of a ballpoint pen.[*] The building was of Victorian design, a burgundy clapboard construction with cream paint on much of the ornately scalloped wood surrounding the peaked roof. The clock face in the cupola up top suggested that it was nearly lunchtime, but she wasn't really hungry. The station sign creaked a little on its hinges, and the melancholy sound made her sigh. She was thinking what to write to Aunt Bea and Uncle Frederick. It had been several weeks since she had left on her travels, and she had promised to keep her aunt up to date with events as well as she could. Of course, she would only give the highlights, as she didn't want to admit to hitchhiking a ride with Reggie or sleeping under the stars, for fear of worrying the poor Westie half to death. As she pondered, a train pulled up to the opposite platform. She looked up momentarily and caught sight of a cat inside pulling down the window.

"Hey there, George, how's things?" he shouted.

Winnie looked around and saw a marmalade cat sweeping the platform. He stopped what he was doing and engaged with the passenger.

"I visited a fortune teller at the weekend," the cat on the train continued. "Told me I would come into some money...just hoping it didn't mean I'd find a fifty pence piece on the ground! The way you keep this station so clean, I think there's no chance of that."

The station cat smiled and waved cheerily as the train began to chug away, then continued with his duties, humming away happily.

It was unlike Winnie to be lost for words for her letter, but she was finding things to be a bit difficult in general. Lottie had gone on her way with Ted, the Irish setter, and she was feeling rather lonely and sad. Her aspirations for the whole trip abroad were now rapidly falling apart. She had hoped Douglas would join her, but that hadn't happened yet either. Winnie didn't want to admit to Aunt Bea that she was now travelling alone, so she decided it might be best to wait before sending anything. A moment later the sound of the broom sweeping the platform came close by, and the station cat spoke.

"Hello there," he said in a cheery voice. "I think you might want to make a quick trip to the bathroom, lass. You are in danger of turning into a Smurf if you carry on like that." He waved a paw at the blue ink stain across her top.

Winnie looked down in embarrassment. "Oh dear, I'm a terror. I'm always doing that when in deep thought, thank you. I'm Win-Win—oh, I mean Winnie." She laughed a little as she realised that she had just called herself by Lottie's pet name for her.

"Pleased to make your acquaintance, Winnie. I'm George," the cat replied, tipping his cap slightly.

After giving herself a clean-up in the station facilities, Winnie returned, smiling at George, who had disposed of his broom and was now up a ladder cleaning the concourse windows.

"That's better, all sorted," he said, as he looked down at the dachshund. "Happier now?"

"I must say," Winnie said, "your lavatories were spotless. I've found it quite rare to find a place so clean and presentable. Normally..." she paused. "I won't say. You know what I mean?"

George stepped down the ladder and peered critically at a window that looked spotless to Winnie. Inside were some newly painted station signs leaning against the wall, alongside some cans and carpentry tools in what looked like a tidy workroom. The cat gave the glass an expert rub and stepped back, nodding with evident satisfaction. "Why thank you, I'm here to please. My passengers deserve the best, and I can't abide by a messy station. What would my grandfather think?"

"Grandfather?" Winnie asked.

"Oh, yes, the station dates to the Victorian age. My grandfather helped design it. He was called George, too. Immensely proud of the place, just as I am. Railways are in our blood, you know. Things happen like that sometimes—I couldn't dream of doing anything else. After father passed away, I became the custodian in a sense, and I live in a carriage in the sidings. The station primarily served the locals as a commuter line, but back in the sixties it was shut down.[†] As much as I tried, I couldn't keep the place up on my own, so a group of locals saved it from demolition, and we eventually managed to raise some money to restore the exterior to its original condition. It's a labour of love I suppose. The station is run for the community, and there aren't a lot of services. Most trains fly by nowadays, but it keeps me busy, and there's always something to do."

"Wow, I'm impressed. So, it was you inside the ticket office earlier, wasn't it? And now you are the handyman! You certainly do wear many hats," Winnie remarked.

"I do, all part of being the station master," he replied. "Keeps me out of mischief, as the wife always says."

George put his bucket away and leaned comfortably on a railing near Winnie's bench, his eyes scanning the tracks expertly. For a moment, she was reminded of Bertie, never mind that George was a cat. "I must be homesick," she thought, and then remembered with a bit of a pang that Bertie wasn't back at home, anyway.

George broke into her thoughts. "So, where are you heading?"

"I really don't know," Winnie replied in a slightly dejected tone. "I had grand visions of travelling merry old England, discovering new places, seeing new things, but, I… I'm kind of at a bit of a loss now. I'm not sure what to do."

"Really, that is a predicament, but there's no problem that can't be sorted, I always say." George looked at her kindly. "I saw you waving a cockapoo friend off earlier, so you must be feeling a mite lonely. Perhaps you'd care to join me at the railway café for a spot of lunch? A problem shared is a problem halved, you know," George said, pointing to the two chairs and a small table outside the office. Winnie looked puzzled.

"Oh, when I say 'café,' I may have been exaggerating things a tad, but I make a lovely pot of tea, and I'm more than happy to share my sandwiches with you. Salmon Saturday, I call it," the cat said, licking his lips as his whiskers twitched. "Not as nice as Tuna Tuesday, but it will have to do. Oh, and for afters I have something new. I found a place not far from here that sells oyster ice cream, sounds a treat. I've not tried it yet, and the wife swears blind that it will be awful, but you never know."

"That would be nice," Winnie said, her smile returning. She was always happier with pleasant company.

*Pawbury Railway Station:** The railway station referenced in this chapter was based on the one found in Swampscott, Massachusetts. It is an historic railroad station originally built in 1868 for the Eastern Railroad but is no longer in use. It was designed by George W. Cram, a Boston housewright. The depot was renovated by a group of locals in the 1980s to save it from demolition, but the work was only temporary. In 1997, a town committee raised money to restore the exterior to its original condition, but no interior work was done. Since 1998, it has been on the National Register of Historic Places.

†**Beeching Axe:** The Beeching cuts, also known as the Beeching Axe, was a plan to increase the efficiency of the railway system in Great Britain. Two reports, *The Reshaping of British Railways* (1963) and *The Development of the Major Railway Trunk Routes* (1965), were written by Richard Beeching and published by the British Railways Board. Each report was very controversial. The first recommended thousands of miles of railway line and stations for closure to stem the losses of the nationalised railways against its competition, in the form of motorways. The second report identified routes to invest in and was less well publicised. Most of the the reports' recommendations were enacted, and Beeching's name remains synonymous with the mass closure of the railways.

Chapter Forty-Nine
Cat Amongst the Pigeons

"My eldest," George said in a comfortably chatty sort of way, as he pulled out a seat for Winnie and disappeared into the office to grab his sandwiches. "Now, she used to travel on the train to get to school. It was only one stop down but too far to walk. One winter the train was delayed, but it was no obstacle, I just telephoned down the line and convinced the signal dog to stop a goods train in the station, allowing my Dottie to travel home on the footplate."

"Really," Winnie said. "That was kind."

"Oh, we railway people stick together, it's like an extended family," George explained. "Here, try one of these." He unwrapped the foil from some brown bread sandwiches filled with cress and salmon and handed one to Winnie.

"Do you ever get any awkward passengers, then?" Winnie asked.

"Oh, lots of them, but many a time they make for an interesting anecdote. For instance, we had one cat come in and ask for tickets to Ireland. 'Ireland' I said, 'that's across the sea! Trains don't travel on water you know.' 'Haven't you ever heard of a boat train, then?' she retorted and went away in a quite a huff. I doubt she ever got there."

"Oh dear," Winnie laughed. "You do have some funny ones, don't you?"

"That's not even scratching the surface, my girl. Back when we had catering carriages on the route, a passenger once activated the emergency alarm. When the furore was over, he was asked why he'd done it. Can you guess what he said?"

Winnie shook her head.

" 'The wretched tea is cold! The trolley steward should be ashamed of himself.' "

The doxie burst into giggles.

"Well, as you can imagine, he was ejected from the train with a big boot up the backside by the rather grumpy guard who wasn't having a good day. I felt obliged to offer him a proper brew, and he left a happy bunny after that."

"Marvellous," Winnie said. "I once got stuck on a train back near Badger's Bay when a dog got his Christmas tree wedged in the train doors."

"Oh, dear me," George said, munching on his second sandwich and licking his paws contentedly. "That was delicious. Ready for some ice cream?"

Winnie was slightly unsure, but not wishing to let down her gracious host, she accepted with some trepidation. She seemed fated to have to try the stuff. George came back outside with two bowls, each containing a rectangle segment of ice cream and a wafer stuck in the top.

"Tuck in," George said as he grabbed his spoon.

Winnie slowly scooped up a small piece of ice cream and placed it in her mouth. For a moment, as it melted, she thought it tasted quite pleasant. But then the flavour really kicked in, and as she gulped it down, she coughed several times.

George was watching Winnie and could see from her expression what she thought of the delicacy. "Ewwww, that is disgusting," he groaned as he put the spoon back in the bowl. "What was I thinking? I am sorry."

"Oh, so glad you agree, I didn't want to appear rude," Winnie said between chokes. 'I wonder if the donkeys thought the same,' she thought as she quickly washed away the flavour as best, she could with her tea.

Just as the pair finished laughing, they heard flapping behind them as several new passengers entered the station. George looked up and noticed a family of pigeons coming towards him, lugging their bulging suitcases, and looking rather miffed.

"Why is there no one in the ticket office? The next train is due soon! I've got the whole family here needing tickets," the father said, plumping his chest out and displaying his purple plumage, not that it needed much plumping as it was already rather sizable to say the least. George excused himself temporarily to deal with the rabble rousers. Winnie turned back around and just caught sight of something flicking across her vision, down from the end of the platform. Two whippets were throwing a ball to each other extremely near the track. She realised this was quite a relatively unused railway, but all the same, it was an extremely dangerous thing to be doing. George was tied up dealing with the troublesome pigeons, and no one else seemed to be bothered, so she felt she had to take things into her own paws.

Winnie approached the dogs carefully, as she didn't want them running away across the tracks. Even though she couldn't hear any diesel locomotive coming, a train travelling at speed would be there within seconds once it rounded the bend just up the line.

"Hey there," she said calmly and in a low enough voice not to cause alarm. The dogs looked up, noted the small dachshund and then continued what they were doing. "Well, if you don't want the free ice cream they are handing out at the station, then it's your call," she shrugged. "There's probably none left now anyway." With that, she turned and walked back up towards the platform.

The whippets stopped and looked at each other, each certain that he knew what the other was thinking. "I'll get there first," Robbie said.* "Not if I get there first," Albury replied, and they shot up past the sauntering Winnie. When she got back to the seats, she and George had recently vacated, she could see the two dogs scooping up the ice cream from the bowls she and George had left. They were shovelling it into their mouths as if they hadn't eaten for days. In the short time it took for Winnie to get back to the table, the pair had gobbled the lot and were looking incredibly pleased with themselves.

"That was delicious," Robbie said.

Winnie was quite amused, as her original rather devious thought had slightly backfired. George returned, having placated the family of fowl, though they were still arguing amongst themselves about who would get the window seat when the train arrived.

"Mmm, now what have we got here then, causing some troubles are we?" George said.

"Oh, no sir, we were eating this lovely free ice cream that was on offer," Robbie replied.

"Got any more?" Albury asked.

"That depends," George said. "I haven't seen you two before. What are your names?"

"I'm Robbie and he's Albury. We've just moved in," Robbie said, smiling.

"Mmm, don't think I didn't see you two up there near the tracks. You know how dangerous that can be, don't you? Makes no difference whether you are new here or not."

Robbie and Albury held their heads down, feeling very ashamed of themselves. "We, er, we were only playing, no harm in that, is there? We weren't going on the tracks."

"Quite the opposite, but I'm not going to lecture you on the matter. I think you are bright enough to realise the dangers. All I will say is that if I ever catch you doing anything like that again, there will be trouble, okay?"

"Okay," the whippets replied in unison.

"And if you promise to stick to the rules, then there'll always be some ice cream here for you too, understand? Now run along home," George said.

"Oh, yes, definitely," the whippets said and left with their ball.

George returned his attention to Winnie. "That was a fine bit of diplomacy there, I must say, marvellously done, young Winnie. Now, what are we going to do about your problem, then?" He looked at her in a fatherly manner. "I'm sure I could ask Hal to let you hitch a ride up the line if you wanted to visit London. Have you been yet?"

Winnie shook her head. "I'm not sure I'm quite ready for that," she said.

"Arh, no one is ever quite ready for London. But I've insisted that each of my kits go when they were just about your age. Does 'em a world of good, broaden their horizons, that sort of thing. All will be well, you'll see." And George rubbed his paws together eagerly. "Now, let's just sort out your ticket, shall we?"

---

*"**Robbie**": One of the whippets in this chapter is named "Robbie," about a 13-minute-long film first made by British Transport Films in 1979. The

film was shown in schools all over Great Britain to encourage rail safety. It tells the story of a young boy who trespasses on the line and suffers a disfiguring and/or fatal accident. Three different versions were made to demonstrate the dangers of both electrified and non-electrified lines. Peter Purvis originally narrated the films but was later replaced by Keith Chegwin during the revisions. The films were a replacement to the very graphic and controversial film "The Finishing Line," which dealt with the same issue.

Chapter Fifty
Any Old Port in a Storm

Badger's Bay primary school was not a large building, but it was sturdy and a safe distance from the water. Only about twenty kits and pups were looked after by two teachers and a head. The head was away on holiday, so it was left to Cilla, the white and brown tabby, to organise the troops. The gymnasium had been opened to accommodate the majority of those in need of shelter, with blankets and bedding provided by local volunteer groups. It was a real team effort.

Cilla couldn't rest until she had done a thorough scout around the hedge bordering the school's playground to check for any wayward youngsters. This done, she slipped back inside the gym, looked down at her muddy paws and shook her head. She'd had to crawl on all fours under one rather overgrown bush. "You're as messy as one of the kittens," she muttered and gave herself a thorough washing up before taking up her post by the door. As most of the village's youngest cats and dogs appeared, Cilla welcomed them in with her customary cheerful demeanour, also noting down their names in her little notebook.

"You'll all be safe as houses in here," she assured them, her heart going out to a doleful-looking Dandie Dinmont who had just entered. "Your mums and dads are busy just now making sure everyone has a place to stay, but they'll be back for you when the storm's over, don't you worry. In the meantime, there are plenty of books and toys for everyone."

Stanley wasn't best pleased to think he was going to have to share his new digs with anyone, let alone a rabble of noisy youngsters. He'd grumpily found a perch in the corner of the room furthest from any activity and looked forward to this ordeal being over as soon as possible. From the window, Cilla could see the trees shaking in the wind, while overhead wires were being whipped up and the roads were already forming into small rivers. She double checked that the door was firmly closed and looked around to see if there was anyone in need of assistance, comforted by the fact that several kittens had already taken up residence in a small tepee in the reading area.

Several the pupils that attended the school had joined the group in the shelter, some were looking a bit scared, others more annoyed that they had to come to school on the weekend. Stan watched from his vantage point and tried to keep himself to himself.

"So, what do you want to be when you grow up?" Cilla said to a little group, trying to keep them engaged.

"Oh, I want to go into space and explore the universe. I love discovering things," one pup replied.

Stanley watched, interested in hearing more. He doubted that this little thing could find his way to the bathroom on his own, let alone piloting a spacecraft.

"Yes, I want to be the first dog to land on the sun," the pup continued.

Cilla was a bit taken aback by the naivety of the comment and smiled. "Surely it would be too hot for that. Maybe Mars would be more suitable?"

"Oh, I'm only four but even I know that the sun is roasting hot, so that's why I'm going to go in the middle of the night, see."

Stanley smirked at the innocence of this pup and started nibbling on a Garibaldi biscuit that he had grabbed from his case. Cilla continued her path around the room, checking up on the children, whilst being followed by a little black pup. She stopped and spoke to a somewhat sulky Samoyed. "Haven't you made it up with Cammie yet? She is over there, and I'm sure she would enjoy playing with you."

"No," came the short reply.

"Why is that?" Cilla asked.

"She's not talking to me, so I'm not talking to her," came the reply.

"Well. Nothing will get sorted out at this rate, will it? It can't be that bad. Let me go and find out what the problem is." Cilla wandered off in Cammie's direction, again closely followed by the black pup, and returned five minutes later.

"I think I have got to the bottom of it. Cammie has just told me she dreamed that you two had a falling out. When she awoke, she was convinced it was real and so has been ignoring you. You know she has a stubborn streak, and I think she is feeling a little embarrassed. Perhaps you could go and give her this as a peace offering?" Cilla pulled out a small plastic brooch from her pocket, the type that wouldn't look out of place in a Christmas cracker, and gave it to the pup, who got up and did as she was told.

"Gosh, this is hard work," Cilla said out loud, without realising Stan was watching. "Are you still here?" she said as she looked down at the Dandie Dinmont. "You are following me around like a little lost soul. Would you follow me over a cliff?" she said rather jokingly. The pup looked up and smiled. "Oh, of course I would, just to make sure you weren't hurt after your fall. And I'd want to make sure you hadn't lost your pretty yellow scarf." He reached out and touched one of its green tassels fondly. Stanley laughed. There really was no reply to that. Cilla looked up at the plump budgie and walked over to him.

"Hello there. Sorry, I scarcely noticed you in all the rush," she said kindly. "You look like you could use some company. And little Cyril here needs some looking after. I'm pretty busy just now, so I'm thinking you could give me a bit of assistance. Oh, and I know for a fact that Garibaldis are Cyril's favourites," she added with a wink before hastening away to do a patrol of the corridor.

Chapter Fifty-One
Kindergarten Coop

Stanley took umbrage at the notion of sharing his biscuits with the little pipsqueak and quickly shifted them deep into the shadows of his corner. He was even more put out when he realised that he had inadvertently become a babysitter for the Dandie Dinmont, who was staring at him in a most disconcerting manner. Strangely, that look of Cyril's brought back some old memories. In his youth, Stan could often be found at the arcades, where he was employed as a sort of watch-bird. He would sit perched up on the ceiling lights, out of sight. Any trouble he spotted he would nip in the bud by alerting security before anything got out of hand.

The arcade had a range of novelty games and amusements to keep customers entertained, from pinball to the claw and even an old "What the Butler Saw" device. In the centre stood a set of "Penny Falls" machines. There was always someone playing these. They were quite addictive, always luring youngsters with glowing lights, shiny coins, the mesmerising action of the sliding coin trays and the possibility of a coin falling off by chance as the pile was pushed ever closer to the raised edge. If anyone took it upon themselves to accidentally bump into the casing to disturb the coins, Stan would be there, squawking at them. Often those pups that had used up all their pocket money elsewhere would begin watching others pop their coins in. If there was a windfall, they might be given a coin so they too could have a go. This Cyril's face wore the same hopeful expression, so Stan took pity on the poor little chap.

With an unaccustomed impulse towards generosity, Stan reached back into his case, pulled out a Garibaldi biscuit and handed it to Cyril, who immediately gulped it down whole. "Blimey, you do have an appetite," Stan remarked, somewhat surprised. The dog licked his lips and started panting for another. Now Stanley found himself with a dilemma. If he fed this dog any more of his treasured biscuits, they would soon run out.

Worse, he could see that some other young dogs were beginning to take notice.

"Now then, Cyril, me old mate, I can't be handing these out like candy or there will be none left." The pup did not seem to be particularly bothered by this situation, but Stanley hopped anxiously from one foot to the other, struggling to think of a way to divert attention away from his biscuits. He looked around at the walls of the gym at various drawings and paintings the students had created and had an idea.

"I know, go and find me something beginning with 's,' " he said. Surely these little ankle biters had learnt the alphabet, and if not, he would be quid's in anyway, as it would give him time to get a bit of shut eye. Cyril yipped happily and, looking like he knew what he was doing, bounded off to another corner of the room to investigate. As the scampering dog disappeared, Stan turned back to his suitcase, patted it fondly, and, certain that his stash was safe, allowed himself to close his eyes.

He awoke with a start, having been nudged in the side rather unceremoniously. Rubbing the sleep out of his eyes, he could see six dogs and cats all staring directly at him. It took a moment before he remembered the challenge, he had set Cyril. A pug pushed forward first, sliding a rather disgusting slug his way. "What the…?" Stanley said, stopping himself just in time. A Labrador puppy was next. She picked up her snail and threw it up to Stan's perch, who instinctively batted it away. It crashed against the climbing bars and cracked on the hard floor. 'Whoops,' Stan thought, as another dog raced over and gobbled it up.

A kitten jumped up and carefully dropped a spider onto Stan's head. Brushing vigorously to get it out of his feathers, he knocked it down in front of him, and the kitten pounced. The spider didn't fare too badly, running off behind the radiator with seven of its legs intact. A couple of caterpillars and an ant managed to find their way into the competition— obviously, Chinese whispers had led to some confusion about the initial letter, but at least there were no snakes. At last, it was Cyril's turn. He pulled out a small half pint bottle of silver-topped milk and handed it to Stan.

'What's this?' Stan wondered. This kid obviously had got completely the wrong end of the stick, although at least he had had the sense to offer something a bit more civilised. "This doesn't begin with 's,' " he called out. Cyril then threw up a plastic straw and barked.

"Oh, I suppose that is quite clever," Stanley admitted before congratulating them all on their endeavours. Cyril barked again which caused the others to start too, meows mixing with yaps, and all were looking at the bottle. Stan wasn't exactly partial to the white stuff, preferring it to be accompanied with a large amount of hot water and a teabag, but decided he had better do as instructed for fear of pandemonium breaking out. He picked up the blue straw, pierced the bottle top and began to drink. The milk tasted rather sour, but Stan could see the pups and kittens were now cheering and stamping their paws as he drank, almost as if he was at a pub drinking competition. Stan laughed and nearly choked on the milk, but continued drinking until the last drop, satisfying the crowd with a slurp and gurgle. A couple of seconds afterwards, he let out a large burp, which went down very well indeed, and he was hoisted aloft and carted round the gym like royalty. Thereafter, he was inspired to show off his various accomplishments, from the "Bumbling Budgie" act to napping upside down, although even he really couldn't fall asleep amid all the racket. Cilla watched from afar, smiling, as the wind battered the windows and rain slapped against the glass. Thanks to a rather unlikely entertainer, the little refugees from the storm were oblivious to the destruction raging outside.

Chapter Fifty-Two
All at Sea

Percy sat in a sunny corner of the Lower Grosvenor Gardens, where he had arranged to meet Hans in a half-hour's time. Victoria Station was nearby, and he could have waited there, but he much preferred the comparative calm in this little jewel of a spot. His bench was positioned near a whimsical shell-encrusted hut* from which a gardener emerged with a pair of secateurs. Percy nodded and smiled at him. 'Quite a few steps up from the allotment shed,' he thought, and reached out to touch the intricate geometric pattern on the wall next to him, tracing it with his paw. His mind roved back to a conversation he'd had with Hans some days ago after the series of untoward events at his house and allotment.

"It's all a bit too much to take in, Hans. I think I need a break away from here," he had said, his head in his paws.

"Understandably. Did you have anywhere in mind?" Hans replied.

"I think I told you that I've always had a hankering to revisit my childhood haunts, especially back in Hastings. Perhaps that is a good place to start?" Percy suggested tentatively. "I would miss London life, of course, the theatre and the bright lights, but perhaps I'm just not cut out for it any longer."

"What about your allotment? You don't want to leave that, do you?" the younger dog asked.

"One can grow flowers anywhere. Maybe I could even find a place with a proper garden. Most of the members would be quite happy to see the back of me anyway—it could easily have been one of them who did the damage, just out of spite," Percy said.

"Possibly," Hans replied, not sounding that convinced. But he remembered that he had offered to paint a portrait of Percy if he was ever back near the sea, so maybe this was an opportunity to spend a few days on the coast with his friend.

"What about booking in at one of the sea front hotels for a few days, give you some time to clear your head and have a think? If you like, I could come for the weekend, have a stroll around. I could even paint your portrait. What do you say?" Hans asked.

Percy's face brightened a little at the thought of getting away and the offer of some company.

Hans noted the dog's change of mood and continued to press the point carefully. "There are any number of trains that will take us there in no time at all. Just think, in a few days' time we could be living it up in sunny Hastings."

Percy laughed at the notion that Hastings had a thriving nightlife, although he really didn't know, it could have changed a fair bit since he was there. He looked out the window at the uninspiring fog and decided that he would allow himself to be persuaded. He really didn't feel comfortable returning home just yet and also didn't want to burden Hans by staying at his flat for too long.

"Excellent!" Hans said. "Let's celebrate our decision with a glass of wine. I haven't got any in the house, but there's a very cosy wine bar not too far away."

The pair passed Murdo as they exited the building, giving him a cheery wave and hailing a cab when they were on the street. He could guess who the Welsh terrier beside him was, not exactly what he had been expecting, but you could never quite tell what a dog looked like from the sound of his voice alone.

Hans touched Percy's arm and smiled at him. "I wasn't asleep," he said, a trifle defensively, rising quickly from the bench. Then he laughed at himself. "I suppose every dog over a certain age says that when caught lazing in the sun."

At the station they found the usual crowd of Londoners doing just what they were, escaping the confines of the city for outings either in the country or at the seaside. The young scampered about with abandon, whilst their elders either panted along behind them, burdened with baskets and bags, or just watched helplessly. Hans had prevailed upon Percy to don his boater for the occasion, and the dog looked quite in keeping with his fellow travellers in their madras shorts and floppy sun hats. Hans smiled and reflected that perhaps Percy had just been in the wrong setting for too long and would feel more at ease among the holiday makers of Hastings. Setting was everything, he mused, remembering a painting of an elegant Sphinx cat named Alice that he could never seem to get right—she had an elusive quality that defied any sort of ordinary backdrop.

He was startled out of his reflections by the conductor's whistle. "Oh, excuse me," a small dog said with a smile. "I believe this is yours. I saw a pup up on his dad's shoulders knock it off." She held out Percy's hat after hastily dusting it off.

"Why, thank you, young lady," Percy said, fixing it more firmly on his head.

"Of course," she said. "Have a good trip." The two gazed after the little reddish-brown dog for a moment before continuing their way.

"Who says American tourists are unpleasant?" Percy remarked. "Many's the time several of them have stopped for a chat with me after my routine. And then there's Bertie...well, he's nearly an American." He smiled, thinking of the peculiar occasion when they had met.

Hans had secured them seats in a second-class carriage and hoisted their kit up onto the luggage rack. He stood aside so that Percy could take the window seat. "Oh, no, you take it," Percy said. "I have seen this route many times in my life. I'd like for you to have the view." Hans smiled and slid into the seat. Percy leaned back against the white headrest.

"Oh, you do remember I had promised to paint you when we get to Hastings?" Hans asked.

"I do," the terrier said and then, by degrees, nodded off.

Hastings was a riot of colour and noise and smells, mostly pleasant, though there was always an underpinning of rubbishy odours from bins. Above it all was the startling screams of seagulls. After they had found their rooms at the hotel, Percy, his hat back on his head at a decidedly jaunty angle, immediately made for the pie whilst chattering like a schoolboy on holiday. All the while, though, he was taking in various changes: high rise blocks of flats, rather more concrete than he remembered and coaches full of sightseers chugging past on the main thoroughfare.

"Here we are," he said, with an expansive sweep of his paw. Hans took in the pleasing aspect of the domed and cupolaed buildings, with curved, arcaded "arms" on each side that embraced all comers. "It looks like something out of a fairy tale," he said admiringly. The two made their way through a turnstile and joined the masses surging to and from the end of the pier. Upon closer inspection, Hans noticed signs of decay and the odd patch-up job, flaking paint and rotting timbers here and there. And even he was a couple of decades older than the average holidaymaker here. Cats lounged against the railings in wide-legged jeans and flat caps, whilst a clutch of leather-clad dogs eyed them ominously from the opposite side. A bit of graffiti, some of it quite accomplished to Hans's eye, decorated several otherwise blank walls.

He noticed Percy visibly drooping, and he didn't at all like the rather unfriendly stares they were getting from all sides, so he nudged his friend gently. "What say we go find some lunch?" he suggested. "And I've got a hankering—I think that's the word? though it always sounds like 'handkerchief' to me—for an ice cream. Then we've got some work to do, as you know. I happened to see a perfect spot just along to the left of the pier, and it's not too crowded."

"Sounds a plan," Percy agreed.

*Shell Huts, Grosvenor Gardens:** The two shell huts referenced in the chapter do indeed exist and were built in 1952 as part of a re-landscaping of the Lower Grosvenor Gardens. The huts were said to be 'in the style of small pavilions that were known as *fabriques* in eighteenth-century France, an old French term which is known as a 'folly' in England. The park itself was designed by the then architect-in-chief of the National Monuments and Palaces of France, Jean Moreux. Some of the shells adorning the huts were brought over from France, whilst others taken from English beaches to reinforce the Anglo-French alliance. The huts themselves were used by the park's gardeners, one designated for the storage of tools and the other for the attendant.

Chapter Fifty-Three
Luxury's Lap

George smiled to himself in satisfaction as he returned to his ticket window. Not only had he gotten Winnie safely onto a train bound for London, but he had secured her a seat in a first-class compartment. There were always so many that were left empty, and he had exercised his prerogative as stationmaster to upgrade her lowly third-class ticket. He could do this, at his own discretion, a couple of times a month, and the wide-eyed wonder he'd seen on the doxie's face convinced him that he'd made the right choice. After he had waved her away, the cat had slipped into his office to make one or two calls to the city.

Winnie gazed around the compartment in awe. She'd never seen such splendour in a moving vehicle. Compared to the spartan railway cars back in New England, with their linoleum floors and slippery vinyl seats, this was the epitome of luxury. Glossy wood panelling and polished brass fittings bespoke opulence. Instead of standard fluorescent lighting, there were three small lamps on each side with conical matte glass shades. The plush velvet purple cushions were so soft to sit on, she thought she could fall asleep in seconds if her head so much as touched the back of the seat. Not wishing to do that and miss the sights from the window, she stowed her bags in the luggage rack above and perched on the edge of the seat.

But her observations of the lush fields and villages nestled among hills were interrupted by a light but insistent tap on the compartment's half-glass door. Winnie turned to see a Dalmatian's head, topped by a jaunty pillbox hat, discreetly looking away. She fiddled with the handle and pulled the door open. Dressed in a purple tunic with brass buttons marching up the front, the Dalmatian tipped his cap.

"Everything to your liking, Madam?" he asked. Winnie flushed a darker red under her whiskers with the pleasure of not being called "Miss."

"Oh, yes," she answered, trying not to gush too much. It wouldn't do for him to know that she was new to this sort of thing.

"Would Madam care for tea?" he enquired, whilst deftly rearranging her luggage on the rack. Winnie reflected that such an indulgence may not have been included in the price of her fare, which had really seemed very low even by her naive standards. She hesitated.

"Well, maybe a cup—"

"I'll just get it, then, shall I?" And the Dalmatian whisked away with an affable nod. Winnie reflected that she had been rather frugal thus far and was confident that she could afford a cup of tea and a cake. She turned her attention back to the window and smiled to herself when she saw a sprinkling of sheep on a hillside. 'Lottie's nemeses,' she thought. In no time at all, the distinctive tapping came again, muffled, she now realised, by the attendant's white gloves.

"Tea for one," the Dalmatian said, but he had nothing in his paws. She looked at him, puzzled, and he stepped aside to reveal a small, wheeled table covered with a white cloth and bearing a three-tiered tray, silver teapot, and various dishes.

"Heavens to—" Winnie exclaimed, and put her paw to her mouth just in time to stop herself from saying "Murgatroyd."

The Dalmatian looked at her questioningly. "I hope this meets your expectations, Madam. I fear that it is only the standard offering with this fare, but I trust that you were made aware of that when you purchased your ticket. I can of course fetch anything else you might like." He pushed the table into the compartment and expertly poured the tea, first holding the teapot close to the rim and then pulling it up high, even with his nose. "Here we have Assam, but if the lady prefers, I can bring a pot of China tea in its place. On the house...er, train."

"Oh, no, this is—splendid. Thank you," Winnie said, recovering herself. She reached for the napkin, folded into the shape of a swan, and regretfully shook it out into her lap, nodding at him as he departed. She was not exactly famished, having just shared George's salmon sandwiches a couple of hours before, but she was enchanted by the pastel macarons and miniature scones. She made plans to secrete the finger sandwiches in her backpack for later, since she hadn't the slightest idea if she would be able to find dinner in London. And as she sipped her tea, she realised that she now had something to relay to Aunt Bea that would not have to be heavily edited.

As the train pulled into the station, Winnie's heart began to beat a tattoo. What had she been thinking, coming to a metropolis like London all on her own? She hated to admit it to herself, but she was half wishing that Lottie was with her. The cockapoo at least gave the appearance of knowing what she was about and could usually bluff her way through sticky situations. Winnie shook her ears and chided herself. "I can do every bit as well," she murmured as she joined the sea of travellers on the platform and felt herself carried along as if on a tidal wave. Jostled this way, elbowed that way, she was sure she would be a bundle of bruises before she even caught sight of the exit. A straw hat sailed in her direction, and by a miracle she caught it and returned it to its owner, who was just a few paces ahead. Then she broke free from the crowd and gazed upward at various signs. Her trusty Baedeker had informed her that she could catch an underground train from this station, but to where? She pulled out a note George had given her with some pointers scrawled on it, but in the dim light and in her present state of confusion, she couldn't make head or tail of it.

She suddenly realised that she was standing rather conspicuously in the middle of an open area ranged around with various newsagents and food stalls, so she retreated towards a pillar. 'I wish I'd asked that nice pair of dogs where I should go,' she thought

"Is that Winnie? Or Winifred?" someone called out.

Winnie whirled around, bewildered, wondering how anyone in London could possibly know who she was. There must have been some mistake.

"Arh, I'm not wrong, then." A British blue cat in a tweedy flat cap extended his paw genially. "Tully, here, at your service. Shall I take your luggage, miss?"

For a moment, Winnie was inclined to hold her bag very tightly with both paws. Tully saw her hesitation and grinned. "Never fear, though you can never be too careful these days. I'm a bona fide London black cab driver, you know, here's my card. George down at Pawbury— think you met? — phoned up my boss and requested my services specially. So here I am," he said with a wink.

Winnie relaxed visibly. "I'm sorry," she said. "Thank you."

"No apologies necessary. Old George loves to fix things up for folks, but he's usually too shy to let them know what he's up to, and that can lead to some confusion. I've told him so, time and again, but does he listen?" Tully continued in this vein as he easily scooped up the bag and led the way to his waiting cab. "Now, you just make yourself comfortable back there, and I'll pop this in the boot. Where are we off to, then?" he enquired, glancing at the dachshund in his rear-view mirror. Before Winnie could open her mouth to give the address of the cheap but cheerful sort of hotel she had seen an advert for at the train station, Tully smacked his head with his paw. "Why am I asking you that? Force of habit, I suppose. Don't worry your head about it. I'll have you there in two shakes of a tail."

Winnie furrowed her brow. Where was "there"? This was turning out to be a most surprising day, though not an unpleasant one. Tully negotiated the traffic with ease, and Winnie gazed out the window but could scarcely take everything in. They'd just made it round Piccadilly Circus when Tully restarted the conversation. "So, has George caught any fish lately? He has the patience of a saint, that one, sitting by the water and dangling his rod for all that time. Wouldn't catch me doing that. I just hie me down to the nearest fish and chips shop. Slap-up meal and no bother. But I guess I'm what you Americans call a 'city slicker,' can't help myself. Get pretty fidgety in the country. Aha, here we are," he said, as if somehow he'd surprised himself.

Winnie craned her neck to look up at the grand edifice beside them. "Are you sure?" she said, hesitantly. "I don't think…" and then she looked straight ahead at the glowing sign, letters picked out with individual bulbs. She felt a little dizzy. "No, this is definitely not the place," she said.

"Now, then, I was told to take you to the Ritz, and I happen to know there's only one in town. I'll just make sure that uppity-looking porter there takes good care of your bag, and I'll be off for my supper," Tully said, as he slipped out of the driver's seat. He handed the porter something and gave Winnie a parting wink. "If you need anything, the numbers on the card. Don't hesitate." And with that, he was gone.

Chapter Fifty-Four
Landing Among the Stars

Tully's whiskers twitched with pleasure as he eased back into traffic. "All in a day's work," he chuckled to himself. He, George and Harry had really managed to work a little magic between them. The call from Pawbury had given Tully an idea. Surely there couldn't be two little American red dachshunds named Winifred rattling around England just now. He'd impulsively pulled over at the nearest phone box.

"Harry, you rascal. Glad I was able to get you out from under that Fiat. I've got a plan. Can you get hold of Bertie and Muriel? Sharpish? Good. Now listen to me."

By some miracle, Harry had just received a postcard and did happen to know where Bertie was, and a couple of quick calls was all that was necessary. The result of all these benevolent machinations was that a bewildered Winnie was now standing in the middle of a glorious suite under a crystal chandelier, gazing open-mouthed at an enormous gold and white Louis XIV bed with a marble fireplace at its foot. A slipper chair upholstered in blue striped satin and edged round with golden fringe occupied a nook before a tall window. All of this for the cost of a room at The Trafalgar Arms, the very modest hotel she'd planned to stay at. She felt more than a little dazed, and the gilded mirror across the room assured her that she looked it, too.

The bellboy had imparted all sorts of information in the five minutes it had taken to find her room and deposit her luggage, but now she wasn't sure if dinner was at 7 o'clock or 8, and what was it he had said about the dress code? Her head was in a whirl. She ventured over to the bathroom and beheld a roll top bath and what looked like acres of marble. Turning back to the room, she sat gingerly on the bed's silk coverlet. 'This would be marvellous for Lottie and Ted's honeymoon,' she thought, 'if they continue to get along as they are at the moment.' But for her?

The bellboy had efficiently built a fire and instructed her as to how to turn on the gas, so she slipped off the bed and turned the knob. Flames sprang up instantly, and she sat on the deep-pile carpet with her feet touching the fender, leaning comfortably against the end of the bed. If this was the way it was going to be, she thought she might be able to get used to it—at least for a few nights.

Winnie felt too sleepy to face the well-heeled patrons of the glittering dining room, which she'd caught a glimpse of on the way up to her room. The obliging bellboy had mentioned room service, but she worried that it would cost the earth, so she made herself a cup of tea with the thoughtfully provided electric kettle and pulled out the sandwiches she'd squirreled away in her backpack. Curling up on the slipper chair, she gazed out at the lights of the city and the comings and goings of beautiful dogs and cats in dazzling attire. It was a world she knew so little of and would never feel comfortable in, but she loved having what felt like a box seat to observe the whirl of life below. She thought of Muriel, to whom this sort of splendour was almost commonplace, and wondered where she and Bertie were at this moment. Snuggling back into the cushions, she pulled some sheets of crested hotel stationery from the table next to her, and, using her Baedeker as a lap desk, began to write, her thoughts flowing at last.

The morning brought with it a realisation that she had arrived in the capital of the country and didn't really know what she was going to do next. Winnie had hoped to see Douglas during her stay, although she couldn't see herself turning up at the palace unannounced and putting him in a difficult position. Unbeknown to her, something was already afoot in that quarter. The bellboy called at the room at 8am and handed Winnie a breakfast tray. On it were a teapot and a china cup and saucer along with an egg and toast. All looked delicious, and her eye caught a small envelope balanced against the teapot. Winnie thanked the bellboy, who disappeared, restoring her privacy. She eagerly tucked into the breakfast, giving the egg a satisfying bash before peeling off the broken shell pieces—she never understood why others simply sliced the top off. After cutting up the toast into soldiers and dipping them, as she had seen Bertie do long ago, she reached for the letter, which was addressed to her personally.

Dearest Winnie,

Your carriage will be waiting at the lobby entrance at 10am.

A friend

Winnie turned the letter over and then looked more carefully at the envelope. She wasn't sure what to make of it, as the handwriting didn't look familiar. 'It's certainly not from Douglas,' she thought, with a little stab of illogical disappointment—how could he know she was at the Ritz? Could it be something George had organised? Surely not. Only those that cared for her knew where she was. But the note was too intriguing to be ignored, and she had nothing else to do. "Why not?" she said aloud, a bit surprised at the determined note in her own voice. Certainly, there was no harm in discovering what this was all about. She sprang from the bed, almost forgetting the breakfast tray but catching it in the nick of time. Whatever the day held, she decided that a good soak in the roll top bath was a necessary precursor.

Chapter Fifty-Five
A Date with Destiny

Winnie arrived in the lobby on the stroke of ten. The dog at the entrance greeted her and held open the door, and she could just see a metallic light blue Rolls Royce Corniche convertible with a cream hood waiting outside. To her surprise, the driver was another dachshund who waved and beckoned for Winnie to join her. She walked up to the car and took a seat in the sumptuous and spacious interior. The fine Connolly hide with blue piping was as striking as it was comfortable, and Winnie admired the shiny burr walnut woodwork and intricate chrome dials on the dashboard.

"Hello Winnie. My name is Molly Engelweiss. I believe we have some friends in common."

Winnie recognised the name instantly and smiled, remembering back to several letters she had read from Bertie. Although she had never met the doxie, she was immediately set at ease. Molly had warm dark eyes and a lovely smile.

"We're off on a little trip, if that is alright with you?"

Winnie was overcome with emotion and beamed at the thought that someone she had never met was prepared to take such trouble for her. After taking a moment to collect her thoughts, she didn't hesitate to nod in agreement. 'Maybe we'll go to the British Museum or Natural History Museum or even the National Portrait Gallery,' she thought. Perhaps Bertie had told his friend that she was interested in the history of the country. The car moved off, and Winnie recognised the start of their route, The Mall. They proceeded at a leisurely pace and passed famous locations, from Buckingham Palace, up to Marble Arch, along Oxford Street and past Trafalgar Square, before crossing Westminster Bridge and seeing Big Ben. Winnie gazed, enraptured, at the architecture and the fascinating faces of the many passers-by. St Paul's Cathedral was next, then the Monument and the Tower of London. All the while, Molly was giving a suitably interesting commentary of the area. The car crossed over Tower Bridge and turned right, passed through some of the less distinguished areas of London along the Thames and pulled into the Royal Botanic Gardens at Kew.

Molly led Winnie on a trail up to the Great Pagoda, where they stopped to take in the spectacular views across London, then through the Palm House with its remarkable indoor rainforest and array of tropical plants. They meandered through a rose garden and rock garden, both with beautiful flowers about to bloom, and finally came to the home of the oldest sculptures at Kew. The Queen's garden was enclosed in box hedges and featured a number of stone ornaments, the most spectacular of which were a Venetian wellhead and marble satyr. There they sat, chatting pleasantly and watching the clouds roll by as if they had known each other for years.

Meanwhile, Nap was busy preparing the second part of the little plan that he and Molly had concocted with Bertie and Muriel. He needed to get Douglas to the Ritz dining room without raising any suspicions, which was no mean feat. He would have preferred to have made a reservation for the pair at one of any number of his favourite little cafés, but Molly had prevailed on that point. "Winnie will wonder what is happening if I take her to the Café Camille," she pointed out. "This way she will be in the dark until the last moment, thinking she's just returning to the hotel after a pleasant afternoon and having dinner with me." In the end, Nap had had to concede that she was right, and it would indeed make for a unique experience. He was sure Douglas was familiar with the fine cuisine offered, given he would undoubtedly have seen it and perhaps even tasted it at the palace. Nap had of course frequented the dining rooms himself on many an occasion and knew the spectacular setting would enchant them, what with its towering marble columns, sparkling chandeliers and soaring floor to ceiling windows which overlooked the calm oasis of Green Park. It really was the perfect meeting place for the young couple.

Nap decided he would meet Douglas outside the palace gates after work. The evenings were light enough for him to see the staff exiting, and he liked to be during things, watching the hurly-burly of London as working dogs and cats poured into the streets after hours. As he waited, he reflected on his approach. Douglas was a bright chap, and after some deliberation,

Nap had thought it safer to steer as close to the truth as possible, so as not to provoke curiosity with an over-elaborate scheme. That morning at breakfast he had told Douglas that he wanted to take him out for an evening meal, though of course he didn't say where and didn't actually say that he would be the other dinner guest. He hadn't done too badly on short notice, he thought with satisfaction, stroking his whiskers and readjusting his mauve waistcoat.

Nap had lapsed into a reverie and was startled when the corgi appeared. "Hello, Uncle Leon. Gosh, I'm glad we're going to eat. Cook gave us prawn sandwiches for lunch, and I couldn't stomach them. Where are we off to? And you really should let me pay my way, you know."

Nap smiled indulgently at Douglas. "No, you must let your old uncle have his pleasures, *mon ami*. I know you'd be happy enough at a pub or carvery, but my tastes run a little to the higher end of the scale, so it will be my treat. This way," he said, gesturing with his paw. Douglas's ears grew pointier when they came to a stop outside the arcaded entrance of the Ritz, and he looked inquiringly at Nap. "Ah. Here we are," the mouse said nonchalantly. Douglas instinctively reached for one of the great glass doors but was not quick enough. A liveried porter pulled it open with a practiced flourish and a slight bow.

As the pair entered the hotel's opulent lobby, Douglas realised he was dressed less for the occasion and more as if he were about to start work there. This thought was quickly brushed aside by Nap, who had a quick word with the maître d'hôtel and explained that there would be a short wait. "*Sacre bleu!* I do believe I see an old friend of mine just over there! But one of us must stay in sight of the restaurant, or they may forget us."

"Go on, I'll wait here," Douglas assured him.

"Ah, *merci, mon ami!* My friend would be most annoyed if I did not acknowledge her. There is quite a comfortable settee just there by the stairs and lift. I've sat there many a time when the Baroness Blumenthal has been, what is it Americans so charmingly say? 'Fashionably late.' I will return *tout de suite*." And he vanished.

Douglas smiled after him and sat on the extreme edge of the settee. This was just the sort of furniture Palace staff were forbidden to use, he thought. He amused himself by watching the hotel's guests descending and ascending the grand staircase ahead of him. Various British accents mingled with foreign ones, and he caught his breath when he glimpsed a well-known and dazzling stage actress on the arm of a particularly unkempt-looking wolfhound, who probably classed himself as a bohemian. For a moment, the stairs were clear, and Douglas lowered his eyes to the complicated pattern in the carpet. Just then, despite the hum around him, he heard, clear as a bell, a voice that sounded familiar and was certainly American, even though it only pronounced the word "Oh."

Raising his eyes slightly, he caught sight of a pair of red silk slippers, and a thrill began at the top of his head and travelled down to his tail. He knew those shoes well. He lifted his head, and there she was, slender in a simple white silk dress, her eyes bright and ears perked. Douglas sprung up, heard another "Oh!"—this time in another tone—and was at the bottom stair just in time to get an armful of Winnie.

"Oh, I'm such a klutz!" she said breathlessly. "I'm sorry, Douglas."

Truth be told, Douglas was not altogether sorry about the situation. But he set her down gently and retrieved the slippery shoe from the step. "I believe this will fit, Cinderella?" He said with a smile. Winnie blushed under her whiskers and took the offending piece of footwear, quickly sliding it back on. They had scarcely had time to recover themselves when the maître d'hôtel came their direction, his face betraying no knowledge of the scene that had just transpired. "Monsieur Pembroke? Mademoiselle Wigglesworth? Allow me to escort you to your table."

As the pair followed the tuxedoed Siamese into the dining room, Molly stepped out from behind a palm, and Nap from behind a pillar, each smiling. "*Bien joué*," said the mouse. "Good show, if I may say so myself, and I do. Now, I did take it upon myself to book a cosy table at the Café Camille. Will you join me there, Mademoiselle Engelweiss?"

"With pleasure," she said.

Winnie and Douglas sat opposite each other, the evening sunlight illuminating the crystal glasses and making a bit of a rainbow on the crisp linen tablecloth. Winnie was feeling especially shy, and Douglas hadn't really said a word yet. A supercilious waiter had placed enormous menus before each of them so that neither could see the other. Winnie peeked around hers and caught Douglas doing the same. They both smiled and then spoke at once.

"Uncle Leon…"

"Molly…"

"We've been cleverly tricked," Douglas grinned.

"Indeed, we have," Winnie replied, putting her menu down. "In the nicest sort of way." She wanted to ask about the postcard she had sent weeks ago, with the address of the hotel she and Lottie had stayed at longest during their stint on the coach tour but thought it best not to. There was an awkward pause.

"Strangest thing happened," Douglas said suddenly, as though he had read her thoughts. "I got a postcard from you just the other day, but the postmark was from ages ago. Can't think what happened to it. It wasn't coming that far. But from the dates you gave, I knew I'd missed my chance to send you a reply. I'm sorry about that. You said you had lunch at a castle?"

Winnie relaxed a bit. "Oh, yes. Well, sort of. You see—"

"Have mademoiselle and monsieur made their selections?" A supercilious-looking Borzoi gazed down the considerable length of his nose at them whilst shaking out the napkins with a flourish and settling them on their laps. He turned his head to the side and gazed at the pair out of one eye in an unsettling sort of way.

"A few more minutes, if you please," Douglas answered, in what he hoped was a tone that bespoke ease and familiarity with the grandeur of their surroundings. The Borzoi didn't deign to reply but turned on his heel and disappeared. Winnie smiled to herself but thought Douglas had carried it off rather well. The fair bit of culinary French he'd picked up from

Napoleon stood them in good stead as they turned their attention to the menus, and when the waiter returned, he was disappointed by the corgi's flawless pronunciation of *boeuf Bourguignon* and *pommes de terre*.

"May I interest Monsieur in a bottle of Liber Pater Blanc?" he enquired hopefully. "If not, the sommelier has several recommendations he can offer you." The mouse had seemed the sort who would spare no expense, he thought. But Winnie had happened to see the eye-watering £500 on the wine list and vigorously shook her head at Douglas. He declined, and the Borzoi sniffed as he spirited away their menus.

Douglas moved the towering vase of calla lilies to the side and shifted in his seat a little, his foot accidentally touching Winnie's under the table. They both blushed. "So, I have managed to save a little time off," he said, after recovering. "You seemed to have quite a full schedule when you wrote, but if you have a couple of days free…"

"Oh, I do!" Winnie broke in, and then looked down at the little rainbow, which had shifted a bit. She was embarrassed by her enthusiasm, but she had to acknowledge to herself that she had missed Douglas and had been trying hard not to get her hopes up. "I mean…I can check my schedule, but I'm pretty sure," she amended.

Douglas was utterly unaware of her discomfort. "Spiffing!" he said, relieved that this new Winnie, despite looking so grown up in evening dress, hadn't altered too much. "I'll square it with the boss, and then we can start planning. Where have you been so far, and what have you been up to?"

Winnie launched into a recital of her exploits with Lottie, somewhat expurgated but not as fully censored as her letter to Aunt Bea. There were no more awkward silences as she recounted their hole-and-corner antics with Artie and Lottie's various escapades. Their giggles drew both glares and indulgent smiles from the diners around them.

Nap would have been most disappointed had he seen their utter inattention to the exquisite entrees before them, but his eyes twinkled contentedly as he wrung all the details of the evening from Douglas the next day at breakfast. "Ah, *mon ami*, and I have a confession to make," he said as he brushed bits of croissant from his waistcoat. "That postcard. Oh, *mon Dieu*, so frightfully embarrassing. The postcard I put on your dresser the other day...well. It spent about a week languishing behind the hall radiator. The housekeeper most fortunately found it." He looked so disconsolate that Douglas hastened to reassure him.

"No harm done," he said. "The Royal Mail took the blame, and Winnie was a brick about it."

"I am glad. But I really must teach you how to refer to a lady, *mon fils*. Sometimes I despair of you."

Chapter Fifty-Six
When One Door Closes

The desk clerk hailed Winnie as she left the breakfast room. "Miss Wigglesworth, I believe?"

"Yes," she replied, a bit shyly, amazed that he knew who she was. She hoped he didn't recognise her merely because she seemed to be one of the least formally dressed dogs in the hotel.

"Telegram for you, miss." Winnie smiled and took the slender envelope. For a moment, her heartbeat faster. Surely nothing was wrong? A host of suppositions flashed through her mind as she slit open the envelope. Her paw shook a bit as she read the contents. The message was quite brief.

Winnie: Nap says you are enjoying yourself. Please stay at the Ritz as long as you like. It will give us pleasure if you do. Love, Bertie & Muriel

Relief pulsed through her, and then overwhelming gratitude. No wonder she had been living like a princess on the paltry bit she had been paying for the last couple of nights. She would have to find a way to thank them.

Rising from her chair, Winnie walked by a dog polishing the marble floor and stepped into the lift. Just as she was about to press the button for her floor, a young pup hopped in, pressed all of the floor buttons and then dashed off, never to be seen again. Slightly bemused, she realised that she might be better off taking the stairs but decided to stay. As the doors began to close, an extremely stiff and formal though rather plump dormouse put his paw on the side panel, enabling his companion to slide by.

"Just in time," Winnie said, trying to break the awkward silence that always seems to occur between guests travelling in elevators. The black and white cat adjacent to her turned her head, nodded gently and resumed her rather statuesque pose. The dormouse sitting on her shoulder turned to Winnie and looked at her up and down. "Ms Arabella does not like to engage in idle chit chat. If you would kindly refrain from talking to her, it would be greatly appreciated."

Having delivered himself of this request, he turned away and noticed that the lift buttons were all lit up. He frowned at Winnie and tutted, before reprising his position. She reluctantly stayed quiet, resisting the urge to tell the mouse that it wasn't her doing. Instead, she allowed herself to glance again at the cat, peering around the mouse's bulky exterior to get a better look at the mysterious creature. Yet again she incurred his displeasure and began to think that he must be a bodyguard or minder of some sort. He glared menacingly back at the poor dachshund, as if to remind her of what he had said only a few seconds ago, and then pointed to a badge on his lapel. "If you can read this, you are standing too close," it said.

From her brief glimpse, Winnie had spotted distinct black markings around the cat's mouth and under her chin, as well as a pair of intelligent green eyes that flashed behind tortoise-shell glasses. She was wearing long white socks, a short grey skirt, with a cream leather jacket to finish off the ensemble. On the front and sleeves of the jacket was a curious perforated pattern that looked a bit like shamrocks. In her hand was a hardback book with a colourful scene on the cover, but Winnie couldn't make out the title. A silver chain with a Cross of Lorraine pendant swung from her neck.

A few seconds later the lift jolted, the lights dimmed for a second and it began to move. The only sound that could be heard was the rattle and coiling of the cable as the carriage ascended. Within a few moments, a pinging noise could be heard, and the doors opened as it reached the first floor. Two guests waiting outside in the corridor peered inside, gasped and made as if to enter.

"I'm sorry, ladies," the dormouse said. "We're going all the way up to the penthouse, so perhaps you'd care to take the other lift?" He slipped down the arm of the cat and punched impatiently at the already lit penthouse suite button. The doors closed quickly, much to his satisfaction, and they began to rise again. Winnie grabbed the chrome handrail, as she wasn't really keen on confined spaces, remembering back to when she rescued Solomon at Caesar's Head. Fortunately, the Ritz, wasn't a tall building, and it would only be a few more minutes before she could get out. The lift pinged again at the second to top floor, and the bodyguard was surprised that the dachshund hadn't vacated the space. For some reason he got rather angry. "Really, this is quite uncalled for," he said, looking daggers at the rather shabby dog. "Don't your sort have better things to do than stalk famous cats? Pests," he muttered. As the doors opened, he moved towards Winnie and ushered her unceremoniously out. "Now, go back to wherever it is you came from and leave us alone. I'll be calling security once I get to the room, and they'll be sure to hear about this," he said gruffly, before the doors closed and she was left standing in the alcove outside the lift.

As much as she was rather perturbed, to say the least, about being pushed out of the lift, Winnie let it lie and took the stairs back up to her room. On exiting the stairwell, she found herself looking down the corridor at the small number of exclusive hotel rooms beyond. Ms Arabella was waiting patiently whilst her bodyguard was fumbling about for the key.

Winnie approached cautiously and heard the dormouse speak.

"Drat and blast! I've mislaid the key, I'm so sorry."

Ms Arabella folded her arms and sighed. "You had better go back to reception sharpish then, hadn't you, Dunston? I suppose you will expect me to take a seat on the floor and wait," she said huffily.

Thankfully, the dormouse rushed past Winnie without taking a second glance, too engrossed in his own dilemma. Winnie approached the black and white cat with some trepidation, as she had to pass her to get to her own room. She felt rather awkward, wondering if Ms Arabella would think, like Dunston, that she was after an autograph or the like. Not that Winnie had a clue who this cat was—and she could hardly assume she was well endowed, just because she was staying in an upper-class establishment, given her own circumstances. Not wanting to appear rude, she gathered her courage and spoke.

"I'm sorry, I didn't mean to overhear, but would you like to come and stay in my room while you wait? I'm only a door along," she asked.

The cat was taken unawares, but when she looked at Winnie's sweet face, a flash of recognition came over her, and she quickly took her up on the offer. Winnie unlocked the room and allowed Ms Arabella to enter first.

"Ah, quite charming, 'The Prince of Wales' suite. I've always wondered what it looks like, very similar to my own room, of course. I expect your agent is around here somewhere too, not hunting for keys like Dunston," she said.

Winnie wasn't sure what the cat was talking about so just nodded in agreement. She inspected the rest of the room, glanced at herself in the vast mirror, fluffed her fur and then sat down on the striped sofa next to the fireplace.

"These book signings, they are a necessary evil I suppose. It's in my contract after all, and I've gotten used to them over time, but what a nuisance! I'm sure you know all about that too, although I wasn't quite expecting to have to share the stage with some other authors, were you?" Ms Arabella remarked languidly. Before Winnie could reply to clear up the confusion, the cat spoke again. "Oh, where are my manners? I do apologise. My name is Daphne Arabella Pussett III but do just call me Oreo—and before you ask, it's a long story."*

"Winifred Wigglesworth," Winnie replied, rather embarrassed at not having her own double-barrelled name, and half wondering if she should have made something up.

"Winnie, oh that's a lovely little name, isn't it? Of course, of course. I should have guessed you wrote under a pseudonym. We writers do like our privacy, don't we?"

"Erm, yes… we do," Winnie replied, feeling a bit uncomfortable and pondering whether she should correct the misapprehension—or, given that she would be unlikely to see the cat again, let her continue. There seemed to be little harm in the latter option. She tried to remember from her frequent visits to the library what the titles of this cat's books were.

"I didn't notice you down in the lobby. I expect you were just networking, getting some ideas from others. I do that myself, doesn't hurt to show your face about," Oreo said, patting down her skirt. "But if you want to take some free advice, I'd try and smarten up a touch. I know there is a certain laid-back style these days, but one must always try to create a good impression."

Oreo had placed the book she was holding in the lift on the glass coffee table. Winnie looked at the title, *The Empath's Doppelgänger*, and saw it was one of a trilogy. Racking her brain, she was just able to recall another title—*It's Not Always Black and White*—from the same mystery series. Stuck for something to say, she ventured what seemed to be a safe comment. "So, I see you have completed the third book in the series?"

"Oh yes, you must read it! Here, you can take this copy if you like, I'll even sign it for you. Have you a pen?"

Winnie picked up the pen which had been right in front of the cat and handed it to her, wondering if she required Dunston's services to get her dressed in the morning, too. She put her paw to her mouth to hide a smile at the thought.

"There, 'To my darling Winnie, with Love.' It'll be worth a fortune in a couple of years," Oreo said with a confident smile. "Actually, I found the book quite hard to write. I lost my impetus somewhere along the way and wasn't happy with how I ended it, but the publishers were on my back to get it finished." She sighed a touch dramatically. "I'm sure the fans will like it though, and I'm already being hounded to start a new one."

"Really?" Winnie said.

"Yes, but I'm not sure, I need a change. Do I really want to continue writing about secret passageways, dark corners of London and creepy villains? There is only so much I can think of without resorting to plagiarism, and I'll not stomach that. Besides, I don't want to be—what is it they say about actors?"

"Typecast?" Winnie said.

"You are a sharp one. Yes. I must spread my wings," Oreo exclaimed, with a sweeping gesture that very nearly upset the crystal lamp on the side table.

Winnie's eyes widened, but she recovered quickly. "Perhaps a romance novel?" she suggested.

"Oh, I'm really not sure about that, my dear," the cat said, putting her head to one side. "Anyone can write that sort of thing. I do have my pride."

"Oh, nothing too risqué," Winnie hurried to assure her, and thought quickly. "I think there are marvellous love stories everywhere. Take my friend Bertie, he's been in love with a dorgi, Muriel, since he was a pup, but only now after years and years have, they got back together. They are travelling the world at the moment. He gets into all sorts of scrapes. The stories he could tell would fill many a book."

Oreo leaned forward slightly, her whiskers twitching. "Oh, that does sound interesting," she said in a thoughtful tone. "Bertie, you say. An older chap, in his dotage, a second wind." Oreo's mind was awash with ideas and her body language animated. "Muriel, the beautiful maiden, albeit a bit mature, whisked away by her true love. I could call it *A Springtime in October.* Perfect! I can see it now, featuring Bernard and Maud— 'A romance that took fifty years to blossom.' "

Winnie was not sure if the cat was just humouring her, but she certainly seemed serious. "I've got a picture of him somewhere," she said, searching her pockets for her wallet. "Here it is. He's standing next to his dory, Duchess Muriel. I've sailed in her too."

"It gets better and better!" Oreo exclaimed delightedly. "He can sail, marvellous." She snatched the photo eagerly. "Oh, what a handsome chap, bit rough around the edges perhaps, roguish, maybe," she continued. "Have you got a photo of his lady-love?" But they were interrupted by a knock on the door. Winnie got up and pulled it open, only to find Dunston standing there, wearing a pugnacious expression.

"You," he said. "Now you're really pushing it, sneaking round the rooms of the rich and famous! They'll lock you up for that and throw away the key."

"Dunston, is that you?" Oreo called, as she got up and headed towards the dormouse. "Now, that is no way to speak to our fellow writer here. Apologise at once. Winnie has been telling me all about her friend and even suggested I write a romance novel. She is a flower among dogs."

Winnie didn't know what to make of being called a flower, but it certainly wasn't objectionable.

Dunston subsided, looking rather ashamed of himself. "My apologies, er, Ms Winnie," he said with as good a grace as he could muster. He eyed the dachshund keenly, and his brain began working furiously. Perhaps he was looking at an undiscovered talent? She must be doing well, or she couldn't have been assigned one of the most expensive suites in the hotel. But what was all this talk of a romance novel? What sorts of half-baked ideas had this dog been putting in Ms Arabella's head, just when the mystery gambit was paying so handsomely? The dormouse turned his back on Winnie, and with a flick of his tail, he followed his employer.

"Now come along, Dunston, we have work to do," Oreo called back. She had already disappeared with a wave, buoyed by the possibilities of her newfound subject.

Winnie sighed with relief and leaned back against the door after it closed noiselessly behind them. Then came the realization of what she had done. "Heavens to Murgatroyd!" she exclaimed aloud. "What will Bertie say?"

The phone rang shrilly and startled her out of her uncomfortable musings. "Winnie, darling, I'm so sorry to ring you when I was just there, but—silly me—I forgot to make an appointment to talk again," Oreo said. "I'm enthralled by your ideas! You must meet me for tea in the Palm Court tomorrow at 3 o'clock."

Winnie made a strangled sort of noise.

"Splendid! See you there! Ta!" And her new acquaintance rang off.

*Oreo: There are some subtle references in the chapter relating to the chief character. The Oreo is an extremely popular American sandwich cookie consisting of two chocolate wafers with a crème filling. The name's origin is not certain. Some suggest a derivation from the French word or, meaning "gold," while others have suggested that it is from an Ancient Greek root meaning "mountain." Another theory is that the name derives from the Latin *Oreodaphne*, a genus of the laurel family, given that an original design of the Oreo includes a laurel wreath. The symbol of the cross of Lorraine is embossed on the cookie to this day.

Chapter Fifty-Seven
In the Palm of her Paw

"You do look young for your age, Winnie darling. You must tell me your secrets sometime," Oreo purred as she eyed the mouth-watering selection of sandwiches before them. Winnie had picked an exquisitely light and flaky pastry and couldn't help but think of Stan, who would have devoured every one of the delicacies without much of a care what they were.

"I always find the selection here makes it so difficult to choose," Oreo continued. "But I'd recommend eating the scones while they're still hot—with plenty of Cornish cream and jam, of course."

Winnie nodded in agreement, thinking that the homely cakes were really her favourites. She wasn't used to such fine food and couldn't help enjoying what was on offer. Even so, she felt like she was getting a little too used to the high life and surroundings. She reminded herself that she had been sleeping under the stars only a week or so ago.

"So, Winnie, you were going to tell me more about your friends, Betty and Malcolm...oh, I am sorry, Bertie and Muriel. I'm already thinking up new names for them. I am a one, aren't I?" the cat said.

Winnie shifted in her chair uncomfortably. This was the moment she had been dreading. She had been certain that the invitation to afternoon tea had been a bit of a ruse, an opportunity for Oreo to pump her for details she could work into her romance novel. She half wondered if Dunston was lurking behind a palm tree, listening to their conversation. She wasn't against the idea of helping this kindly cat—far from it. 'If only I hadn't mentioned Bertie and Maud...Muriel," she thought. But the damage was done, the cat was looking at her expectantly and the silence was becoming uncomfortable. She needed to talk her way out of this mess, quickly.

"I was?" Winnie questioned, "Oh, yes, erm, shall I start on Muriel?"

"Please do," the cat said, relaxing into her chair and sipping her Darjeeling.

Winnie looked around the room for inspiration. An Afghan hound at the next table was flicking the hair from her eyes, and she was instantly reminded of Alfreda and Artie from the coach trip. A plan began to take shape in her mind.

"I haven't actually met Muriel, but by all accounts, she is a sophisticated basset hound, perhaps rather ostentatious too, a very colourful dog in more ways than one." Winnie wondered if she should really have made such a drastic change to Muriel's appearance. But 'in for a penny in for a pound,' as Bertie would say. "She was an east end pup and would visit him at the docks, where he used to work at the fish market."

Oreo was letting her tea grow cold and avidly listening.

"Muriel once fell into the river, and Bertie pulled her out, although he was surprised at her colourful language on that occasion. It even made him blush. Water has played a big part in their story. When they were out on a boating lake, somehow or another they had lost their oars and drifted into a rather hidden away spot. Bertie always thought Muriel had loosened the rowlocks so she could spend an uninterrupted moonlit evening with him. They stayed there until dusk, and Bertie began to get restless. He decided he would swim to the bank and pull the boat along too if he could manage it. When Bertie leapt over the side, he found he was standing in only two feet of water. Muriel was in hysterics, as she had known all along."

Oreo laughed out loud. "Oh, I do love this Bertie of yours, he does find himself in a pickle, doesn't he? Please do continue."

"As much as Bertie didn't like being in the water, he was fine being on it, so much so that he joined the Royal Navy. He became Ensign Bertram, for that was his real name." Winnie blushed a bit at yet another little white lie but plunged ahead. "He travelled on a number of vessels and enjoyed life at sea. The only thing was, he got a nickname, 'Unsinkable Stanley.' " This embellishment was even bolder than the last and would have undoubtedly horrified both Stan and Bertie, but no matter. She was starting to have fun.

"Why was that?" Oreo asked.

"I'm glad you asked," Winnie said, turning her attention to a teacake that was sitting rather forlornly on the cake dish before her. His ships had the habit of always being sunk. The only saving grace was that he always survived and found a new bunk soon enough. His crew mates believed he was a lucky charm, and as much as they didn't look forward to being hit by a torpedo, they at least knew that if they stuck with Bertie, they would always be safe."

"Golly," Oreo exclaimed. "What a story And I expect he always wrote to Muriel back home?"

"Quite," Winnie nodded.

"Without tooting my own trumpet, I think that will work out well. 'Love letters from round the world.' How marvellous," Oreo replied, her eyes taking on a faraway look.

Winnie continued unabated. "As you can imagine, the long-distance relationship was hard going, especially over so many years, and they lost touch. Muriel bumped into a fish sales dog whom she found to be a loveable rogue and ended up marrying him. He was like Bertie but didn't have his kind heart. He got in with the wrong crowd, and eventually ran off to Australia after getting into one too many scrapes with the law. Muriel was ambivalent. On the one paw, she was free again, but on the other, she was lonely. She later had various flings with other dogs but nothing stuck."

"Oh, poor Muriel," Oreo feelingly interjected.

"Bertie had tried to forget all about Muriel. He had heard through the grapevine that she had married, and he decided to shun England in favour of the bright lights of America. He found himself touring in a travelling circus of all things, was quite handy on the tightrope by all accounts. Must have been all that sailing that made for good balance. But he was happiest when performing various stunts on his motorbike and wowed crowds by riding the 'Wall of Death.' He had no fear.

"Marvellous, just marvellous. A daredevil, too," Oreo sighed.

"Oh, yes, indeed. He became quite famous, by all accounts, and eventually married a film starlet, Billie Babington. I'm sure you've heard of her?"

Winnie continued, without stopping for a reply, just in case Oreo picked her up on the falsehood. "They met at some awards ceremony, a red carpet 'do. Bertie had been a stunt double for many famous actors, of course. They had a star-studded life together for a while, the handsome, loveable rogue and the beautiful actress. As with many high-profile couples, though, they grew apart. She had her career; he had his burgeoning responsibilities and the like. You know the sort of thing." Seeing that Oreo sat in speechless wonder, she went on. "Bertie eventually injured himself after falling off one too many buildings, and unfortunately his career ended. He opted for the quiet life at an exclusive beach resort, sun, sea and sand."

"Bertie, a stuntman. This gets better and better," Oreo remarked. "So, if you don't mind me interrupting your story, how did he ever meet Muriel again?"

"I'm glad you asked," Winnie replied. "In fact, Muriel had become an air hostess, working out of London. In a way, she had followed in Bertie's paw prints, travelling all over the world, but by plane instead of by boat. Maybe she secretly hoped to meet him in some far-flung place. Out of pure coincidence, she had an overnight stop in New York before having to set off for Toronto one weekend, and Bertie was at the same hotel at the same time. He was at a birthday bash for an old friend, or something along those lines. Muriel was at the bar drinking cocktails with the captain of the Boeing 747, and Bertie was at the other end drinking beer and singing karaoke. I'm sure you can use some poetic licence to add a song of your choosing," Winnie smiled.

"Indeed, I can think of many that would be suitable," Oreo replied. "Oh, you have been so helpful, Winnie! My head is simply buzzing with new ideas now—storylines, plot lines, etc., etc. But I've got to get off to another awful book signing, more's the pity. I can see Dunston waving his paw and looking rather anxious. Thank you so much."

"A pleasure," Winnie replied, very thankful that she would not be called upon to invent anything further.

"Now, the next time you are in London, we must catch up again. Here, takes my card. I'll let Dunston know...toodle-oo for now."

Winnie sat back, looked up at the glittering chandeliers and elegant mirrors, and exhaled for what seemed the first time in ten minutes. She felt secure in the knowledge that Oreo was highly unlikely to bump into the real Bertie and Muriel. 'And really,' she mused, as she nibbled the last of her teacake, 'perhaps I should become a writer myself.'

Chapter Fifty-Eight
Taking the Long Way Down

The wind was rattling the windows and moaning around corners, reminding Winnie of the coastal storms at home. Despite the luxuriously smooth sheets, silken eiderdown, and satin pillowcases, she was tossing about restlessly. The series of events that had brought her to the Ritz were replaying in her mind, but with everything turned upside down in unsettling ways. George was driving the taxi, Ted was leaving Lottie at the station, she herself was gobbling up all the oyster ice cream, and the misbehaving pups were scolding her for her greediness, while Tully had steam puffing from his ears and was covered in coal dust. Shaking her head to clear these half-dreams, she kicked the covers off, sat up and flicked on the little bedside lamp. She was in no mood to peruse the Baedeker, and the television in the corner did not tempt her.

In truth, she was feeling a bit restless and lonely. Now that she had seen Douglas again, she was eager to spend time with him, but he would not get leave from work for several more days. That couldn't be helped, so she tried to divert her thoughts. 'I wonder if anyone would mind if I explored a little?' she asked herself, and suddenly realised that, as a paying guest, she didn't need to ask anyone's permission. The little china clock on the mantel shelf had just chimed twelve. 'Surely most of the hotel's guests will have returned from their evening's entertainments and now be safe in their beds?' she mused, innocent of the late-night ways of a metropolis.

With uncharacteristic impulsivity, she leapt out of the bed, misjudging how high it was and landing with an ungraceful thud. Pulling on yesterday's clothes, she slid her room key in her pocket and slipped soundlessly into the plushily-carpeted corridor. She waited and listened, but all was very silent, almost unnaturally so. The thick, panelled doors deadened any sounds from within the adjacent rooms. She made her way to the mirrored and gilded lift doors.

They opened with a pneumatic wheeze, and she was startled when a pair of King Charles's spaniels emerged, identically dressed in brown and cream evening gowns, though one appeared to be some years older than the other. The younger one, her crocodile handbag embossed with a gold "L," looked Winnie up and down with a patronising air and took the other dog by the elbow. "The youth these days," she uttered in a voluble whisper. "No elegance at all."

"If you say so, my dear," her companion replied.

Winnie's ears drooped for a moment as she caught a glimpse of herself full-length in the elevator doors. Her jumper was rumpled, and her jeans creased, and there was a black smudge on one knee. 'I do look a sight,' she thought unhappily. 'I must find a way to get my laundry done.' Not keen on meeting anyone else on her rambles, she opted for the stairs, having forgotten that she was on the fifteenth floor.

Whatever her sartorial shortcomings, Winnie had become quite strong during her holiday, and she was halfway down before she needed to stop for breath. Leaning against the railing, she was surprised to hear a soft noise. She quietened her own breathing and listened carefully. The sound was quite familiar, really. It brought back a memory of an afternoon at Bertie's cove that seemed very long ago. A somewhat louder sob brought her back to the present.

Not wanting to startle whoever it was, Winnie tiptoed down the next flight of stairs, keeping close to the wall. Once at the landing, she peered through the ornate iron railings and down the dizzying twists and turns of the stairwell. Nothing. She listened again, and all was silent. Not a firm believer in ghosts, she decided it best to make herself known and see what happened next. "Hello—please don't be startled. Is everything okay?" she said in a friendly tone and in a volume, she hoped would carry to whoever it was, but not too loud.

Silence again. But then Winnie thought she could hear the faintest suggestion of a sniffle. In the subdued light she was sure she saw a shadow move another flight down. "Are you in trouble? Can I help?" She continued edging her way down as noiselessly as possible, glad that she was wearing her plimsolls and not her stouter walking shoes. As she approached, a small, huddled form shifted and detached itself from the surrounding gloom. First an aquiline nose, then wide, round eyes, and finally a pair of long ears emerged into a pool of light from the sconce on the wall. Above these features was a neat white cap, and below the chin, just above a starched collar, was a striking streak of white.

"Hello," Winnie said softly. "I'm Winnie. I'm sorry to have disturbed you." The dog turned her head to one side and looked down, embarrassed to have been found in such a state. "Hello," she replied. "I'm not supposed to talk to the guests. You'd best be getting on."

"I don't have anywhere in particular to go," Winnie answered quite truthfully. She sat down on a stair near the unhappy dog, who she could now see was quite as long as herself, only with lustrous ebony fur.

"Neither do I," the dog said with a sigh. "But I'm sorry to have gotten in your way."

"Not at all," Winnie said kindly, fishing a packet of tissues from her jeans pocket. "Here, take these. Now, what is your name?"

"I'm Gretchen Schwartz, and I'm—I mean I was—a kitchen maid here."

"I'm happy to meet you," Winnie replied. "But 'was'?"

"Oh. I've been sacked. And it's all my fault, really. But it's really not a remarkably interesting story."

Winnie considered a moment and then stood up. "Well, interesting or not, it won't do to sit here any longer. You must be feeling very stiff and uncomfortable. I was thinking of exploring the rooms on the main floor, but I think I'd rather get some fresh air. Would you like to join me?"

Gretchen eyed the dachshund warily. She certainly didn't look like a habitué of glamourous hotels, but you never could tell. She knew that some absurdly wealthy dogs were eccentric enough to go about wearing tatty clothes, as if they were somehow apologising to the world for their good luck. "You're an American, aren't you?" she said, forgetting her manners for a moment. Perhaps that accounted for the dog's oddly democratic ways. "Have you been here before?"

"Never," Winnie replied, still aware of the smudge on her knee and trying to angle herself so that Gretchen wouldn't see it. "To tell you the truth, I feel a bit overwhelmed by this place. You see, I didn't plan to stay at the Ritz at all. I had a booking at the Churchill Arms."

This was not at all what Gretchen had expected to hear, and she was intrigued. The Churchill Arms was rather seedy, by her standards. What an odd dog. Not wanting to discuss her troubles or even think about them any longer that night, she rose and shook herself a little. "Well, I could show you about a bit and keep you away from the worst spots, if you'd like," she offered. "I often walk home at night, so I know what's what around here," she said with some pride. She was feeling ashamed by the awkward first impression she'd made, sobbing in a heap on the stairs.

"That would be fabulous," Winnie exclaimed, bouncing down the next flight of steps, her heart lighter for having found a companion and possibly distracting her from her sadness.

"Hang about," Gretchen said with a giggle. "I have to change out of this lot, as it no longer belongs to me anyway, and then we can go. Follow me."

Gretchen set quite a pace. Winnie admired her stature—the doxie was rather longer than herself and quite athletic. The light became murkier as they descended. Bare bulbs, some flickering, replaced the elegant fixtures of the floors above, frayed carpet was in evidence, and the paint was beginning to blister and peel off the damp walls. Gretchen came to a halt in front of a splintering door and turned to Winnie. "I'll just be ten minutes, then, if you don't mind waiting here."

"Of course not," Winnie replied. The door closed behind her companion, and she stood rather at a loss in the insalubrious surroundings. She surmised that the kitchen must be close by, as there was a curious mixture of food odours wafting along the corridor.

"Gretchen! Where 'ave you been? I hate to complain, with you bein' so generous, but I've only got use of the van for a little longer, and then me mate Donny needs it back." Winnie whirled around and looked for the speaker but saw no one. "Gretchen?" the voice repeated.

Winnie was too confused to answer. Was there an intercom in the wall? Where was the voice coming from? She felt a little tug at her jeans and looked down. "Oh, you're—you're not Gretchen. Sorry, you have exactly the same profile, darn difficult seeing things in 'ere. Oh, well, never mind. Sorry to bother ya. I'll just take meself off, then." In the dimness, she could just make out a grey mouse, a bit scruffy in well-worn white overall and stained trousers, as he turned on his heel and began scurrying away.

"Wait!" Winnie called after him, her curiosity roused. The mouse came to a halt, almost comically frozen in place, and glanced back at her. "Gretchen is just sorting something out, but perhaps I could help? I'd hate for you to have a wasted trip."

"Wot? Oh, er, I don't think so. No. Nothin' you can do, luv. Now just forget this 'ole business, don't worry your pretty 'ead over it. Nothin' of importance." And with that, he vanished.

Winnie frowned after him. What was that all about? 'Not quite cricket, as Bertie would say,' she thought. She wasn't very suspicious by nature, but the mouse had seemed distinctly nervous. And what did Gretchen have to do with him? She seemed a decent sort of dog, at least on short acquaintance, not one to be mixed up in shady dealings. Engrossed in her thoughts, she scarcely heard the squeaking of the door behind her. In a moment, Gretchen was by her side.

"That's done and dusted," the dog said, with somewhat forced cheerfulness. "Returned my key, put my uniform in the laundry, tidied up my locker. 'Let's blow this popsicle stand,' as they say in the movies."

Winnie didn't like to air her suspicions—it seemed hardly the thing to do when she'd just met the doxie and she had been so distressed. But she felt compelled to at least tell Gretchen about her encounter. "Someone was looking for you just now. A mouse," she said, somewhat abruptly. "He didn't give me his name. Looked like he works in a café, or something like that."

"Oh, I did forget about poor Gerard," she replied, and then was silent for a few moments. "Well, you may as well know. He's part of the reason I was sacked. Now, come along, and I'll tell you the gory details as we walk."

Chapter Fifty-Nine
Kind Hearts and Charity

The service door closed behind them, and Winnie was met with the acrid odour of the rubbish bins behind the hotel. This was certainly not the Ritz envisioned by the hordes of tourists that passed through the glamorous arcades at the front. She nearly slipped on a leaf of lettuce.

"I should have warned you to be careful," Gretchen said, catching her paw. "Sorry to bring you out this way, but I wasn't allowed to use the guest entrance even when I was employed here, of course."

"Oh, don't worry about it," Winnie said and thought almost guiltily of the suite she was occupying.

Once they were outside the gate, Gretchen broke into her thoughts. "So, you met Gerard. You must be wondering about that."

"Oh, not really. He seemed nice enough," Winnie replied. Now that she might discover the truth, she wasn't sure that she wanted to, here, in a dim alley that smelt rather foul. What had she gotten herself into? She'd only meant to be kind.

"He is, actually. One of the nicest mice I know." Winnie could scarcely see Gretchen in the darkness, save for the white patches, so it was almost as if the voice were coming from a void. She shivered. "I know he was probably acting rather shifty, but that was just for my sake, really," her companion continued.

'That doesn't explain much,' Winnie thought, but stayed silent.

"You see—well, a place like the Ritz can afford to buy more than it needs for its guests. I watched so much get wasted, day after day, tossed out heedlessly like that bit you nearly slipped on back there. I'd been seeing so much hunger on my route to and from work that I could scarcely stand it.

251

Here I was, with meals provided on the job and acres of food everywhere, every day, while so many creatures were going without. I began to save my evening meal and leave it on a park bench where I knew a group of mice gathered every evening, busking for a few meagre coins."

This had not at all been what Winnie had expected to hear, and she was now disgusted by her suspicious thoughts. Still, though, there was the question of Gerard. She nodded as they passed an anaemic streetlamp, hoping that Gretchen had seen her and would continue her tale.

"I always tried to do this before the little band arrived, not wanting to embarrass them, but on one occasion the mouse who seemed to be their leader came a bit early—it was the end of British Summer Time, and he'd forgotten to put his clock back. Of course, he spotted me."

Engrossed by the tale, Winnie unwittingly said, "Gerard."

"Yes," Gretchen said, stopping for a moment at the main road. "It was rather awkward. 'Thank you, but we do work for our food, you know,' he said a little stiffly. 'If you like our music, then that's a kind sort of payment, but I've never seen you before.' He put down his saxophone case and looked at me challengingly. I didn't really know what to say, realising how patronising my actions may have seemed.

"I apologised and turned to depart, feeling rather low, when the mouse called me back. 'That was churlish of me,' he said, holding out his paw, which I tried not to crush with my own. 'I'm Gerard.' 'Gretchen,' I said. 'And I have heard your music. I'm no judge, but I do enjoy it.' 'Much obliged,' he replied, with a friendly smile. 'You should come to our little café sometime, luv. I think there'd be room for you.' I was surprised by this mention of a café but assured him that I would love to. 'I'm afraid it's not very lively. We're not doin' a roarin' business at present. So many mice in this area 'ave lost their jobs and can't afford to come even once a week. And really, we don't 'ave too many funds to buy supplies for the place. But we could certainly knock up a decent meal for you in thanks for your generosity.' "

A seedy looking dog slouched by unsteadily, singing "One Hundred Bottles of Beer" in a voice that made them impulsively stuff their paws in their ears, and Gretchen suddenly seemed to recall that loitering at the opening of an alleyway wasn't the best idea. She beckoned to Winnie to turn right onto the main thoroughfare. The pavement reflected vast rectangles of warm light emanating from various posh establishments. Winnie was entranced by one of them, piled high with hampers and displaying a smorgasbord of delicacies, from every sort of pickle imaginable to delicate cakes and bottles of champagne.

They had fallen silent, but the sight of such abundance seemed to recall Gretchen to her tale. "I'm nattering on," she said apologetically.

Winnie turned from the window and shook her head. It had been some time since she'd been in the company of someone who had so much to say and told a story well. Lottie had many strong points and had kept her laughing at her antics, but fascinating conversation really wasn't her forte. "Oh, no, please do go on," she urged the doxie. Now that they were in a brighter place, she could see how warm Gretchen's large brown eyes were, and she knew that she'd been wrong to doubt her.

"If you're sure," Gretchen said with a grin. "I suppose it's a relief to tell someone about it, really, and I can tell that you're a trustworthy sort, even if you are an American," she teased. Winnie smiled back, not taking offence. "Well, I did go to the café on my next afternoon off," Gretchen continued. 'It was indeed mouse-sized, and I'm not as petite as you are, but I just managed to squeeze in. I felt a bit like Alice after she had drunk the potion, I must say. The Narrows is built right above the pavement, set into the foundation of a green grocers. A large dog minding its own business could easily miss it. I was fascinated by how cosy and well-appointed it was, with chequered tablecloths, gleaming cutlery, and a comforting wood stove set in an inglenook where a large oven used to be. The place had belonged to the grandfather of one of Gerard's friends, you see, and was rent-free. At one end was a little dais with a couple of stage lights, nothing fancy. 'We have music here some nights, usually provided by ourselves, as the budget don't stretch far,' Gerard told me. It was then that I had an idea."

Winnie could see the garish lights of what Piccadilly Circus must be ahead, with flashing two-story advertisements for soft drinks, chewing gum and various shows taking centre stage. Even long past midnight, the traffic whirled around in a dizzying manner, headlights cutting across whatever darkness was left by the billboards and marquees. They both instinctively stopped, as they knew that if they continued that direction, the noise would make conversation impossible. Gretchen caught the eye of a police dog on his beat, a capable looking yellow Labrador. "Hello, Sam. Just out for a stroll with my friend here. Everything going well?" she asked with a familiarity that surprised Winnie.

"All tickety-boo," Sam said with an affable nod. "Nice little spot over there if you need to take a load off your paws for a minute." He gestured toward a well-lit bench with his helmeted head.

"Thanks, Sam! Think we may take you up on that," Gretchen answered, waving as they moved off. "He looks out for me," she explained. "Friend of my brother's. Knows I go home this way and keeps an eye out."

Winnie nodded, somewhat relieved, as the darkness had felt a little forbidding. The harsh brilliance of the area ahead hadn't seemed too congenial, either.

"So, what was your idea?" Winnie prompted.

"Ah, yes, well. Here's the bit that got me into the fix I'm in now. This area is a haven for creative mice—writers, musicians, actors, painters. Gerard told me. And his first words when I met him came back to me one day when I was emptying the leftovers into the hotel bins. Just a few paws full of the beautiful, untouched food I was tossing out could feed so many mice. Well. The café is open all hours because it serves customers with odd schedules—you know how artists are. Shall we go and have a look?"

Winnie was feeling braver after their encounter with Sam and felt sure that Gretchen knew the streets of London well. She eagerly assented, and they took a winding but short route to a rather rundown street. At first, it seemed to be completely dark and quiet, but as Winnie's eyes and ears adjusted to her surroundings, she noticed a small patch of light just a few feet away and heard a voice. It was singing sweetly—in French, she thought. Gretchen drew close to one window and beckoned Winnie to the other. As they watched, a little grey mouse in a red beret bowed to the diners and took a seat at one of the tables, where a plate of food already awaited her.

Moments later, a somewhat tubby white mouse wearing a spotted cravat took the little stage and began to tell a story while illustrating it on a large pad of paper propped up on an easel. When he finished to a round of applause, he also found a steaming dish at his place. Winnie was entranced. As they stood looking in, the mouse in the beret finished her meal, waved a genial goodbye to the other diners and came toward the door. The two dogs pulled back into the shadows as she came out and went her way humming.

"I think I understand," Winnie said softly. "They 'sing for their supper.' "

"Exactly. "Or tell stories or do whatever they like to amuse the others. No money changes hands."

Winnie was silent for a moment. "So, Gerard was there with the van to take the food you'd saved for him."

"Yes," Gretchen replied. "But I went too far this time, and I was caught out by the sous chef. Apparently, a whole meal was sent back because the steak was garnished with a few shrimps. The waiter said that the diner made quite a fuss and swore she had told the hotel of her dietary requirements. She would not touch the food. I thought that I was alone when I scraped it into a tin for transport, but I was not. The sous chef came looking for the shrimp, saying that he could use them in a salad, saw me near the empty plate with my tin, and came to the obvious conclusion. I don't know what I or the café will do, really."

As they left the little space of warmth, light, and comfort behind, Winnie pondered her new friend's dilemma. She most certainly would not have been given any references, and jobs were scarce. Winnie had seen enough newspapers during her stay to know that. It came to her quite suddenly what she must do. By hook or by crook, she must get in touch with Douglas.

Chapter Sixty
One Good Turn

Gretchen felt rather small and insignificant in the shadow of the looming ironwork gates that marked the "working" area of the Palace, but she drew herself up to her full size and breathed deeply. 'This is the chance of a lifetime,' she thought, 'and you're not about to spoil it by wobbling now.' As it turned out, she didn't have time to let her anxiety get the better of her. She was whisked inside, taken through a series of labyrinthine but not unpleasant corridors and left outside a door marked with a name that she was too muddled to read. She lifted her paw and knocked.

A bright-eyed black and tan dog opened the door and beckoned her inside. "Gretchen Schwartz, isn't it?" Her voice was warm, and the doxie surprised herself by taking an immediate liking to her. And she couldn't help but admire the feathery bits of fur at each dainty ankle, atop smart but sensible boots. Still in a bit of a daze, Gretchen didn't quite catch the dog's full name as she introduced herself, though she knew that she must be the head housekeeper for the Palace. "...But you can call me Kit," she said. "We may serve royals, but we do not stand too much on ceremony amongst ourselves. Here, please do take a seat."

The interview passed in a blur. Gretchen told Winnie afterwards that she truly had no idea what answers she had given nor indeed what the questions were.

There was a profound silence after the questions and answers ceased, during which the ticking of a little brass clock on the mantelpiece was the only sound to be heard. Gretchen felt her paws shaking a little. How could she have dared to think that she could find a place here? Before Winnie had put the idea into her head, she would have counted herself lucky to have found a chambermaid's post at the Churchill Arms. She steeled herself for an inevitable if courteous rejection. After what seemed an eternity, Kit placed her pen down on the desk and spoke. "We shall be glad to have you join our staff and certainly would like to do all we can to help a worthy cause, too. Shall we go and visit the kitchens so you can see where you will be working?"

Gretchen's eyes widened, and, quite speechless, she nodded, not trusting her voice. It was difficult to believe that a chance encounter with a fellow dachshund on the stairwell of the Ritz could have led to such a wonderful outcome. Her old bosses weren't uncaring people, but they had rules to follow, and she had to admit that she had stepped out of line. At least now everything was on an even keel. She hadn't even met Douglas and certainly owed him a favour of gratitude, too. Perhaps she could take him to The Narrows—he might enjoy the music. 'Oh, and Winnie did mention that he lives with a mouse, so I do think he'll be sympathetic to the cause,' she thought as she trotted after Kit.

The kitchen, one of several as it turned out, was a surprisingly cosy place, despite the soaring ceiling and grand proportions. Battalions of copper pots winked cheerily in the afternoon sunshine from the tall windows at one end, and there was a homey sort of muddle on the zinc countertop, where a flour-bedecked border collie was dexterously wielding a rolling pin. She interrupted her labours and wiped her paws on her apron as she saw Kit approaching with Gretchen in her wake.

"Frankie," Kit said, "this is your new assistant, Gretchen. She comes to us from the Ritz and is exceptionally professionally qualified. Gretchen, Frankie has been with us for many years and has been commended more than once by Her Majesty. You are sure to learn much from her." Frankie nodded at the dachshund, and it was difficult to tell from her shrewd expression whether she approved of her new colleague or not. Gretchen quietly took the apron that lay over a nearby stool and began to peel the apples piled high at the end of the counter. "Tha's right, get stuck in thar, and you'll be alright," Frankie said in a broad northern accent. "But tha's not wanta peel those, just slice 'em. Her Majesty's fond of the skins." And thus, began Gretchen's first lesson in the vagaries of royal cuisine.

A few days later, Gerard arrived early at one of the Palace's service entrances, which he devoutly hoped was the right one. He'd had a message from a chap named Douglas, and there'd been a handy map sketched in it.

But Gerard hadn't really got a head for maps, preferring to follow his nose most of the time. The comings and goings of so many dogs and cats awed him. Of course, it would take quite a retinue to prop up such an institution, but he'd never really thought too much about it. Not wanting to attract unfriendly attention from passers-by, he edged himself halfway behind a bit of box hedge whilst he waited.

"You, there! Step onto the pavement, please. Did you not read the sign?" Gerard did as he was told and noticed, too late, a rather conspicuous sign warning errant pedestrians to 'Keep off the Grass.' He also couldn't help but notice a burly tom in what looked like very official garb looming over the sign. Despite his fear, Gerard had the urge to point out that the cat was himself transgressing, but he swallowed this impertinence. "And what exactly is your business here?" the tom enquired, in a tone that suggested that there could be no satisfactory answer to his question.

Gerard lifted his chin and refused to be bullied. "I 'ave an appointment with Mr Manners," he said, pleased that there wasn't a hint of a squeak in his voice. "I'm just a bit early."

"Oh, you do, do you?" The cat regarded him for a moment. "Well, if that's how it is, why don't you just step this way, Mister…?"

"Geoffrey. Gerard Geoffrey."

The cat nodded indifferently and pressed a button near the door. "Mr Manners. Chap named Mr Geoffrey to see you."

"Fine, fine, let him in," came a harassed-sounding voice. The cat stood aside with a bit of a smirk on his face. Gerard edged past him into what looked like a never-ending corridor with hundreds of doors on either side. The tom had closed the door swiftly behind him, so there was no hope of help from that quarter. He began making his way down the hall, his head swivelling from side to side as he read the name plaques. As it turned out, he did not have far to travel. A lean German shepherd emerged into the hallway, and his eyes grew wide.

"Who are you?" he said sharply.

Gerard was tiring of this sort of treatment and answered shortly, "I'm Gerard. Gerard Geoffrey. I'm 'ere because...I mean, I was meant to meet someone in the kitchens."

"There is absolutely no reason for you to be here!" Mr Manners barked. "No mice in my kitchens! What are you talking about? Out, out this instant! Why ever did that wretched cat let you in?" And he suited his actions to his words, marching Gerard before him.

"I say!" Gerard began, but Mr Manners was in a particularly bad humour after having had a very trying morning and roared over his objection.

"You'll say nothing! I don't want to hear it."

Gerard drooped, and he was just about to push out the door when a corgi appeared. "Mr Manners? Is everything alright?" And then his gaze dropped to the harried-looking mouse. "Oh! You must be Gerard." He extended his paw. The German shepherd looked from one to the other in bewilderment.

"What is the meaning of this, Master Pembroke? Explain yourself."

Douglas straightened up and faced his employer. "I sent you a note days ago," he said. "It explains everything. Gerard thought he had every right to be here, sir."

Mr Manners' expression changed, and he patted his pockets. "Oh...I do remember something of the sort," he mumbled. "Do remind me."

Within a few minutes, Gerard had been ferried to the kitchen where Gretchen had already made herself indispensable to Frankie. Together with Douglas, he emerged triumphant with two baskets of spoils and an assurance from Gretchen that she would join them at The Narrows for a slap-up Sunday lunch.

The next afternoon saw Winnie, Douglas, and Gretchen happily, if a little cosily, ensconced at a table in the midst of nearly fifty mice. In lieu of individual performances, most of them had opted to participate in a sort of cabaret, and the little room resounded with singing and laughter. As Gretchen swayed happily to the music, her eye caught a movement at the window, and she was just about certain that she had seen a corgi's face there, one that was familiar to every British citizen. She edged over to get a better look but caught only a glimpse of a pair of sensible black pumps disappearing into the depths of a distinctly upper-class motor.

Chapter Sixty-One
Let's Ride

Douglas wheeled the two bikes he had borrowed from a friend into the station with some difficulty, juggling them and his luggage, too. He was thankful to prop them up on their stands and wait for Winnie. As much as he would have preferred to have rolled up on a Harley Davison or even a lowlier Honda Cub, he still hadn't got the means to buy his first motorbike. Realising how many miles there were between London and the coast, he had dismissed the thought of riding all the way there anyway, and it would be far more comfortable having a snooze on the train.

Winnie arrived, bouncing along, suitcase at her side, and was immediately visible by her yellow hat. She stopped, said hello, gave Douglas a peck on the cheek and then admired the bicycles.

"Wow, they look like motorbikes. I wonder what made you choose these?" she teased.

In front of her were two similarly sized Raleigh Choppers, one metallic light blue, the other deep purple with striking luminous writing. Both were sitting on their kickstands, which gave them the stationary look of a parked motorcycle. The front wheels were smaller than the rear ones by some inches and had red lines around the sidewalls. The chrome mudguards shone brightly. Both had long padded high-back seats and the most notable feature, the 'ape hanger' handlebars, which Winnie recognised from the American motorbikes that Douglas so loved.

"Which one is mine?" she asked enthusiastically.

"I think the purple one, it's a Mark II, slightly newer, and the seat is closer to the handlebars. It'll probably suit you better. I've got the Mark I, with a knob to change gears," Douglas replied.

"Oh, I see, that's rather cool, we change the gear down, there do we?" Winnie said as she fiddled with the stick on the middle of the frame. "So, ready for the trip?"

"Yup, I've got the tickets, we'll put the bikes in the guard's van and find a seat in the carriage. Can't be sitting on the wooden floor or standing for the whole journey," Douglas said.

"No, that wouldn't do," Winnie smiled, as she helped Douglas on with the bikes. The guard was on the platform waiting to signal the train's departure, watching for the pair to finish. "Mind my paraffin stove, won't you, I'm going to get my spuds on the boil after I've walked through the train and checked the tickets."

"Oh, of course," Winnie replied, as he shut the first of the double doors behind them, stepped up and pulled the other one to. The guard cried out, "Close the doors down the front please," and then blew his whistle. The train gave a clunk as it picked up the slack and then steadily pulled out of the station.

"Tickets please," the guard said, looking at Douglas and Winnie. "Yes, that'll do."

Winnie looked around and her eyes were drawn to the two large boxes stacked in the corner. She looked at the guard. "Are they what I think they are?"

"Yes, that's right," he replied. "Coffins."

Douglas jumped back slightly, and the pair's faces both revealed what their next question was.

"It's okay, they are empty," the guard said, laughing. "Just dropping them off for somebody, but I have had the odd fare dodger chancing their luck from time to time, gave me a right shock the first time it happened too… Anyway, can't stop here gassing any longer, tickets to check. See you anon."

Winnie and Douglas walked in the other direction, and the minute the pair entered the closest carriage they knew they were going to have an interesting journey.

"Excellent, excellent, I'm so glad you came in when you did," the rather flamboyant husky said, dressed up to the nines, as he turned around from his seat and looked up at Douglas and Winnie. "I was hoping we'd get a couple more passengers boarding. Mr Bickerstaff has let us down, and Miss Shuttleworth has got a most terrible cold. Her sister was adamant she shouldn't come."

Winnie looked at Douglas. Neither had any idea what the dog was talking about.

"Oh, I do apologise, you must think me awfully rude. My name is Mr Anthony Fortescue-Berringer, Tony to my friends. I'm the producer here at the Rustington Amateur Dramatics Society, and we're just embarking on our first tour of The Scarlet Pimpernel. It's so exciting, I can't tell you how much I'm looking forward to it all."

"My name is Winnie, and this is Douglas. A pleasure," Winnie said, hoping the pair could continue along the aisle and find a window seat, preferably with a table, in the middle of the carriage.

The husky had other ideas, though. He lightly touched Winnie's elbow.

"Oh, please, could I ask you a huuuge favour? As I mentioned, we are a couple of members down, until we get to Wellbury, at least. I could really do with help from both of you. Just as stand -ins, you understand, to do a read-through. I've got the scripts right here, no need to dress up or anything."

"Well…" Winnie said, looking at Douglas, "I suppose we could help you out, we aren't getting off for a long while yet." She wasn't at all keen, really, but Mr Fortescue-Berringer was so eager that it seemed churlish to refuse.

Douglas didn't look too pleased at the prospect, but the die was cast. The husky leaped up for joy, handed both dogs a script and ushered them along to meet the others. He clapped his hands and turned them by the shoulders to face the clutch of disaffected-looking actors variously lounging about with magazines, sipping tea from paper cups or gossiping in pairs.

"Duckies, duckies! May I have your attention! Look here, I have excellent news. We have stand-ins for poor Miss Shuttleworth and that rotter Mr Bickerstaff, and you all know our star Mr Dankworth is joining down the line. We can now rehearse during our journey—isn't it wonderful?"

Various dogs and cats looked up at the new arrivals, whilst several groans could be heard further down the carriage. "And there I was thinking we'd get a sleep on this trip, no rest of the wicked," one said, whilst another whined, "Stunning, it's only the hundredth time we've rehearsed this darn play."

"Ignore them," Tony said. "Let's get started, shall we?" He looked at Winnie and Douglas. "I'm sure you know the story, set in England and France during the French Revolution's Reign of Terror, yes? Set in 1792. Well, I've followed the original and haven't changed much at all. Places everyone, I'd like us all to start at Calais. Sir Percy Blakeney—that's you, Douglas—is approaching Citizen Chauvelin at an inn. You have just met and are trying to escape. Make it real. You are offering Chauvelin a pinch of snuff... Ready?"

Douglas looked bewildered, as he hadn't even managed to find the right page. Winnie, who had read the book and was well versed with the ins and outs, stifled a smile at Douglas's conundrum.

"Just read it as best you can. I'm sure you'll soon pick it up," Winnie said as she flicked through his script and found the right place to begin. A dog in the next seat began.

" 'Indeed, Monsieur, you are most gracious.' "

Douglas started to speak in a hesitant monotone. " 'A pleasure... a pleasure indeed. You are a dog of fine distinction, and I wish you every success in your search.' Sorry, I'll try that again. 'I wish you every success in your search for the Pimpernel. Now I must be going, I have urgent business to attend. Tootle pip.' "

Eyes began to roll as the cast members heard Douglas fluff his next lines.

"Tony, Tony, are you sure we can't wait? This, this, erm, for want of a better word, imposter, really isn't right, you know," whined a languid poodle.

"We don't have much time. Now, what would you suggest? I can't read it now can I, I need to watch the interplay between the cast, make sure everything is proceeding as I anticipated." Mr Fortescue-Berringer lifted his paws helplessly.

"Divas, the lot of them," Douglas whispered to Winnie. "Can't we just go and hide back in the guard's van or something? I'm not enjoying being the centre of all this negative attention."

Winnie laughed. "Perhaps I can read in your place," she offered, as she pulled the script from Douglas's paw and continued reading his lines. Tony looked back up, wondering why he was hearing the feminine voice of the young dachshund, but then actually smiled and nodded. She read the lines as though she had been born to play the role.

The rather odd rehearsal continued. Winnie's confidence gradually increased, and she even started putting on some accents as she read the parts of the Scarlet Pimpernel's many disguised characters. Douglas began to relax, watching from his seat, leaning against the window.

"This is going so well," Tony said to the group, "really, really well. Now, you know we have a dress rehearsal later this evening at the hotel. Mrs Miles has done a sterling job with the outfits; her stitch craft is second to none. And I'm reliably informed that the Fortune Theatre, near Canterbury, where we are debuting, is under new ownership. American chap—he's had it refurbished since the last time, so no repeats of those tatty curtains and flea-bitten seats. Oh, and more good news, they have obtained the services of a young lad who is training to be a lighting engineer. He can't be any worse than the last one, who always seemed to have the spotlight trained on the wrong cast member."

A rather unintelligible announcement came over the tannoy that the next station stop for Wellbury was ahead, where the train would terminate. Winnie and Douglas knew they were going to have to change for their onward journey. The members of the amateur group gathered their belongings and made for the exits.

Mr Dankworth was waiting on the platform as promised and waved to Tony the minute he saw him in the carriage. The jubilant director smiled, glad his star had been true to his word, and pushed through the group to be the first to greet him properly. In his haste, his foot slipped as he stepped off the train, and he found himself dropping his suitcase and lying spread eagle on top of poor Mr Dankworth. A rather indiscreet tear in the seat of Tony's trousers had appeared, and his spotted pants peeped through. His personal belongings had fallen out of the now open suitcase. Douglas rushed to his aid and helped him up, unharmed, but the same couldn't be said for Mr Dankworth, who lay in a state of shock. Douglas soon pronounced that he had more than likely sprained his ankle and would need to put his leg up for a couple of days. Tony gasped as he gathered up his smoking jacket and five starched shirts from the platform. "Oh, my goodness, Dickie, what's happened? The show, the show... all my hard work..."

Winnie watched as the producer fussed around the actor, although it was clear he was more upset by the fact that Mr Dankworth would be confined to his hotel room than by his obvious discomfort. He turned as Winnie stepped down and rushed over to her. "Winnie, oh there you are, my dear! Poor Dickie here has had an accident. I'm at your mercy. Will you please understudy for him, just this once? We have our first matinee performance tomorrow afternoon."

Winnie realised she was in an awkward position, as she was not really particularly good at saying no to others. Despite Douglas's glare, she found herself assenting to Tony's request.

Chapter Sixty-Two
Curtain Call

A bit of a scuffle erupted in the stalls just as the curtain was about to rise. Trying not to think about the flutter in her stomach, Winnie peeped out and saw a pair of dogs arguing with two already-seated theatregoers. She slipped down the stairway next to the stage to see what the fuss was about, keeping to the shadowy outer edges so as not to be seen in her powdered wig, knee-breeches, and embroidered waistcoat.

"I repeat, you are in our seats! Will you kindly move? The show is about to start," the irate dog said, pointing to the door. The cat sitting in the closest seat dismissed the suggestion and called for the usher, who was already approaching.

"What seems to be the problem?" he asked.

The dog explained the predicament, and the usher asked for the tickets to check if he was right.

"You are quite right; you have booked seats 7D and 7E. There are only two slight problems," he continued. "Firstly, these tickets are for the play When the Dark Turns to Night and not The Scarlet Pimpernel. Secondly, they are for the Garden Theatre in Dukes Street, and not the Fortune Theatre, which is where we are now."

The dogs squinted at their tickets again. "What about those seats over there," one asked, pointing to a couple of empty places nearby. "Can't we just stay and use those?"

The usher shook his head vigorously. "Oh no, that is quite out of the question—no, that wouldn't do at all. Now, please leave."

The dogs, looking rather foolish, removed themselves from the auditorium as quickly as possible, and the seats' rightful occupants settled in more comfortably. "Strange, really," one of them said. "You did notice that those seats were bolted open, didn't you?"

"Oh, I expect they're just stuck. These old theatres, you know. Always things out of order," the other replied and buried her nose in the programme.

The house lights began to dim, signalling that the play was about to start. As Winnie turned back to the stage, she was nearly mown down by a young Jack Russell terrier who was shoving something in his back jeans pocket and grinning from ear to ear as he made for one of the exits. "Excuse you," she muttered, reaching up to make sure her pompadour was not in disarray.

"Places please, everyone," Tony called out. "Douglas, you have an important job. I need you to give the grips some help between scenes and be prompter during them, as we discussed. I do hope you know your way around the script by now," he said with a wink. Douglas took the teasing in his stride and gave Winnie's paw a squeeze.

"Break a leg," he said. "Or don't. I never know which is right." Winnie gave him a nervous smile as he disappeared into the wings and took his post.

The curtain rose, and Winnie gave Sir Percy Blakeney's opening lines without faltering, lounging against a settee and drawling in a perfectly foppish sort of way that reminded Douglas uncannily of some of the real aristocrats he saw on a daily basis at the palace, albeit they didn't wear hose and buckled shoes. He watched with admiration as she strutted convincingly offstage, enthusiastic applause echoing after her.

Chauvelin slunk in next, a pointer smoothing his curling moustache. He clumped about, airing his grievances against the aristos and sitting down briefly to write a letter. He was just punching the air with righteous indignation against the Pimpernel when a loud and unmistakable "thoing" sounded into the rafters. The actor's eyes bulged, and he tried again, with the same effect. This time tittering erupted from some of the less well-mannered members of the audience. Shaking his head, the dog bravely attempted a recovery. A pimpernel flower lay on the desk next to him, proof that his enemy had been there quite recently. He picked it up and spat a curse at it, preparatory to tossing it on the floor. But before he could grind it under his heel, as per the script, the flower spurted a dark, inky substance up into his face. Chauvelin began dashing hither and thither about the stage with his paws out, looking rather too frantic to be a scheming villain. Douglas, who had had an unobstructed view of the scene, hesitated, but then took pity on the pointer. He nodded to the cat managing the curtain from above, and as soon as the red velvet had descended, guided the temporarily blinded dog off the stage. He could hear a rustle of whispers and seat-shifting in the audience.

"What is the meaning of this?" Tony shouted, as the troupe gathered round the unfortunate pointer. Winnie offered him a wet towel and guided him to the bathroom. "Is there a prankster among us? I'll have you know that any losses we incur will come straight out of your pocket, whoever you are. This is monstrous!" And his blue eyes, usually good humoured, flashed frostily at first one and then another of the actors.

"Now, Tony, why would any of us want to do that?" Ms Deronda said in what she meant to be soothing tones, though they sounded to Douglas's ears like nails on a chalkboard. The poodle patted the director's arm. "It's our play, too, you know."

"I'll check the props over carefully before they go on," Douglas offered. "No one was really watching the stage just before we began. Maybe a mischievous pup switched out the flowers. And any number of toys could have made that noise from somewhere in the audience."

Somewhat mollified, Tony wiped his brow with a purple handkerchief and waved them away. "We'll sort everything later. The show must go on!"

The curtain was raised several minutes later with the actors in place, and the murmurs of the audience stopped. Marguerite stood alongside Chauvelin, who was asking for her help to find the elusive Scarlet Pimpernel in exchange for her brother's life. Ms Doreen Pinkerton, a svelte Weimaraner, played the part well, even though the pointer left a large black paw print on her sleeve as he pleaded his case. She picked up a small mirror and adjusted her hair as Chauvelin continued.

"I can arrange a pardon for this brother of yours, Armand, as long as you promise to tell me the true identity of the miscreant," Chauvelin said. "And you know what will happen if you fail me," he continued, pointing at something beyond the window.

Behind them was a rumble, as the spotlight swept away from the pair to the guillotine and turned the stage red. The blade fell to the accompaniment of a tremendous "bong" of the sort usually heard at the fairground after a successful attempt at the "Test Your Strength" booth. The audience gasped as a pumpkin rolled across the stage, leaving its straw-stuffed body behind.

"I can but try, Monsieur, if you will be true to your word," Marguerite replied, wondering why the prop had been activated at the wrong time. The lights dimmed and then lit up the stage again. Marguerite was now alone, standing near a window lit by three candles. Hunting around a chest of drawers in Sir Percy's private study, she found a ring engraved with a Scarlet Pimpernel. She held it up to the light. "Oh, my husband! How I have misjudged you!" she exclaimed in heartrending tones. On cue, Sir Percy entered, bedecked in an elegant blue frock coat over a double-breasted waistcoat and buff breeches.* He was nearly toppled by Marguerite's enthusiastic embrace. In the end, only the gentleman's wig fell off, and his ladylove unceremoniously crammed it back on in a jiffy.

The audience seemed not to have heeded this minor mishap, and the troupe relaxed into their parts again. In the final, affecting scene by the cliffs, Sir Percy shed his last disguise and was reunited with Marguerite. The two stood centre stage in a rapturous attitude as the lights began to dim, and a ripple of clapping began.

The applause was short lived, drowned out by the strains of a Wurlitzer organ, rising slowly from beneath the floor, directly in front of the stage. Its multicoloured lights glowed, and the fickle spotlight shone on the empty music stool as the strains of "For He's a Jolly Good Fellow" poured out and the keys danced.

As the music died away, there was utter and unnatural silence in the theatre. And then thunderous applause, stomping feet, cries of "Bravo!" and "Encore!" and other unmistakable sounds of approbation. Winnie and

Doreen recovered themselves and bowed. The curtain fell and rose again on the entire cast several times before the last claps died away.

Tony watched, flabbergasted—horror-struck, really—and when the actors at last left the stage, they found him seated on a gilded drawing-room chair with his head in his paws. "I'm finished," he moaned pathetically. "We're finished. It's the end of the Rustington Amateur Dramatics Society." From nowhere, a maniacal laugh sounded. "Oh, stop that," he shouted irritably, "whoever or whatever you are."

Winnie was inclined to see the humorous side of the affair but could never bear to see someone humiliated. She tapped the distraught husky gently on the shoulder. "Mr Fortescue-Berringer, what sort of dog was hired on to do the lighting and sound?"

"Oh, I don't know," he groaned. "Excitable young chap but seemed bright enough."

"Maybe a Jack Russell?" she prompted.

"Why yes, I think so. Larry, I think his name was. Where is he? He must be behind this!"

"Maybe some of it, but he wasn't at his station when the play began. I saw him near the stage," Winnie said decidedly.

Douglas, who had done a little investigation of his own, came and stood by her side. "Just saw a St Bernard slipping out from up there," he offered.

"Bickerstaff!" shouted several of the actors in unison.

"But what about the guillotine? I'm sure it was offstage for that act?" Ms Pinkerton asked.

"It was," Douglas assured them, puzzled himself.

There was silence as everyone contemplated this conundrum. "Well," Ms Deronda said, "it's the audience that pays us, and they were happy."

"Oh, but Cecil Crumper was in that audience," Tony replied, morosely. "And he'll make mincemeat of us, just you watch."

Early the next morning, Winnie and Douglas made their farewells somewhat reluctantly, as they hated to leave the troupe whilst they were still under a cloud. They returned to the station to collect their bicycles and board their next train. Winnie purchased a paper from a hawker near the entrance. "I do like a crossword once in a while," she said, when Douglas looked at her questioningly. Once they were settled on board, she folded the pages back and chewed her pencil end thoughtfully. "What's a 5-letter word for...Oh, look! There's a review of the Monday night plays just here!"

Douglas read over her shoulder.

Monday, 21st April 1978

Pandemonium at the Palladium

Last night I was obligated to watch a new play put on by the Rustington Amateur Dramatics touring group at the Fortune Theatre. I was expecting a rather dull affair from a set of actors that would normally be walking the floors of the local bank or office rather than treading the boards of the stage, but I have to say I was pleasantly surprised.

Mr Fortescue-Berringer's adaptation of the classic Scarlet Pimpernel was experimental to say the least. Having taken my seat early, I watched the usual array of mishaps that precede such performances. The prompter was searching manically for his script, the runner was busy dropping props and there was even some light entertainment before the start as two dogs with tickets to a different play were sent off with a flea in their ears.

The curtain finally rose on Sir Percy Blakeney eloquently reciting his lines with panache and poise, quite the little starlet in the making, mark my words. Other actors joined the fray, and I stayed riveted by the dialogue until one of them stepped on a mousetrap and yelped out in agony. Later on, an unfortunate incident with a flower caused the show to be paused, as Chauvelin fumbled about the stage in dismay. Recovering from adversity is always a sign of great strength, and this little troupe soldiered on with only a few further oddities. I'm not sure why the poodle was wearing a dirndl, rather Germanic, but funny nonetheless, and I could definitely see a Chihuahua under the desk flipping the script over for one of the lesser actors to read. Perhaps, for all I know, this was all part of Fortescue-Berringer's avant garde vision for an otherwise rather tired classic drama. Unfortunately, he declined my request to interview him.

I won't spoil the grand finale for readers who may be intending to visit in the coming days. All I will say is that the audience were in raptures.

Cecil Crumper

Theatre Critic, The Wellbury Chronicle

***Superstition and Theatres:** The chapter makes note of two theatre seats that are unoccupied and fixed in their downward position. This is a reference to the superstition that many theatres have resident ghosts; in particular, the Palace Theatre in London keeps two seats always bolted open to ensure that the spirits are accommodated. Additionally, some believe that theatres should remain empty at least one night per week, traditionally on Mondays, to placate any ghosts that haunt the site. Three lit candles are also a sign to be wary of, and according to theatre lore, the person closest to the shortest candle will either pass away or be the next to marry. Marguerite uses a real mirror, a prop which some believe is a cause of performance disasters, including forgotten lines and broken sets. Finally, Sir Percy's frock coat is blue, which is said to be an unlucky colour to wear onstage, unless counteracted by something silver. The superstition is believed to date back to the early days of theatre, when blue dye was expensive and difficult to acquire. If actors wore blue, you could assume that they were successful. However, many companies donned the colour to fool their audiences into thinking they were more popular than they were. Only the most prosperous theatre companies had blue costumes accompanied by real silver thread, fabric, or lace.

Chapter Sixty-Three
Capturing the Castle

"I'm gasping for a cuppa," Douglas panted, as he dismounted and laid his bicycle on the side of the road.

"Haven't you got water?" Winnie asked. "I can lend you mine."

"I don't need water. I need tea," Douglas grumbled. "I'm shattered."

"We're almost there," Winnie said reassuringly, refolding her map and pushing her Baedeker into her pocket. "And it's all downhill from here." She began pedalling forward, ready to coast down toward the village below.

"You can say that again," Douglas mumbled.

"What was that? You've been an absolute bear since breakfast." Winnie halted her progress and looked back at the corgi; her head tilted.

"I don't know that I'm so keen on all this 'authentically English' business. That's the problem. It is all a business. You just can't see that because you're not from here," Douglas replied, kicking at one of the bike's wheels in a dissatisfied way. " 'Ye olde England' and all that. It's rubbish. If you've seen one picturesque village in the South of England, you've seen 'em all. And you know they're teeming with toffs sniggering at the likes of us."

"Oh, don't be such an old misery guts. Let them snigger. There's real history here, so much more than in America. And my guidebook says Castle Frithorpe isn't just a tourist trap. There isn't really even a high street."

"Good thing you didn't talk Lottie into coming here, then," Douglas smirked.

"Really, Douglas, I'm beginning to wish I'd left you to stew back at the hostel. I'm going to see what there is to see. If you plan to grouse the whole way, then maybe you should stay here."

Not really wanting to separate, and slightly ashamed of his attitude, Douglas harrumphed. "I just hope there's a tea shop, then," he muttered, as he struggled to catch up with Winnie, who had gotten a head start. "Wish I had a motorbike. That would really wake this place up. Raise some eyebrows."

Despite her bravado, Winnie was troubled by her companion's mood. "It's not my fault," she said to herself, though she inevitably felt that it was, somehow. Shaking her head and ears, she tried to push her worries to the back of her mind and gave herself up to the pleasure of speeding down a quiet lane, wind rushing through her fur, with buttercups nodding sleepily on both sides. In no time at all, the road opened out, and the village lay before her, still and silent yet quietly welcoming, like a kindly maiden aunt.

She skidded to a stop and admired the colour of the stone in the afternoon light. The buildings themselves were low, with a multitude of gables jostling each other in a companionable way. To her right, alongside one of the wisteria-hung doorways, a little table was laid with cakes and biscuits under a glass cloche, with an honesty box discreetly tucked alongside. Their breakfast had been very early and rather skimpy, once they'd put aside half of it for lunch, and that was now a distant memory, too. Winnie felt her tummy rumbling and heard the screech of Douglas's brakes as he drew up alongside her.

"Arh, that looks good," he said, immediately noting the edibles on offer and rummaging in his jean's pockets. "Drat it all! I left my money at the hostel."

"Good thing you've got me around to fund you, then," Winnie teased, producing a pound from her purse. Douglas brightened, and she put it behind her back. "But I'll only share if you promise to give this place a chance." 'And give me a chance,' she thought. She had planned the excursion with care and felt irritation fizzing just beneath the playfulness.

"Alright, deal," Douglas replied.

They took their repast to the covered market cross and sprawled there comfortably, Douglas examining the peculiar granite blocks nearby, and Winnie taking photos of the winding street beyond. "I think those were for mounting one's horse more conveniently," she said, noticing the direction of his gaze.

"Your Baedeker must be pretty thorough," Douglas said, watching Winnie look at the travel guide.

"It is. But there's also a little plaque right above your head."

Douglas laughed, and the tension seemed to be broken. "Where to next? I will follow wherever you lead, my fair lady."[*]

Winnie blushed a little. "To the church, then," she said briskly.

Once inside the empty but gracious stone building, they wandered around the perimeter, admiring the stained glass and stone carvings. They stopped in front of the mechanism of a clock that claimed to be nearly five hundred years old, according to the nearby placard. It whirred and ticked away inside its glass case. "Uncle Nap would love this," Douglas said, craning his neck to see around the gears, while Winnie attempted to get a photo despite the dimness. "Hmm. It doesn't have a face." They leapt backward as the bell tower bonged twice, echoing off the stone walls.[†] Douglas instinctively thrust a paw in front of Winnie.

"It's a masterpiece of engineering, isn't it?" came a voice behind them. A corgi had appeared as if from nowhere and was eyeing them curiously. "Don't mind me. I'm just here to wind it up. The mechanism controls the bells rather than keeping exact time. Rhys is the name," he said, extending a paw toward Winnie. She took it and made the necessary introductions. He was a striking dog, still youthful, with a brindled grey and white face and rather unsettling pale blue eyes.

"Actually, the church has some notoriety in these parts," Rhys continued. "It has the tallest tower in the area. A number of years ago there was a storm, and a tree came crashing down on a neighbouring church, destroying its belfry. The parishioners all pulled together and over time raised enough money to rebuild the structure. They decided to increase the height of the new tower, making it the tallest in the county. This church would then no longer be entitled to that accolade."

Douglas started fidgeting, but Winnie was enthralled.

"A pair of dogs were sent in the middle of the night with a long rope to climb the roof and measure the height of this tower. Pleased with their achievement, the parishioners began to boast that their church would be seen from all around the valley as a shining example of triumph in the face of adversity. A rather bold and canny dog, who shall remain nameless, decided to put an end to these taunts. How do you think he did that?"

Winnie decided that this was a rhetorical question and said nothing, not wanting to steal the dog's thunder. Douglas, annoyed by Rhys's manner, was not so accommodating. "Probably sneaked into the vestry of the other church and chopped off some of the rope," he blurted.

Rhys looked at him for the first time, and his gaze was none too friendly. "Ah. Yes. Shaved one metre off of it, in fact. After the renovations were complete, there was a grand reopening, and everyone sung the praises of the workmen, until they finally realised their mistake.

"That is some story, but we were just on our way out," Douglas said. Winnie looked at him questioningly. "Much more of the village to see before we go," he added. Nodding to Rhys, he opened the heavy oak door.

"I wanted to ask him a few questions!" Winnie exclaimed with a slight frown, as they picked their way through the crooked gravestones. "You didn't have to be in such a darn hurry." But Douglas scarcely heard her. Outside the quiet and calm of the church, an unearthly clamour reigned: laughter, the deafening screech of badly oiled wheels, and a few cheers. Winnie trotted ahead and peered through the lych-gate, and Douglas soon fetched up behind her. "Jumping Jehoshaphat!" she yelped.

The once-deserted street was now populated by cats and dogs of all stripes, most supplied with overflowing pints, and all of them focused on some sort of kerfuffle a little way uphill. Winnie followed the direction of their gaze. About fifty metres away, five bonneted heads reared up over the sides of as many tricked-out prams. Not only heads—long legs dangled over the fronts, and paws waved every which way. Three dogs and two cats, all in fancy dress, two nurses, a pirate, a rector and a Lord Mayor, were guiding their cargo swiftly down the slope. The pram in the lead, brashly painted red with flames on either side, nearly had an upset when the beagle passenger, well past puppyhood and sporting a bath towel nappy, attempted to high-five a spectator. He then began honking an air horn at intervals.[‡]

Douglas shook his head. "Here's a bit of authentic England for you," he shouted with a bit of a smirk. "We'll never get anywhere with this lot clogging the pavement."

"We have to try," Winnie replied, as loudly as she could, and pulled the gate open determinedly. "I want to get to the stone bridge. They say it's the best spot for a photo of the village." The pair emerged into the surging throng, edging their way gingerly along the building fronts.

Winnie pulled her yellow hat far down over her ears, trying to block out some of the noise. She saw a bit of a gap and plunged through it, then crossed the road and made for the bridge. "Oi! Watch where you're goin,' missy!" a gruff voice called after her, and she felt a slosh of liquid seeping through her jumper.

"Bleh!" she said to herself, disgusted that she now smelled of beer. Pausing for a moment to catch her breath, she scanned the somewhat less crowded pavement just behind her, sure that Douglas couldn't be far behind. But she was wrong. He was nowhere to be seen. She pondered whether she should wait for him and decided that he'd probably meet her at the bridge.

Away from the worst of the clamour, she breathed a sigh of relief and pulled her hat off to cool herself. The bridge was just a few metres away, and she slowed her pace, soothed by the gurgling of the stream to her left. The sun had been playing hide-and-seek all day but suddenly grew tired of the game and thrust aside the clouds. At the bridge's parapet, she turned and gazed up the street, readying her camera for a shot. As she focused and zoomed in a bit, she saw something which nearly made her drop it in the water below.

For there was Douglas, lounging comfortably against the bay window of a tea shop, with three almost identical poodles, dressed to kill, ranged around him in various admiring poses. One had put her paw familiarly on his arm. And he was laughing.

*Castle Frithorpe:** This location bears a strong resemblance to Castle Combe, where the 1967 movie *Doctor Doolittle* (starring Rex Harrison) was famously filmed. Harrison was also well-known for his role in *My Fair Lady*, a musical based on George Bernard Shaw's play *Pygmalion*.

†**Church Clock:** The clock mentioned here is modelled on one in St. Andrew's Church in Castle Combe, but it can also be compared to similar ones at Exeter Cathedral and elsewhere. The mechanism was originally in the church's bell tower and was moved to the nave in 1986, but for the purposes of this chapter, the authors have placed it there in 1978.

‡**Pram Race, England:** Windlesham in Surrey is well known for its pram race, an annual event in which teams race around the village, stopping at every pub along the way. The event has been going for over fifty years and usually takes place on Boxing Day, starting in the morning and running throughout the day. Funds raised through entry fees and coin collections during the race are distributed to local charities and organisations.

Chapter Sixty-Four
Growing Pains

Winnie felt herself go cold inside, and then suddenly warm with a hot flush. She forgot all about her photo and turned to face the opposite direction. Leaning against the ledge and looking over the burbling water, she gazed unseeingly at a particularly handsome garden near the water's edge, ablaze with tulips. 'I'm an absolute idiot,' she thought, her head and ears drooping. Seeing her reflection in the stream from a rather unflattering angle did nothing to cheer her, but she didn't look away.

Suddenly there was another face alongside hers, one with memorable blue eyes. "Hello—is that Winifred?"

Winnie looked up, startled out of herself. "Yes," she said, without thinking. "Oh, Rhys. Hello."

"Are you lost?" he asked, adjusting his shirt collar slightly and looking at her as though sizing her up. "Can't imagine it. You look clever enough to find your way around. This ruckus won't go on much longer, don't worry."

Winnie didn't know what to say, so she kept silent. She found Rhys's gaze a little disconcerting and looked away. "Has anyone ever told you what a lovely profile you have?" he asked. She shook her head. "Especially when you're looking pensive, as you are now. I'm something of a portrait painter, you know, just a hobby, so I have an eye for such things. Is something wrong?" The corgi edged a little closer and peered down at her questioningly.

Winnie's head was spinning. She didn't quite know what to think of this dog, but at least he offered a distraction from her unhappy thoughts. But she was suddenly conscious of the fact that she smelled of someone else's beer, and that her jeans hadn't been washed for a couple of days. "I'm fine," she replied at last. "Just waiting for my friend to catch up."

"Oh, I think I saw him. He's rather busy now," Rhys said with a hint of a smirk. "What say you we go find a cup of tea? I know a lovely place just round the corner. Nice old barn, done up very cosily. We can have a chat and wait for Douglas. I'm sure he'll check there. There aren't too many places to hide in this village."

'Why not?' Winnie asked herself. 'Maybe he'll tell me more about the church clock. No good moping about here.' And she astonished herself by taking Rhys's proffered arm. "I'd like that," she replied, this time looking him squarely in the eyes.

Rhys held her a bit more tightly to his side than she might have liked, but in her present mood, Winnie didn't much care. "So, are you traveling with any other friends?" he asked.

"Oh, yes," she replied airily, if a little mendaciously. Their hostel housed nearly twenty other young dogs and cats, though they were not actually spending much time all together, except at evening meals. "We're backpacking around, seeing the sights."

"It's just that you seem a little lonely." Rhys turned to look at her, and she evaded his glance.

"Ah! Is this it?" she asked, her voice a bit unnatural. Ahead of them was a long, low building with a cheerful sign directing potential customers around to the front for "Teas." Several dogs and cats were already making their way there, having seen the race upset by the "rector" and his charge. They had kept the course by refusing the various libations on offer as they sped past the surging crowd.

"Looks a mite busy," Rhys commented, as they passed the gate. "I know of a nice little place just the next town over. Let's go there."

Winnie withdrew her arm. "This looks lovely, and I'm a little tired," she said, making her way toward the big stable door. "Mmm. Smells wonderful too." Rhys looked less than enthusiastic but had no choice except to follow her. A sprightly Russell terrier cross sporting a blue and yellow spotted apron greeted them cheerily. "I've got the perfect table for two just over there near the fire. It's turning a little nippy out there, isn't it? I'll fetch you a pot of tea. Won't be a moment."

"Well, now, that's satisfactory, I suppose," Rhys said, scanning the room. He ordered cream teas for both. "So, tell me a bit more about yourself."

Winnie felt bolder now, and, pushing Douglas out of her thoughts, found that she was talking quite freely about Badger's Bay, Bertie, the Wagminster Library, and the rest. Rhys nodded and smiled and made appropriate noises. His eyes never left her face, and she found herself warmed by his attention. Really, he was rather like Douglas, she thought, and not just in appearance. Or at least like the old Douglas. "So why have you come here?" he suddenly asked.

"Oh, you know, just for the adventure. See a bit more of the world," she replied, looking down at her cooling tea and feeling her heart sink again. Rhys took the paw she had left on the table, and she didn't pull away.

"Well, you needn't be alone, you know," he said softly.

Just then, the terrier bustled up. "Oh, excuse me," she said, twinkling at them. "These are for you, miss. Handed to me by a handsome young devil, if I do say so myself. He told me to deliver them safely to the pretty red doxie at the corner table, and I'm guessing that must be you, dear. Woe betides me if I'm wrong. He was most anxious and urgent, but he left before I could ask his name."

Winnie looked at the dog in utter confusion. Thrust toward her were a bunch of buttercups in a small jar with a folded paper doily tucked among them and a plate with a heart-shaped scone. "I'll just be leaving that here, then, dearie," the terrier said. "Seems you've got a secret admirer. Some dogs have all the luck," and with a wink she whisked away to the kitchen. Rhys pulled his paw away and looked at Winnie quizzically. She sat as if turned to stone.

"Well. Aren't you going to read the note?" he asked, his tone a tad less warm than it had been. He leaned back in his chair and thrust his paw over the back. Winnie recovered herself and looked down at the pool of yellow. She didn't want to read whatever the mysterious note had to say directly under Rhys's cool gaze.

"I feel a little chilly," she said. "I'm going to sit on the fender for a few moments."

As she left the table, she deftly pulled the note from along the flowers. Sitting on the edge of the little seat by the fire, she unfolded the doily.

W.—You are the only flower for me. —D.

Her eyes blurred, and she looked at the fire for a few moments. The image of the three poodles loomed large in her mind's eye. Looking up at the mirror opposite, she saw Rhys get up and leave the table, carelessly brushing against the jar of buttercups and knocking them over as he passed. She dove over to save the flowers, picking them off the floor from among the glass shards, and in that moment her mind was made up. Cleaning up the mess as best she could, she left a few coins on the table. "Don't you worry about that, love. I'll tidy it up. Just you go find whoever gave you those," the terrier said. "And don't forget your scone. That's the last one today, and I'll be tempted to eat it myself." She wrapped it in a clean napkin and put it in the paw that wasn't gripping the buttercups.

Winnie burst out of the stable door, relieved to see that Rhys was well and truly gone, and looked about her, breathing in the crisp late-afternoon air. A forlorn figure, head in paws, sat on a bench across the lane. She trotted over.

"Hello there," she said. "Seems you lost these." And she held out the little bouquet.

Douglas looked up at her. "Why did you disappear like that?" he asked.

For a moment, Winnie felt cold inside once again. "I saw you were with some friends," she replied, as evenly as she could. "And Rhys passed by and invited me to tea."

"That dog is a menace. I saw him in the tearoom staring at you."

"He was nice enough," she said, taking a step back and beginning to regret her decision. "We just talked about my life back in America."

Douglas looked away for a moment and then straight at Winnie. "The three dogs I was chatting with—they work at the Palace," he said. "Milly, Minnie and Myrtle. They're triplets and a little eccentric, and everyone else laughs at them behind their backs. They saw me and insisted I pass the time of day, and, well, I didn't want to give them the cold shoulder."

Winnie's paws fell to her sides. "I understand. It just looked a bit different through my viewfinder."

Douglas gave her his lopsided grin. "I know, and I'm sorry. What you couldn't see was that they're all about fifty years old. Hard to tell at a distance, I know, as they're already white and tend to dress rather youthfully."

Winnie sat down next to him and smiled back. Unwrapping the scone, she broke it in half. "Here," she said. "Thank you for rescuing me. Rhys was beginning to be rather a bore." She tucked the buttercups into her jeans pocket.

And they sat side by side, paw in paw, munching contentedly and watching the golden afternoon sun slanting across the honey-coloured stone, turning it to gold.

Chapter Sixty-Five
Snake Charmer

Since the little group had left the spot overlooking the submerged village, the way had become rather steeper, and everyone except Sweetie was beginning to lag a bit. The trees and undergrowth formed almost impenetrable walls on either side, blocking any views of the valley. Muriel was beginning to get rather sore but was loath to admit it, so she tried to distract herself by making conversation with Ani, who was also looking a bit weary. The path had widened slightly and could safely accommodate two side by side, so she fell into step with the cat.

"I was fascinated by your first name when we met," she said. "I don't think I've ever come across it before."

Ani glanced at her from the folds of her scarf and hesitated a moment. "Actually, my full given name is Anipe Schäfer, and my Christian name means 'daughter of the Nile,' " she explained. "I no longer go by that surname, though. My aunt on my mother's side married a cat named Amourby, and I chose to use that instead. It was just easier when I was young and at school," Ani replied.

Muriel was pleased that Ani seemed to be more at ease than she had ever been before. Perhaps the peace of their natural surroundings had made her more comfortable. She wanted to seize the opportunity to find out more about her walking partner, but Bertie's voice broke in.

"How far are we going?" he called out to Sweetie.

"We have a good few miles of trekking left yet, assuming we go to the right place. But the sun is out and it's not too cold. Now you know why I insisted on bringing some tents and provisions—we could be out in the wilderness for the night. But don't worry, I've done this many times," Sweetie replied. She stopped and rummaged around her backpack, producing a map.

"Look, we have moved a bit past Beckenstein, here we saw the village underwater. This is where I think we need to get to," she explained, pointing to a spot further up the map.

"That far?" Muriel asked.

"Yes, and I must warn you that we will be treading our own path soon. There are no gravel footpaths once we get closer, and more woods too," Sweetie said.

At that moment there was a shriek from behind Bertie. Ani was bending over, clutching her leg.

"What's happened?" Sweetie asked, looking concerned.

"It's my leg, I... I think I've been bitten," Ani replied.

Sweetie rushed over to Ani as the cat continued, "I stepped on something and am sure I saw it disappear off into the undergrowth."

"A snake could have been sunning itself on the rocks and was disturbed. Let me look," Sweetie said, apprehensively. "We have several breeds of snakes in Germany, although..." she stopped, realising her next words might frighten Ani further. She had already seen for herself and confirmed her suspicions.

"Sit down on the rock, Ani, and rest your leg," Sweetie told her, pulling off her backpack and unzipping a pocket. "Now, do you feel any tingling sensation?" she asked.

"A little. It's stinging more than anything," Ani replied.

Sweetie could see that the bite had begun to swell and showed pinkly under Ani's fur. Snake bites were common, really, and most were not fatal. She applied a pad and then rolled a bandage tightly around the limb.

"You must stay calm and still," Sweetie said, looking directly at the poor cat. "And don't be anxious." Muriel and Bertie looked on in dismay, wondering what would happen next.

Sweetie pulled them to one side. "I'm really sorry, but we will have to turn back. There are several snakes in these parts, and while most are harmless, a couple are venomous. I don't think there is any great danger, but we have no way to tell what type had bitten Ani. The pain she is experiencing will more than likely spread within a few hours, and her leg will be tender and inflamed. She needs to be kept as still as possible, and under no circumstances can she walk. That would only help spread any venom. Do you know if she is allergic to anything?"

"We only met her a while ago, so we really don't know her that well," Muriel replied.

"We have to get back to civilization as soon as we can, just to be safe," Sweetie said decisively. "If she has a severe reaction we could know in a few minutes, but it can also be delayed for many hours. We need to watch out for symptoms such as nausea and vomiting, light-headedness and loss of consciousness."

"Of course," Bertie said. "I'll carry her back if I have to."

"That's very heroic of you Bertie, but I don't want any more incidents," Sweetie replied firmly. "We've travelled a good few miles, but I'm just thankful it's happened now, early on in the day. We have plenty of light, the weather is fine, and the path back is clear. We could go back for help, but there are enough of us to carry her back, if we create a makeshift stretcher from our hiking sticks and tents. It will have to do."

Muriel nodded and returned to Ani's side. "We are all in agreement that it's best to return," she said. "You are in no position to carry on, and we can always return another day."

Ani looked up gratefully. "Of course," she said. "Although I hate to have wasted your time like this." As she spoke, she tried to get up unaided and fell backwards again. Bertie caught her deftly. He had anticipated her movement, guessing that she did not like to have to depend on others.

"We are having none of that. Just stay where you are, and we'll get this all sorted," he said.

The group all took stock of the situation and stayed calm. Sweetie expertly fashioned a stretcher and after a thirty-minute rest, Ani was carefully placed on it, her leg kept as low as possible. Bertie took the front whilst Muriel lifted the back.

Suddenly, Bertie cried out. Muriel, her nerves on edge, nearly dropped her end of the stretcher. "What was that, Bertie?"

"Oh, don't worry. A frog jumped out on the path and made me jump, that's all," he replied, sheepishly, and then laughed. Relieved, the others joined him.

"I'm sure he was more frightened of you than the other way around, Bertie," Muriel said with a smile. "How's the leg now?" she asked.

"Still hurts, but I'll survive," Ani said bravely.

Fortunately for her, Bertie and Muriel were larger and stronger than the two cats, and she really didn't weigh too much. Any of her equipment that wasn't required was left behind.

Seeing things from a different perspective, the travellers enjoyed the views of the lake from the reverse direction. It was slow going, though, and Sweetie continued to check up on the patient. She offered to take over the carrying duties, but both the dogs refused. "You are doing fine as you are, Sweetie," Bertie assured her. Muriel was coping just as well, but she made sure that Bertie's headstrong attitude didn't keep them going without adequate breaks.

Sweetie conceded this point and kept her place in the lead. They all fell silent for a while, anxiety and a sudden rain shower dampening their spirits. Truth be told, Muriel and Bertie were beginning to feel a bit of fatigue, and they were picking their way with extreme care over the now more slippery ground. Lost in their thoughts, they were surprised to hear a flute-like soprano floating back to them.

Ani shifted a little on her stretcher, and Muriel looked at her with concern. But she began humming, as if to soothe herself, and Sweetie's voice carried on: "*Schlaf, Kindlein, Schlaf.*"*

Bertie raised his brows a bit. 'Funny old world when cats from two different hemispheres both know something like that,' he mused.

On returning to the post office, Sweetie called for an ambulance. It was the best precaution to take. Once Ani was in hospital, her bandage could be removed, and her blood hopefully tested for any venom. In the safe hands of a pair of German Shepherds, Ani was placed in the back of the vehicle, and Muriel hopped in, promising to update them as soon as she had some news. Ani waved as the doors closed, whilst Bertie and Sweetie smiled back, hoping for the best.

*"**Schlaf, Kindlein, Schlaf**": This old German lullaby, which translates to "Sleep, dear child, sleep," first appeared in print in 1611. It was set to music by Johann Friedrich Reichardt in the eighteenth century and remained surprisingly popular with rock bands in the late twentieth and early twenty-first centuries. The authors imagined the cats to be singing the version by Reichardt.

Chapter Sixty-Six
All About Ani

After several hours, Muriel called from the hospital to relay the good news that Ani would be fine. The bite had been analysed and appeared to be from a European Adder, but the doctors were just awaiting confirmation. Ani was feeling somewhat better, and fortunately she hadn't experienced any of the symptoms Sweetie had described earlier in the day.

There is so little to do in a hospital room, really, and Muriel thought that perhaps now was the time to resume the conversation they had begun earlier. Talking might also serve to distract Ani from her discomfort. She pulled her rather uncomfortable vinyl chair closer to the bed. "So, you lived with your aunt, chiefly, you said?"

"I did. I'm sad to say that I don't know too much about my mother. Her name was Sanura," Ani began. "She met Elias at the library in Alexandria when they both were studying archaeology and history. They both adored those subjects and were always off on digs all over the world to further their knowledge."

Muriel noted the way Ani used her father's first name rather than calling him "father," but didn't say anything.

"Elias was on a field trip when they met, and they fell in love and were married soon after. They continued travelling together until I was born. Elias was always very guarded when talking about mother. He didn't like bringing her up and most often changed the conversation when I did, which made me quite sad. I don't really know what she looked like. Aria, my aunt in America, had some photos of her from when she was a kitten and she was incredibly beautiful, but it's not quite the same. When I look in the mirror, I often wonder if she looked like me or if I inherited Elias's features."

Ani's scarf had slipped far from her chin in the course of the afternoon's events, and she had made no effort to adjust it. Muriel noted a lovely tan mark just below her mouth and thought privately that she probably did favour her mother. "So, you were brought up by your aunt and uncle. What have you been doing since?" she asked.

"I became an historian, followed in my mother's paw steps, really. I've always had an interest in the past, what may lie only a few feet beneath the surface. I was a terrible one for pawing up things in my aunt's garden and would even bury little treasures so I could dig them up again a year later. You would be amazed at what has been found in shallow digs. It's a slow process, but it can be extremely rewarding," Ani said.

"Oh, I can imagine," Muriel said. "Why, Bertie and a friend found a gold bracelet not too long ago when fishing. It's not quite the same—they weren't looking, and it was quite by accident, but it was thrilling to know they unearthed a treasure. You must have a chat with him soon. There's really quite a tale about it, and he'd love to tell it, I'm sure." Ani smiled up at her and relaxed a little. She had told very few about her odd personal history, but it felt right to be confiding in this gentle dog.

A few miles away, Bertie was sitting with Sweetie in her chilly office, trying to while away the time. "So, what's your story? How did you end up here?" he asked.

The afternoon's events had shaken Sweetie a bit, and she surprised herself by replying to this polite inquiry with more directness than she ordinarily would. "I grew up around these parts. I was brought up by my grandparents from the age of three, after my mother died whilst serving in the First World War. I don't remember my father, Thomas, a 'wrong un' by all accounts. In any case, he didn't want me and was all too happy to let nanna and grandpa take custody. I don't know what happened to him and really don't care. I'm sorry if that sounds harsh." As Sweetie said this, her paw shook, and she accidentally dribbled some boiling water from the kettle onto herself. "Bumblepaws," she muttered.

"Not at all," Bertie assured her, feeling that perhaps he should have tried a safer topic of conversation. "You have every right to feel any way you wish."

Sweetie handed Bertie a cup of tea and was silent for some moments, as if considering what, if anything, she should say next. "My earliest memory is from school. The teacher, a Miss Williams, used to hold up a card with a letter on it, and all the class who were sitting on the floor in a semicircle around her would repeat it, along with the sound. She made the cards herself, and many of the pictures illustrating the letters were hand drawn images of local landmarks, flora and fauna. My love of nature and history came from my surroundings. This is such a beautiful part of the world. Why would I want to leave?"

"It is, but there are lots of places to explore," Bertie said, leaning forward a bit in his eagerness. "Some are just as beautiful, you know. Have you ever considered broadening your horizons?"

"I've been asked that from time to time. I've just never felt the urge to up sticks and travel. And perhaps at my age it's too late, really." Sweetie put down her cup with a resigned air.

"Oh no, you are never too old. Look at me, I travelled the world myself when I was young and in the merchant navy, of course. But look at me now—I'm doing it again. And until recently, I lived all alone in my cottage with only a budgie for company," Bertie replied.

"A budgie?" Sweetie said. "That's a bit of a coincidence. I have a good friend named Robyn. She's a hummingbird who lives in these parts."

"Really? Does she eat a lot and chatter incessantly about food?" Bertie asked jokingly.

"Oh, no, she's quite the silent type, but we get along, and we often go on hiking trips together."

At that moment, the phone rang. It was Muriel again, wanting to speak with Bertie. He nodded from time to time. "Of course, I'll do that," he said. When he had rung off, Sweetie looked at him questioningly.

"Good news I hope?"

"Yes, the doctors have confirmed that the bite was from an adder and have given Ani the necessary medication. The bite area will be painful for a while, but the anti-venom will prevent anything worse. She will be kept in for observation given she had no place to go, apart from the hotel in the village. Muriel is going to come back to freshen up and get a couple of hours sleep before returning."

"That is excellent news," Sweetie smiled.

"There is one other thing," Bertie continued somewhat hesitantly. "Ani has asked if you and I would be prepared to go back and retrieve the item she was after from the cave, assuming we can find it, that is. She does not think she is going to be up and about that soon and certainly will not be able to travel that distance. Without being too formal about things, she wondered if you would consider doing it, since she booked with you for a week, and you will be at a bit of a loose end."

"I think I can agree to that," Sweetie said. "I like to see things through to the end. Please tell Ani that I'll be happy to continue the quest."

"Maybe your friend can come along, Robyn, wasn't it?" Bertie suggested.

Chapter Sixty-Seven
Douglas Gets Butterflies

Douglas was sitting inside the station, waiting for Winnie to come back from the newsagents. She had told him she wanted to get something to read for the journey ahead. At Napoleon's urging, they had decided to take a short excursion to Paris. "You cannot be so close, *cheri*, and not see the finest city in the world. It would be too, too horrible. And Douglas, you must go in memory of your Auntie Sam. She was so happy in France."

Accordingly, they were taking the train to Dover. He was slightly apprehensive, not because he minded the journey or feared seasickness on the ferry. He just really didn't like London railway stations. Having witnessed the abduction of his mother when he was just a pup, he found that such places made him both anxious and melancholy.

Douglas tried to divert his attention by studying the Victorian architecture inside the station. The red brick building was adorned with scores of pointed-arch windows, each with its finials and elaborate cornices, all fine examples of secular gothic style. Large ironwork structures stretched down the platform, holding up the glass roof on carved metal pillars. The glass was stained with green mildew in places and covered in soot, filtering the light and casting peculiar shadows on the platform surface. There were one or two passengers standing about aimlessly, either waiting for their train or for a loved one to arrive on the next train. The large wooden doors that served as the goods entrance were open, and the station porter was helping load a set of crates into the guard's van of the waiting train.

None of this distracted him fully, and he retreated into his thoughts. Winnie had managed to convince him that the past was now behind him; his mother was back in his life, and he must try and let the painful past go. Step by step they would overcome his fears together, she had assured him. Her smiling face and happy demeanour certainly helped in this regard.

Exiting the ticket office was a rather fine-looking whippet wearing a checked jacket with tan leather patches at the elbows. Firmly grasping a medium sized box with puncture marks on top, he sat down on the other end of Douglas's bench and carefully placed it in the gap between them. Douglas's interest was sparked in spite of his troubled frame of mind, and he found himself trying to work out what might be inside the box. He couldn't really see anything without putting an eye to one of the holes, though, of course that wasn't an option. The whippet smiled at his ill-concealed curiosity and began to talk.

"I usually get that reaction when I carry around my little parcels," he laughed. "Would you like a peek?"

Douglas backed away a moment. "There aren't spiders in there?" he questioned, warily.

"Oh, no, far prettier, although don't let me hear you say that around my arachnologist friends! For some reason, they seem to take great delight in giving their spiders pet names, and woe betide you if you say they look creepy. My name is Mr Hollands, by the way. Pleased to make your acquaintance."

"Douglas," the corgi replied.

Mr Hollands lifted the lid carefully on the box and brought it up slightly closer to Douglas's face. "There, can you see?"

Douglas peered inside, half wondering if this dog might be a prankster playing a trick and ready for a coiled snake to suddenly spring out at him. But he was wrong. Inside a group of velvety jet-black caterpillars were crawling around.

"Oh, be careful, don't touch them. These are quite special. They have short, prickly little spines to help protect them from predators, and if they really feel threatened, they have the ability to come together and jerk their bodies in unison so that they appear to be a larger creature. It's quite amazing to behold."

"What are they?" Douglas asked.

"In contrast to their currently rather dark appearance, these will turn into beautiful brightly-coloured peacock butterflies," Mr Hollands said.

"What are you doing with them, then?" Mesmerised, Douglas kept his eyes on the little wriggling mass.

"Oh, I'm taking them to a school to show the children. Actually, it's my hobby. I'm an amateur lepidopterist, and my friend let me 'borrow' them. I'm a geography teacher by day, you know. Actually, for my sins, I did take one of the year groups on a little expedition into the countryside, but it didn't turn out too well."

"Don't tell me," Douglas said. "You met a large bull in a field?"

"Not quite. For the most part, the pups and kittens learnt a great deal on our field trip, and I was pleased with the interest they took in nature. The school hired a coach to take us to the destination, and a farmer nearby was kind enough to allow us to go investigating on his land. We had the usual mixture of students, some that wanted to learn, some that wanted to play and some that, unfortunately, just wanted to cause a little trouble."

Douglas tried to remember back to his earlier years and thought that, if it had not been for Auntie Sam, he would have ended up in the latter category. He smiled as he fondly recalled his aunt teaching him all sorts of interesting facts. She would no doubt have been able to find something fascinating to say about a speck of dust.

"Anyway," Mr Hollands continued, pulling him from his reverie, "a small group decided to go off on a little adventure of their own and broke away from the class. Whilst Mr Green kept an eye on the rest of the youngsters, I went in search of the others. I was sure they would probably be found in the nearby woods, a great place to go and hide and have some fun on their own away from the watching adults. I wasn't wrong. After following the trail, a short distance, I heard some excited kittens, and there before me the ring leader and his cohorts stood looking upwards to the top of an oak tree."

"Spotted a squirrel?" Douglas enquired.

"If only," Mr Hollands said. "No. In fact, one of the other kittens had been dared to climb the tree and looked to be stuck in the centre between the branches. The others saw me coming and were calling up and telling her to stop messing about and come down as soon as she could. I spent a short moment assessing the situation and decided that I had to go up myself. I told the others to return to the group at once and that there would be trouble when I got back. Fortunately, the warning was enough to make them do as I said."

Douglas chuckled quietly, and this didn't go unnoticed by Mr Hollands.

"I can see what you are thinking, my lad. A great dog like myself climbing trees—not exactly built for it, I know, but I have my moments and managed it just fine. When I got up there, I discovered that the poor thing wasn't stuck at all. She was just a little embarrassed. Unbeknown to the others, there was a hole inside the trunk, between the branches, where the locals must have lit a fire and burnt it out to make a hollow or den of sorts. The yellow dress the kitten was wearing was covered in black marks. I had a devil of a time coaxing her out, but eventually succeeded, even if the others below did pull her leg when she returned."

"My, my," Douglas said, thinking back to his puppyhood and fondly remembering the many trees he'd climbed. So, all's well that ends well."

"Not quite," Mr Hollands said. "We returned to the field and got the rogue pupils back on track with their classmates, or so we thought. Mr Green and I managed to keep things in order, shepherded the students back onto the coach and sat back to relax for the journey back to the school. I was just nodding off when a commotion at the back of the coach first alerted us. Various kittens and pups started cheering and shouting, and within a few minutes the whole class was trying to see what was happening. We heard calls such as 'go on you beauty, you can do it' and 'no, not that way, you silly creature!' I got up with a sigh, as I do like to get a little shuteye after these things and went to take a look at the reason for the disturbance. After clearing the students from the aisle, I could see the same troublemakers from earlier in the day lying on the seats and looking towards the floor. As I stepped closer, they stopped cheering and looked up, sitting back up in their seats as if nothing was going on. 'Hello sir, enjoying the ride?' one quipped. I smiled as I studied the vicinity, and out of the corner of my eye I spotted something crawling along the floor. They had only gone and smuggled some caterpillars back from the field and were placing bets on which one would make its way across the back of the coach the quickest."

"Troublemakers indeed," Douglas chuckled.

"Once again, I had to intervene, and the perpetrators had detention to look forward to. The funny thing is, we all thought that was the end of the story, but it wasn't."

"Oh, why is that?" Douglas asked.

"A few weeks later, the coach company called up the school with some news. One of their drivers was taking the same coach on a trip away. He'd driven the vehicle to the terminus to pick up all of the passengers and was about to load the coach up with the suitcases. When he opened the side luggage compartment hatch, he was greeted by some half dozen monarch butterflies emerging from the darkness within."

Douglas looked at Mr Hollands in wonder.

"Well, that's my train, so I'll be getting along now. Safe travels, my lad!" And with a wink and a tip of his cap, the whippet was gone. Douglas gazed after him, an imaginary vision of gorgeous black and orange wings obscuring the dimness and dinginess of the station for a moment. Suddenly his daydream was replaced by Winnie in her checked coat, smiling at him. She put her paw lightly on his. "You were away with the fairies, weren't you?" she said playfully.

In that moment, seemingly from nowhere, a black speck caught Winnie's eye, and she felt a tickle as it came to rest on her paw. Douglas noticed where her attention was and then held out his paw and let the caterpillar walk on. The pair held their breath and smiled at each other. Douglas got up, looked around and then walked towards a large planter close by. The little creature slid from his paw onto a branch, and he at last felt the burden of the past easing from his shoulders as the caterpillar continued its journey.

Chapter Sixty-Eight
Passageways and Paraffin

The hummingbird flittered behind the steady stream of water splashing over the ledge at the cave's opening and then reappeared quickly.

"There's definitely a crevice behind there, quite narrow, but it opens out into a small space, and a tunnel leads off it," she proclaimed. Robyn was wearing the type of outfit any self-respecting hiker would wear in the circumstances and looked well prepared. Her ruby-coloured throat shone, and her iridescent feathers glowed as the sun peeked in and out of the drifting clouds. The brief period under the waterfall hadn't drenched her. "I've got my own waterproofing," she had told Bertie, when he'd asked if she had a mackintosh.

"At last, I can stretch my feathers and go spelunking," she said eagerly. "I haven't been for a good while. I hear you have a certain letter. Now that we are here, may I look?"

Bertie handed Ani's letter to the hummingbird and watched. Sweetie looked over the bird's wing to take another peek at it herself.

"We had better get the lanterns out," Bertie said, as he unfastened his backpack and reached inside. "Have you been in this cave before?"

Sweetie looked up from the letter. "I have, actually, but it was a good few years ago. In fact, folklore in these parts suggests that this is the location of a crystal cave, which is why I've been here before.* One would think that the geology of this country does not support the notion that such a place could exist, but over a hundred years ago some miners looking for phosphorite stumbled upon an underground cave that was so big, the church we passed getting here could have fitted in it. It seems that because this was not the mineral the miners were looking for, they filled in the entrance, and the exact location was forgotten. Over time, word did spread of the place, and—" Sweetie stopped rather abruptly and turned away, her eye-catching Robyn's briefly.

"That sounds like the stories I've heard about sea monsters and pirate treasure on the ocean floor," Bertie replied with a smile.

"It could be. But I like to think that it may be there after all, and that it isn't guarded by some mythical creature," Sweetie replied lightly.

Robyn had been listening to their exchange but now continued studying the letter. What most didn't know was that she had expert knowledge of symbology and history, having taught herself when her applications to study at various universities had been rejected. She was determined to someday show the academic world how wrong they'd been about her.

"The letter says to follow the signs. Look, his handwriting is not exactly easy to read, and the folds in the paper don't help. But here, the way he has underlined these letters and used uppercase on those others...I think he's telling us something."

"Yes, and those plus symbols," Sweetie agreed. "There is definitely a pattern of clues here. I think all will become clear when we enter the cave and see for ourselves. Ready, Bertie?"

The three of them ducked through the water and started their journey into the relative unknown. The protector lanterns lit up the cavern, which was nothing more than a damp hole with slimy walls and water dripping from the ceiling. Bertie shuddered to think why others thought this was a fine way to spend a fine spring day. He didn't mind tight spaces or getting dirty, but it was rather eerie and cold. He had no way of knowing if the search was going to be fruitful, but he had agreed to do it and followed, albeit reluctantly, thinking hopefully of a time when he could sit back in a comfy chair near a crackling log fire in the hotel room and have an evening tipple.

Sweetie shone her lamp around the walls and headed off into the darkness. After fifteen or so metres, she stopped, as the passageway ahead split into two, and they needed to decide which route to follow. She lifted her lamp up in the air and studied the dripping rock walls. Robyn did the same.

"Look here," she said, "does that look like a marking to you?"

Sweetie moved her lamp down to get a better view and passed her paw over the rock where Robyn had indicated something.

"It certainly looks like something cat-made. I don't think erosion would account for it," she mused.

Not one to hang about, Robyn had already flitted to the entrance of the second passageway. "There's another one over here," she called out. "Now that can't be a random occurrence, can it?"

"That does present a conundrum," Bertie said. "There's one on the wall near the last passage, too. Do we know what they are?"

Sweetie looked at them both and studied the shapes. "The first looks like a square, the second an oval and the last a saw."

Robyn considered for a moment, hovering with wings a blur, as she often did when thinking. Bertie found it dizzying to look at her. "They used a hieroglyphic system of writing from around 3000 BC in Egypt, of course. Did Elias study that era?"

"I'm sure Ani would be able to tell us more detail, but I think it would be a valid assumption to make," Sweetie said.

Robyn pondered again for a moment and then spoke, "A saw shape represented 'N,' the oval was, ooh, let me see, possibly 'R' or 'S' and a square...I'm sure that was a 'P.' "

Sweetie looked at the letter again in the dim light. "The first clue in the letter appears to be the underlined letter 'P.' There are several of them. I think our choice is made; don't you agree?"

The two others nodded, and they all headed down the tunnel on the right, though not before Sweetie made a note in her jotter of which direction they had taken. Any light that had shone through from the outside was now gone, and without the lamps, the three would have been in total darkness. Bertie wasn't afraid of the dark, but he didn't like the eerie silence and atmosphere of the caves. To soothe himself, he imagined that the passageway might open up into a mythical Eden, with lush green shrubbery, fruit-laden trees, pure blue water and the sun shining in from a small hole above. But he was sure that he was very much mistaken. Before long they would be climbing and crawling their way through the endless dark, winding tunnels of the cave, exploring a part of the world no one had ever seen, except perhaps one brave cat, Elias.

Deep in that labyrinth, a side passageway presented itself. They stopped and studied the surrounding walls, but nothing out of the ordinary appeared. Bertie ventured a comment. "We should probably continue looking for symbols that correspond to clues in the letter, then?"

"Oh, yes, I think so," Sweetie replied.

When they came to another division, she quickly surveyed the sides of the tunnels and spotted two more signs, a twisted wire and a semi-circle.

"The upper-case letters are 'T.' Which one should we head down now?" Sweetie asked.

Robyn cocked her head, despite no one seeing. "The right one, of course. Already moving on."

Bertie wondered if Ani's altercation with the snake a stroke of luck after all had been. Sweetie's choice of a new caving partner seemed on the face of it inspired, although he was sure that the cat knew her onions, too. As his waterproof brushed against the tighter tunnels, he realised that he was the largest member of the group—the agile hummingbird certainly had no problem traversing the spaces underground. He just hoped that Elias had been a large tom. After another ten minutes of trudging along, the next slit in the passageway revealed itself. This time there were symbols at the entrances of two of the tunnels. Sweetie showed her prowess and announced the leftmost symbol looked like 'Ka,' a hieroglyph with a shoulder and arms bent upwards at the elbow, while the one on the right looked like 'The Crescent' and appeared as the shape of the moon. The third clue in the letter referenced 'plus' symbols, and their arrangement on the paper looked to be like the 'Ka' symbol. The way forward was now clear.

Continuing for what seemed like an eternity of gloom, they finally reached what Bertie hoped was the last puzzle. The walls glistened a bit as water from above seeped through the rocks, and the air was becoming acrider. They came to a fork in the tunnel which was even narrower than the previous ones. Bertie was reminded of a book Sam had once read to him in which the heroine had found herself in a hole underground, and he wondered whether the corridor was getting smaller, or they were getting magically larger. "I really hope we are nearly there," he said rather anxiously. "You do realise there aren't any more clues in the letter?"

Sweetie and Robyn were too busy looking at the walls before them to pay him any heed. Four new passageways, two markings. Robyn hovered near each in turn. "This one looks like a star, and this one, a sun and lines. Do you know what, they're rather crude, but symbols, nonetheless? If my memory serves me correctly, the 'Seba' was used to decorate several tombs and temples and is associated with gates and doorways and the concept of learning, whilst the 'Amenta' is a rather unique symbol representing the land of the dead."

Bertie shivered and didn't know if it was the draught or the mention of the dead. "I know which passage I think we should take," he said.

Sweetie pondered, "I think you are right. We are on a journey to learn something, and I don't want to overthink the situation."

Ten more minutes passed, and Robyn was now leading the way, flying deeper underground as the path sloped downwards. She was unaware of how slippery it had now become for her companions. Up ahead, the light that was reflecting off the tight walls disappeared and was replaced with a glowing hole. Sweetie, closely followed by Bertie, now found themselves in a small cavern. With all three of their lanterns shining brightly, they could see stalagmite and stalactite formations and the long shadows they cast on the surrounding walls. The three marvelled at them for several minutes, noticing the various shades of beige, brown, red and grey that were reflected by several shallow pools of water.

"It looks like this is the end of the road. I can't see any more paths," Robyn said. A search of the space revealed what appeared to be a deeper, greenish pool that had formed in a corner. Bertie put his lamp down at the water's edge, knelt and put his paw in, feeling for any objects beneath. It didn't take long for him to touch something wrapped tightly in rubbery plastic, and he pulled it up. Sweetie and Robyn watched as he turned towards them and the dripping object appeared in the light of their lanterns.

"Is this what we are looking for?" Bertie asked, as he untied the frayed cord and sheet of plastic. Inside was another wrapped object and a tired old leather journal with the name 'Elias Thomas Schäfer' embossed on the cover.

Sweetie examined them and smiled. "In think so, yes. Now I believe we should get them to Ani and let her look first. After all, she was the intended recipient. Shall I pop it all in my rucksack?"

Bertie felt a wave of relief. They'd accomplished their mission, and they could now hopefully get out as quickly as possible. 'I do hope Sweetie's notes will keep us from getting lost,' he thought uneasily. The atmosphere of the cave had wreaked havoc with his nerves.

*Crystal Cave: On the northern edge of the Taunus mountains, above the Weilburg district of Kubach in Germany, the Kubacher Kristallhöhle lies about 50 to 70 meters below the earth's surface. The cave in this chapter is a notional reference to this one, which is believed to be the only calcite crystal cave in Germany and is adorned with countless crystals and pearl drop stones.

Chapter Sixty-Nine
What's in a Name?

Bertie placed his rucksack down on the couch in the hotel room and felt very relieved. Muriel had left a message with the front desk attendant which he had read as he took the lift up. Ani would be able to leave the next morning and Muriel herself was due back soon. He took off his muddy boots and kicked them to the corner of the room, and the minute his head touched the pillow he fell fast asleep. When he awoke, he found himself covered in a blanket and saw Muriel lying on the couch with a pillow under her head. Glancing at his watch, he realised that he must have slept from late afternoon until late morning. Long gone were the days when he would be raring to go and up-and-at-them, he thought ruefully. Instead, he was feeling rather old and still tired from the past day's exploits. He was about to snuggle back up under the blanket and catch another forty winks, but he saw Muriel stir and felt duty bound to relinquish his soft bed and make some morning tea. After all, she had thoughtfully taken the couch rather than wake him in the night by slipping into the bed. And she did look a bit tired, her ears drooping and her eyes not quite open.

"Looks like I'm not the only one who needed some beauty sleep?" he teased.

"Yes, I think everything is finally catching up with us, isn't it? My arms are still aching somewhat from carrying Ani all that way—how about you?" Muriel asked.

"I hate to say it, but I'm feeling about the same," Bertie said, yawning widely. "There was me thinking we'd be lying in the sun cruising the Mediterranean, and instead I've been trudging around dark caves underground. It has been a bit more of an adventure than we bargained for."

"Always seems to be when I'm with you," she teased.

"Ah, but you wouldn't have it any other way, now, would you?" he replied with a wink.

"I'll have to have a think about that," she said, taking the mug he offered her. "Oh, just what I needed. Yes, maybe I'll stick with you after all."

Bertie chuckled and sat down beside her. Muriel looked at the package, now on the dresser. "You found it then. I knew you would."

"Yes, but I don't think it would have happened without Sweetie and Robyn. Ani made the right decision when she chose her guide," Bertie said, yawning again as he picked up the journal. "I hope this is worth the journey, along with whatever is still wrapped up in the other package." As he flipped through the journal, a folded piece of paper fell to the floor. He bent to retrieve it and cast an eye over it without thinking.

"Bertie, put it back, quickly. We mustn't read that. It's not ours," Muriel chastised him. He obediently slotted it back in the front of the journal.

The pair washed and dressed and made their way to the breakfast table. Their hopes of making it a quick meal were dashed when they were approached by a fellow tourist who seemed convinced that Bertie looked exactly like her second cousin (once removed) and insisted he was rather pale and in need of a generous helping of Schwarzwälder Schinken and several slices of cheese. These were generously piled onto his plate, and she sat nearby eyeing him while he polished it off. Extricating themselves from her attentions with some difficulty, they set off to meet Ani.

They found the calico waiting at the entrance to the hospital, eager to find out about the past day's exploration. She greeted them both warmly and gave Bertie a big hug, thanking him not only for his efforts inside the cave but also for carrying her all the way back to civilization. It was all Bertie could do to keep from burping rather unceremoniously, like a baby, after his hearty morning meal. Muriel quickly took hold of Ani's hand and led her away. "There's a café in the village. I thought, as it's such a nice day, that we could get tea or coffee and sit down at the stream? We have the things Bertie found with us, of course, and we want to let you have them as soon as possible."

"Sounds good to me," Ani said, eagerly looking at the bag Bertie was carrying and trying to peek inside. "Sorry, I've always been a rather inquisitive cat, despite being rather shy."

Once they were all settled on a stone bench outside the café that overlooked the rippling water, Bertie handed Ani the packet. She pulled out the journal, tracing over the embossed name with her paw, and for a moment she was stuck in her thoughts, wondering what lay inside. Would it be details of Elias's travels? She thought this was most likely. Or perhaps it might tell her a little more about her mother—she really hoped for that. Ani skimmed through several faded yellow leaves inserted into the front of the journal, most of them faded and crumbling handwritten notes, until she came to the beginning of the bound pages. She read aloud a note that she found there.

My darling Anipe,

If you are reading this, then you have found my journal. I'm so glad. Inside you will find the musings of an eccentric old explorer, sometimes too blinkered in his efforts to search for distant treasures when all along he had one right by his side. For this I am truly sorry. If you read on, you will learn the truth about the item hidden alongside, which is your birth right, and also about something else from my past. I hope you can find it in your heart to forgive me.

Your loving father,

Elias

Ani sat thinking for a while, the paw holding the letter shaking a bit. She reached in the bag for the item and unwrapped it, quite speechless at what she saw. In her lap was a paw carved figurine of an ancient Egyptian Bastet cat sitting upright, fashioned in bronze. The artefact stood about twenty centimetres tall and weighed about one kilogram. It was a beautiful work of art and craftsmanship.

"That looks magnificent," Muriel said, "and very old."

"Indeed," Ani replied, with a tear in her eye.

"Do you know what it is?" Bertie asked tentatively.

A flicker of a memory crossed Ani's mind, "I don't, but it does look vaguely familiar," she lifted the figure up and looked at the base. Underneath she saw her initials, 'AS,' crudely imprinted. "I think it is something from when I was a kitten, but..."

"Maybe Sweetie can help, she knows about Egyptian history. Or perhaps Ms Durcheinander," Bertie suggested.

"Durcheinander," Ani flinched. "Did you say Durcheinander?"

"Why yes," Bertie said. "Without her, I'm sure we wouldn't have found the journal."

Ani was now looking rather apprehensive, and she pulled up her scarf and tried to cover her face slightly. Nervously she reached into her pocket and took out a letter. "I should have shown you this before. I'm sorry." And she handed it to Bertie.

"What's this?" he questioned.

"It's a second letter. It came with the other," Ani replied. Bertie hesitantly read it aloud.

Ani, my journal will give you more information about my past, but if you ever decide to follow my instructions, then steer clear of Durcheinander. Elias.

"Have I read that correctly?" Bertie asked. "Surely not?"

Ani looked up unhappily. "I thought it was a place that I couldn't find on any map... somewhere too small to mark up or an old name for a town, perhaps like the place under the water at the reservoir...somewhere that no longer exists. Until just now."

"Oh, my goodness," Muriel exclaimed. "What does it mean?"

"It means we have a few questions for that hummingbird," Bertie said with a determined face.

"I think you are jumping the gun, Bertie. We need more than an old note to start casting aspersions on the poor bird," Muriel said. "We have the journal. Ani will need to read it and find out more, if there is more to be known. In the meantime, we just have to be on our guard, perhaps even find somewhere else to stay."

Ani calmed down slightly, thankful that Muriel was being protective of her. "Oh, but what about Sweetie? I still need to settle up with her and thank her, too."

"I can take her the money, Ani," Bertie said. "She is a nice cat, seemed completely hospitable and all, but is it really wise to put yourself in harm's way if you don't have to?"

"Oh, but… surely not, she doesn't seem the type to be mixed up in whatever this is all about," Ani said unhappily. "I'm sure she would be interested in this figurine too."

"Maybe she would, a bit too interested," Bertie said. "We can't risk anyone else knowing about it just yet, now, can we?"

"I suppose you're right," Ani agreed with a sigh.

"I think we need to leave Ani in peace, she needs some rest. Let's buy ourselves some time, Bertie—you go and see Sweetie, let her know that Ani is doing well, and if she asks, she hasn't yet opened the package. Tell her that she should be present for the unwrapping, too, since she took such trouble to retrieve it. We can arrange to meet again in a day or so's time when Ani is up to it. That's a believable little white lie, I think. If we find something in the meantime that something untoward is going on, then we can leave," Muriel said, logically.

Ani agreed that she favoured this "softly" approach and thanked Muriel and Bertie for their concern. Once they had exacted a promise that she would return to the hotel soon, she waved to them, opened the journal and began to read.

Chapter Seventy
What Bertie Heard

"I've told you, Robyn, it's just not something I want to do. You know how I feel. It's not right!" Sweetie said rather angrily.

Bertie was just trotting up to the shed behind the post office, but on hearing the raised voices, he stopped. He had an envelope in his paw already to pay Sweetie for her services, but the argument caused him to hold off knocking on the door. By the same token, he couldn't bring himself to move out of earshot.

"That is not what you said before," Robyn replied. "The look on your face, the amazement at what we had found in the cave—and now you turn around and say it's not right? There's money to be made, here, can't you see that? You could find yourself a real office, maybe even a new business, and I could—"

"That is as maybe," Sweetie interrupted her. "But I just don't think it's something I can do. It feels like a betrayal. I've got a trusted position now, and it doesn't even belong to us, does it?" Sweetie said, dejected.

"It doesn't belong to anyone. That's the point!" Robyn paused for emphasis, and Bertie fancied that he could hear her wings beating furiously. "It mustn't be hidden any longer. A discovery like this deserves national coverage. If you don't do something about it, then I will take matters into my wings. I will have no choice. I'm not getting any younger, and opportunities like this don't come along that often. You are just being very selfish!" Robyn shouted. A nearby window opened, and the bird flew out in a rage.

Bertie stood before the door for a moment or two, frozen, trying to process what he had just heard. Mechanically, he turned the knob. Sweetie was sitting inside with tears welling up in her eyes. She looked up and saw the wire-haired dachshund looking straight back at her.

"Oh, Bertie, I'm sorry, did you hear that? I do hope not. I'm not very good when it comes to confrontation, not like our feathered friend there. She is a dab hand and can get rather aggressive, but she doesn't mean it, really. Now, what can I do for you, and how is dear Ani?" Sweetie said as she reached for a tissue.

Bertie was rather upset himself after what he had just heard, and he wasn't in the mood to be too polite to this wretched charlatan. He handed Sweetie the envelope and told her the money Anipe owed her was all there. He didn't mention that he and Muriel had added a sum to express their gratitude for her services, since he now regretted it. The offer of a cup of tea and several Berliner cakes was not enough to tempt Bertie to stay.

"I'm expected for tea, I'm afraid. Ani is doing much better, but we don't like to leave her for too long. Goodbye." Sweetie looked taken aback at this rather brusque answer and was about to respond, but Bertie turned on his heel and walked back out of the shed. He sped back to the hotel before he forgot a word.

"There you are Muriel. I've been looking all over for you," Bertie said, agitated, as he paced up and down the lobby.

"Whatever is the matter? I've just been browsing the shops and was going back to our room," Muriel replied.

"It's Sweetie and Robyn. I overheard them—couldn't help it. They were there in the office when I got there, having an almighty argument. They were talking about the figurine. They want to sell it," Bertie said animatedly.

"Sell the cat statue? Why, they haven't even seen it," Muriel said.

"They must have looked on the way back from the cave, no other explanation. Sweetie carried it in her rucksack, and they were both behind me on the walk," Bertie continued. "To think I was starting to like her! You never can tell, can you?"

Muriel wasn't sure. She didn't like to contradict Bertie but really couldn't imagine that the tabby could be so devious. "So, what should we do, and how can we resolve this? And, more to the point, how do we tell Ani?" she asked.

The last question resolved itself, as Ani had crept into the lobby quietly and stood there with a slightly worried look on her face, holding the journal.

"Tell me what?" she questioned.

Bertie felt that he should be the one to break the bad news, given that he had witnessed the argument. After telling Ani word for word what he heard, he felt relief from the burden, but he was slightly puzzled by Ani's reaction.

"I don't know what to think about that," she said. But it's not the only mystery. I have a couple of things to show you. Shall we find somewhere a bit less public?" Ani asked.

The three of them walked into the hotel snug, a sparsely decorated room with a traditional brick fireplace and a small number of easy chairs. A couple of bits of farming equipment were tastefully hung on the walls alongside framed pictures of alpine scenes. They each took a seat and waited for Ani to begin.

Chapter Seventy-One
Symbols and Suspicions

Ani gazed thoughtfully into the hissing fire for a moment and then looked at Muriel and Bertie, smiling before she began to speak. "Firstly, I want to thank you properly for what you have done for me over these past few weeks. I don't think I would have been in the position I am now if it hadn't been for you. I'm a shy creature by nature and rarely have enough trust in others to get to know them, but I feel a real connection with you both. I hope that our friendship can continue after we part ways—if you feel the same."

The two dogs nodded. "Of course," Muriel assured her.

"I am very glad," Ani said, impulsively reaching out and squeezing the dorgi's paw. "True friends are not always easily found at my age." She inhaled deeply, shifted in her seat and placed the journal on the table between them. "I've had a chance to read through much of this and have discovered a lot of answers to questions I had when growing up. Elias lived a simple life, loved his work and wasn't extravagant, taking each day as it came, really. After I was sent off to America, he spent much of his time abroad, visiting digs and helping colleagues. I'm now sad that we lost contact, and I should have known better than to think that he didn't want to be reunited with me. He did, and often mentions in the journal that he missed me and wanted to know how I was getting on. Alas, he never found out."

"That is unfortunate," Bertie said, though he wondered why Elias hadn't simply written to his daughter, aside from the one final letter to the solicitor that had gone astray. 'Not that I can say much,' he thought ruefully, remembering his sister's many unanswered missives.

"I can't change the past now," Ani continued. "I have to look forward, and that brings me to a couple of things I would like to show you."

"Whatever could they be?" Muriel asked, intrigued.

Ani opened the journal to the first page, withdrew two grainy black and white photographs and handed them to Muriel.

Muriel took the first one and studied it. It was an image of a mosaic depicting a dog resting on his hind legs next to an upturned Greek vessel. He was looking rather sheepish, as if he were the cause of the supposed accident.*

"I think it's from one of Elias's digs," Ani said. "He must have unearthed it at some time or other, I assume."

"Look, Bertie, proof that Egypt was home to dogs even in ancient times," Muriel said as she passed over the photo. He looked and smiled at the character before him.

"Looks like something my friend Nipper might have done, by accident, of course. He was always getting into trouble like that."

Muriel studied the second photo, "Why, is that Elias? I assume it is. He looks like you and is wearing the type of outfit I would expect from someone at an archaeological dig," she commented.

"It is," Ani said.

"Hang on a minute," Bertie chipped in, as Muriel passed him the photo. "Look…" He pointed to a rather dishevelled bird shielding its face from the sun with its wing, perching near Elias. "That's…"

"Who?" Ani asked.

"Well, it can't be Robyn, but how many hummingbirds can there be in this part of the world?" Bertie said, his brows beetling. "Do you know who that bird is?"

Ani looked at him seriously. "I do. The name is written on the back—Klaus Durcheinander. He was Elias's friend and colleague, and he has been mentioned in the journal a fair bit, too. I couldn't help but take notice after reading Elias's warning note. You may well be right about the connection with Robyn."

"I'm sure of it," Bertie muttered as he handed back the picture.

"I suppose we had better ask Sweetie about it," Ani said. "And then there's this…" She passed a newspaper cutting to Bertie, and Muriel read over his shoulder.

"I'm afraid I don't know many German," she admitted.

"I don't either," Ani said. "But with my dictionary and grammar, I worked out that it is an article about a cave— 'discovered by Frieda V., a native of this town.' You see that the paper is badly worn just there on the crease, and I couldn't make out the rest of the surname."

"No photograph. Perhaps it was a local sort of paper, as it does not mention the town's name, either. A bit odd," Muriel said, her head cocked to one side. "And no date. All rather peculiar."

"Yes," Ani agreed. "It's such a short piece, not much more than the bare facts, really, so there's not much to go on. I really am at a loss. I wish I knew why it was important to Elias."

"Perhaps she was a colleague," Bertie surmised, rubbing his whiskers thoughtfully.

"Perhaps," Ani said. "But there's no mention of her anywhere else."

"We seem to have more questions than answers," Muriel mused.

"Well, the journal does explain why the figurine was hidden, but it essentially says just what Elias wrote in the letter. It was given to him when I was born by a high-ranking official from Egypt. He was a friend of Elias's and had worked with him to unearth some historical mysteries over there. Then there are some odd little symbols at the tops of various pages," the cat continued. "I've been looking at them a long time, trying to work them out. I'd dismiss them as random scribblings, but Elias's writing is very neat, no stray marks anywhere. I feel as though I'm missing a clue."

"How many are there?" Muriel asked, her eyes betraying her curiosity. And she and Ani moved their chairs closer together so that they could examine the book together.

Bertie shifted uncomfortably in his seat and thought longingly of his worn leather chair back in Badger's Bay. Nor was he in a comfortable state of mind, despite the cheery crackling from the hearth. This Elias had been entirely too fond of riddles for his liking. He'd really had quite enough of those during the underground expedition of a few days before. Which reminded him of his previous worry.

"This is all very interesting, but I think that we need to talk about Sweetie and Robyn," he interjected. "I still don't trust them. Especially Robyn. And now it turns out she may have a relative about who may be as bad as she is."

Muriel sighed. "You may be right. But what do you suggest we do?"

Ani had closed the journal and was looking into the fire again. Then she sat up very straight and said in a quiet but decisive voice, "I know what I mean to do. Bertie, you said yourself that Sweetie's knowledge was invaluable when you were searching the cave, so too Robyn's. I am going to ask Sweetie for her opinion of these symbols. I am sure that there is something more that my father was trying to tell me, and I don't know anyone else to ask."

Bertie looked at her quizzically. "Well, I don't suppose she has any reason to mislead you," he admitted. "Unless it all has something to do with that blasted figurine."

"Perhaps you can show that to her, too," Muriel suggested, taking a cue from Ani's newfound boldness. "And watch her reaction closely."

"Absolutely not!" Bertie exclaimed. "Too risky. I won't stand for it."

But the cat and dorgi were already gathering their bags and making for the door of the snug. "Are you coming?" Muriel asked, and there was in her voice a determined quality that Bertie recognised and knew he was powerless against.

"May as well beard the lioness in her den, I suppose," he murmured.

*Egyptian Floor Mosaic:** The floor mosaic mentioned in the chapter does exist and dates from 200-100 BC. The central medallion depicts a dog and a knocked-over gold vessel. It is made up of minute stone cubes, ranging from one to four millimetres, and was fashioned using the opus vermiculite technique. The motif is the only one of its kind to have been found on a floor mosaic in Alexandria. The image bears a striking resemblance to "*Nipper*," a dog who served as the model for an 1898 painting by Francis Barraud titled *His Master's Voice*. The image was the basis for one of the world's best-known trademarks.

Chapter Seventy-Two
An Imposter in Paris

The day had turned very fine, and Paris seemed to be putting on its best face for those tourists who had been a bit battered during their channel crossing. Winnie felt her spirits rise as she stopped to admire the *bouquinistes*, metal book stalls that stretched for miles along the banks of the Seine. Douglas was allowing Winnie to indulge her pleasure whilst he looked over the water and watched the boats toing and froing. Still a bit unsteady after the ferry, he wasn't in the mood to hop on another boat just yet, content instead to take in the fresh air and try to relax.

Entirely in her element, Winnie admired the array of volumes before her, some wrapped in cellophane to protect their leather bindings. Cheek-by-jowl with these august tomes were brightly covered paperbacks, well-worn and seeking new readers on their journey to a new bookshelf. Almost as iconic to the capital as Notre Dame, this vast river library was a place where Winnie could mix with Parisians and tourists alike and feel at ease, imagining a time when peddlers might have hawked second-hand books from wooden carts along the Quai du Louvre. So many dogs and cats had exchanged bookshelves for television sets these days, but she hoped that the humble paperback would always remain a true symbol of knowledge and intellect.

As she almost skipped with happiness between the stalls, she found herself standing before one that was selling new books and had half a mind to ask the bookseller why he thought such monstrosities would make good bedfellows with the antiquarian books nearby. What stopped her was the picture on the back cover of a book titled *Room 34: An Odyssey*. A young red dachshund looked out at her; head tilted to the left in a thoughtful pose. Picking up the volume, she saw that the author, Dahlia Dalrymple, had written several other books, too. 'No wonder Oreo mistook me for her back at the Ritz,' Winnie thought. She put it down, hoping that none of the other bibliophiles around her would notice the resemblance, and searched for Douglas. He was looking dashing as always, leaning against a parapet in a statuesque pose, a letter in his paw. She waved at him happily, and he nodded in acknowledgement, seemingly embarrassed to wave back.

"The water does remind me of Bertie. I wonder how he is getting on. It's rather hard to keep in touch when we are both on the move all of the time," Winnie said as she re-joined Douglas.

"I was thinking the same, but also about this letter," Douglas said as he handed it to Winnie. She recognised the paw writing—it was from Sophia.

25th March 1978

My darling Douglas,

I have some wonderful news to tell you. Eddie has proposed to me. I'm so happy. We haven't set a date for the wedding yet, but it goes without saying that I would like you to give me away. Would you be willing to do that for me?

Dino and Augie are doing fine, growing like weeds and still talking of your visit. I do hope you can come back soon.

Your loving mother

"Wow, I didn't see that coming," Winnie joked. "I'm only surprised it's taken this long for Eddie to propose. Looks like you are going to have a dad. It's wonderful news, isn't it?"

Douglas wasn't sure what to make of it and had a slightly distant look in his eyes, head drooping. "I suppose."

"Why didn't you show me earlier? You must have been hanging onto it for a few days now?" Winnie asked.

"I have," Douglas replied, "I guess I was just thinking back to my childhood. Brought back memories, that's all."

"Oh, you mustn't dwell on the past, look to the future, Douglas. Dino and Augie will have a new dog in their lives, and Sophia will have someone to look after her. It's wonderful news, it really is. I've known Eddie for quite some time, and he is a good sort. Mark my words."

Douglas had forgotten that Winnie knew Eddie much better than he did and allowed himself to be comforted. Banishing his angst, he smiled warmly at her. "Shall we try the Eiffel Tower next?" he said, putting the letter back in his jacket pocket and changing the subject.

"Oh, I would love to, but it is rather on the chilly side, and I've not brought my earmuffs or gloves. Perhaps a brisk walk to Rue de Montmartre and up the steps to Sacré Coeur Basilica? It would give us an appetite for lunch," Winnie suggested.

"Mm thought you would have liked the views from up there," Douglas said. "But I'm sure we can go another day. Lead the way."

Winnie had suffered no ill effects from their journey over and set such a brisk pace that Douglas was out of breath halfway up the steps and stopped, panting hard. "Are you okay?" she asked, pausing next to him. He nodded and waved her on. "I'll just meet you up there when you're ready, then" she said. Eager to look out over the city from the forecourt, she reached the top in no time and found herself amongst a tour group from a school, all giggling and laughing amongst themselves. A street artist flattered some of them into sitting for him, and Winnie wandered away, glad to disengage herself from the crowd and trying not to mind that he hadn't bothered asking her. Not that she had expected him to. She was not a vain dog and still lacked confidence about her appearance. Douglas sometimes looked at her in a way that made her think that he found her pretty, but she really wasn't certain. Shaking her head to clear these thoughts, she leaned over the balustrade and looked out over the rooftops, losing herself in the loveliness of the view.

Winnie was startled out of her reverie when a rather woolly-looking Spanish water dog approached her and lounged against the railing nearby. "What are you thinking of?" he asked, without so much as a hello or an introduction. She looked at him in confusion and didn't answer. "Ah, well, I like a lady who can keep secrets," he said with a half-smile. "I noticed you because you are not like the silly creatures over there, clamouring after that artist fellow. But you look a little melancholy. Perhaps a stroll about this lovely place will cheer you up?" He offered his arm, and to her surprise Winnie found herself following his lead. The dog continued to talk pleasantly for a while and then tried to kiss her, but Winnie turned away, coming very quickly to her senses. "I have to meet my friends and go back to the hotel," she said, disengaging herself, grateful that there were plenty of others around. Retracing her steps, she noticed the rather grotesque caricatures the artist had painted of the school pups and would have laughed if she hadn't felt a little shaken.

"There you are! I've been looking all over. So many tourists! Shall we find somewhere a bit more peaceful?" Douglas was at her side, still puffing a little, but his eyes had brightened on seeing her.

"Oh, I'm sorry, I… er…was a bit distracted. I was having a look at the architecture around the basilica's entrance," Winnie replied, feeling her face grow warm. What had she been thinking, wandering off like that? "I wonder if Uncle Leon would like a postcard. What do you think? I'm sure they must sell them here."

"Oh, I think he would probably find it odd, receiving a postcard from somewhere so familiar, don't you think?" Douglas said.

"Perhaps, but I must get one for Aunt Bea and Uncle Frederick. I'm sure they would be interested," Winnie replied. "And you must get one to reply to Sophia," she instructed.

"I suppose you're right," he said, although he had been trying to put his mother's news from his mind. He would have to sort his feelings on the matter out at some point, but now was not the time. "I'm so glad to be here with you, *mon cheri*," he murmured, and, taking her paw, kissed it lightly.

Chapter Seventy-Three
Truth and Consequences

Sweetie unwrapped the figurine carefully and marvelled at what lay in front of her.

"This is rather unique," she said, "I've seen some relatively recent copies, but this looks much older. I wouldn't care to hazard a guess as to its age. Bastet is the beloved and benevolent Egyptian Cat Goddess, worshipped in Bubastis in Lower Egypt. For the Egyptians, the goddesses Bastet and Sakhmet were two aspects of divine power. Sakhmet, the lioness, represented the powerful warrior, a force that could either protect or destroy, whilst Bastet, the feline of the house, incorporated the gentler characteristics."

Bertie was listening intently. 'Two halves of the same, interesting,' he thought. 'And which are you, I wonder?'

"See here," Sweetie continued, pointing to the right ear. "It is pierced with a gold ring and suspended from its incised necklace is a wedjat-eye or an 'Eye of Horus' pendant, which is an ancient Egyptian symbol of protection, royal power and good health."

"Interesting," Ani said. "You know so much."

"I find Egyptian religion fascinating," Sweetie said. "But I wish I knew more." She turned the cat around and held it up to the light. "An impression of majesty is created by the animal's erect and almost regal pose. It is a very graceful piece, but..."

"There's always a 'but,' " Bertie said, still wondering if he could trust this cat. She had seemed genuinely surprised by the object. 'But then she's no fool,' he thought. He wondered to himself why he had such strong feelings on the matter and wasn't entirely sure. Sweetie continued.

"...there is a fine crack at the neck. It goes right around. I didn't spot it to start with. I was too enthralled with the piece. But it looks like it's been repaired well, and the break must have occurred a long time ago. I think that's all I can tell you about it, really. I'm not sure if it is valuable or not. I suppose it is damaged, but given it is an historic piece, perhaps that won't be such an issue. Also, if I'm not very much mistaken, there seems to be a slight rattle inside, perhaps a broken piece of the bronze. Robyn could probably give us more information when she arrives."

Muriel and Ani looked at each other. Did Robyn know it was valuable, or had she missed the break, too? Bertie harrumphed to himself, still suspecting that the cat was bluffing.

"What was the other thing you wanted to show me?" Sweetie enquired.

Ani produced the journal and handed it to Sweetie. "We wondered if you could work out what the symbols on the pages mean. You seem to be something of an expert."

Sweetie took the journal, and as she opened it, the newspaper cutting fluttered to the floor. She stooped to pick it up and could not help but see the headline. Her eyes swept over the brief article. "Oh, sorry. I meant to tuck that away properly," Ani said.

Sweetie looked startled and began talking, as if to herself, really. "Gosh, this was a long time ago, I'd nearly forgotten about that." But she showed no inclination to say more.

"You know something about it, then?" Bertie asked, his curiosity getting the better of his suspicion for a moment.

Sweetie blushed a little. "Oh, well, I may," she replied, and paused to read the full article. "Oh yes, this was in the area where I lived as a young cat. I was out for a walk in the hills and found it quite by accident, really. A sinkhole appeared above ground, as it had been raining heavily. It was just by luck, really, that I happened upon it. The newspaper claimed I had made a discovery, but it was just a big hole and a couple of tunnels, nothing else, and all related to previous mining in the area. I can't claim to have found anything that wasn't already known about a century or so ago. I was rather embarrassed, to be honest."

Muriel smiled at Sweetie's modesty. "But why did Elias have the cutting in his journal—and what about the name? I believe you initially introduced yourself as Johanna."

"I really couldn't say why it's here," Sweetie said, looking a little baffled and scratching her head. "Just a matter of local interest? And as for the name, my grandparents used to call me by my middle name, Frieda. I didn't know my first name until I was older. Once they had passed, I decided it suited me better."

'Arrh, I wonder how many other names she's got,' Bertie thought. But he held his tongue.

Sweetie turned to the journal itself. "Symbols, you say. Let me see." She studied the pages that Ani had marked with slips of paper, not reading them, but flicking between and then turning back again to retrace her steps. "Yes, these are hieroglyphics again, like we saw in the cave... rather small and slightly indistinct, though." She started scribbling on her notepad, now oblivious to the three pairs of eyes watching her intently. "There, I think that is all of them. Sorry, I might have rushed a bit." She showed the three what she had produced.

"Means very little to me," Bertie said grumpily.

"Or me," Muriel agreed.

Ani was alert to this hidden message. "What does it say?"

"The letters...Truth Lies Within."

"Is that it?" Bertie asked. "Another riddle?"

"I think it's right, but the meaning is a mystery to me too," Sweetie said. The moment she finished speaking, the door opened, and in flew Robyn. She perched herself on the bookshelf.

"Good afternoon. Quite the crowd here. I see you began the party without me," she observed, rather sarcastically. "I'm sure you know best."

Sweetie wasn't in the mood for another argument so ignored the implication.

"Now, what's all this about? I'm a very busy bird," Robyn continued. "And what's that? My, my." She flew down and landed on the table.

Bertie refrained from interrogating the hummingbird, but he couldn't help blurting out, "you know exactly what it is!" and fixing her with his gaze.

"What? Of course, I do. It's a Bastet figurine. Glad you have some faith in my abilities. Excellent quality, indeed, fine craftsmanship. Is this what was hidden in the cave?" she asked.

Sweetie nodded.

"I'm glad it wasn't damaged, after having been in a cave so long. This is a work of art. It deserves to be in a museum," Robyn muttered as she hopped around the statue and eyed its details more closely.

Bertie couldn't help himself and rather rashly accused the bird of having seen the item before. "And you were planning to flog it. Sell it to the highest bidder!" he cried.

"Sell it! What do you mean, you hairy buffoon?" Robyn began hovering near him, her wings a blur.

Riled by her denial, Bertie carried on, ignoring Muriel's pleas for him to stop.

"I heard you, right here in this very room! You had every intention of stealing this. Sweetie too, both of you! Don't act all innocent. I was right outside the door, and I heard everything," he growled.

"What?" Robyn screeched. "What right do you have to accuse me of something like that? Why, if I was younger, I'd bash your ears to the other side of the country."

Bertie wouldn't let it lie. All the pent-up frustration boiled over. "You're nothing more than a common thief!" he yelled, the force of his voice beating the still hovering bird back a bit.

"Take that back right now... or I'll..." the bird looked around desperately, wondering what she could do after this attempt at character assassination. "...Or I'll throw this figurine on the floor, yes... that's right... I'll smash it into pieces, just to show you how much I care about it," she exclaimed, flying up in the air and holding the object in her claws.

Ani leapt up and opened her mouth to say something that might calm the two. But as she did so, Robyn flicked around, thinking Bertie was attacking her, and the Bastet cat dropped from her grasp. Everything then seemed to happen in slow motion. Ani gasped as the figurine fell onto the edge of the table and toppled to the floor. Muriel reached out but only managed to prevent the object from crashing to the ground with more force. Luckily, it hit the wooden floor, base first, but the damage was done. The head of the cat broke off along the old crack and rolled under Sweetie's paw.

"Now look at what you've done!" Robyn shrieked. "You clumsy oaf!"

Muriel looked on, aghast, and felt for Ani. Sweetie carefully picked up the head and placed it on the table, and Bertie handed her the body. Robyn had flown back to the relative safety of the bookshelves, out of Bertie's reach, just in case. In the meantime, something strange was happening. Ani was chuckling. The group momentarily forgot about the damaged figurine and stared at the calico cat, wondering what sort of reaction this was to the events that had just unfolded.

'Must be an American thing. Laugh in the face of adversity?' Robyn thought. 'Or she's in shock.'

Aware that everyone was staring at her, Ani tried to compose herself. Everyone waited, the room now seeming profoundly silent after the noise of the past few minutes.

Ani broke the silence first. "I do apologise. It's just that at the moment the figurine crashed to the floor, an old memory came back to me. I told you earlier that the item looked vaguely familiar, and now I know why."

Sweetie and Muriel looked at her expectantly, while Bertie continued to eye the hummingbird on the shelf.

"The crack along the neck...it was my doing!" She paused a moment. "I've just remembered. I was still just a kitten, and I was so intrigued by the figurine that I picked it up to look more closely at the carvings. But it was too heavy, and I dropped it, just as happened here. Dad didn't scold me, though. He seemed almost glad," Ani smiled, recalling her father's face at that moment. She paused again and then continued more quietly. "I've also just recalled that he did something odd. He picked the pieces up and said, almost to himself, 'no one will care about you now.' I think I believed he was talking about me, and he did leave on his last trip soon after. I must have blocked out all memory of the incident."

Muriel and Sweetie sat amazed at the revelation. And it occurred to Muriel that Ani had used the word dad for the first time. "That can't have been what he meant," she assured her, seeing that the cat was looking at the floor and no longer smiling. Bertie had been about to say something to the effect that it seemed like they had wasted a lot of effort just to find a kitten's broken trinket, but he wisely stopped himself.

Robyn left her perch to join the group. "I think I may have something to add to the story," she said, glancing down at the two pieces rather contritely. They all looked at her in surprise. "I am rather ashamed to say that Bertie was right to be suspicious of a Durcheinander. My Uncle Klaus was Elias's colleague."

"Ah, yes, we saw a photo of him," Bertie said, regarding her curiously.

"I have a copy of that one, too," Robyn said. "I grew up in awe of him and his love of archaeology. He was a fine and clever bird, but he was very unhappy in his later years. He felt he hadn't gotten the credit he deserved for his achievements, and he grew bitter and twisted. When Elias was given the figurine, Klaus became very envious, so much so that he was the one that started spreading the rumour that his friend had come into possession of it unlawfully. I didn't learn of this until after his passing, but I am ashamed."

Bertie raised his brows in disbelief, realising he could have misjudged this bird.

"After Elias died Klaus took it upon himself to search his house. He was a persuasive bird, and he convinced the solicitors that he was Elias's most trusted friend and should be the one to sort through everything, since there was no will. As a colleague in the same field, Klaus would make sure that nothing important was thrown away. It was a painstaking job no one else wanted, so they gave him free rein, and he went in prepared to remove anything of historic value. He didn't find anything apart from notes and papers, all of which he ended up burning. His bitterness eventually got the better of him, and he died a broken bird."

"I'm sorry," Bertie said, sincerely. But he was still wondering about Robyn's argument with Sweetie. Realising what Bertie was thinking, Muriel decided to broach the point.

"So, it seems you knew nothing about the figurine, so what was the argument about, if I may ask?"

"Oh, that. I suppose I inherited a bit of my uncle's lack of tact. I have already apologised to Sweetie." The cat nodded in agreement.

"Maybe I should explain," Sweetie offered.

"Please do," Bertie said.

"A few years ago, we were both exploring some new passageways underground in Germany. We came upon a calcite crystal cavern surrounded by limestone and adorned with countless crystals and pearl drop stones. It was the very one I mentioned earlier, and truly breath-taking. We were both exhilarated by the discovery and could scarcely believe what we had found. Naturally, we both had ideas about what should be done about the find. As you could tell, Bertie, those opinions do not coincide, and that is what the argument was about."

Bertie sat silently, looking out the window and trying to replay the argument in his mind. Had they mentioned the figurine at all? Or had he just jumped to conclusions, his head too full of recent events?

"Oh my," he said apologetically. "I think I am in the doghouse. I am so sorry."

Muriel patted his paw and saved his blushes by saying, "He meant well. I'm sure you can all see that?"

"Of course," Sweetie replied, and Robyn nodded in agreement. "Think no more of it. Let me make us all a pot of tea."

"I'll help you," Ani said, feeling a little fidgety after the excitement of the past hours. The two cats rose simultaneously and jostled the desk ever so slightly. Two paws shot out toward the figurine, which rolled toward Sweetie. They all exhaled in relief as she grasped it with both paws.

"I think we need to find a safer spot for this," she said with a smile. "It seems a bit accident-prone." She turned it slightly in her paw and glanced around the room. Ani put her head to one side and gazed at it intently.

"Sweetie," she said, "look. It doesn't look completely hollow."

The cat held the body of the figurine up to the light, taking care not to tip it. "You're right. The inner wall looks thicker than it should."

"*Truth Lies Within*," murmured Ani. "Could there be something in there?"

"Doesn't really look like it," Bertie said. He was beginning to feel peckish, and Sweetie's offer of tea had roused hopes of a plate of custard creams. Muriel nudged his elbow and shook her head. He sighed.

Sweetie reached a paw inside, delicately, and felt around. Then she handed the object to Ani and pulled open her desk drawer. "This should do it," she said. "Just hold it up—that way—perfect. Now, if I can just..." She deftly manoeuvred the razor around the edge. "That's just papier-mâché," she said. "A layer of it, adhered to the inside like a lining. Now, do we have something soft that we can put under it?"

Chapter Seventy-Four
Letters of Love

Ani hesitated for a moment and then untied the scarf from around her head and neck. She folded it several times and placed it in the centre of the desk. Muriel's eyes grew wide, and she exchanged a knowing glance with Bertie, who had now forgotten all about custard creams. "Excellent," Sweetie said quietly, scarcely daring to breathe as she tipped the figurine over the scarf and shook it gently. Two heads bent over the desk in anticipation, their faces bearing almost the same look of concentration.

Two tiny packets slid out, each bearing a seal. Closer inspection revealed an ornate letter A on one and a similarly decorated J on the other. Bertie and Muriel rose to get a better look. "I don't understand," Sweetie said, standing back a little. "Well, Ani, you should open them."

Bertie was intrigued, and he'd also noticed something no one else had. "There's still something in there," he muttered. "See that little bit poking out there?"

Ani peered at the figurine again. "Yes, a little corner of something. Do you have any tweezers, Sweetie?" The cat nodded.

"In my first aid kit, yes." She produced them quickly and handed them to Ani, who tugged very gently at the corner until a small square of paper came free. On it were two ovals, apparently clipped and pasted on. Muriel caught her breath, for the resemblance between the photos was suddenly more than obvious. Under each, carefully printed, were the names of the two cats who now stood transfixed, staring at the paper. The two ovals were linked to Elias's name at the top, with the names of their mothers to his left and right.

Ani and Sweetie looked at each other in a dazed sort of way, and Sweetie sat down heavily in her chair. "I still don't understand," she murmured.

"How…?" Ani began.

"Perhaps the packets will explain everything," Muriel suggested, smiling.

Ani looked at the two little objects still in her paw. "This must be yours," she said shakily, handing Sweetie the one embossed with J. After looking at each other once again in disbelief, they opened the packets with care. Ani shook hers out onto the scarf first, and then Sweetie. There lay two gold pendants and two wedding rings. The pendants each formed half of a heart and appeared to fit together like puzzle pieces.

"There's something engraved on mine," Ani said, holding it out to Sweetie.

"My half has hieroglyphs for the letters *s*, *i* and *s*," Sweetie replied. "And yours—*t*, *e* and *r*."

Muriel suggested that each packet should be unfolded fully and with permission did just that. "They are letters," she said, holding them up. The paw writing was small but matched that of the journal. Judging that both cats were in too much shock to do much about the letters, she asked if they wanted her to read them aloud. They both nodded. Muriel began with Sweetie's note.

My dearest Johanna,

If you are reading this, then I can only apologise that I was not there for you when you were a kitten. Hannah, your mother, was a kind and beautiful cat, tragically taken from us so young. I know that she would have wanted her husband and daughter to be together. However, her parents had been against our marriage from the start, and when Hannah died while serving in the medical corps, they took you from me. I wrote many letters pleading with them to allow me to see you and even engaged a solicitor to see what could be done, but it was hopeless. By the time you were old enough to receive letters, they had turned you against me.

When all else failed, I asked one of your mother's closest friends, your godmother Isolde, to keep me apprised of your doings. She kindly did so, even sending me snapshots which I treasured, happy that you resemble your lovely mother. When Isolde told me of your interests, so many of which we shared, I sent her some of my books to give to you. I think that you will know which ones they are. If you look at the pages corresponding to the date of your birth, you will find messages from me. It was so little, but it was the best I could do.

I trust you can forgive me, my darling Johanna, and hope you can develop a happy relationship with your half-sister.

Your loving father,

Elias

Sweetie was looking down, clasping her paws so that they would not shake. "I had no idea that he wanted me," she said in a choked voice, a tear falling to the floor. "All those years." Bertie found that his own eyes were misting over as he passed her his handkerchief. Muriel laid a paw on her shoulder, and they all sat in silence for some minutes as the golden afternoon sunshine dappled the room.

"Please don't mind me," Sweetie said, embarrassed by her show of emotion. "We must hear Ani's letter."

It was a shorter missive, as was appropriate, given Elias's other messages to Ani. Muriel read the few lines to them.

My dearest Anipe,

If you are reading this, then I hope with all my heart that in the not-too-distant future you will be able to find your half-sister and do something I could not. Her name is Johanna Schneider.

Your loving father,

Elias

The pair of cats looked at each other. Her shyness fully evaporating, Ani did something she had refrained from doing for so long and embraced

Sweetie in a warm and loving hug. Both were crying, and neither could speak, but they knew that the loneliness of many years would be no longer.

Chapter Seventy-Five
Vagaries in Venice

Bertie was pleased to have left the Volkswagen in Germany and to have travelled in style in a Pullman carriage to the Santa Lucia station on the north western edge of the city of Venice. He had admired Muriel's ability to adapt graciously to various modes of transport during their journey thus far, but he was pleased that she had had a chance to relax in comfort. They had agreed that Ani and Sweetie needed space, and they could continue their tour around Europe without any remorse or worry about leaving their friend behind. Sweetie already had plans to take her sister to see the wonders of the crystal cave, and the cats had two lifetimes'-worth of history to share with each other. Of course, Muriel made sure to exchange contact details before they left, and they all spoke of meeting again to find out how the cats were getting along, perhaps in London—or even in America. "Maybe a road trip," Bertie had suggested, though with the memory of their adventures in the Transporter still fresh in their minds, Ani and Muriel let the comment pass.

It was a glorious afternoon for having a look at the ancient city. Bertie and Muriel left their bags at their lodgings near the station. "Let's not go up to our room just yet," Muriel said, and Bertie agreed. A pleasant, half-hour stroll brought them to a smattering of merchant stalls along the Grand Canal, extremely near St Mark's Square. Artisans were hawking their wares, everything from watercolour prints of picturesque local scenes to Murano glass necklaces and hats. Muriel decided to buy Bertie a Venetian-style boater as well as a hat for herself. He briefly resisted the idea of wearing such a thing but gave in when he saw a certain determined look in her eye. Placing it on his head at just the right angle, Muriel stood back to admire the effect and was inevitably reminded of Percy. She made a mental note to write him when she had a spare moment.

The arcaded walks on two sides of the piazza offered welcome shade, and they craned their necks to gaze at the several domes of St Mark's Basilica. The sinking sun picked out four gilded arches and threw the domes into relief. It also reminded them that they had had a light lunch and no tea. "Though I suppose tea is not quite the thing here," Bertie observed.

"Shall we have gelato instead?" Muriel suggested, as she gazed longingly in the direction of a shop with an inviting striped awning over its window. Bertie looked at the place a tad suspiciously.

"Is it really ice cream?" He looked at her with bushy brows sceptically raised.

"Oh, Bertie, come and find out for yourself," she said with a laugh, grabbing his paw and leading him to the door. The proprietor waved them in.

"I give you free gelato," the pointer said with a buoyant smile. He thrust two small cups toward them, and they realised that it was only polite to accept.

"*Grazie*," Muriel said. Bertie, eager to prove that his tastes were cosmopolitan after his hesitancy, plunged the little spoon in and took a mouthful. Muriel approached hers more delicately. They looked at each other with eyes wide. Bertie gulped.

"Ah! I can see you like it very much. When I heard you speak *Inglese*, I knew. Gelato from your country! Perfetto!" Bertie insisted on paying the dog in lieu of purchasing anything else. As they hastily left the shop, Muriel's eye caught a small poster next to the door touting "Baker's *Speciale Ostrica Gelato*," and the grinning mollusk in one corner left little to the imagination.

When they returned to their hotel, a message was waiting for them. Having booked ahead before they left Germany, Muriel had informed Wagmore of their whereabouts. The greyhound had taken great pleasure in writing a short telegram, which was waiting at their new hotel when they arrived, informing them that Bertie's cottage had been flooded in a storm. Wagmore himself didn't really know what the state of the building was; the call from America from a bumbling budgie called Stanley was all rather broken up by the clamour of kittens and pups shouting something about drinking more milk. 'Quite a strange fellow,' Wagmore thought, but no matter. He had the opportunity to cause Bertie as much distress as possible by hinting at what a lot of damage had been done.

The message had its desired effect. Although he hadn't been back to Badger's Bay for quite some time, it was still the place Bertie called home, for the time being at least. He tried to think what time it would be in the United States if he called at that moment and decided he would contact Chief first to get a clear and calm explanation. Stan would more than likely say whatever he could to persuade him to return.

Muriel looked at him with concern. "I know you're upset, Bertie, but there's nothing you can do just now. Best to have a good night's sleep and call tomorrow. You know Chief is an early riser, so you can call just before lunch." Bertie nodded in agreement, feeling sleep overcome him despite the bad news.

After a relaxed morning sunning themselves on the hotel's terrace, Muriel decided to go for a walk whilst Bertie rang up Chief. The square was full of tourists, pigeons everywhere. She found it quite a contrast from the green hills in Germany and it struck her that she would soon have to return to London and find a similarly busy place. She felt it disconcerting to be surrounded by the birds flocking in groups to have their photos taken, pushing by, generating a lot of noise, and jostling for position. She decided to head to the basilica in hope of finding some peace. The cool interior dazzled, especially the mosaics underfoot, on the walls and on the ceilings. But the floors were curiously wavy, as a result of the city's shifting water levels, and she started to feel slightly nauseous. Bertie would have been right at home, accustomed as he was to tossing about on the Atlantic, but Muriel felt off kilter and decided to find the nearest seat.

The gold leaf decorations inside the building shone gloriously in the afternoon sun and Muriel was quite happy admiring them until a pair of cats appeared, each holding a fish cicchetti, and she was overpowered by the smell. Holding her mouth, she rushed out to get some fresh air. Wandering through some charming stone alleyways, she eventually found herself in a courtyard with only one exit, an archway looking down into one of the numerous canals which make the area famous. She crossed to it to look for gondolas and promptly slipped on the algae which grew along the edges of the water and fell in.

After recovering from the shock of the experience, Muriel clambered back onto the bank. She was wet through but thankfully only her pride was hurting.

"Are you okay?" a familiar voice next to her said, and a paw grabbed hers to help her up.

"Estelle! What are you doing here?" Muriel asked, thankful to see a friendly face.

"Looks like I arrived in the nick of time, doesn't it?" she beamed. "And there I was thinking you were searching for buried treasure down there."

"Not quite," Muriel replied. "I think I would have brought my bathing costume, or perhaps a diving suit."

"Now then, you do look a sight. I think you had better hand me some of your garments, and we'll go and dry off in the sun. We can buy you some replacements at the market rather than traipsing back to the hotel. Come along now," Lady Effingham instructed.

Across the way, Bertie was perusing the streets of Venice, trying not to think too much about his conversation with Chief, when he noticed a stunning Italian Renaissance building. He didn't recognise the name, Fondaco dei Tedeschi, just that it looked very grand. The most striking thing was not the building itself or its opulence, however, but rather a large sign at the entrance advertising a book signing that was going on inside. Bertie decided to investigate, as he was at a loose end, and Muriel wouldn't be back for a while. The glorious building oozed history from every angle, with a walkway that led through a large, rounded arcade into a central courtyard. Looking up, Bertie could see several floors. In the corner of the square a small crowd had gathered, and most of them were queuing, so out of interest he walked over to investigate what all the fuss was about.

He noticed a couple of cats staring at something behind him, so he turned and saw an advertisement nearly one story high displaying an enormous picture of a book titled *A Springtime in October*. Beneath the image, in bold capitals as tall as Bertie himself, was a brief description: "The tale of Bernard and Maud—a love story that took fifty years to come to life." On the book's cover was a strapping Doberman standing on a sun-drenched beach with a sailing boat in the distance and a female Basset hound relaxing under some palm trees. A couple of standout quotations surrounded the image: "Mills & Boon, eat your heart out," "WOW, sensual, seductive and superb, a must-read" and "Daphne does it again!!!"

'Surely not,' Bertie murmured to himself. 'Must be a coincidence.' He looked over at a black and white cat sitting at a desk who was busy scribbling on title pages for her adoring public. At that moment, the cat looked up and gazed across the room, and Bertie was sure she was looking directly at him. He gave a friendly wave and made his way out of the courtyard.

Once outside, he decided to continue strolling around the winding cobbled streets and many bridges. Like many a tourist before him, he was charmed by the quaintness of the historic city, the stucco houses with geraniums in the window boxes, and the many stone footbridges. He spotted a commotion in the distance, where a small crowd had gathered, but he didn't particularly want to gawp at any unfortunate incident so continued in his way. As he approached the water's edge Bertie was reminded of Badger's Bay. It wasn't as iconic a place and certainly didn't have the history, tradition or romance of Venice, but that didn't matter. He couldn't resist the urge to jump aboard a gondola and remind himself of how it felt to sit in a small boat, gently rocking up and down as the traffic streamed by on the busy Grand Canal. Although black was the official colour, many other ornately decorated craft passed by whilst he basked in the atmosphere and relative comfort of the seats with blankets. But his idyll was all too brief. The boat was moored only a stone's throw from St. Mark's Square, and a group of five tourists hopped into the boat with him. Bertie looked up from under his straw hat and wondered why they were all staring at him.

"We're ready," the oldest dog called.

"What?" Bertie replied. "I don't understand."

"Let's go, we haven't got all day," the dog repeated.

After a moment of confusion, Bertie realised he had been mistaken for a gondolier. Not wishing to disappoint and not seeing any sign of the boat's owner, he decided it could do no harm to oblige. He unleashed the rope and pushed the boat away. It didn't take long for Bertie to adjust to standing up to pilot the boat, within a short time he was rowing with the single oar out along the narrow channels. It was cooler on the water, and Bertie lost himself, forgetting about the passengers in front of him and ignoring their questions. After twenty minutes he had woken from his daze and realised he had better get back to the spot where he had found the boat.

When the group got back to dry land, Bertie held the boat and the passengers disembarked, all with rather glum faces, except one who had managed to pick up a straw hat floating in the water and was quite pleased with how it fitted. The older chap approached him, grimacing. "I had an image of a singing gondolier, a one-of-a-kind experience. You've absolutely ruined our day, and I shan't be paying you one cent," he growled, striding off to re-join his family. "Drat this hat," Bertie said, and then realised that it had been several hours since he had seen Muriel.

Chapter Seventy-Six
Calm Contemplation

"I've just had some slightly sad news, Hans," Percy said as he returned to his seat on the seafront on Hastings's promenade. "I made a call to check up on Bertie and Muriel. I didn't speak to Muriel's butler, who has always been a bit terse to say the least. Instead, I got hold of Nightingale, her driver, and he told me that the pair are safe and sound, still travelling around Europe, but over at Badger's Bay Bertie's cottage has suffered some damage in a storm. He was a bit light on detail, having heard it second-hand, but it's still rather disconcerting all the same."

"That is bad luck," Hans replied. "It's so far away, but I suppose that's the trade-off of living by the coast and in such a beautiful place. Like here, the weather can change so quickly."

"Indeed," Percy replied. "We nearly got caught by that shower when you were sketching my picture." Although he didn't want to pressure his friend, he allowed himself this oblique hint, as he was keen to see the fruits of Hans's labour.

"Ah yes. I've just finished that, and I brought it along to show you." Hans pulled out a small parcel wrapped in brown paper and handed it over to Percy. "Here, it is. I do hope you like it. If not, you can always sell it, might make a bob or two."

"Oh, I'd never..." Percy tore off the paper and looked at the portrait. The painting was not quite what he had expected, though he thought it flattered him too much. There he stood, gloves in one hand and hat in the other, in the stance he adopted at the end of his routine. But his face was in profile, and he was looking out to sea, away from the Hastings Pier.

"Is that really how people see me, do you think?" Percy said.

"I think we all see things differently," Hans replied. "Do you like it?"

"If I'm honest, I think I look a bit sad," he murmured. "I'm sorry, maybe I am, and you've captured exactly how I feel. It's not that I don't like it, it's a fine piece of work. I think it just reminds me of how old I am, how grey my fur has got."

Hans could see his gift hadn't quite got the reaction he had anticipated. Perhaps he should have tried to make it livelier. He kicked himself for not realising the impact it would have on Percy. He adjusted his glasses and resolved to speak. "Look, Percy, I didn't want to mention this, but now is as good a time as any. I just happened to have gotten a letter from Leonard—oh, you don't know him, do you? He was a theatre director I was very friendly with. Bit of a rolling stone took positions all over the place, and then suddenly decided he couldn't abide professionals anymore and upped sticks to New England. He is just starting up an amateur dramatics troupe up in Cape Berkeley. Says he's happy as a clam, as they apparently put it over there."

"Is that so?" Percy responded thoughtfully. "It does sound like great fun, so long as one has the patience for it." Hans looked keenly at Percy for a moment and thought he saw a flicker of something he'd never seen before in his face.

"I had a thought. What do you say I give Leonard a call? I'm sure he could use someone with your experience to lend a hand. Maybe it would help Bertie out too, perhaps you could be a temporary liaison across the ocean and make sure any repair work goes to plan?"

"I... I don't know," Percy replied, momentarily taken aback by this proposal. Could he really leave everything here? But what had he got left, really? Then he sat up straighter in his chair, as if invigorated by what Hans had just told him. "Would you come and visit, too?" he asked with the beginnings of a smile.

"I think I could be quite easily persuaded," the younger dog said, his eyes warm.

'This is the type of son I wish I could have had,' Percy thought.

Chapter Seventy-Seven
Speaking my Language

Muriel had a last look in the mirror of the market stall, admired some of the Murano glass on the stall next door and patted her new attire down to pull out some of the creases. She re-joined Lady Effingham at the café table she had managed to acquire.

"So, what brings you to Venice?" Muriel asked, now feeling rather more comfortable, if not a little embarrassed.

"I decided to follow your lead and have a little break. London is normally so glum at this time of year, and I needed some sun to cheer me up," she replied.

"I can't argue with that, as you know. I'm here with Bertie, after a rather eventful trip, which I won't bore you with now," Muriel said.

"Oh, you know I'll want all the details, so we must catch up when you return. How is Bertie? Keeping well, I hope. And you both are still getting along? Speaking of such things, I did have another reason to take a leave of absence from my usual routine. I have recently made the acquaintance of a chap called Charles, a rather handsome cat, but a little too forthcoming for my liking. We met at Christmas; you know. I was shopping for some gifts in a jeweller in town, and he was at the counter waiting to collect a piece that needed cleaning, so we got chatting."

"Quite unlike you," mused Muriel.

"Indeed. He was telling me about a story he overheard from one of the shop assistants whose sister works at the tourist office in some part of the country. She was Spanish, and an elderly couple came into the information centre and started looking at items in the glass cabinets and flicking through the pamphlets, appearing to be interested. The sister of the assistant approached the wife—she assumed they were a married couple as they were bickering—would like any information on the castle pictured on the leaflet the dog was holding. She nodded and listened to the short spiel. The customer began asking various questions herself, interested in visiting and booking a ticket."

"Interesting. What happened next?" Muriel asked.

"Well, the couple said they would think about it, given the tour was fairly expensive, and left the store. The next day they were back, this time wanting to look at country houses. The assistant's sister obliged, answering all their questions about historic events and dates, convinced they would want to go along and see for themselves. Unfortunately, the customers politely left the centre again without scheduling a tour. They returned a third time and looked at theme parks, supposedly for their grand pups, but left as before, without making any arrangements."

"That is strange," Muriel said.

"Charlie continued, enjoying the look of interest on my face and seeing that I was rather enthralled. I was almost wondering if he had made the whole thing up just to keep chatting with me. Anyway, I'll continue. The assistant decided to follow the couple out of the store and ask them why they had been acting so strangely. Whilst standing in the doorway she heard them chatting to each other, so stopped to listen. 'I'm sure she is from Russia, and you think Italy, but do the Italians use the word antique? Isn't that French? I reckon she's French, she must be, let's listen more carefully the next time, maybe we can ask her about dinosaurs, that's a hard word to pronounce. We'll go in again tomorrow, as I do love her accent, even if I don't have a clue what she is telling us.' "

Muriel laughed. "How quaint. That is a lovely story, but what happened with Charlie?"

"Oh, we did meet up, and ever since he has been sending me flowers. I don't mind the attention, you understand, I'm an attractive lady. But when I find him singing outside the front door in the dead of night, I think you will agree that it's a bit much."

"Oh, don't you think it is somewhat romantic?" Muriel questioned.

"No, I do not," Estelle said. "It's all I could do to keep from throwing a bucket of water out the window at him. At least the neighbours didn't see him—what would they think? Hopefully they didn't hear him, either. I did a little bit of asking around, and it seems like he is a bit lovesick to be honest. He's recently moved his business from France and broken up with his fiancée. I do hope he will get the idea soon enough and find another cat who will return his affection."

"Quite," Muriel smiled. "Let's hope he's an 'out of sight, out of mind' sort of chap."

"Oh, I do hope so. And now that I've bumped into you, I should mention poor Percy. It appears he has had some bad luck recently."

"Bad luck? What do you mean?" Muriel asked, worriedly.

"Well, I didn't hear it first-hand, mind, but I trust the source. You know that Nightingale comes round sometimes to have a chat with my driver, and before he left, he asked to speak to me. He'd had a call from Percy about Bertie and Muriel, and the older dog let slip that he had had some squatters for a few days. They have gone now, but it shook him up somewhat. I didn't know what to do. I did call, but he wasn't there. A neighbour said he had gone away to spend time with a friend, but she didn't know where and when he would be back. Perhaps Bertie can look in on him when you return?" Estelle suggested.

"Of course, I will tell him when I see him," Muriel said, her face full of concern.

"Well enough of this nattering," Estelle said as she stood up and hugged Muriel. "I've got a book signing to get to. My favourite author just wrote a marvellous new romance." And with that she whisked herself away, leaving Muriel to ponder what she had heard.

Chapter Seventy-Eight
A Bridge Too Far?

Bertie leaned on a parapet and watched the gondolas gliding past, each with a gondolier either regaling his passengers with fabulous tales of dubious historic accuracy, or singing the likes of "Funiculi, Funiculi" with a gusto undiminished by hundreds of repetitions each season. Some of the less inhibited tourists joined in the rousing chorus. He shook his head at his own silent turn as gondolier. No wonder his customers had not been satisfied, he thought with a wry smile, as he slipped off his hat. A few of the boats had obviously been hired by couples, and one was decorated with a spray of roses and baby's breath. The gondolier tucked a rose in his hatband as he waited for the bride and groom to appear. To his surprise, he noticed some fins protruding from the wash, and within a few moments he saw the bodies of two dolphins emerge and then disappear again as they swam past. He didn't know if it was his lucky day or if someone from the wedding party had somehow commandeered them from a zoo for the occasion. Looking up at Bertie, he gesticulated in the direction of what he had seen, and Bertie nodded, sharing his wonderment.

After gazing out for a while and not seeing the dolphins again, Bertie turned away and sought a shady bench nearby. Something had been playing on his mind for some time since he came back to England in fact. Would he ever get married? He had always considered it an impossibility. Living all on his own with only Stanley for company, the chances of him meeting anyone were as remote as his cottage. But things had now changed. Winnie had made sure of that, bless her. Did he enjoy his new life? Yes. Did he hanker for a return to the old days? No, but there was still a nagging doubt that haunted him. What if things went wrong? And could he really live in London—or would Muriel be open to finding somewhere a bit more tranquil, maybe in the country? He supposed he should already know the answers to these questions, but he honestly didn't. He was on holiday with Muriel, he could spend as much time as possible with Muriel, but it wasn't the same as living with her every day. Bertie had realised very quickly that he certainly couldn't live in the same house as Wagmore, but would Muriel be happy to relinquish her butler's services, and for that matter, Harry's? More unanswered questions. How could he find the answers without making himself look a fool, or worse, ruining his relationship?

Bertie wandered back to the Piazza San Marco and looked up at the iconic bell tower just as it began to toll the hour. He almost bumped into a dog in pink corduroy trousers who was doing the same. "So sorry," he mumbled.

"As you should be," she answered in a voice he knew well. Turning, he first saw a baggy "I Love Venice" t-shirt and then a pair of laughing eyes above it. "Do you like my new look?" Muriel asked.

"Most befitting," he replied. "What happened? I'd swear that you were quite a different dog when you left the hotel this morning."

"Amazing what clothes can do," Muriel said, rather reluctant to tell him the whole story. "Shall we go for a walk? I'd like to see the Rialto bridge."

"Of course," Bertie replied.

The pair walked paw in paw amongst the throng of other visitors. When they got to the crest of the bridge they took in the gorgeous view, the gondolas and vaporetti passing under the bridge, the sun reflecting on the water. Bertie was rather overcome with it all, and he turned to Muriel, who was gazing out thoughtfully.

"Marry me?" he blurted out, surprising even himself.

Muriel stood still, stunned. The wire-haired dachshund was on one knee, his deep brown eyes looking up at her, and she was caught quite off guard. An eruption of cheers and cries occurred as others around them realised what was happening.

"Where's the ring?" was the first thing Muriel could think of saying, though she felt rather an idiot. "I think it's customary to have one to paw when one makes such a proposal?" she said, with a laugh and a blush.

"Errum, I... it was a spur of the moment thing. Oh, dear," Bertie replied.

Pausing for a moment, Muriel's face changed, and her voice was serious. "I think we need to have a chat before we take things any further. Let's find somewhere a bit more private." The pair found a small jetty looking over the water and sat down. "I need you to listen, Bertie. Please don't interrupt and let me try and explain a few things that you aren't aware of," Muriel continued calmly.

"You already know I was married to Peter and that it was really a marriage of convenience. What you don't really know is what happened later. We were never close, though he was a decent enough dog, and some years later he asked for a divorce. He didn't say why, and I wasn't particularly curious. I agreed, and he added the proviso that no one was to know of it. He had his place as an equerry to consider, he said, and chaps had been ousted for less, he said. In return for keeping up a sham marriage, he insisted on settling his estate on me."

'As he should have,' Bertie thought. 'The rotter.'

"Very little changed, except that Peter was free to live as he chose, within certain bounds. Wagmore was the only dog who knew of the arrangement, and he stayed on as butler. Unfortunately, he grew quite infatuated with me. It wasn't mutual, I hasten to add. Throughout this time I grew lonely, and I longed for companionship. I threw myself into my charity work and social life and gradually started having some rendezvous with other dogs. It was just male friendships at first, but over time it developed into more with one particular hound, Everett Walker."

Bertie sat silent and still. He had known in his heart that Muriel must have had other relationships. He hadn't been the only dog in Muriel's life.

"Things got problematic," Muriel said.

"Why?" Bertie asked, then realised that he should not have spoken.

"An amazing thing happened. I had a pup and named him Rupert, but Everett didn't want to know, and he left me the minute he found out I was expecting. I struggled and found it very difficult to cope, what with having to keep everything secret. I began to see a warmer side to Wagmore, and he helped me through some hard times. I fell ill, postpartum, and over a short space of time Wagmore had gotten it into his head that we could become a family, but that was the furthest thing from my mind. He was furious at my rejection. Rupert was adopted, apparently with my consent. I had been considering adoption up until the birth but changed my mind the minute I saw his little face. I couldn't do it. In my daze, I thought I was signing something to do with some household matters and was too unwell to read it closely. I discovered my mistake and was horrified."

Bertie looked at her downcast face and felt a wave of sadness for her.

"I had so many visitors, doctors, friends—my memory of the events is hazy. Wagmore could have been involved, but I have no proof of anything. I did all I could to reverse the decision, pleading with the orphanage, but the authorities dismissed me as a silly and unstable dog."

Bertie wrapped his paw around Muriel and tried to comfort her. She dropped her head on his shoulder and cried, heedless of the one or two passers-by.

"You've been carrying this for so long. Why didn't you tell me before?" Bertie asked quietly.

"I wanted to tell you, Bertie, I really did. I've tossed and turned many nights worrying over it, but the right moment just never seemed to come along…until now."

Bertie handed her a handkerchief. Once her sobs had subsided a little, he ventured another question. "So what became of Rupert?" Bertie asked.

"That's a difficult question, Bertie, "I don't know, and it hurts me to think about where he is and what type of life he had since birth." She paused. "Would you still want to marry someone with that sort of past?"

Bertie was relieved that Muriel had confided in him and was determined to help her through this, whichever way that might be. He took her paw and thought about her question, but not for long.

"We can't change the past. We can only look to the future and live in the present. Of course I would still like to marry you. I think I knew we would be together from the minute we met all those years ago at the palace. It's just taken many years for the jigsaw to fall into place."

Muriel smiled and was comforted by Bertie's words.

"I suggest we ask your friends for some help. They won't jump to any conclusions or judge you, if you write to them and explain. Then when we get back from our break we can get together and discuss our future. Perhaps an intimate gathering, Molly, Lady Effingham, Nap, Douglas—and as Winnie is in London, perhaps it would be a good chance to meet her, too. I know she wants to meet you," Bertie suggested. "It goes without saying that we don't want Wagmore around, so perhaps we should send him a message, tell him we plan to stay longer on our holiday? Say that he deserves a holiday himself and should go away somewhere?"

Muriel pondered on the idea. She had kept her secret so long and been afraid but looking into Bertie's kind eyes and knowing she had true friends, she decided it was time to face her demons and was determined to banish them, once and for all.

Chapter Seventy-Nine
London Calling

Lady Effingham had arrived at twelve on the dot, and Molly had arrived early, as was her way. Winnie and Douglas had received the telegram and had come straight back to London after their trip to Paris. That only left Napoleon, who was fashionably late, on account of a mix-up with the taxi driver, who had taken him to Kennington instead of Kensington. The new valet at Dolphin Square would be reminded to get his facts right next time.

Nightingale appeared in the doorway, having somewhat reluctantly disengaged himself from a tune-up of the Fiat and changed his oily overalls for a respectable grey suit. Just before he stepped into the room, he looked down and groaned inwardly. His work boots...he had forgotten to change. They were not greasy, but he'd taken a muddy shortcut this morning. He was about to turn back when Molly appeared at his side. She'd slipped away from the others and taken a copy of the Times from a nearby side table. "This should do the trick," she whispered, holding the newspaper out to him. He met her eyes and wondered why he had never noticed how lovely they were before. "Just the thing," he agreed with a smile.

Muriel had dismissed Peel and Flora for the weekend, and Wagmore had not hesitated to take them up on the offer of a long weekend cruise. He chose Amsterdam via Bruges, as he had some new business in that area to take care of. He felt particularly pleased with himself for securing a cabin on the Odyssey, which was certainly not going to be full of hip young things making noise at all hours and sniggered at the memory of Bertie and Muriel's debacle.

The lady of the house entered the drawing room unobtrusively and gazed at her guests for a moment. The formalities of the introductions were over, save for one, and the atmosphere was convivial and friendly. Bertie looked dapper in his beige tweed blazer and blue shirt. Douglas had refrained from donning his leather biker's jacket and was wearing something quite formal too, not wishing to stand out. Winnie—for there she was at last, looking more poised and even prettier than in Bertie's favourite photo—sported a smart striped outfit and red slippers. Muriel caught Bertie's eye and made her way over to the trio, a Parisian silk scarf floating behind her. He extended a paw to her.

"Muriel, I am delighted to introduce you to Winifred Wigglesworth, without whose imagination and irrepressible optimism we three would not be standing here together."

"Hear, hear," Douglas added, quietly, in an aside to Winnie, who was feeling a bit like her bashful old self and lifted her eyes to Muriel's kindly ones with some difficulty.

Muriel smiled and stepped closer to her. "We owe you so much," she said, and overcome with a wave of maternal tenderness, enveloped the dachshund in a warm embrace. Winnie felt herself relax immediately; her awkwardness gone. Muriel was as lovely as she had imagined her to be.

"I'm so happy to finally meet you," she replied, simply but with feeling. And then with a touch of mischief, she added, "I've been eager to make your acquaintance ever since I first saw Bertie's dory."

Muriel looked at Bertie inquiringly, and he raised his bushy brows. "Oh, well, that's a story for another time," he said evasively. She gave him a sidelong glance and grinned.

"I think I might know how that tale goes. Now, Winnie—I may call you that, I hope?" Winnie nodded. "I would like you to have something as a token of my gratitude, a reminder that love can close distances and transcend time." Her voice wobbled a little, and she held out a small green box to the dachshund. Winnie took it wonderingly, slid off the cover and caught her breath. Inside lay the golden collar she had seen long ago in Bertie's memory cabinet. "You will do it justice, with your lovely fur," Muriel said.

Winnie squeezed the dorgi's paw in thanks and wrapped the collar twice around her wrist. "I'm honoured," she said.

The other guests had been keeping a discreet distance during this interlude, but Muriel now beckoned them to partake of the food and drink supplied by caterers in the absence of her usual staff. Nap picked up one of the *hors d'oeuvres* and commented to Bertie, "these look delicious, have you tried one?" As Bertie's palate was not as discerning as Nap's, and he preferred to stick to something more familiar, he changed the subject. "Do you know, I once went to a party where a guest got rather tipsy. He didn't want to drive home but had forgotten his wife needed the car the following day. Fortunately, it was a classic mini, so he decided to push it three miles home. Odd chap. But at least it was a good, solid thing to lean on, kept him from falling over."

Nap laughed. "Ah. I remember a party where the hostess had been called to her neighbour's house to help with an outfit. The zip had stuck on the lady's fancy dress costume. The hostess saw several the guests arriving and called out from the bedroom window to tell them they would be down in a moment. Unfortunately, the guests thought she was waving and welcoming them in, so they proceeded to enter the property and make themselves at home in the lounge. They had a terrible job to convince them all that they were in the wrong house."

"Oh, if you are talking about party stories," Douglas interjected, "I had a friend whose birthday was coming up, so we decided to throw him a surprise party. We knew his sister had a birthday close by and even invited him to help with ideas. He didn't suspect a thing, even gave suggestions for entertainment. His family and friends congregated in the church hall and waited quietly in darkness. When he arrived and turned the lights on, everyone shouted 'SURPRISE!' 'You silly lot,' he laughed. 'My sister's birthday isn't until next week.' "

"Speaking of birthdays," Bertie said, "do you know it's Muriel's sixtieth next year? Now don't tell anyone."

"Surely not," Winnie replied. "She looks so young."

Meanwhile, Muriel had moved into the conservatory with Estelle and Molly to discuss the letters she'd sent them from Venice. She had decided that she really didn't want to mention the matter in front of Winnie or Douglas.

"I was sorry to hear of this Muriel," Molly said, putting her paw on Muriel's.

Estelle nodded in agreement. "I have some friends who could look into it for you, Muriel," Estelle said. "Perhaps they could find Rupert?"

"That is kind of you Estelle, it would help set my mind at ease, although it won't be easy. I have even heard of stories of children being sent as far as Australia. I hate myself now for doing what I did," Muriel replied.

"You were confused and unwell. What of this Everett Walker? Do you know where he is nowadays?" Molly asked.

"After so long, he could be anywhere. He might not even be alive. But I'm not thinking about him. He doesn't matter."

"Of course," Molly replied, wondering how her special skills could be put to good use to help resolve this sad situation. She tried to remember something she had heard at the hair salon, some whispers about a detective agency involving mice. 'Now what was it called, Anonymouse? No... The Great Ratsby? No, that is just silly. Oh dear, I really can't recall.' She would have to find out. Maybe Napoleon would know. She sipped her glass of wine and admired the flowers that had begun to bloom in the garden.

Muriel felt lighter for her friends' thoughts and caring, and she began to wonder if she had been living for too long in the shadow of her guilt and sadness.

"Come along, I think we've hidden away long enough. We should join the others," she said.

The cat and two dogs returned to the lounge and found Douglas laughing at Nap's impression of a seahorse, of all things. Winnie was chatting away with Harry, and Bertie was looking at his friend's footwear with an amused expression. As Muriel approached, he could see that she looked much happier, her worried look replaced by a genuine smile. He looked around to make sure everyone's glasses were full and then held up own. "To us all. May we enjoy our health and friendship and future adventures," he said, winking at Muriel and smiling at Harry, who had shifted closer to Molly. They all raised their glasses and wished for the same, chinking them all around. As each took a sip, Bertie looked about him and at the lengthening shadows beyond the windows. "What time is it?" he asked. "Oh, don't let's think about that," Harry said, nudging him. "You haven't got any trains to catch now, have you? It's odd, but holidays can make you think too much about the clock, I say." Bertie nodded.

Having heard this exchange, Muriel suddenly thought of something. She put her glass down and slipped through the door into the hall. The little French clock on the mantelpiece had stopped, long neglected by Wagmore, and she reached for the key to wind it. Something swung down with it, attached by a red ribbon. She held it up to a shaft of light and saw a delicate gold band with several tiny flecks of diamond embedded in it. Nearly dropping both the key and the ring, she felt Bertie's paw take hers.

"Yes," she said, simply, looking into his warm brown eyes. "In case I didn't make myself very clear before."

"I've had the ring ever since I bought this," Bertie said, touching the timepiece fondly. "Seems it's found you at last." He took the key and wound the clock. "Prospice will be our motto now, I think. "

Muriel nodded and kissed him. "I'm sure we'll get up to all sorts."

"I do hope so," Bertie murmured.

Cast of Characters
(in alphabetical order)

Albert Longfellow (Bertie), wire-haired dachshund; Samantha's brother

Ms Alfreda Chasemoore, Afghan hound; Coach passenger

Anipe Amourby (Ani), calico cat; Historian

Mr Anthony Fortescue-Berringer, husky; Producer, Rustington Amateur Dramatics Group

Arthur Barclay (Artie), Airedale terrier; Coach passenger

Augie, bulldog; Sophia's foster son

Barney, grey mastiff; Hired hand

Bertram Percy Hamilton (Percy), Welsh terrier; Bertie's friend

Charlotte (Lottie), cockapoo; Winnie's friend

Cilla, calico cat; Primary school teacher

Daphne Arabella Pussett III (Oreo), black & white cat; Author

Dino, pug; Sophia's foster son

Douglas Pembroke, corgi; Samantha's protégé

Dunston, brown mouse; Oreo's agent and minder

Elias Thomas Schäfer, calico cat; Archaeologist/Ani's father

Everett Walker, corgi; Muriel's romantic friend

Edward Kimber, Great Dane; Head librarian

Estelle (Lady Effingham), Birman cat; Muriel's friend

Gabe, grey tabby cat; Wilbur's friend

George, ginger tabby cat; Station Master

Gerard Geoffrey, grey mouse; Co-owner of The Narrows café

Ginger, ginger tabby cat; Brother to Tango

Gretchen Schwartz, black dachshund; Kitchen maid at the Ritz

Hans Fischer, Wowauzer (Welsh terrier/miniature schnauzer mix); Artist

Harry Nightingale, golden retriever; Muriel's chauffeur

Mr Hollands, whippet; Teacher

Johanna Frieda Voigt (Sweetie), tabby/white cat; Half-sister to Anipe

Kit, mixed breed dog; Head housekeeper at Palace

Klaus Durcheinander, hummingbird; Elias's friend/Robyn's uncle

Mr Louis Belcher (Wagmore in disguise), greyhound; Percy's cleaner's husband

Miss Louisa Meredith Hunter, King Charles spaniel; Muriel's school friend's mother

Miss Lucille Meredith Hunter, King Charles spaniel; Daughter of Louisa Meredith Hunter

Mason, bull terrier; Hired hand

Molly Engelweiss, smooth black dachshund; Muriel's friend

Murdo McLoughlin, cat; Doorman/security guard at Hans's block of flats

Muriel (Duchess of Berkshire), dorgi; Captain Peter Randolph's widow

Nadine Lefevre, white mouse; NiceMice operative

Napoleon, grey mouse; Samantha's friend, Douglas's mentor/'uncle'

Captain Peter Randolph, corgi; Muriel's deceased husband

Reggie, chow; Driver for Beeliner Tours

Rhys, cardigan corgi; Portrait painter

Robyn Durcheinander, hummingbird; Lecturer/Professor/Spelunker

Sanura Amourby, calico cat; Anipe's mother

Sophia Pembroke, corgi; Douglas's mother

Stanley, budgie; Bertie's housemate

Ted Tierney, Irish setter; Lottie's friend

Tango, ginger tabby cat; Brother to Ginger

Tully, British blue cat; Harry's friend

Wilbur, tabby cat; Winnie's friend

Winifred Wigglesworth (Winnie), smooth red dachshund; Aunt Bea and Uncle Frederick's niece

Zach, **Zofia**, and **Zosia**, white mice; Founder of '*NiceMice*' and his sisters

Also Available

The Tales of Bertie & Winnie, Book One

Bertie Longfellow is an old sea dog, a wirehaired dachshund to be precise, hiding away in an idyllic coastal cottage far from his native England. He is a bit set in his ways and wants nothing more than a little peace and quiet. Having put his past firmly behind him, he spends his days in his dory or by his fireside with only a talkative budgie for company. That is, until a shy young red dachshund named Winnie Wigglesworth comes along and turns that world upside down.

A charming tale told chiefly in stories and letters, *The Tales of Bertie & Winnie* enchants its readers with memories of long-lost love, far-flung relatives, tantalizing royal connections, a whiff of intrigue - and the extraordinary efforts of one long dog and her friends on both sides of the Atlantic to "rewrite" it all with a suitably happy ending.

Also Available

The Adventures of Bertie & Winnie, Book Two

Bertie has jetted off to England to meet his long-lost sweetheart, Muriel. His return to London is not quite as he expected, fraught with complications of all sorts, from comic gaffes to the connivings of Muriel's nefarious butler, Wagmore. Back in idyllic Badger's Bay, Winnie is growing up and facing challenges of her own. The adolescent dachshund finally meets Douglas, the corgi of her dreams, and the pair contend with a threat from his mother's past, whilst also finding themselves entangled in a kidnap plot with a cross-Atlantic twist.

A heartwarming story in which the present is never far from the past, *The Adventures of Bertie & Winnie* tells of friendships new and old and hardships overcome, all the while reminding us that though the course of true love never does run smooth, it is an adventure worth having.

www.ingramcontent.com/pod-product-compliance
Lightning Source LLC
Chambersburg PA
CBHW030633020726
47493CB00006B/1698